Praise for THE HOMECOMING

WINNER OF THE 2023 AUSTRALIAN ROMANCE READERS FAVOURITE HISTORICAL ROMANCE AWARD

While it's hard to pick a favourite in this series, I feel Stuart's outdone herself here with the tension and drama, wrapped with a murder and a major flood...This really is an excellent addition to the Maiden's Creek series and establishes Stuart's place as one of Australia's great historical novelists.

    Bettter Reading

What another excellent Australian Historical Romance by Alison Stuart! I really enjoyed *The Homecoming* which is the third instalment of the Maiden's Creek series. There is a lot packed into this novel set in 1892: floods, the missing mace, romance, mystery, murder, class and family/relationship issues. It is also a story about sacrifice and the difficulties women faced in an era when wanting to have a career and possibly a marriage, too, was highly unacceptable. The plot demonstrates the damage that can result from revenge, jealousy, deception and keeping secrets, too. But the rewards that can be reaped through honesty are still very real. There are some unexpected twists in the story that you might not see coming: good and bad outcomes that are appropriate to the crimes, actions and times.

    — CLS Review

THE HOMECOMING

THE WOMEN OF MAIDEN'S CREEK

ALISON STUART

The Homecoming: An Australian romantic historical mystery

(The Women of Maiden's Creek Book 3)

Copyright ©2021 by Alison Stuart

ISBN (PRINT): 9780975640753

First published 2022

This (second) edition: Oportet Publishing 2025

Cover Design: Fiona Jayde Media

Spelling and styles throughout is US English

Discover other titles by Alison Stuart at

Author website: http://www.alisonstuart.com

About the Author

Alison Stuart writes historical romances and short stories set in England and Australia and across different periods of history. She is best known for her English Civil War stories and also THE POSTMISTRESS , THE GOLDMINER'S SISTER and THE HOMECOMING, stories set in the Victorian goldfields in the 1870s.

She also writes historical mysteries as A.M. Stuart and her popular Harriet Gordon mystery series is set in Singapore in 1910.

Alison lives in Melbourne, Australia. In a past life she worked as a lawyer across a variety of disciplines including the military and emergency services. She has lived in Africa and Singapore and, when circumstances permit, travels extensively-all for research of course!

To discover more about Alison Stuart visit her website or follow her on any of the social media accounts below.

DEDICATION

This book was written through the depths of the 2020/21 COVID pandemic and, as the subject matter I chose for the theme for this story was the medical profession, there can only be one dedication and that is to our amazing doctors, nurses and frontline workers who stood beside us and steered us through that frightening and uncertain time.

PROLOGUE

MENZIES HOTEL, MELBOURNE, VICTORIA SATURDAY 5 MAY 1883

Charlie O'Reilly stood ignored at the door of the most talked-about event in Melbourne, overwhelmed by the knowledge that despite her beautiful dress and her kindly patrons, she did not belong. What would her mother say? Something about silk purses and sow's ears?

In her last term at the East Melbourne Academy for Young Ladies, Charlotte O'Reilly, Charlie to her closest friends and family, had no idea how her benefactress, Eliza McLeod, had secured an invitation to the social event of the year, a party thrown by the prominent member of the Legislative Council, Caleb Hunt and his wife Adelaide to celebrate both the safe return of their eldest son, Daniel, from his travels abroad and his coming of age.

When the invitation had arrived, Charlie cracked the seal on the heavy cream envelope and withdrew the stiff, gilt-edged card with *Miss C. O'Reilly* inscribed in copperplate at the top. Her school friends *oohed* and *ahhed* and told her how lucky she was, but she knew that behind her back they probably laughed and sneered.

Eliza McLeod took her to a dressmaker in Collins Street, as excited as any mama would be about a daughter's first proper ball. Madame tutted at Charlie's height—*"Too tall!"*—and lack of feminine proportions—*"Too thin!"*—but the green silk evening dress she produced was the most beautiful thing Charlie had ever owned. Eliza smiled and said it brought out the green in Charlie's eyes. Eliza's nine-year-old daughter, Cecilia, who had accompanied her mother on the shopping expedition, clapped her hands and declared that Charlie looked like a princess.

On the night of the party, those of her schoolmates not invited to the party helped her to dress. They twisted and curled her hair into fashionable ringlets and gushed over the lustrous emerald earrings and necklace that Eliza McLeod had loaned her. For all her physical failings, Charlie thought, as she turned to admire herself in the mirror, she had scrubbed up quite well. Her mother would not recognize her.

But nothing in her rough-and-tumble upbringing or even the years at the academy had really prepared her for such a high-society party. Several girls from the school were there, dancing attendance on the scion of the Hunt household, but even with Eliza and her husband Alec McLeod beside her, Charlie felt awkward, out of place, and alone.

She peeked over her fan at the center of attention. Although the McLeods and the Hunts were close friends she'd not met Daniel before tonight. On the very few occasions she had been in the company of the Hunts, Daniel had been at school and, in more recent years, at Oxford.

He was not as tall as his father, Caleb, a handsome man with dark hair, greying at the temples, and a taste for colorful waistcoats. Daniel's hair was a lighter brown. In fact, it struck her, he looked nothing like his father, more closely resembling his mother with her striking light grey eyes.

Eliza and Alec McLeod were distracted by people they knew and, overwhelmed by the crowd, Charlie accepted a glass of champagne and retreated into an alcove, sliding down the wall to sit on the floor behind a large potted palm where she could watch unobserved as her school friends simpered and cooed around Daniel Hunt and several of his male friends.

She had no way of knowing if he enjoyed the attention. He had been far too well brought up to give any sign of discomfort. In the room next door, the orchestra struck up, and Charlie strained to see if Eliza and Alec were taking to the floor.

Too late, she looked up to see Daniel Hunt looking down at her, a bemused smile on his face.

"What on earth are you doing?" he asked.

A perfectly reasonable question in the circumstances, but words failed her and the heat rose to her cheeks.

"I... I..." she stuttered.

"Who are you?" he said.

"Char... Charlotte O'Reilly."

She tried to smile but, conscious of how strange she looked sitting cross-legged behind a potted palm, clutching a glass of champagne, her smile faltered.

Daniel Hunt considered her for a long moment.

"I'm Danny Hunt."

"I know."

"Mind if I join you?"

She moved over and he squeezed in beside her, drawing up his knees. They sat in silence for several long minutes, drinking their now warm glasses of champagne.

"It's your party," Charlie said.

"I know, but I hate large crowds of people, and I don't know half of the people here. Do you know anyone?"

Charlie shook her head. "No one. Apart from Mr and Mrs McLeod and a couple of girls from school."

"Duck," Danny said. "Mother is looking for me."

They pulled in tighter to the shadows of their hiding place as Adelaide Hunt came sallying forth.

"It's time for the speeches. Has anyone seen Daniel?" Charlie heard her ask one of the other guests.

Beside her Daniel groaned and rose to his feet. "I better get back to it. Nice to meet you, Charlotte."

"And you."

He smiled down at her. "May I claim a dance later?"

She nodded and handed him her empty card. He penciled his name beside a waltz and left her sitting in a crumpled heap on the parquet floor in her lovely green silk dress, with an empty glass in her hand.

ONE

T hey say you can never go back.

Charlotte O'Reilly, Sister O'Reilly to her colleagues and Charlie to everyone who knew her, couldn't recall where she had heard that aphorism but now every clack of the train seemed to echo those words.

Don't go back. Don't go back.

And yet that was exactly what she was doing... returning to Maiden's Creek, back to the memories of a miserable childhood, back to... somewhere safe and familiar. She needed the familiarity of the steep valleys and the mountains, the perfect place to hide... to forget... to escape from the ill-judged relationship on which she had once built so much hope. She had foolishly thought a few years of exile in London long enough to mend her broken heart, but while her heart had mended, she had not counted on the man's arrogant belief that she had returned to him.

She leaned an elbow on the sill and stared out at the passing scenery —a blur of tree ferns and vertiginous gullies, little creeks and tall mountain ash. The scent of the eucalypts on the cold winter air mingled with the smoke drifting back from the train engine. She breathed it in and knew, whatever her reasons, she needed to return, to lay other, older memories and ghosts to rest and, maybe, to prove, if only to herself, that the child that everyone dismissed as lost had been found.

The train whistle screeched, echoing around the valley, and she smiled. She would never have imagined a train would come to Maiden's Creek. The only way out of the little town that nestled in the steep, impenetrable valley had been a treacherous road plied by Amos Burrell's stagecoach from Shady Creek. The journey from Melbourne to Maiden's Creek would take two to three days if the weather was good, longer in winter.

Now it barely took a day.

Too fast to travel back in time. She needed those long, slow days of travel to reflect on what waited for her. Without that time, she felt she had been uprooted from her position at the Women's Hospital in Melbourne, to be replanted into a town she no longer knew and would probably not even recognize.

Around her the other passengers, more familiar with the train line, straightened in their seats and began reaching for bags and parcels as the train rounded a bend and a neat station painted in cream and burgundy came into view.

"Made such a difference, having the train now," the large woman who had been sitting opposite Charlie said. "We get daytrippers now! Who'd have thought it. You ever been to Maiden's Creek?"

"A long time ago," Charlie replied.

"What brings you back?"

Memories, Charlie thought.

The woman stared at her expectantly, so she smiled and said, "I've taken a position at the hospital."

The woman's eyes widened. "The hospital? Plenty to keep you busy, dear. Are you a nurse?"

Charlie nodded and added, "It's only for a couple of months while Matron Birch takes leave."

The woman gave her a knowing look.

"It's that kind of town, isn't it? No one stays."

That much was true. Charlie's mother had left to marry a farmer down near Korumburra, her uncle had gone... who knew where? Her benefactors, Eliza and Alec McLeod, had long since moved to Melbourne.

But some people remained, and she alighted from the train into the warm embrace of a small, elderly woman.

"Welcome home, Charlie," Netty Burrell said.

Shaming tears sprang to Charlie's eyes. Home... what a strange, alien concept, and yet Maiden's Creek was as close to a home as anywhere she had lived.

"That your box, love?"

The burly man standing behind Netty pulled off his hat, a broad grin on his face. The red hair had faded to white but Amos Burrell, along with his beloved horses, was an institution in Maiden's Creek and instantly recognizable.

Before she could reply, he had hoisted her traveling box onto his shoulders as if it weighed nothing.

"You're coming with us."

Netty tucked her hand into Charlie's elbow before Charlie had a chance to say that she had a room booked at the Empress Hotel.

Amos strode ahead with Netty and Charlie following. Charlie looked around, searching for familiar landmarks. Was it possible for a town to change so much? The buildings on Main Street, although still predominantly wooden, had an air of prosperity about them and there was even a brightly painted bandstand built high above the ground, occupying a prominent position in a small park in the bend of the creek.

But some things remained the same: the ceaseless beat of the mines' batteries of stampers, the wood smoke from the many boiler fires and the unrelenting stench from the heavily polluted creek. Charlie put a hand to her mouth and nose and coughed.

Netty chuckled. "You've forgotten, haven't you?"

Charlie nodded. "Was it always this bad?"

"This is better than it used to be," Netty said. "Depends which way the wind's blowing."

"Where's the hospital?" Charlie asked.

Netty pointed up the hill to their right, where a long, low white-painted building perched above them.

"The town can thank the Hunts for that," Amos said. "Pretty much their money what built it."

Charlie had met Caleb and Adelaide Hunt occasionally, through her own benefactors, Eliza and Alec McLeod. Caleb had been the doctor in the town for a short time, and Adelaide its postmistress, but that was many years ago. All four were shareholders in a successful mine, the Shenandoah, and lived very different lives now.

But in their own ways, the Hunts and the McLeods had never forgotten what they owed this little town and had given back wherever and whenever they could, such as the Hunts' support of the hospital or the MacLeods' provision of scholarships for the more gifted school-children to go on to education in Melbourne.

Only a few others had benefitted from the success of the Shenan-doah, including Netty and Amos Burrell, but despite the generous returns on their shares, they still lived in a cottage at the back of a shop on Main Street.

The comforting smell of recent baking greeted Charlie inside Netty's warm, familiar kitchen. She hadn't eaten since breakfast, and her stomach growled in response to the cornucopia of food laid out on the kitchen table beneath an embroidered lace cloth.

Netty bustled around, tying on an apron and ordering Amos to take the box through to the spare bedroom while she took Charlie's hat and coat, hanging them on the pegs beside the door.

"Let me look at you," she said, holding Charlie at arm's length. She nodded approval at what she saw. "Always told your mother that you'd turn into a beauty."

Charlie, unused to compliments, colored, but before she could respond, Netty continued, "When your ma wrote and told us you were coming up here, I said to Amos that we'd be sure to be the first to greet you. Not that you'd know many people now."

That's probably a good thing, Charlie thought, grateful there wouldn't be many people who would remember her as a child.

"Sit down, sit down..." Netty waved at a chair and hoisted the kettle onto the stove to boil. She whipped off the cloth covering the food. "Help yourself. You must be starving, and by the look of you, you need a good feed."

Charlie removed her hat and the jacket of her neat dusky pink suit that she had purchased at great expense in London.

An indignant and very pregnant cat voiced her disapproval as Charlie lifted her from the chair.

"Don't mind Flossie," Netty said. "She thinks she owns the place."

Charlie gave Flossie a cuddle before setting her on the floor.

"Cats do," she said.

A lengthy stay with Netty Burrell and she would need a whole new wardrobe, Charlie thought as she piled a pretty floral plate with sandwiches, biscuits and cakes. Amos sat down with a grunt as Netty placed the brown teapot, which Charlie remembered from her childhood, in the center of the table with a woolen tea cosy over it.

"Good to see you, lass," Amos said. "And you a nurse and all. Who'd have thought?"

Charlie smiled. Who, indeed would have thought that the child everyone dismissed as a lost cause would be sitting here today, a qualified nurse and midwife.

"So, you're taking Matron Birch's position?" Netty said.

"Only until she returns from England," Charlie said.

"Why would you want to give up your post in the city to come all the way back out 'ere?" Amos asked the question to which Charlie could not give an honest answer.

Running away, she thought.

Instead, she smiled and said, "April Birch is a friend and I thought the responsibility of matron, even of such a small hospital, would be good experience."

"I think you'll find it quiet after the city," Netty said.

Charlie smiled. "I don't mind quiet."

Netty pushed back her chair and stood up. "Any more tea?"

Two

Charlie slept badly in the unfamiliar bed, the ceaseless beat of the stamper batteries driving her to distraction as her mind and stomach churned in anticipation of her first meeting at the hospital the following morning. When she eventually drifted off, it was to nightmare images from her childhood. She woke heavy-eyed and feeling far from her professional best for the interview that morning with the hospital committee.

After washing away the dregs of her troubled sleep, she did up her hair in the severe style expected of those in the nursing profession and dressed in the formal navy blue walking-out uniform of the Women's Hospital. To complete the ensemble, she fastened on the dark blue cape and matching hat with its long trailing veil. The uniform served two purposes; it gave her power and anonymity. No one saw the woman beneath the hideous hat, just the authority of the sister's uniform.

Netty stared at her.

"Don't you look the part," she said.

"That is my intention," Charlie said.

She turned down Netty's offer of breakfast and stepped out onto the busy main street of Maiden's Creek. A few passers-by cast her curious glances, but she tightened her grip on her leather handbag, containing her references and professional qualifications, and set out with purposeful stride for Church Street, the winding lane that led up past the Church of England, St. Thomas on the Hill, to the new hospital.

As she passed the Britannia Hotel, a young man wearing a brown apron over his clothes paused in sweeping the boards of the front porch and leaned on his broom, watching her with a frown. Charlie would have known Joe Trevelyan anywhere. His bowed leg and club foot made him instantly recognizable.

She smiled and waved.

"Good morning, Joe. Don't you recognize me?"

The frown deepened. "No, ma'am. I thought for a moment you may be someone I knew..."

"Charlie O'Reilly perhaps?"

Joe's mouth fell open and his eyes widened.

"Charlie! Bless my soul. Look at you... a proper lady and all."

Charlie smiled. "I'd like to stop and chat, Joe, but I am expected at the hospital."

"The hospital? Are you ill?"

"No, nothing like that. I am taking the matron's position for a few months."

"I heard Matron Birch was going away and I thought one of the girls up there might fill in... but here you are. Charlie O'Reilly—a nurse and all. Who'd have thought it. Come back and tell me everything," Joe said. "We've a lot of catching up to do."

Buoyed by her encounter with Joe and the memory of the kindness he had shown her in those dark days of her childhood, Charlie strode up the steep hill and came out onto a wide cut in the steep hillside on which the hospital had been built.

Her initial impression of the hospital seen from the main street had not been wrong, and she was struck by the pretty building with its two wings and a broad, sheltered verandah between affording a wide view of the valley. A garden, dominated by a huge old eucalypt providing shade, presented a pleasant outlook over the town, and she paused at the gate and took in the aspect with a professional eye. The position of the building high above the town made the hospital a perfect place for healing away from the pestilential depths of the valley.

Taking a breath to steady her nerves, she stepped up onto the verandah. Despite the cold July day, a couple of male patients sat in the shelter of the verandah in comfortable rattan chairs, blankets over their knees and around their shoulders, smoking pipes. They returned her cheery greeting with noncommittal grunts and nods.

A distant bell tinkled as she pushed the front door open and entered a wood-paneled hallway. A door to her left opened and an older woman in the unmistakable starched apron and cap of a matron came out to meet her.

April Birch smiled. "Look at you, Miss O'Reilly. Ready to take on the world."

"I don't know about the world. I rather hope it is just the hospital committee," Charlie said.

April Birch took Charlie's cape and hat, hanging them on the hall stand. She indicated the door across the hallway.

"They're waiting for you. I have been plying them with tea and cake."

Charlie glanced at her watch. "I'm not late, am I?"

"Not at all. They came early for a look around before they met."

Matron Birch directed her into the room across the corridor. Two men and a woman were seated on one side of a heavy wooden desk. With Charlie and April Birch to make up the numbers, the room felt overcrowded and the fire burning in the grate added to the fug.

Introductions were made and hands shaken, and Charlie took a seat before the chairman of the hospital's board, Councillor Sloan from the Maiden's Creek District Council, Doctor Linacre, the senior doctor and medical officer at the hospital, and Mrs Crabtree. Mrs Crabtree was afforded no official title, so Charlie was left to assume she was one of the local ladies of 'good works' who had been the bane of her mother's existence.

Councillor Sloan perused Charlie's references and passed them to Doctor Linacre.

"You worked in London?"

"I did," Charlie replied.

"Sister O'Reilly is a Nightingale trained nurse," Matron Birch put in. "You'll find none better."

Doctor Linacre nodded. "My experience with the Nightingale nurses is they are thoroughly professional and well trained. Better than some doctors of my acquaintance. How long did you work in London, Miss O'Reilly?"

Charlie gave the man a small smile. He was a good-looking man in his late thirties, dark hair greying at the temples, sharp grey eyes and an arrogant twist to his mouth. He had an unnaturally high color that may have been accounted for by his proximity to the fire—or something else. Charlie had encountered many Linacres in the course of her work, but, oddly, he was not the sort of doctor she thought to find in a small cottage hospital in an isolated town like Maiden's Creek.

"I left for London in January 1888. I trained in midwifery at St Thomas and worked in St Bartholomew's for a couple of years before returning to Melbourne late last year to take up a position of charge sister at the Women's Hospital and Infirmary for Diseases of Women."

Doctor Linacre laid the papers down.

"You are eminently well qualified, if not overqualified, Miss O'Reilly. What on earth induced you to apply for this position?"

Charlie smiled at April Birch. "I initially trained under Matron Birch at the Royal Melbourne Hospital and we have kept in touch over the years. When she knew she had to return to London, she asked if I would be interested in taking on the role." When she got no response from any of the committee members Charlie continued, "I am always looking for new challenges, and I lived here in Maiden's Creek as a child."

"O'Reilly?" Mrs Crabtree frowned. "No. I don't recall the name."

Thank heavens, thought Charlie. She didn't need anyone to remember 'Mad Annie' and her ruffian child.

"Who were your parents?" Mrs Crabtree persisted.

Charlie took a breath. The details of her helter-skelter childhood were no business of these people. "My father died not long after I was born, and my mother and I moved here from Tasmania. My mother remarried and settled down in Korumburra." That sounded respectable.

Mrs Crabtree had been going through the references. She picked one out and looked up at Charlie. "You have a reference from Dr. Caleb Hunt," she said. "I presume you are aware that Doctor and Mrs Hunt are great benefactors of the hospital? Are they personal friends?"

"Doctor Hunt is an acquaintance," Charlie said carefully.

The reference from Caleb Hunt had come from Eliza McLeod's recommendation rather than close personal acquaintance.

The woman straightened. "As far as I am concerned, if you come recommended by Doctor Hunt and Matron Birch, then I see no impediment to your appointment."

The others nodded in agreement.

"That all seems in order," the councillor said. "We will confirm your appointment in writing. It is, of course, on the understanding that the position remains Matron Birch's should she wish to return to it?"

April Birch nodded but said nothing, and Charlie wondered if the lure of the home country might not keep her friend.

"The position of matron comes with use of a small cottage on the hill behind the hospital. I am sure Matron Birch will have no objection to you occupying it during your stay," Mrs Crabtree said.

"None at all. I have already packed away my bits and pieces, and as I leave tomorrow, I have taken a room at one of the hotels. You are welcome to move in today," April Birch said. "It's small but cosy, and a girl comes up from the town to clean and do the laundry. You can take meals here at the hospital, or there is a small stove if you wish to cook for yourself."

"That all sounds quite acceptable, but I wasn't aware you were leaving so soon," Charlie said, trying unsuccessfully to hide her disappointment.

"No point delaying," April said. "I have a passage booked from Melbourne at the end of the week. If I wish to see my dear father still alive, I must make haste." She smiled. "I have every confidence in you."

"You will be under the guidance of Doctor Linacre, of course, but as he has a busy practice, he only visits the hospital once or twice a day, so responsibility for the day-to-day running, the budgeting, the meals and management of the staff will all fall to you, Miss O'Reilly." Councillor Sloan's moustache twitched. "Should I say, Matron O'Reilly."

As one, the committee rose and, duly dismissed, the two nurses adjourned to the matron's office, the pleasant room beside the front door, on the opposite side of the corridor to the office used by the doctors in which her interview had taken place.

April Birch left Charlie perusing the hospital records and returned with a teapot, two cups, and a plate of biscuits on a tray.

"Can you brief me on the other staff members?" Charlie said as April handed her a cup.

"Sister Mary Keegan is our most experienced nurse." April paused and took a bite from a biscuit. "Although probably not our most loved."

Charlie smiled. She knew the type.

"Then there is Lily Roberts and Janet Becker. They are the youngest and, I should say, silliest. Margaret Campbell is by far the most reliable."

"Margaret Campbell?" Charlie repeated the name.

"Do you know her?"

Charlie shrugged. "The name is familiar. And ancillary staff?" she asked.

"We have a live-in handyman and orderly, Alf Kimble. Then there is the cook and a girl who does the laundry and cleaning who comes in daily. Finally, there's a young lad, Eddie Williams, who helps with the cleaning, does odd jobs, and runs errands. It's not like the old days when nurses were expected to do the cleaning and got paid less than the wardsmen," April said. "We've come a long way, Charlie."

"Where do the nurses live?"

"The two youngest, Becker and Roberts, board with a widow in the town. Sister Campbell also boards in town. Sister Keegan has her own small cottage to the north of Main Street."

"What about the doctors?"

"The town has three doctors. Dr. John Linacre you have just met. Then there is Dr. Elliott." She shook her head. "He is somewhat lacking in experience while Dr. Dixon is much older and set in his ways. They run their own clinics in town and don't have much to do with the hospital, but no doubt you will meet them both in due course. As for the hospital itself, we have an operating theater and two wards with six beds, one for men and one for women, with attached bathrooms. There is also a single room for acute cases."

"You sound very well set up," Charlie said.

"The town raised most of the money for the building, but the fitting out has come from a trust set up by the Hunts. They have seen we want for very little." She sighed. "But hospitals do cost a great deal of money to run, and we must budget accordingly." She leaned back in her chair, holding her teacup in both hands. "I am curious as to how you know the Hunts?"

"I don't know them well. They are friends of Alec and Eliza McLeod, who have been very good to me over the years. I believe they were all partners in the Shenandoah mine." Charlie paused, waiting to see if that name meant anything to April Birch.

April nodded. "Ah yes, the Shenandoah mine. That's the one up at Pretty Sally? It closed recently." She set her empty cup down and waved a hand at the door. "Shall we proceed, Matron O'Reilly?"

Charlie smiled at the new title. It would take some time to get used to.

In the men's ward, she was introduced to Sister Becker, a pretty, sweet-faced woman some years younger than Charlie. Of the six beds, two were occupied by pneumonia cases, and the two recovering typhus cases were the men Charlie had seen on the verandah.

The operating theater was small but airy, well scrubbed, and adequate.

The women's ward only had two beds occupied, one by a new mother and baby and the other by a pregnant woman.

Charlie admired the baby and asked after the mother.

"A breech birth," the matron said.

Before Charlie could ask about the other patient, an older nurse in a crisply starched apron and cap and a collar so high and tight that it threatened to strangle her, entered the ward, carrying a bedpan.

She stopped at the sight of Charlie and her gaze flicked to April.

"I do apologize, Matron. I just stepped out to fetch a pan for Mrs. Coghlan." Her voice betrayed a strong Irish accent.

"Sister Keegan, please meet Matron O'Reilly," April said.

Sister Keegan was the opposite of Sister Becker. Older than Charlie, she had a tightly drawn face that looked like it would crack if she smiled and fading red hair, wrenched back from her face into a tight bun at the back of her head.

She acknowledged the introduction with a quick nod of her head.

"Excuse me, I have a patient to attend to."

And she swept off with a crackle of starched apron, pulling a screen around Mrs. Coghlan's bed.

"You'll get to know her," Matron Birch said after they left the ward. "She's not as fierce as she likes people to believe. Our other two nurses, Sister Campbell and Sister Roberts, are off duty but you'll meet them in due course."

Behind the women's ward was the service area, a storeroom, and a large homely kitchen dominated by a well-scrubbed table. Two comfortable chairs stood in front of the fire, and an old day bed covered in a blanket had been placed against the wall, under the window.

A heavily pregnant woman stood at the stove, stirring a pot with one hand while the other supported her back. She looked around as the two women entered.

"Morning, Matron," she said.

"This is our cook, Geraldine Ryan. Mrs. Ryan, the new matron, Miss O'Reilly."

"Pleasure," Mrs. Ryan said with genuine warmth. "Kettle's always on the hob, and there's always cake or biscuits in that tin on the table."

"This is where the staff eat and take our time off," Matron Birch said. "We live on tea and Mrs. Ryan's excellent baking."

"When is the baby due?" Charlie asked the cook.

Geraldine Ryan ran a hand protectively over her bulge. "Sometime in the next few weeks. I've had eight so I reckon I'll know when the time is come."

"You'll need some time off," Charlie said.

Mrs Ryan shrugged. "A couple of weeks perhaps, but I'm hoping you won't mind if I bring the baby up here with me. It wasn't a problem last time. In the meantime, my eldest girl Lizzie will do for you. She's as good a cook as any. Lizzie!"

A girl of about fifteen appeared from a back room.

"Yes, ma?"

"This here's the new matron, Miss O'Reilly."

Lizzie bobbed her head. "Welcome to Maiden's Creek. I do for the matron's cottage as well as help out with the cleaning and laundry here."

"Lizzie cleans the cottage and makes sure I always have something in the larder," April said. "Not sure what we would do without the Ryans."

"I've no problem with the baby coming with you, Mrs Ryan, as long as you are well enough," Charlie said. "If there's anything I can do, I'm a midwife."

"Thank you, but Ellen Bushby's delivered all me bairns. She'll see me right."

April Birch's lips compressed. "Most of the mothers give birth at home, and Ellen is the one they call for."

Charlie stared at her. "Ellen Bushby is still here?"

"Do you know her?" April asked.

Charlie nodded. "I do. She saved my mother's life."

The matron's eyes rested on her face. "Did she indeed?"

"She delivered my sister... not me. That was nearly twenty years ago."

Memories of the horrific night when Sarah had entered the world still haunted her nightmares.

"Ellen's been a great asset to the town but she's no longer in the best of health, and frankly, her practices are outdated," April said. "It will be good to have someone with modern midwifery training in the town."

The kitchen opened onto a courtyard with outbuildings built hard up against the rise of the hill. They consisted of a laundry and stable and living quarters, and workshop for Alf Kimble beside a woodshed. There also appeared to be a workshop, a storeroom, and a locked, windowless room April called 'the morgue'.

"It's a hospital. People die, and we have to put them somewhere until the undertakers can collect them," she said with a shrug.

Charlie stood looking into the dark room and shivered.

After completing the tour, they returned to the front door. April unhooked a bunch of keys from her belt and handed them over.

"There you are. It's all yours now, Matron O'Reilly. I'll be gone in the morning. Bring your box up to the cottage and settle in. I'll be on the early train tomorrow."

The two women embraced and said their farewells.

As the front door of the hospital shut behind her, Charlie walked to the edge of the garden and stood looking out over the town of Maiden's Creek, the rhythm of the battery stampers reverberating around the hillsides. The noise, the smells... everything awoke the memory of her childhood, and she surprised herself by realizing that, in a way, it felt right to be back.

It had not been a mistake after all.

THREE

L ike many of the miners' cottages, the humble matron's cottage consisted of two rooms. The small bedroom was furnished with a single iron bedstead, a battered chest of drawers, and a rough cupboard built in the corner with hanging space. A rag rug beside the bed saved the feet from the cold nip of a Maiden's Creek winter morning. The living room doubled as the kitchen with a compact, well-polished stove, a pine dresser, a food safe, and an all-purpose table with two chairs. Gingham curtains hung by the small square-paned windows, and two well-worn but comfortable chairs had been placed beside the fireplace.

For Charlie, who had known only rudimentary nurses' quarters or rough lodgings, it may as well have been a palace.

No trace of April Birch's presence remained save for a jar with a sprig of bright yellow wattle in the center of the table and a shelf of medical textbooks next to the fireplace. The 'good strong lads' procured by Amos Burrell set Charlie's box down in the middle of the floor and stood expectantly while she fished in her purse for the promised coins. Anyone who had to lug heavy luggage up the steep tracks of Maiden's Creek deserved their sixpence.

Amos set the basket he carried down on the table and saw to the lighting of the fire while Netty began unpacking enough food to see Charlie fed for the next week: pies, cold meat, cheese, tea, cake, butter, jam, bread and a jug of milk accompanied by a commentary on which purveyors in town were the most reliable.

Only after Netty had checked the dresser and satisfied herself that the cottage "would do" did she take her husband by the arm and leave Charlie to her unpacking.

Charlie's own belongings were sparse. She had been too much on the move in her life to accumulate much ephemera. She unwrapped a framed photograph of her family and set it on the shelf above the fireplace. The studio portrait had been taken some five years earlier and she brushed a finger over the much-loved sepia faces: Annie Woods, as she now was, with her husband Joshua; Charlie's sister Sarah, still a gawky youngster with her hair in plaits; and cradled in Annie's arms, the baby, Amy.

Charlie had taken Sarah for tea in Collins Street before leaving Melbourne. In her final year at school, Sarah, who had taken Joshua Woods's name, was bright and beautiful but cursed with her father 'Black Jack' Tehan's mercurial nature. Not that Sarah had ever known her real father. There were many evenings when Charlie wondered what had become of her charming, handsome and unreliable paternal uncle, Jack Tehan. Jack had walked out of their lives on the night Sarah had been born and had not been seen since. He had sent money to Annie on a semi-regular basis but had never come looking for his daughter. Charlie often wondered if her mother had told Sarah about her father or if Sarah herself had ever asked.

Beneath her neatly folded clothes was a patchwork quilt of unmatched hexagons, originally made by Annie's mother on the voyage from England. Convict women were often provided with the means to pass the voyage making a quilt for their new life, and if Charlie looked closely, she could make out the name of the ship, *Coromandel*, and the date, 1843, picked out in tiny stitches on one of the patches.

The quilt was now much mended and faded, and Annie had sewn an old blanket to its back to give it strength and warmth. It was almost the only possession Annie had brought with her when she had fled her abusive man in Tasmania and come to Victoria. When she had married Joshua Woods she had passed it to Charlie. The quilt had accompanied Charlie to London and home again, and as she laid it on her bed, she ran a hand over the faded fabric, feeling the love of her mother and grandmother through the stitches.

Charlie kneeled and lifted the very last item in the trunk, a once elegant box from the very best dressmaker in Melbourne, tied up with string and much battered from its travels. She set it on the bed, undid the string, and lifted off the lid. Beneath the layers of tissue paper was the one beautiful thing she had ever owned, a green silk evening dress.

She had worn it once... a long time ago. She could have disposed of it years ago or had it converted into something more practical but she had held on to it. Running her hand over the beautiful fabric brought back memories of the night of Daniel Hunt's party: The dread feeling of social isolation in a crowded room tempered by the quick, easy smile of the young man who had sat with her on the floor behind a potted palm.

That timorous girl was long gone. With a quick intake of breath, she restored the tissue paper and secured the box lid once again, returning it and her memories to the bottom of the trunk.

She had just settled in front of the fire with a cup of tea, a slice of Netty's cake, and a copy of the *Maiden's Creek Chronicle* when a knock on the door startled her. She set the cup down, wiping spilled tea from the front of her dress as she went to answer her visitor.

A woman of much her own age stood in the shelter of the lean-to verandah dressed in a plain dress of good-quality dark green wool. She smiled and held out a package tied in string.

"A housewarming gift," she said. "I'm Margaret Campbell. I apologize for not being at the hospital when you arrived, but I had done a long night duty."

Charlie frowned. "I know you, don't I?"

Margaret returned the smile. "I may have changed a little since we last met. We were at school together at the East Melbourne Academy. I was in the year below you. My sister, Louisa, was in your year."

Charlie had never met anyone who remembered her from the school that had saved her from a life in the gutter. Even at that wonderful school, Charlie had been the odd one out—the scholarship girl in the second-hand clothes who preferred study to parties.

She took a moment to study Margaret Campbell, recalling now a girl in braids with slightly buck teeth, always in trouble for absconding from the school or some misdemeanor or another and sullen and resentful along with it. Her sister, Louisa, had been a beauty with no interest at all in school—or Charlie.

The Campbell girls came from a wealthy Western District farming family. Surely by rights, Margaret Campbell, like her sister, should now be presiding over her husband's dining table in a mansion in Toorak, not tending to the sick and injured of a mining community in western Gippsland. In Charlie's opinion, that made Margaret Campbell interesting.

She stood aside and invited the young woman in, offering her tea, which Margaret accepted.

"It's very basic, but Matron Birch never complained," Margaret said, looking around the cottage as she seated herself in the chair Charlie had claimed as her own.

"It will do me just fine. I've only ever lived in hospital accommodation, so it is a pleasure to have a place of my own," Charlie said, handing her the cup.

"I board with Mrs. Butler and her family. Her husband has a carpentry business, and they take in lodgers for a few extra shillings. She's a good landlady and makes sure I'm fed and my laundry is done." Margaret took a decorous sip of the tea and set the cup down, turning it on its saucer as she said, "You're probably wondering what I am doing here in Maiden's Creek."

"The Melbourne nursing community is not so very large. How is it I've not come across you before now?" Charlie asked.

Margaret gave a dismissive shrug of her shoulders and smiled, a curious, tight-lipped, humorless smile. "My parents and I had different ideas about my future. They had a brilliant marriage all but organized, but I didn't want to exchange one prison for another and, as you know, there are not many options for girls. My father refused to allow me to go to university. I could have become a teacher, but I hated school so much the thought of spending the rest of my life pandering to girls like me..." She gave a dramatic shudder. "So, in a moment of madness, I told them I wanted to be a nurse. I held out until I was twenty-one, and only then did my parents relent enough to send me to Edinburgh to train at the Royal Infirmary. They wanted me out of the way of polite Melbourne society with the hope that the reality of working in a busy Scottish hospital might cure my obsession. They were wrong. I returned to Melbourne about twelve months ago, and I've been working at the Alfred Hospital, but I wanted a different challenge, so when the opportunity to come here presented, I took it."

"And is it the challenge you expected?"

Margaret shrugged. "I've only been here six months and the environment is certainly different." She looked around the cottage. "I am very good at what I do, and I had expected—" She broke off and bestowed a winning smile on Charlie. "I warn you, winter is dreadful. We've had a couple of days of snow on several days in July and a spate of chest infections. In summer, we get overrun with typhoid cases. Then there are the accidents and the babies... so yes, plenty to challenge us, Matron."

"We're off duty, please call me Charlie."

Margaret colored. "Oh, I couldn't. You were Charlotte at school."

"I am only ever Charlotte when people are annoyed with me," Charlie said.

She wondered what Margaret's expectation had been. To succeed Matron Birch as the acting matron? Even in this short conversation, it seemed to Charlie that Margaret Campbell was a restless soul who would never be truly content while the prospect of something more interesting loomed on the horizon.

Margaret rose to her feet and set the cup down in the enamel washing basin.

"Welcome to Maiden's Creek, Charlie. I hope you enjoy your time here."

"I'm sure I will," Charlie said.

After Margaret had left, Charlie unwrapped the housewarming present the nurse had left—a box of chocolates from an expensive shop in Collins Street. She opened the lid on the pretty box and shook her head. The chocolates had the ashy bloom of age on them. Margaret must have purchased them on a long-ago trip to Melbourne and forgotten about them. Still, chocolate was chocolate, and Charlie gave in to her sweet tooth. They may not have looked the best but they tasted just fine.

FOUR

SATURDAY 16 JULY

Joe Trevelyan and Charlie sat on the wall opposite the schoolhouse. Over the years other buildings had been added to the site, although the original single schoolhouse Charlie had known still formed the hub of the complex.

"They have over one hundred and fifty children there now," Joe said.

Charlie shook her head in disbelief. What had it been in her time... seventy?

"Flora Donald still lives here," Joe said.

His tone was casual, but the look he shot her told her that he had not forgotten the injustices meted out to Charlie by Miss Donald.

Charlie flexed her left hand as if she could still feel the leather tawse and see Flora Donald's face crumpled with hatred.

"Is she still teaching?"

Joe shook his head. "No. She married a clerk from the Bank of Victoria. He left her a widow with a son after five years of marriage."

Charlie wondered if she was supposed to express some sympathy for Flora Donald, but she recalled no kindness from the woman, and she had the unchristian thought that the poor man had probably given up and gone to his God in the hope of some peace and quiet.

"What about the others?" she asked.

Joe pointed up the hill at the now weathered corrugated iron buildings of the Maiden's Creek Mine. "Bert Marsh is a leading hand up at the mine. He's married with three bairns."

"I hope he is kinder to them than his father was to him," Charlie said, remembering the bruises on the boy's arm.

Joe shot another glance at her. Bert had not been the only child who came to school with bruises, although Charlie's bruises had not come from her mother but from a vicious brute of a man who had terrorized her mother—and her—for the better part of a year.

He'd been hanged in Melbourne for his dark deeds.

"What about the Mackies?" Charlie ventured.

"The old man died about five years ago, and his missus sold the shop and moved to Melbourne." Joe hesitated. "Martha's still here."

Martha Mackie. Of all the children at the school, Martha had been Charlie's particular nemesis. The prissy child who had called Charlie's mother 'a filthy whore' and worse. It had been that incident that had led to Flora Donald and the tawse.

She didn't want to know any more about Martha. She imagined that Martha now lived in one of the nicer houses at the top of the hill with a loving husband and a tribe of children, little girls in immaculate pinafores and boys with shiny shoes. She and Martha were always destined for different roads.

"We've talked about everyone else, but what about you, Joe? Is your family still here? Your father was the mine foreman, wasn't he?"

Joe gave a short shake of his head and looked away. "They're all gone, Charlie. Pa was killed in an accident at the mine the year after the mine collapse and Ma and my sister went the following summer. Typhoid."

Charlie put a hand on his arm. "Oh, Joe, I'm so sorry. You must have still been so young."

He hefted a heavy breath. "No one wanted a useless cripple but Yorkie Oldroyd and his wife took me in. Their children were all grown and left town and Mrs. Oldroyd had too big a heart to see me left on the street. She died a few years ago, so it's just Yorkie and me now. He's a good man, Charlie. I owe him my life."

They sat in silence for a few moments sharing the grief of lost childhoods.

Joe shrugged his shoulders. "I'm doing all right, Charlie. Got a nice girl and we've got plans."

Charlie smiled. "Glad to hear it."

"And how's your mother? Haven't heard any news of her since she left town to marry that farmer," Joe said.

The townsfolk had called Charlie's mother 'Mad Annie' but the circumstances of Sarah's birth had tamed her, and she'd worked for Netty as a seamstress for a while before marrying Joshua Woods of Korumburra. It had hardly been a love match. Recently widowed, Joshua had advertised for a wife to look after his three children and keep house for him and Annie had answered. However, despite this inauspicious start, the marriage had been a success.

"She's happy," Charlie said.

"And your sister?"

Charlie smiled. Sarah had never known the grinding poverty, squalor or violence that had marked Charlie's early years. Her life had been one of love and relative comfort. Like Charlie, Sarah attended the East Melbourne Academy for Young Ladies, courtesy of a scholarship provided by the McLeods.

"Sarah's still at school in Melbourne," Charlie said.

"That fancy place you went to?"

Charlie smiled. "Yes. It is our hope she goes to university to study medicine."

That was a vain hope. Sarah had at one point muttered something about studying medicine, but her interests were more artistic and literary than scientific, and unlike Charlie, she had not excelled academically. Her dubious success had been social, and she was a popular choice for parties and theater excursions. Annie had high hopes that she would marry well.

Joe whistled through his teeth. "A lady doctor, eh. Who'd have thought it."

"There are a few women practicing medicine now."

Although she tried to sound casual it was hard to ignore the familiar stab of envy that caught at Charlie's heart. The ability to study medicine had not been available to her, but if it had, she would have seized it with both hands. She had had to settle for nursing as a second best.

"Tell me about your girl, Joe?"

A smile twitched the corners of Joe's mouth. "I never thought any girl would want a cripple like me."

"Any girl would be lucky to have you. So who is she?"

A pink flush colored Joe's cheeks. "Between us, it's your Sister Becker. She's a corker."

His eyes shone and Charlie smiled and patted his hand.

"She's a nice girl, and I am sure she deserves you, Joe."

"What about you, Charlie?" Joe asked.

"Nursing doesn't leave much time for friendships, let alone anything else, Joe."

"So there's never been a bloke for you?"

There had been a bloke, but that interlude in her life had been a bitter mistake, one that she suffered for every day.

She smiled and rose to her feet.

"No one that mattered. Now, I need to get back for lunch and prepare my uniform for work. This has been nice, Joe."

He stood up. "I'm glad you're back, Charlie. I've often thought of you, wondered what you were up to."

They ambled back into town and parted at the Britannia. Charlie watched her old friend, a gentle soul who knew more than others the harsh life of this goldfields town, as he limped up the steps to the front door. It was reassuring to learn he had a girl, and her few interactions with Janet Becker had impressed her. If she cared as much for Joe as he did for her, there was hope that he might escape his fate.

She quickened her step, conscious that she had only half an hour before she should be on duty at the hospital. As her mind raced through the list of things that needed to be done, she almost collided with a woman and child coming out of the library at the Mechanics Institute.

"Watch where you are going, young lady."

Charlie's blood froze. She knew those harsh Highland Scottish consonants and the sharp face that turned to her in righteous fury, even though it had been the older woman who had not been watching where she was going.

Flora Donald.

A flicker of something that may have been recognition flashed into the woman's eyes and dissipated.

"Don't you recognize me, Miss Donald?" Charlie said.

"It's Mrs. Fraser now." She narrowed her eyes. "Do I know you?"

Charlie took a breath and said, "Charlotte O'Reilly."

Flora froze, the color draining from her face. Her shoulders stiffened and her mouth tightened in the old familiar way that made Charlie shiver.

"Never," she said.

"The same." Charlie had to admit she was enjoying the woman's discomfiture. "The same little girl you said would never amount to anything. I'm the new matron up at the hospital."

Flora gathered herself together and she sniffed. "Are you now? All I can say is you were fortunate in your friends. That Eliza McLeod saw to it that she dragged you out of the gutter where you belonged."

Why, after all these years, did the woman's sharp tongue and harsh words still have the power to hurt? Suddenly Charlie was ten years old in ragged clothes and cracked boots, holding out her hand for an undeserved lash of the cane.

She turned her attention to the boy who was looking from his mother to Charlie with a frown. He looked about ten, the same age Charlie had been when she had fallen foul of Miss Donald. If Flora had married late then this child would have come to her when she was nearly forty.

"What's your name?" she asked the boy.

"Archie," the child replied.

Charlie looked up at Flora. "Congratulations, Mrs. Fraser."

Flora looked down at her son and squeezed his hand and Charlie caught a flash of genuine tenderness in the look she bestowed on this precious child.

"Aye, I have been blessed," she said and, as if she remembered who she was and who Charlie was, she straightened. "Congratulations on your appointment to the hospital, Miss O'Reilly. Come Archie, we will be late."

As Charlie watched the woman hurry away, the child cast her a backward glance, and she smiled and gave a small wave. Had she caught the faintest note of derision in the *Miss* O'Reilly? She sighed. She didn't care, or at least she shouldn't care what Flora Donald thought of her. She hadn't cared nearly twenty years ago, and now...?

No, the good opinion of Flora Donald, or Flora Fraser as she now was, meant nothing to her.

FIVE

Daniel Hunt, barrister at law, stood on the steps of the Supreme Court of Victoria and swept the hot, scratchy horsehair wig from his head. He hated the damn thing.

Jenkins, the Crown Prosecutor in his recent case, joined him.

"You did a good job, Jude."

Danny scowled at the lawyer. He knew his fellow barristers called him Jude behind his back, after Saint Jude, the patron saint of lost causes, but he didn't appreciate being called it to his face.

The case of *Regina v Palmer* had been a particularly lost cause in a long line of lost causes. His client, Harry Palmer, a lad of fifteen, had been part of a cattle-stealing gang. Harry's part in the racket had been holding the horses. A confrontation with the rightful owner of one particular herd had led to a shooting that had left the cattle owner, John Allen, dead and Harry Palmer with a bullet in the leg. His fellow gang members, including two of Harry's brothers, had fled, abandoning the boy to carry the blame for the man's death.

Danny had managed to create sufficient uncertainty about who had fired the fatal shot to save his client from the noose and Harry had received the relatively light sentence of three years for his part in the affair. In the circumstances it was as good an outcome as Palmer could have expected and he was suitably grateful.

Danny bid Jenkins good day and stepped out onto the street. A burly young man with a heavy, dark beard barred his way. The deceased John Allen's son, twenty-year-old Micah Allen. Micah was not alone. With him was his mother, John Allen's wife, Mary. They had both attended every day of the court case and created such a fuss when the verdict had been announced they had been forcibly removed.

Mrs. Allen raised her hand, her face contorted with anger. Danny caught her wrist before she struck his face.

"Now, Mrs. Allen," he said as she strained against his grip.

Prevented from slapping him, she spat in his face.

"My husband's dead and Palmer should have hung for it," she shrieked.

Danny pulled out his handkerchief and wiped the tobacco-tainted spittle from his eyes.

"That was our livelihood he was stealing. Thanks to him, I've lost the farm. How am I going to support the farm and the children now he's gone?" Mrs. Allen demanded.

The anger had dissipated, and tears welled in her eyes.

"Where's the justice for me father?"

Micah Allen pushed in front of his mother and poked a finger at Danny, who stepped back in time to avoid the digit imprinting itself on his chest. He knew Micah's type, recognizing the danger in the too-small eyes and the pugnacious tilt of the young man's jaw.

Danny straightened and looked from one angry face to the other.

"I'm sorry, Mrs. Allen, but hanging Palmer does not bring your husband back. Palmer is still to serve three years in Pentridge," he said. "Nobody wins or loses in cases like this. Now, let me pass."

"Need some help, sir?" A large constable ambled towards the belligerent little group.

Danny glanced at him with some gratitude as the Allens stepped back.

"Thank you, constable, but there's no problem here," Danny said.

The constable fixed Micah Allen with a hard gaze. "Let the gentleman pass."

Micah stepped aside, but not far enough forcing Danny to jostle him.

The man leaned in and said in a low voice, "You watch yourself, Hunt. I can't get Palmer but you're going to pay for Dad's life."

SIX

The unsettling encounter with Micah Allen preyed on Danny's mind for the next few days. He knew he had nothing to reproach himself for. Hanging young Palmer would have served no purpose except revenge on the miscreants who had really killed Allen's father but he knew grief did strange things and that guilt probably played a big part in Allen's reaction. It had come out in court that the young man had been in town getting drunk at the pub, leaving his father and younger siblings to confront the cattle thieves alone.

At breakfast a week after the trial, he sat munching toast and going through the morning mail. His stepfather Caleb Hunt, in town for a sitting of Parliament, sat across from him, absorbed in *The Argus*. He lowered the newspaper when Danny let out an involuntary gasp.

"Something the problem?"

Danny pushed the envelope he had just opened across the table. Caleb extricated a rifle bullet between his thumb and forefinger and inspected the envelope. As Danny had discovered it contained no note, just his name printed on the outside. No address. The sender of the letter knew where he lived and had probably pushed the letter through the slot in the front door sometime during the night where it was gathered up with the morning mail.

Caleb held the bullet up and said in his most languid Virginian drawl, "Now, Dan, who have you annoyed?"

For a moment Danny could think of nobody but then the threat from Micah Allen came back.

"It might be connected to the Palmer case," he said. "I told you that Allen's son was not happy that my client got off so lightly."

"He wants an eye for an eye?" Caleb raised an eyebrow in query.

"I can't take it seriously, Caleb," Danny said but a cold chill ran down his spine as he said the words.

Caleb leaned back in his chair and rang the bell to summon the housekeeper, Mrs Brown.

"Is there something I can get you, sir?" she enquired.

Caleb held up the envelope.

"Do you know when this was delivered?"

The woman took the envelope and looked at it. She shook her head as she handed it back.

"No. It must have been on the mat with the other mail."

"Have you seen any strangers hanging around the street in recent days?"

Mrs Brown looked aghast. Strangers in this respectable part of East Melbourne?

"No, sir." Her eyes widened and she raised a finger. "Wait. Young Daisy who helps in the kitchen said she'd been accosted by a ruffian wanting to know if this was the house where Mr Daniel Hunt lived."

"And Daisy, being Daisy, said it was?" Danny suggested.

"I suspect so. It was only when she got into the kitchen that she thought it was strange enough to mention it to Brown and me."

"Fetch Daisy, please," Caleb ordered.

The kitchen maid was produced, hurriedly pulling her sleeves down and trying to tuck a loose strand of hair behind her ear.

Danny asked her about the man she had encountered, and she repeated the story Mrs Brown had just related. With some prompting from Danny, she went on to describe a young man in his early twenties with a heavy dark brown beard, scuffed work boots and hands with dirty fingernails. The description was general enough to cover Micah Allen... and a hundred others.

Daisy looked from Danny to his father. "Did I do wrong, sir?"

Caleb gave the girl a reassuring smile. "No, you didn't, but be sure to tell one of us if you see this man again."

"Now you mention it, I saw him yesterday," Daisy volunteered. "When I was heading home. He pulled into the shadows by the gates of number thirty-one, but it was him all right."

Danny thanked the girl and she scuttled back to the kitchen.

"You too, Mrs Brown, if you or Brown see this fellow, let me know," he said to the housekeeper.

"I don't like this, Dan," Caleb said as Mrs Brown closed the door behind her.

"He's just trying to scare me."

Caleb gave him an appraising glance. "Admit it, Dan, this has got you rattled."

Danny picked up the envelope with the bullet.

"Words are one thing, Caleb. Words don't bother me. But this...?"

"I think you should report it to the authorities and go up to the farm for a little while."

"I'm not running away," Danny said. "Besides which, I've got a case in a couple of days."

"I'll have a word with Hussey Chomley—"

"There is no need to bother the chief commissioner of police," Danny said, rather more sharply than he intended.

Caleb lapsed into silence, his long fingers drumming on the table.

"Wait here," he said.

He left the room, returning with a canvas-wrapped package, which he set down on the table. Danny knew what the package contained. He'd handled it often enough in the past. Caleb had carried the Colt revolver through the long, difficult years following the American war and it had an almost totemic symbolism for him, a connection with an old life he had long put away. He had taught Danny to shoot the weapon and Danny had proven a proficient shot with the old revolver, but it was hardly a practical weapon at the best of times.

"Your Colt? What am I supposed to do with it?" Danny asked.

"It would make me feel better knowing you had it. You're here by yourself."

Danny pushed it away. "I appreciate the gesture, Caleb, but I'm not going to shoot an intruder in cold blood. We do have laws in this country."

Caleb pushed it back. "I want you to have it."

Weaponry had improved in the years since the army of the Confederacy had issued Caleb with the revolver. It was large and heavy and hardly suitable for carrying around, tucked under a barrister's robes, but Danny didn't want to hurt his stepfather's feelings. "Thank you, Caleb. I appreciate the thought."

His stepfather nodded. "I'll find the box of ammunition for it and leave it on your desk and you will do me the favor of calling by the East Melbourne police post and asking the sergeant on duty to send a constable down this street more often. Promise me, you'll at least do that?"

Danny smiled and nodded. "I can do that."

Caleb nodded and sat back in his chair. "Now tell me about this new case. Another one of your lost causes?"

"A servant girl accused of stealing jewelry from her mistress."

"Did she do it?"

"Probably," Danny admitted, "The woman starved and beat her, and she deserves to have someone stand up for her."

"Why don't you take some of the bigger cases? A nice property dispute for example?"

"Nice property disputes can still end with bullets in envelopes, Caleb. Besides, I don't need to take bigger cases."

"Hell of a hobby, Dan."

"It gives my life some purpose. What would I do otherwise? Loaf around the Melbourne Club? My mother used to teach prostitutes how to read and you used to accept chickens instead of payment for your medical skills," Danny pointed out. "Any wonder where I got it from?"

Caleb nodded. "Touché." He pushed back his chair. "A day of fun and games in the Council calls me. I might or might not see you for supper tonight."

As the door closed behind Caleb Hunt, Danny smiled. Caleb loved every minute of the cut and thrust of politics and was an excellent and much-respected member of Victoria's Legislative Council. He'd even renounced his American citizenship to be elected.

He had been the very best father Danny could have wished for, but he still wondered about the man who had come into his life for a few short weeks when Danny had been ten. Danny's memories of the events that had led to Richard Barnwell's dramatic death were hazy. Even now he would wake, drenched in sweat, from nightmares of pursuit, of flames and smoke and serpents with fangs, and always the silent, menacing, faceless figure of the man who had called himself his father.

Following their marriage, Caleb and Adelaide had left Maiden's Creek and wandered the world with Danny in tow. The incident in which the three of them had nearly died was never mentioned. On the few occasions Danny had raised it, he had been told by his mother that it was all in the past and best forgotten.

But some things that happen to you as a child can never be forgotten, he thought.

Danny drained the last of the tea from his cup and stood up, pocketing the envelope with its ambiguous content. He picked up the bundled Colt and weighed it in his hand. He had no idea what Caleb thought he would do with it. He had no intention of wandering the streets of Melbourne with a revolver in his coat pocket.

Upstairs in the pleasant front room he occupied, he found the box of ammunition on the desk. He stowed both gun and ammunition in his chest of drawers and wandered over to the window. The street looked as it always did, quiet and prosperous, the winter trees stark against the gray Melbourne morning. A dog trotted past, its tail held high, but nothing else stirred.

"You're being ridiculous," Danny told himself.

He sat down at his desk and picked up a few pages of the story he was currently writing. He could forget about Micah Allen and the dark specter from his past and lose himself in his imaginings.

SEVEN

MONDAY 25 JULY

"You've a visitor."

Danny looked up from the latest edition of *The Bulletin*. He'd been following the poetical debate between Henry Lawson and Banjo Paterson about the merits of bush life and this edition contained Paterson's riposte, *In Defence of the Bush*. In Lawson's opinion, Paterson was a city bushman who viewed life in the bush with a romantic eye, while Paterson accused Lawson of seeing only gloom and misery. Danny admired both writers and while he himself wrote the occasional piece of fiction for *The Bulletin* under the pen name Thomas Pike, he envied the poets their talents.

Mrs. Brown stood in the doorway to his room, her hands neatly folded in front of her gray woolen dress.

"Who?"

"Mr. Campbell. I've put him in the parlour."

"Robert Campbell?"

"That's correct," Mrs. Brown replied. "That chap you were at school with."

"Oh... right. Do I look presentable?"

Mrs. Brown's eyes narrowed, and Danny hastily pulled his shirt-sleeves down and reached for a jacket. He ran his ink-stained fingers through his hair, but that just made it worse. Giving himself up as a lost cause, he went to greet his visitor.

Danny plastered a smile on his face as he threw open the door.

"Sorry to keep you waiting."

Robert Campbell, known as Bertie to his friends and family, stood with his back to the fire. Seeing Danny, he offered his hand outstretched and wrung Danny's with a force that made the bones in his hand crack, while simultaneously slapping him on the shoulder.

Danny hadn't seen Campbell in a long time and the man seemed to be carrying more flesh than Danny remembered. Good living did that, he reflected.

"Good to see you, Campbell." Danny waved at a chair. "Can I get you some refreshments. Tea...?"

"I'll have a brandy."

Four in the afternoon seemed a little early for a brandy, but Danny poured the man a glass from the crystal decanter and, because it would be rude not to, poured himself one too.

Campbell had made himself at home in one of the velvet armchairs. He sat back, glass in his hand, legs casually crossed, and looked around the room as if appraising it for purchase. The Hunts' East Melbourne residence was certainly not a grand mansion like that owned by the Campbells in Toorak, but it was comfortable... it was home.

"I thought it had been a little while since we caught up, Hunt. Are you doing anything tonight? How about dinner at the Club and on for a bit of sport at Madame Brussels?"

Danny couldn't have thought of two things he would like least. The club Bertie referred to was the Melbourne Club, an elite gentlemen's establishment where he rubbed shoulders with members of parliament, judges, surgeons, and the wealthiest graziers from the Western District but, as one of the younger members of the club, he found the company of the wealthy, and elderly, elite gentlemen of Melbourne, could be... well... boring.

He had only joined because the lawyer under whom he had read for the bar, on discovering Daniel was a young gentleman of considerable fortune, insisted it would be a 'good thing'. But the sort of clients Danny took on were not to be found in the members' reading room at the Melbourne Club, and it never featured high on his list of social interactions.

As for Madame Brussels—a high-class but notorious brothel in Little Lonsdale Street—he had spent too long in the company of prostitutes during his childhood. Knowing the sad stories behind the girls, he would never darken the door of a brothel.

"Sorry, old chap, I'm working on an important case," he lied.

"Surely an hour or two won't make a difference," Campbell cajoled.

Danny shook his head.

"For the life of me I can't understand why you feel you have to carry on the pretense of a legal career," Campbell said. "It's not like you need to work."

Danny forced a smile and shrugged. "It keeps me busy."

Campbell was not alone in finding it odd that a man with Danny's income chose to work, but Danny's good fortune was not something he dwelt on—or took for granted. After a childhood spent in a household where every penny had to be counted, the grandfather he had never met, and who he probably would have disliked greatly, had bequeathed his shipping empire to his grandson.

Having no interest in shipping, as soon as he had come of age, Daniel sold his interest but the substantial private income from the sale of the company coupled with his mother and stepfather's investment in one of the most profitable goldmines in Victoria ensured that as far as the cream of Melbourne society was concerned, Daniel was one of them.

He could have spent his days at the Club or the racecourse or anywhere rich and idle young men like Campbell could be found. Anywhere except the stinking courtrooms of the Court of Petty Sessions, where the lowest of Melbourne humanity, pushed and jostled, cried and spewed anger and frustration, and worse.

But the thought of spending his days in such inactivity filled him with horror. The work ethic had been drilled into him since birth by his own hardworking mother, so he had studied law and now as a barrister of the Supreme Court of Victoria, had the luxury of taking only cases that interested him and, again with the example set by his mother, he chose to take the lost causes, the forgotten women and the frightened boys such as Palmer.

"How is the family?" he inquired, changing the subject.

"Ma is busy with the wedding," Bertie replied, referring to his youngest sister Angelica's spring nuptials. "I think she had just about given up on Angelica but that will be all the girls married off, except Margaret."

Bertie cocked a knowing eyebrow at Danny and Danny's heart skipped a beat at the mention of Margaret Campbell. She was a couple of years younger than him, and in a summer of madness he had fallen madly and deeply in love with her. Her mother had been delighted and done everything in her power to encourage a match.

Danny had made an offer to her only to receive a short polite note thanking him for being so attentive but asking him to dismiss any thought of a future together. Margaret had other plans. She told her parents that she had no interest in marriage and intended to become a nurse. That was that. Danny's heart, or maybe his pride, had shattered into a thousand pieces and never really recovered.

"Is she still nursing?" he asked, hoping his tone sounded casual.

Bertie rolled his eyes and nodded. "She took a position in some beknighted little town in Gippsland. Maiden's something."

"Maiden's Creek?" The old familiar name slipped out almost without conscious thought.

Something in Danny's tone caught Bertie's interest. "That's the one. Do you know it?"

Danny affected a casual shrug. "I lived there for a while when I was a boy, but I wouldn't have been back for nigh on twenty years." He paused, forcing himself not to recall the dark memories of the last few weeks in that town, but instead remember the happier times before his life had changed forever. "I still have friends there," he added.

Bertie brightened. "Really? You're a dark horse, old man." He set his glass down on the table beside him, running his finger around the rim. "I say, are you fearfully busy at the moment?"

Danny shook his head. "No. Just finished a big case in the Supreme Court."

Bertie frowned. "I thought you said you were working on a big case?"

Caught in the lie, Danny coughed and shrugged. "Different case."

Bertie sat up. "I've just had a corker of an idea. Why don't we go and pay Margaret a visit? Ma's always going on about how she hardly writes and seeing you, she might... umm... remember what she left behind."

"Oh God, Campbell, that was years ago. There was never anything in it."

"Not what I heard. She turned you down if I recall?"

Danny rubbed the back of his neck. "I've got no reason to go to Maiden's Creek but don't let me stop you."

Campbell stood up. "Think about it. A jaunt to the bush might do us both good."

Danny shook his head. "Both of us can escape the city any time we choose. Now, if you'll excuse me, I have work to do."

Bertie paused at the door with a hopeful smile. "Are you sure I can't persuade you to join me for some sport at Madame Brussels?"

"Quite sure."

Danny closed the door on his friend and retired to his room with a tray of supper.

He was still working at midnight when the front gate squeaked. He looked up from his desk and peered into the night in time to see the tall, shadowy figure of his stepfather striding down the path to the front door.

Stepfather... father... On marrying Danny's mother, Caleb had formalized the relationship by legally adopting Danny. When Danny spoke of his father, he meant Caleb, never Richard Barnwell.

Doors opened and closed and after a peremptory knock, Caleb entered Danny's room, a glass of American bourbon whiskey in his hand and his coat undone.

"Late sitting?" Danny said.

Caleb grunted. "Those bastards can talk," he said. "Talk, talk, talk... that's all they do." Danny smiled. Even after twenty years in Australia, Caleb had never lost his Virginian accent and the whiskey only served to deepen it.

Caleb wandered across to the desk and picked up the pages Danny had been writing.

"New story?"

Danny nodded. "It's still rough."

Caleb carried the pages across to the armchair and sat down. He set the papers and his glass down and undid the buttons on the flamboyant red and gold silk waistcoat before settling to read what Danny had written.

Caleb Hunt was the only person who knew that the popular scrivener for *The Bulletin*, Thomas Pike, was really Daniel Hunt, and that every penny Danny earned from this endeavour meant more to him than his monthly private income, or the few shillings he earned as an advocate.

When he had finished, Caleb nodded. "It's good," he said. "You've got the character of the old bushman down. Reminds me of that chap we used to know in Maiden's Creek—Mick. Do you remember him?"

Danny nodded. He hadn't consciously recalled Mick while he was writing his story but now Caleb mentioned it, he was correct; the character in his story had come from some deep memory of Mick.

"Funny you should mention Maiden's Creek," Danny said. "Bertie Campbell came by this evening."

"That wastrel, what did he want?"

"He wanted a companion to sport with him at Madame Brussels."

Caleb laughed. "That name just keeps coming up, don't it? They are still going on and on about the theft of the mace. Rumor is it ended up at Madame Brussels where it was used, and I quote, for lewd and improper purposes. Poor old Tommy Bent is having fingers pointed at him."

Caleb referred to the mysterious disappearance, in October of the previous year, of the ceremonial mace used as part of the regalia of the Victorian parliament. It had become a cause célèbre across the colony with differing stories and rumors about its fate circulating wildly, the most popular being that it had appeared at a night of japes at Madame Brussels involving the pompous self-important speaker of the Legislative Assembly, Thomas Bent.

"Your stories about Bent don't instill much faith in the leadership of our colony," Danny remarked.

He had met Bent, and he could well understand how the politician's name would have been dragged into a night of larks that had got a bit out of hand.

"Is the mace worth anything?" he asked.

Caleb nodded. "Five feet of solid silver with a gold veneer? It would be worth a bit but it's also highly distinctive, hard to dispose of."

"Unless it was melted down," Danny suggested.

Caleb nodded. "I'd have to agree with you there. Either that or it's at the bottom of the Yarra. Anyway, what were you saying about Maiden's Creek?"

"Apparently Bertie's sister, Margaret, is a nurse at the hospital."

Caleb raised an eyebrow. "Is she? Small world."

Caleb and Adelaide had, in effect, provided the money to build the hospital and Caleb still maintained an interest as chairman of the board of trustees that managed the funding of the hospital. A local committee dealt with the day-to-day management.

Danny shrugged. "It's a small colony."

Caleb frowned. "Weren't you keen on her?"

"That was years ago. Haven't thought of her in a long time."

"Sure," Caleb said.

He picked up his glass and regarded Dan from over the rim with a knowing quirk of his lips.

"Bertie asked me to accompany him on a visit," Danny said.

"You've never been back, have you?"

"No, and I don't feel the need to do so now."

"Don't be so hasty," Caleb said. "I wouldn't mind a report on the hospital. See how it's going and if they need anything. They're an independent lot down there and don't like to ask for help."

"Really?"

Danny felt himself backing into a corner from which there was no escape. He knew his father's charm would beat him down.

"And then there's the Shenandoah," Caleb continued. "I'd appreciate you checking to see that it's been made safe and that Jones has seen to the disposal of the equipment."

The gold seam mined by the Shenandoah operation had, after twenty years of operation, reached exhaustion and the sad decision had been made to close the Shenandoah the previous year.

Danny capped his fountain pen and laid it carefully on the blotter. If, and that was a big if... if he went back to Maiden's Creek it would be for one reason only. Time to lay the past to rest.

He took a breath. "Is Richard Barnwell buried in the cemetery up there?"

Something flickered at the back of Caleb's eyes.

"He is. Adelaide saw to it that the bast... that he had a proper burial. Headstone and all. More than he deserved. Why?"

Danny shrugged. "Curiosity."

"If you're looking for Barnwell, you won't find any answers up there," Caleb said, his tone unusually defensive.

"I certainly don't get any answers from you or mother," Danny responded peevishly.

Caleb stood up in one swift movement, sending the pages of Danny's story fluttering to the ground.

"He's dead, Dan. I don't see any point in looking at the past. When I left America, I left my past behind and I suggest you do too."

This was how these conversations always went and Danny sighed. He had no reason to drag Caleb into this dark part of his past. The questions, and they were many, were for his mother to answer.

"Besides all of that," Caleb said, "Brown says that man, Allen was lurking in the street again today. It might be an idea to get out of town and let the man cool down before a bullet actually comes crashing through the front door for real."

Danny had made a report to the local constabulary but despite his outward show of nonchalance, he was starting to jump at shadows. Just tonight he thought he had seen a bearded man turning down the lane that ran behind the house and Caleb had just confirmed it had not been his imagination.

"I'll think about it," he said.

EIGHT

Danny spent the next couple of days working on the case of the maid accused of theft. He had put up a spirited defense and discredited the main witness, laying her mistreatment of the girl before the court, but he couldn't get past his client's guilt. The JPs hearing the case had not looked favorably on the girl's mistress, and the lass had got away with one year behind bars instead of the heftier sentence she could have expected.

On Thursday he found a note from his father at breakfast, inviting him for lunch in the member's dining room at Parliament House. Danny studied the note and frowned. Invitations to dine with Caleb were not infrequent but they generally directed him to the more genial surrounds of the Australian Club. This one smacked of a command.

"What's the reason for lunch?" he asked Caleb as he sat down at the table in the grand dining room, where his father already waited, reading a newspaper.

"Does there have to be a reason?" Caleb feigned mock indignation.

"Of course there does," Danny said. "I only saw you last night. You are up to something."

Caleb's lips twitched. "You are so like your mother when you are telling me off," he said. "There is someone who wants to talk with you... and here he is."

Both men stood as an expensively dressed gentleman with a florid face, ample facial hair and a solid girth, a heavy gold watch chain straining across the front of his waistcoat, approached their table. Thomas Bent, the current speaker of the Legislative Assembly, greeted Danny like an old friend, although they had only met in passing on one previous occasion.

The chair creaked ominously as Bent sat, reaching for his table napkin and summarily requesting the roast mutton and best claret. A pair of small, almost piggy eyes studied Danny with an acuity that made Danny shift nervously.

"How are you, young Hunt?" Bent said.

"Fine, thank you, sir," Danny replied, feeling ten years old. "What is it you wish to speak with me about?"

He braced, expecting a request for free legal advice, or worse, free legal representation. Tommy Bent was not widely popular among the social elite of Melbourne. He spoke with a rough uncultured accent and his numerous, and successful, property transactions were viewed with disdain.

"You don't beat about the bush," Bent said. "Let's eat first and then we'll talk."

Danny shrugged but Bent said nothing of importance until their food had been served and the waiting staff were well out of earshot.

Bent bolted through his heaped plate and sat back while Caleb and Danny finished their more modest servings. He pulled his pocket watch from his waistcoat, opened it, studied it, and shut it with a click.

"Got to be back in the chamber in a few minutes so I'll make this quick. There's a lot of people in this town who don't like me," Bent said. "It would amuse them to see me made a fool of. You know about the business with the mace?"

"I do... hardly a state secret," Danny replied.

"Should be," Bent grumbled. "The facts are these. Just after midnight on Friday the ninth of October, Fred Davis and George Upward—"

"Who are...?" Danny interposed, wondering if he was supposed to be taking notes.

"Speaker's messenger and the sergeant at arms. These gentlemen locked the mace in its box. Next day at 1 pm the mace was gone. Upward only thought to report it to the speaker the following Tuesday by which stage the trail had gone cold."

"Any witnesses?"

"The only witness is a tram driver who saw a man running out of the gate of Parliament House carrying an awkward package and by awkward I mean a long, mace-shaped package."

"How big is the mace?"

"Five feet, give or take," Bent replied.

"Hardly easy to conceal," Danny said.

"Turns out the man with the package was Thomas Jeffrey, the electrical engineer at the parliament. He's been questioned and admits to being in the habit of taking home odd pieces of wood for the fire but denies taking the mace. His home's been searched, and nothing found."

Danny shrugged. "Not enough evidence to prove anything against anyone."

"Quite," Bent agreed and his color grew more florid as he spluttered, "There's stories going around that I engineered its disappearance for a night of fun and games at a certain," he coughed, "place of ill repute."

"I had heard that story," Danny admitted. "Madame Brussels I believe."

Bent drilled a fat finger into the tablecloth. "Let me tell you here and now, I had nothing to do with it, but there are those having a good laugh at my expense."

Danny thought he had better defuse the conversation before the man exploded. "And what has this to do with me?"

Bent leaned forward. "What's not widely known is there is a group of young men who are known to frequent that establishment you mentioned. Among their hijinks and japes are frequent scavenger hunts. The police'll turn a blind eye to missing street signs and the like but the whisper I hear is that the mace was top of their list."

"Have they been questioned?" Danny asked.

Bent rolled his eyes. "Such fine upstanding pillars of society? No, they damn well haven't and as it happens one of the names I have been given is Robert Campbell. I believe he's an old school chum of yours."

Danny shot Caleb a sharp reproachful glance. "That's right."

"I don't need to tell you, Campbell is the leader of a bunch of young reprobates who frequent the establishment I mentioned. His father is the member for the Hamilton district so young Campbell has access to this building, knows what's what."

Danny stared at Bent, incredulous. "Are you saying his father is involved?"

Bertie Campbell's father was a dour Scotsman who insisted on a reading from the Bible every night after dinner.

"No, I'm not, but I don't think it would be that hard for young Campbell and his pals to break in and steal the mace... or arrange for someone in need of some extra cash to take it."

"Like Jeffrey, the engineer?"

"Exactly like Jeffrey."

The resounding clamor of bells announced that lunch was over, and the gentlemen required back in their respective houses. Bent rose to his feet.

"Your father tells me you're going on a jaunt with young Campbell," he said, poking a pudgy finger in Danny's direction. "I would be grateful if you could undertake a bit of judicious questioning of that young man."

"He's my friend," Danny protested, "and I haven't made a decision about—" He glared at Caleb, who smiled guilelessly.

"I'm not asking you to turn him over to the police, I'd just like to know once and for all where the bloody mace is and I want it returned, no questions asked. Understood?"

Before Danny could respond, Bent had turned and gone, striding through the dining room.

Danny turned on Caleb. "You have set me up, Caleb. Why should I do Tommy Bent a favor?"

Caleb shrugged. "No reason at all." He smiled. "But admit it, you are curious."

"It would be a coup to solve the mystery of the mace, wouldn't it?"

Danny admitted. "But Bertie is a friend. I'd hate to abuse that friendship."

"If the mace could be quietly returned, no questions asked, we can get back to the business of governing this colony," Caleb said. "It is a distraction none of us need."

"Curse you, Caleb Hunt," Danny said. "Now I am going to have to go to Maiden's Creek."

Caleb laid a hand on his shoulder. "As you said yourself, you need to go to Maiden's Creek, Dan. For your own reasons, if not for mine or Tommy Bent's."

NINE

"What's this nonsense I hear about you going to Maiden's Creek?"

Danny, just returned from his chambers, froze in the doorway of the house in East Melbourne. Standing on the lower step of the staircase was his mother, Adelaide Hunt. Adelaide preferred to spend most of her time at the family's Mansfield property, only making occasional forays to Melbourne to visit her children and accompany Caleb to formal occasions. Neither Adelaide nor Caleb had much time for the social rounds of Melbourne's polite society.

"Good afternoon, mother," he said, carefully closing the door behind him, and hanging his coat and hat on the coat hooks.

"I would love tea," he said, addressing Mrs. Brown, who had appeared at the servant's door. "It's freezing out there today."

He gestured to the parlor and shut the door behind her as Adelaide passed him. She turned to face him, tall and slender, her face still barely lined despite the strands of silver that ran through her hair.

"How on earth did you know my plans? I didn't know them myself until this morning," he said.

"Didn't your father mention that I would be down today? There is a dinner he wants me to accompany him to tonight and I thought I would come down early to do some shopping and see the boys and Nicia. I arrive and find Mrs. Brown in a flap about what to pack for your visit to Maiden's Creek."

Adelaide referred to Danny's half-siblings, Charles and Simon, both at Melbourne Grammar School, and Berenice, known to the family as Nicia, who boarded at the nearby East Melbourne Academy for Young Ladies.

Danny gave a humorless laugh. "Is she indeed? I don't need that much."

"Is it true?"

"Yes, it is. My old school friend Bertie Campbell wants to visit his sister—"

"Which sister?"

Danny's pause might have been infinitesimal but it was enough to send his mother's eyebrows arching as he said in a casual tone, "Margaret... you may remember her?"

Adelaide's eyes blazed. "I remember her. She turned down your offer of marriage. Is she the attraction in Maiden's Creek? And what on earth is she doing there?"

"She's a nurse at the hospital and no, she's not the reason I am going." *Not entirely.* "Caleb wants me to see that the Shenandoah is secure and that there are no problems with the hospital the trustees should know about."

"Don't lie to me, Danny."

He glared at his mother but she said nothing, allowing Danny the space to compose the answer to her question.

"None of that is a lie, Mother, but you're right. It is time I went back. I am thirty-two years old and I need some answers."

"To what?" she asked, her eyes narrowing.

The long-suppressed questions rose to the surface and he blurted out, "I want to know about my father. What happened to me that day?"

He couldn't keep the bitterness out of his voice and felt a pang of guilt as the color drained from her face.

"He came to take you away, Danny but he was a fool and ran into the bushfire. Surely you know the rest."

Danny turned away. "It's not just about the one incident, mother." He turned back to face her. "Remember the lie you told me from the moment I was old enough to understand? My father, the hero, lost at sea. You the grieving widow."

She took a breath and straightened her shoulders. "It's in the past, Danny. Richard Barnwell is of no relevance to you or the man you have become."

"Everyone keeps telling me that, but no one has ever told me the truth. I need to put the events of that summer of 1872 into perspective, Mother."

"You won't find the answers you seek in Maiden's Creek, just a grave."

"No, the answers are standing on that hearth."

A muscle twitched in Adelaide's cheek. "You want to know why I lied about your parentage?"

"Seems a good place to start."

"I did it for your sake, Danny. I couldn't have people think of you as a bastard."

Danny shook his head. "No, it wasn't for me or not entirely. It was about your reputation." He held up his hand as anger flashed in her eyes. "And I understand that, Mother."

"Then understand this. As a widow I had respectability. If the world had known the truth, I would have been deemed a fallen woman. I would have ended in the street... or, if I was lucky, working for someone like Lil." She took a breath and closed her eyes for a moment before she said in a low voice, "And I genuinely believed your father was dead." Her face was still. "You have to understand, Danny, my father would have destroyed me... taken you from my life... sent me to an institution. That's why I fled." She closed her eyes and swallowed. "As for my lies... You kept asking about your father, and what began as the truth—that he was lost at sea—became a game between us. I didn't intend to deceive you, and I certainly never expected he would turn up on my doorstep, alive and... wanting to take you away from me."

Danny couldn't meet her gaze. "And that's why I need to go back to

Maiden's Creek. Mother, I need to know what happened to me there that made me who I am."

Nothing flickered in her face. She stood quite still and straight. "And who do you think you are?"

Danny closed his eyes. "Those events... they made me someone who wouldn't take risks. Did what was expected of me. Never questioned... and now I am questioning. I have carried these secrets with me since the day of the bushfire." The long-suppressed anger rose in his chest. "I have never talked about my father, never had the chance to understand who he was and what he had done to you."

"None of that mattered. You have Caleb."

"And Caleb is the world to me, Mother, but he is only part of the story."

Adelaide turned away to face the fire, poking at the coals with the fire iron. "I don't know what you hope to find there, Danny. It was twenty years ago."

"Netty and Amos are still there."

Adelaide turned back to face him. "You're right, they are. And Netty may help you in your quest but I wonder if we would be having this conversation if Margaret Campbell wasn't a part of the decision."

Danny laughed, but even to his ears his dismissal of the suggestion sounded forced. "Margaret is the reason Bertie is going. I am going to see that the mine is secure and to keep Bertie company—"

The uncomfortable conversation ended abruptly with the arrival of Mrs. Brown and the tea tray.

"If you'll excuse me, Mama, we are leaving on the train early tomorrow morning and I think I should probably see to my own packing." He crossed to the hearth and kissed his mother on the cheek. "I have to do this," he said in a low voice, "but it changes nothing. You are and always will be the very best of mothers."

She smiled, but he thought he could detect a tinge of worry in the crease of her forehead.

"Take care, Danny," she said. "Sometimes the past really doesn't want to be disturbed."

As he climbed the stairs to his room, he wondered if she meant the events now twenty years in the past... or Margaret Campbell.

Ten

If Charlie had been hoping for a challenge in her new role, her wish was granted. An outbreak of scarlet fever at the school had kept the hospital and the doctors busy all week. Fortunately, the cases that had presented were mild, and the school had been closed and the children ordered to stay away from each other, and no new cases had been seen for a few days.

The beds in the hospital were nearly all full and, to add to the strain, Geraldine Ryan had sent a message in the morning to say that she had gone into labor. This had left the nurses on duty to prepare food for the patients, and there had been considerable grumbling from her staff.

At the end of the long, cold, tiring day, Charlie retired to her office to complete and check the endless paperwork that administration of the hospital required. The grind of paperwork and administration was proving to be an aspect of the role of matron Charlie felt ill-prepared for. She preferred the practical, problem-solving aspect of her nursing skills.

Those skills had been called into question only that morning when she had clashed with Doctor Elliott over the treatment of a patient.

Elliott had given orders regarding the dressing of the wound on a miner whose foot had to be amputated. Elliott had ordered only a light dressing to let the air work on drying out the wound. When Charlie had come to change the dressings that morning, she'd found the wound suppurating, so she had made the decision to put a heavier dressing on the wound.

Elliott had stormed into her office demanding she dress the wound as he had directed. Charlie rose to her feet and, keeping her voice as calm as she could, explained the reasons for her decision.

"You are not a doctor, Matron. Do I make myself clear? Linacre..." The older doctor hailed the hospital's medical director. "Please keep your nursing staff in their place."

And with that, he had stormed out.

Any attempt to appeal to Linacre had fallen on fallow ground.

Linacre shrugged and said, "He's Elliott's patient, not mine. You are a nurse and it is not your place to make medical decisions. Kindly obey his instructions and don't argue back, Matron."

White rage boiling inside her, Charlie battled to keep her face composed as she said between gritted teeth, "Yes, Doctor. I shall see to the redressing of the wound."

The argument still rankled, and Charlie closed the ledger and heaved a sigh. She wondered whether she could go off duty or if she should stay a little longer to see the patients settled for the night.

A knock on the door made her start and Sister Keegan put her head around the door.

"Lizzie Ryan's here, Matron—"

Lizzie pushed past Sister Keegan. "Me ma's in trouble. Mrs. Bushby said to send for the doctor. I went to Doctor Linacre's house and his housekeeper said he was here so I went to the other doctors but Dr. Dixon was out and Dr. Elliott said he didn't attend to births and was in the middle of his dinner."

"Doctor Linacre's not here. What's the problem with your mother?" Charlie asked.

"Mrs. Bushby says the baby's stuck."

"How long has Mrs. Bushby been with her?"

"All day."

Charlie nodded. "Wait here. I'll fetch my bag. Sister Keegan, can you send Alf out to find Doctor Linacre?"

Keegan snorted. "I've a fair bet I know where he is," she said.

Charlie didn't have time to ask what the woman knew. "If you can't find him, hopefully, he'll have better luck with the other doctors."

She quickly packed a bag with the obstetrics equipment she would need, grabbed her coat from the hook behind her door and hurried after Lizzie.

The Ryans' cottage was on the far side of the valley, a small timbered building set into the side of the hill. Smoke curled from the chimney and an assortment of children of different ages were gathered around the front door in the gathering gloom of the winter night. They looked up at Charlie with pale, pinched faces, their clothes inadequate for the biting chill.

"Are these your brothers and sisters?" Charlie asked.

Lizzie nodded. "This baby is Ma's ninth. I'm the eldest."

Eight children, soon to be nine, in a two-room cottage? Charlie shivered.

"Can you take them to a friend?" she said. "It's too cold for them to be standing out here."

Lizzie scooped up the youngest, who couldn't have been much more than twelve months old, as Charlie pushed the door open. Ellen Bushby stood at the door to the bedroom, her sleeves rolled up and her apron stained with blood and more. The town midwife had to be in her early sixties, and she was thinner and shorter than Charlie remembered her. Her weather-beaten face bore testament to the strain of her profession. After all, she alone had brought most of the children of Maiden's Creek into the world for nearly thirty years.

"Where's Linacre?" Ellen demanded.

"He'll be here presently. In the meantime, you'll have to make do with me. I'm Matron O'Reilly and I'm a trained midwife—"

Ellen Bushby's eyes narrowed, and Charlie braced for a retort about trained midwives, but the woman's face relaxed.

"You're Annie O'Reilly's girl! I heard the name around town but I didn't make the connection."

"We'll have to save the reunion, Mrs. Bushby. I need to see the patient."

In the ruins of the bed, Mrs. Ryan looked up at Charlie with wide, frightened eyes.

"I've birthed eight bairns," she said. "It's never been like this."

Charlie gave her a reassuring smile. "There's always got to be one with a mind of his own," she said.

It took only minutes to establish both mother and baby were in distress. Forceps would be needed to aid the baby to the outside world and they could not wait for the doctor.

Charlie had begun to lay out her instruments when the front door slammed open and Doctor Linacre stormed into the room.

"What do you think you're doing?" he demanded of Charlie.

"The baby is posterior, I was about to use the forceps to turn him—"

"Matron, what did I say this morning about medical procedures? Let me examine the patient."

Geraldine moaned as another contraction gripped her. Linacre conducted a quick examination—too quick in Charlie's opinion. He stood back.

"No option, I'm afraid. It has to be a cesarean."

Ellen Bushby gripped Charlie's arm. A drastic surgery, particularly one performed in these conditions, would in all likelihood kill Geraldine, and the baby's chance of survival was small.

"Please, doctor," Charlie said. "Let me try the forceps."

"Matron, I am not going to take any advice from you—"

"Let her try." Ellen Bushby stepped in front of Charlie.

Geraldine Ryan pushed herself up on her elbows. "If this babe is going to kill me, I would rather go to my maker in one piece, not cut open like a piece of meat," she said. "I want the sister."

"My good woman," Linacre began. "It is not your decision. Where is your husband?"

"Paddy Ryan's working up at Blue Sailor," Ellen Bushby said. "We've sent a message but he won't be here till morning and it can't wait for him."

"It's my body and my baby, it is my decision," Geraldine roared back.

Linacre looked from one woman to the other. His eyes blazed but Charlie sensed the indecision. He turned back to Geraldine and this time his examination was more thorough.

He stood back. "Very well, Miss O'Reilly. I want you all to bear witness that I take no responsibility for any outcome of the proposed procedure. On your head be it."

Charlie nodded. "On my head be it."

She rolled up her sleeves, washed her hands, and took up the evil-looking forceps. Automatically she crossed herself, sending a quick, private prayer to Saint Raymond Nonnatus, an action echoed by Geraldine Ryan. Ellen Bushby took Geraldine's hand and Linacre stood back, his brow furrowed, as Charlie set to work.

Geraldine's screams came from that deep primeval part of her soul where pain takes over all sense but Charlie persisted and slowly her gentle pressure eased the child and it turned, expelled into the world with a rush of fluid. Geraldine fell back on the pillows, exhausted.

The baby hung in Charlie's hands, limp and unresponsive, and once more she was back at her mother's bedside, her sister, Sarah, apparently dead in her arms.

"I told you—" Linacre began.

Charlie had no time for the doctor as she laid the child down, clearing mouth and nose and rubbing life into the tiny body. It began as a sputter and then an indignant wail, and everyone present in the room let out an audible breath. Charlie swaddled the baby in the wrap that had been set aside and handed the child to Ellen, who laid the baby in his mother's arms.

"Let me see to the afterbirth," Charlie said, "and then we'll see you cleaned up and comfortable."

Linacre left the room, leaving Geraldine in the care of the midwives. When they were done, he re-entered and did a final examination of both mother and baby. When he was finished he looked at Charlie.

"Outside, O'Reilly," he said.

Charlie took a breath, bracing for what was coming. She followed him into the cold, dark night.

He turned to face her. "Let me be quite clear, Matron O'Reilly.

What you did just then was a medical procedure. You had no right... I should report you, terminate your contract—"

"I am a qualified midwife, doctor. You saw my diploma. It was life or death and you could not be located."

Linacre's mouth tightened. "I was dealing with another case," he said.

Liar, Charlie thought. She could smell the pungent mix of perfume and alcohol from where she stood.

"Besides which, there are two other doctors in town who could have been called."

Charlie mentally counted to ten, took a breath and said, "I'm sorry if you feel I overstepped my role, Doctor, but neither of the other doctors were available and you were otherwise occupied. She could have died."

"Miss O'Reilly! That is enough." He held up a finger and waved it in Charlie's face. His shoulders relaxed. "You did good work in there, but one more instance of insubordination, Matron, and I shall see you on the first train back to Melbourne."

"Yes, Doctor," Charlie replied with what she hoped was a suitable tone of contrition.

Linacre grunted, slapped his hat onto his head and stomped down the path, leaving Charlie standing in the cold, suddenly exhausted, but there was still work to do and she turned back to the cottage.

Only when she and Ellen had seen Geraldine Ryan safely into the hands of her neighbors, and all the children had been returned, did they leave.

"I've never forgotten you, Charlie O'Reilly," Ellen said as they walked down the path leading back into town.

"Really? I was eminently forgettable."

Ellen shook her head. "No. Some births stay in your mind and that night with your mother is one I will never forget. You took that babe in your arms, so determined she was not dead."

Charlie stopped, conscious that the tears were prickling the back of her eyes.

"You are the reason I became a nurse," she said.

Ellen Bushby stared at her. "Me? Never. I saw what you did today. I couldn't have done that. I'm fine with a straightforward birth but the town will be a better place for having you here. I know Matron Birch disapproved of me, but the women still come to me. As you have probably worked out, none of the doctors are reliable. If they were any good they wouldn't be here. Elliott is seventy if he's a day and does the minimum amount and nothing more than a scratch. Dixon isn't interested in anyone who can't pay his fee and Linacre..." She sniffed. "He's here because he got into some sort of trouble in Sydney. I think underneath he's a decent doctor, but..."

"Alcohol?"

Ellen Bushby shrugged. "You could smell it on him... and more. He frequents the whorehouses. If you can't find him, that's where he'll be."

Charlie glanced to the north of the town. The mention of the town's brothels reminded her of someone she had been meaning to seek out. She had been too busy to venture beyond the bounds of the town. "Is Lil's Place still here?"

Ellen smiled. "Aye, it is. Lil, bless her, died a few years ago. Took ten men to carry her coffin to the cemetery. It's still known as Lil's Place even though the new proprietor changed the name. There's a few other places of ill repute tucked around the backstreets and it might be worth your while checking on the girls because none of the doctors will, except if it's a business arrangement."

They had reached Main Street and Ellen Bushby took the turn that led to her cottage. Charlie hesitated, looking north along the road that led to Aberfeldy. Tomorrow morning, she would pay an overdue visit.

ELEVEN

Charlie stood looking up at the double-storey weatherboard with a wide verandah edged with iron lace. It had been freshly painted, the boards gleaming with an ochre paint and the ironwork on the upstairs verandah a bright green. They had called it Lil's Place in her day. Now it had a board beside the front door proclaiming it as *The Maiden's Creek Tavern. Music and Dancing girls. Beer and whisky. Licensee E. Taylor.*

Charlie, as a child, had never known what went on behind the walls of Lil's Place, and it was not until she was much older that she had pieced together snatched memories of an enormous woman visiting her mother in her shack on the Aberfeldy road. There had been a brief, angry—on the part of Annie—conversation before the woman left. Annie had slammed the rickety door behind her visitor.

"I'm not a whore," she had said, not so much to Charlie as to the unseen and unknowing world.

Turning on her heel, she had glared at Charlie. "Just you remember that. Whatever people might say about me, your mother is not a whore."

It was the aftermath of the turbulent events of Sarah's birth that

Charlie remembered more clearly. The ladies who had come to Netty Burrell's door with a purse of money for the child.

She pushed open the door. A fire roared in the large fireplace and a couple of men sat at a table playing cards while a girl of about thirteen in a drab brown dress, several sizes too large, swept the floor. She looked up as Charlie shut the door behind her and her eyes widened.

"What do you want?" she demanded.

"I'd like to speak with E. Taylor," Charlie said.

The girl stood quite still, blinking. "The licensee of this establishment?" Charlie prompted.

"Mrs T, Mrs T..." The girl dropped her broom and turned, scurrying into the backrooms.

Charlie looked around, smiling at the two men who were staring at her.

"I don't have no do-gooders—"

A tall woman in a respectable gray woolen dress, heavily corseted and with her red hair piled in curls on top of her head, strode out of the back room, followed by the girl in the brown dress. She stopped short, her hands on her hips, raking Charlie from head to foot, taking in the blue uniform dress.

"Who the hell are you?"

Charlie couldn't help but grin. "Don't you recognize me, Nell?"

"Jesus, Mary, and all the saints," Nell replied, her face splitting in a broad grin. "Annie O'Reilly's girl."

Nell's gaze swung to the two gawping men. "Mind yer own business." She jerked her head at Charlie. "Come through to the back. We've got some catching' up to do."

Nearly twenty years after the brash young woman with the red hair had smiled at Charlie and told her to call her Nell, she sat across from her in front of a cozy fire in a respectable parlor, pouring tea, every bit the well-to-do matron.

"So, Charlie O'Reilly, you've come home," Nell said.

"I don't consider Maiden's Creek home. It was somewhere I passed through on my way to somewhere else," Charlie replied.

Nell sat back in her chair and took a sip of her tea. "You're back for a reason my girl. What is it? A man?"

Charlie must have started because Nell smiled and set her cup down. "It's always a man," Nell said.

"It was a professional opportunity," Charlie said, but she could hear the lack of verity in her own voice. "Why are you still here, Nell?"

Nell shrugged and looked around the comfortable parlor. "Lil died and left the place to me. Going back to Melbourne held no attraction. Why not stay here where there's still good money to be made?"

"I've worked with the women of the Melbourne stews," Charlie said with a shudder. "It's worse since they made soliciting a crime last year."

Nell nodded. "It's driven too many good girls into the arms of some shady characters. There's a few lasses around town who will turn a trick for a few extra pennies to buy grog or food for their bairns. The sergeant's mighty quick to lock 'em up while the men just walk away. It's the way of the world ain't it? Those girls need a good heart to look out for 'em. Still not a crime to run a brothel, thank the Lord. I do what I can, but I can't take in every girl." She sat back. "You come across a German woman, name of Caroline Hodgson, calls herself Madame Brussels?"

Charlie laughed. "Everyone knows Madame Brussels."

"Runs a flash house by all accounts. That's me, love... the Madame Brussels of Maiden's Creek." Nell set her cup down. "I run a good, tidy place but there's a couple of disorderly houses in town that weren't there in your day."

Charlie nodded. "If you tell me where they are, I'll make sure they know I will see to them... no questions asked, and no judgment given."

Nell smiled. "I knew you'd turn out all right. You always had a good heart." Her face sobered. "Sorry about the bloke though."

Charlie huffed out a breath. "Biggest mistake of my life."

"Married?"

"What do you think?"

"They're the worst. Singing hymns in church on Sunday with their wives and tupping the girls on the other nights of the week. One of your doctors is a frequent visitor. Him with a wife and bairns in Sydney."

Charlie didn't ask which doctor. She knew it had to be Linacre.

"Do you know why he is here?" she asked.

Nell quirked an eyebrow. "Killed a patient," she said.

"Patients die," Charlie said with a shrug.

Nell made a drinking motion with her hand. "Gave the man too much morphine. The problem was it was some Sydney bigwig. It was suggested he should make himself scarce for a couple of years."

Charlie had already suspected Linacre was a doctor with a drinking problem. She sighed. He wouldn't be the first and she'd dealt with others, and tidied up their mistakes, but it didn't make it easy.

She set her cup down. "Thank you for the tea, Nell. I need to be on my way."

Nell stood up and held out her hand. "Welcome back to Maiden's Creek, Charlie O'Reilly."

Charlie took the proffered hand and found herself pulled into a warm embrace.

"Welcome home," Nell whispered in her ear.

TWELVE

D anny stood on the platform of the Maiden's Creek train station, looking down the valley to a town that had grown beyond his remembrance. Little houses clung precariously to the treeless hillsides, interspersed with water races and tramways. Tall chimney stacks from innumerable mines belched steam into the cold air and beyond the immediate hills was steam from other unseen mines. He breathed in the scent of woodsmoke—and worse—and smiled. Smell had an uncanny ability to awaken memory and once again he was a ten-year-old boy living in the post office in Main Street.

Beside him, Bertie Campbell pulled a face.

"What a godawful hole."

Danny shrugged. "It has its charms."

Bertie turned a horrified face to him. "Whatever they are, they are not immediately obvious. You, boy!" Bertie hailed a young man who was many years beyond being a 'boy'. "Where's the best place to stay in town?"

"That'll be the Empress in Main Street. Can't miss it," came the curt reply.

Bertie looked around. "Looks like we'll have to carry our own bags. I knew I should have brought my man."

Danny had only a modest carpetbag for his personal possessions and a satchel with his sketching pad and paints, but Bertie had a trunk and Bertie was looking at him expectantly. With a sigh, he stooped and picked up one handle of the trunk and huffed out a breath.

"What have you got in here? Rocks?"

"Just the things a chap requires... evening dress, riding boots... you never know."

"This is Maiden's Creek, not Paris! You're not going to need evening dress."

He hefted his own portmanteau in his spare hand and the pair made slow progress up Main Street. They passed Sones Livery Stables and if Danny had not been lumbered with Bertie and the luggage, he would have stopped to see if Amos Burrell was at his place of business.

Shops and businesses of all sorts now crowded Main Street and it took a moment to recognize the Empress Hotel. The venerable establishment had undergone several renovations in the twenty years since Danny had last seen it. The upstairs balconies were now adorned with decorative iron lace, and the sound of a piano playing a Chopin sonata drifted out into the street.

Bertie left Danny with the luggage on the mud-smeared boardwalk while he went to inquire about rooms. Danny turned to look at the post office across the road. It had been new when he and his mother had moved in and over the last twenty years it looked to have been added to and improved. As the town had grown so had the demand on the mail and telegraph. The little verandah had been fully enclosed and a shiny red mailbox had been placed beside the new front door.

"No rooms," Bertie complained. "The proprietor suggests the Britannia may be worth a try. Do you know it?"

Danny nodded. He knew the Britannia well. Caleb had run his medical practice out of a small room at the front of the pub for a while. It may not have boasted fine iron lace or Chopin sonatas but it did have the advantage of a proprietor who remembered Danny.

"Daniel Greaves," Yorkie Oldroyd said, greeting him with a firm handshake. "Apologies, it's Hunt, isn't it? How are your folks?"

"Both well," Danny said.

"It's been a long time, lad, too long! Joe!" Yorkie shouted into the back of the residence. "You'll remember Joe Trevelyan, Mr Hunt? Took him in after his parents died. He's been like a son to me."

As Joe Trevelyan limped out of the back of the hotel, Danny thought he would have known his contemporary from his days at the Maiden's Creek school anywhere.

"Joe lad, look who's come back to Maiden's Creek. Daniel Hunt, Greaves as you'd have known him," Yorkie said.

Joe Trevelyan had been a steady, kindly boy and Danny saw the same qualities in the man as Joe smiled and held out his hand. "Good afternoon, Mr Hunt. Welcome back."

Danny returned the smile and the handshake with genuine warmth. "It's good to see you, Joe."

Bertie coughed and Danny made the introductions.

"Show our visitors to the suite, Joe," Yorkie said. "Anything you want lads, anything, just ask Joe or me. We serve dinner from seven."

Joe led the way up the stairs to a comfortable suite of rooms, two bedrooms with a small living room between them at the front of the building with access to the wide verandah.

"Why did he call you Greaves?" Bertie asked. "I've only ever known you as a Hunt."

Adelaide's lies again. "My father died before I was born," Danny said. "Caleb adopted me when he married my mother."

To his relief, Bertie asked no more questions and he adjourned to one of the bedrooms to unpack.

This activity took Danny all of two minutes.

He stood looking at the canvas-wrapped object at the bottom of his bag for a long moment before taking it out. Caleb's revolver. He had no fear of it—he just didn't know what he was supposed to do with it. Maiden's Creek was hardly a frontier town and aside from the occasional drunken miner, he didn't think anyone posed any physical threat to life and limb.

It was ridiculous to think that Micah Allen would have followed him to Maiden's Creek, but he remembered the solitary bullet in the envelope and the shadowy figure lurking in the street outside their East Melbourne home. Allen had fixed on Danny as the cause of his family's problems and there was no logic or right thinking when dealing with such high emotion, so he had included the revolver in his packing.

There was no obvious place to conceal the weapon so Danny did the only thing he could think of, lifting the foot of his mattress and sliding the canvas bundle far enough under it so anybody making the bed would not casually come across it.

While Bertie remained in his room, still fussing with his unpacking interspersed with grumbles about his decision to leave his valet back in Melbourne, Danny stepped onto the verandah and leaned his hands on the rail as he looked out over the little town that had been such a huge part of his childhood.

Although the years had changed the town from the raw settlement he had known as a boy, he had the strangest sense that he had never left.

Bertie joined him, throwing himself down on an old chair that had outlived its usefulness inside the hotel and been relegated to the verandah. It creaked ominously as Bertie rested his feet on the verandah rail.

"So, what is there to do in this benighted town? Anywhere a chap can meet a few willing girls?"

Danny glanced at his friend. "You are here to see your sister and, to answer your question, I've no idea. I was ten when I left."

Danny had, in fact, been very well acquainted, through his mother's friendship, with the girls from Lil's Place but he wasn't going to admit that to Bertie. Even if Lil's Place no longer existed, he was certain other similar establishments had taken its place. Bertie could make his own inquiries.

Bertie glanced at his pocket watch. "I think I might go downstairs and have a snifter before our dinner. Care to join me?"

Danny shook his head. "No. I have some old friends to find. I'll be back in time to eat."

"Am I invited?"

"Perhaps not on this occasion," Danny said. There would be time enough for Bertie to meet the Burrells.

The winter sun had already moved away, plunging the valley into a chilly, dark gloom. Danny donned his coat and hat and stepped out onto Main Street, hunching his shoulders against the cold.

They had passed Netty's shop and cottage on their way to the

Britannia. In the same way as when he'd passed Sones Livery Stables it had not been the right time to call in, but now he wanted to see these two old and dear friends with an almost desperate longing. The Burrells had been such a huge part of his life, but over the years he had only seen them on their rare trips to Melbourne.

As he trudged past Mackie's General Store he thought about the tribe of Mackie daughters who had attended the school. He knew one had married Alec McLeod's brother, Ian, and the rest would all be grown now and had probably left town.

He opened the front door of *Mrs. A. Burrell, Seamstress and Dressmaker,* and entered a neat, well-kept shop with a glass-fronted display cabinet filled with ribbons, lace, and boxes of gloves. The bell above the door rang and Netty herself came out from the back, hastily untying an apron.

For all her dapper appearance, she had a streak of flour on her cheek and Danny smiled. Netty... dear Netty... older but unchanged.

"How are you, Netty?"

Netty screamed and flung her arms around him. "Danny! Why didn't you tell me you were coming?"

"It was a last-minute decision—" Danny began but Netty was already pushing him towards the door into the residence at the back, pausing only long enough to lock her shop and turn the sign to Closed.

Seated in front of the fire with a cup of tea and a plate of cake, Danny was once more transported back to his childhood. This woman had all but raised him, and the tender care she had taken of both his mother and himself was the warmest memory of his early years. When they had left Maiden's Creek, Netty had remained to marry her Amos and despite an improvement in their fortunes that would have allowed them to live in comfort in Melbourne, the Burrells had chosen to remain and run their respective businesses.

"The devil makes work for idle hands," Netty had told his mother. "Amos and me would rather earn an honest living."

Danny understood that sentiment.

The back door opened and Amos Burrell stumped in, older, the red hair faded to white but the twinkle in his eye, and the warm, reassuring scent of horse and hay that always followed him, reminded Danny how much he loved these two people.

He rose to his feet, being careful to set down his teacup as Amos folded him in a bear hug.

"What brings you to the Creek, Dan?" Amos said, pouring himself a cup of tea from Netty's big brown teapot.

"I came with a friend. His sister is one of the nurses at the hospital. Margaret Campbell. Do you know her?"

"Aye, I know Sister Campbell," Netty said. "Nursed Amos here through a bad cut to his hand a few months ago. We've been blessed with the staff at the hospital. You be sure to tell your pa that."

"Don't think the town's forgotten where most of the money to build it came from," Amos said, picking up from Netty. "Mind you, I don't think we've ever had a doctor as good as Caleb, have we, Netty?"

"No. One doctor we had back then. Now we have three and not one of them a patch on Caleb," Netty agreed.

Danny smiled. In the very short time Caleb Hunt had been the doctor at Maiden's Creek, he had certainly left a lasting impression. But that was Caleb—once met, never forgotten. Although he had chosen not to practice medicine after he left Maiden's Creek, he still received letters from patients he had treated all those years ago.

They exchanged news. Netty was very eager to know about the younger Hunts and Danny was happy to pass on the family gossip. Simon, Charles, and Berenice had all been born after Adelaide and Caleb had left Maiden's Creek and the age difference between himself and his half-siblings yawned like a gulf. His now twelve-year-old sister had been named for Netty, who had never in her life actually gone by her given name of Berenice. She'd always been Netty, just as his sister would always be Nicia.

He told them that Simon was finishing school at Melbourne Grammar School and hoped to go to university and study medicine.

"Just like his father," Netty said with a nod of approval.

Charles was doing well at sport but didn't have much interest in academic subjects, and Nicia had just started at the East Melbourne Academy that year. As for their parents, Caleb's responsibilities as a member of the Legislative Council kept him busy and Adelaide drifted between the Mansfield property and the town house, busy with charitable work and the demands of her offspring.

The clock on the mantlepiece struck five and Danny realized the midwinter dark had closed in.

"Thank you for the tea." Danny set the cup down. "I better be getting back to Bertie, he'll be wondering where I've disappeared to."

Although he doubted Bertie would have missed him for a moment.

"How long are you staying?" Amos asked.

Danny shrugged. "A few days I imagine. Not sure how I can keep Bertie busy. He bores quickly."

"Why don't you borrow a couple of horses and take him down to the river?" Netty suggested.

"I am happy to rent them—"

"Rent my horses?" Amos looked insulted. "I own the Sones stables, Dan. You can have the pick of 'em. Got a couple of nice geldings that would suit you."

"Champion," Danny said. "We'll be there in the morning."

THIRTEEN

Danny returned to the hotel to find Bertie taking tea in the private parlour of their suite with a young woman wearing the blue uniform of a nurse, her brown hair arranged in the fashionable style, her brown curls drawn up to the top of her head.

His heart skipped a beat as Margaret Campbell rose to her feet and came towards him, her hands outstretched, a broad smile on her face.

"Danny, how wonderful to see you."

He still carried this woman's image in his wallet, taking it out every now and then, crumpled and peeling at the edges. It had been years since he had seen her in person and the fresh-faced girl of his memory had given way to an elegant, mature woman. The smattering of freckles across her nose, which he had found so attractive, were now faded.

He took her hands in his, expecting the connection that flowed between them all those years ago, but he felt nothing. The connection had been severed by rejection and the intervening years but perhaps it could be rebuilt.

He returned her smile and said, with complete candor, "Margaret, you look fine. Your life here suits you."

She smiled and squeezed his fingers. "And you, Dan. Bertie tells me you are still practicing as a lawyer. It suits you."

Danny gave a snort of laughter. "I'm not sure it does. All those days with my nose in the Victorian law reports... but I'm disturbing you. I can make myself scarce."

"Not at all," Margaret replied, resuming her seat with a practiced twitch of her blue serge skirt, a gesture practiced in her mother's drawing room. "Please join us. I'll send for another cup."

"Thank you, but no. I've been visiting a friend and she provided enough tea and cake to keep me going for months."

Margaret's eyebrow arched. "A friend? Here in Maiden's Creek? Who?"

"Netty and Amos Burrell."

Margaret frowned. "Oh yes, Amos was up at the hospital with a cut hand a few months ago." Her eyes widened. "How on earth do you know them? They're lovely people, but not really—" She stopped and Danny wondered if the slight curl of her lip indicated surprise that someone of his social standing should be acquainted with a horse handler and a dressmaker.

"Didn't you know?" Bertie chimed in. "Dan used to live here."

Margaret turned her sharp eyes on him. "Really? You never mentioned it."

"Until the age of ten." Danny pulled a third chair up to the table. "What about you, Margaret... are you enjoying your work here?"

Margaret cast her brother a quick glance that left Danny with the distinct impression that brother and sister had been having words when he interrupted them.

"Very much," she said with a defiant tilt of her chin. "It's a strange place and the work can be challenging. I've been here just over a year now and every day is different."

"When I was a child, there was one doctor and a midwife and that was it," Danny said. "No hospital. In fact at one stage the mine manager used to pay one of the local hostelries to look after injured miners. Going to the Australis Hotel was generally a one-way ticket to the cemetery. Caleb was determined to change that—"

Margaret let out a gasp. "Of course... how stupid of me... your father was the doctor here. The benefactor of the hospital in fact. His portrait is in the front hall. I hadn't made the connection. So you were here when they had the smallpox scare?"

Danny raised an eyebrow. "Is that still talked about?"

"In awed tones," Margaret said. "Caleb Hunt saved the town, they tell me."

Danny shrugged. "He and the other town doctor—their quick thinking saved the town. Sadly the poor woman died. She's buried on the hill above her home."

Margaret set her cup down. "So, with a father such as Caleb, did you ever consider becoming a doctor?"

Danny was on the point of correcting the relationship between himself and Caleb but realized that as far as most of the world knew, Caleb was his father.

Instead he raised his eyebrows in mock horror. "Good heavens, no. I faint at the sight of blood. I'll leave that to my brother. Besides, Caleb never practiced medicine again after leaving here. He preferred life on the land."

Margaret laughed. He had forgotten her pretty, lilting laugh that would be well suited to the drawing rooms of Melbourne society but seemed strangely out of place in this environment.

"You've had plenty of experience now. Is nursing what you hoped?" he asked.

Margaret cast her brother a sharp glance. "As I was telling Bertie, I like working out here. The experience is invaluable and I feel I can be useful."

"And I keep telling her, there are plenty of acts of charity she can perform without the need to get her hands dirty," Bertie responded.

Margaret rose to her feet, smoothing down her skirt with a quick gesture.

"And on that note," she said. "I will leave you, gentlemen. I am on duty tonight and expected at the hospital. I shall speak to the matron about changing my shift tomorrow and hopefully we will be able to dine together in the evening... before you catch the train back to Melbourne on Monday. Bertie."

Danny caught himself before he laughed out loud. Whatever Bertie had hoped to achieve by his surprise visit, his sister had made her intentions perfectly clear. He'd said his piece and he could leave. Margaret was not going to comply and return to life as the daughter of a Western District grazier.

"God knows what I'm going to tell Mama," Bertie grumbled after Margaret had left.

"The truth. Your sister is perfectly happy and doing exactly what she wants to do."

"If that's how she feels, I'll be quite happy to get on a train tomorrow and leave her to it. The sooner I am back in Melbourne the better."

Danny turned the empty plate on which the biscuits had been placed. "One more dinner with her won't hurt and then you can tell your parents you tried. I might stay on a little longer. Caleb's given me a couple of jobs to see to before I leave."

Bertie shrugged. "Suit yourself. How are we going to fill in tomorrow?"

"My friend owns the livery stables and he's lending us a couple of horses. I'll take you down to the Thompson River. We can take some lunch and I'll take my drawing things. It's worth the ride."

Bertie brightened. "Excellent. A ride will do me good. Now, about dinner, I gather the dining room here does a good roast and afterwards we can see if this town has any entertainment." His eyes narrowed. "Joe tells me there's an establishment up the road with music and dancing girls."

Danny's breath caught. "Lil's?"

Bertie shook his head. "He called it the Tavern. May as well have some fun while we're here. What do you say, Dan?"

It sounded like the last thing Danny wanted to do but curiosity, if nothing else, drew him to Lil and her girls. Her mother had been close to a couple of the girls in Lil's establishment and maybe, if they were still around, they may have some answers to his questions.

"Very well, but I'm only going for a drink, Campbell."

Bertie shrugged. "Suit yourself."

FOURTEEN

Lights blazed from every window of the Maiden's Creek Tavern, and music and drunken miners spilled out onto the street. Danny glanced at the name of the Licensee on the board beside the door: E. Taylor.

So, Lil had gone, that larger-than-life madam of the most orderly disorderly house in Maiden's Creek. She had terrified him as a small boy and he'd have liked to have met her again. Danny shrugged off the disappointment and followed Bertie inside. He'd have a quick drink and retreat to the Britannia for a quiet night with a book.

On a small stage to one side of the room, a young woman wearing a corset, scarlet petticoats, and black stockings performed an odd little dance to the accompanying music from a slightly out-of-tune piano played by another young woman in a similar state of dishabille.

Bertie pushed through the crowd to the bar where a tall, red-headed woman in a red satin gown presided. She straightened at the sight of the two well-dressed young men. She bestowed a broad, welcoming grin on them, no doubt doubling the price of everything on offer in the establishment.

"What can I do for you gents?" she said in an unmistakable Yorkshire brogue.

"Two lonely bachelors in town for a couple of nights and looking for some company," Bertie said, setting a couple of banknotes down on the bar top.

The woman palmed the money and gestured to a couple of girls who sidled over to the men. The blonde went straight to Bertie and a brunette with high, painted cheekbones and dead eyes sidled up to Danny, running her fingers through his hair.

Danny continued to stare at the proprietress, if that's who she was, behind the bar.

"Nell?"

The name came from the back of his memory, dredged from a recollection of a red-headed young woman in her mother's parlor. The woman started, recovering her composure and regarding him with narrowed eyes.

"Do I know you?"

"Danny Greaves."

If it was possible to shock the madam of a disorderly house, Danny had accomplished it. The glass Nell had been holding crashed to the floor with a tinkle of splintering glass.

The two girls stopped their attentions to the men and stared at their employer. Even Bertie looked bemused.

"I say, do you know this lady?" he asked.

Danny nodded. "I tell you what, Bertie, you and your new friend go and amuse yourselves and I'll chat to Nell."

"What about me?" the brunette pouted.

Danny handed over a banknote, which she turned over several times before folding it carefully and tucking it down the front of her corset.

"You tend the bar, Elsie," Nell said to the brunette. "This gentleman and me are going to have a drink together."

Nell held up a bottle of American bourbon and Danny shook his head. "I never developed Caleb's taste for it," he said. "A brandy will be fine."

Nell carried the drinks to a quiet table in a corner.

"Make sure you charge Bertie double," Danny said with a smile as she set a tankard in front of him. "He's good for it."

Nell laughed. "Some friend you are, me lad." She sat down with an audible sigh and took a draught of her beer. She fixed him with hard, dark eyes. "What brings you back to the Creek?"

"Campbell's sister works up at the hospital, and Caleb had a small job at the mine for me," Danny said with a careless shrug.

"I heard the Shenandoah's closed?"

"It's worked out. I just need to check it's been made safe."

Nell leaned back, lifting the front legs of her chair from the floor. "There's something else that brought you back here. And don't look at me like that. It's my job to read people, Daniel Greaves. I'd be a poor businesswoman if I took people at face value."

"It's Hunt now, Nell." Danny toyed with his glass, swirling the amber fluid and watching it catch in the light. "Back then... did you come across an Englishman called Richard Barnwell?"

Nell's chair returned to four legs with a resounding thump as she leaned forward, her eyes blazing. "That bastard!"

That had not been the reaction Danny had expected.

"What did he do to you?"

"It wasn't me. It was another of Lil's girls." Nell leaned forward. "And don't dance around me, Danny, I know the whole story about your mother and that... that... lying, cheating, son of a bitch."

Danny tensed. How was it possible his mother had confided her story in this woman?

Before he could formulate the next question, Nell continued, adding emphasis with her forefinger on the scratched table top.

"Let me tell you, that man had only one thing on his mind, and that was your money—your inheritance. He lied outright to your mother, convinced her he had only her best interests at heart. What you don't know, because I'm betting your ma or Caleb never told you, is that he'd come here straight from courting your ma, and he was a vicious bastard. Lil banned him after he took to one of the girls with his fists. He may have been your father but trust me, you and Adelaide were better off without him. She found a good 'un in Caleb Hunt."

Danny sat back. This is what he'd come for. Here at last was the truth about the man he remembered from the Aberfeldy track, wild-eyed and only interested in saving his own skin. His blood ran cold. Had his parents been right? Was this what he'd actually wanted to hear?

Nell's lips quirked. "I've shocked you, Dan, but I'm not sorry. You meet all sorts in this job, but there are a few that you remember for all the wrong reasons and Barnwell was one of those."

Danny took a swig of the hard liquor, relishing the burning sensation as a distraction from his turbulent emotions. He had asked the question and if the answer was not what he wanted to hear, it was consistent with his scattered memories. The faceless man of his nightmares acquired a more corporeal form. He could deal with the real man... it was the ghost who had frightened him.

He looked around the ornate red and gilt room and changed the subject. "You've done all right, Nell."

"There's still a lot of money in these goldfields." She shrugged. "Lil left me the business, so I've stayed on. Got a nice little nest egg tucked away when the time comes to leave." She glanced up at the ceiling. "What did you say your mate's name is?"

"Robert Campbell. His sister's a nurse up at the hospital."

"Sister Campbell?" Nell's lips narrowed. "She's a prissy little miss. Looks down her long nose at my working girls."

That surprised Danny. It seemed at odds with Margaret's professed desire to be useful.

Nell shrugged. "Don't look like that. It's always been the way, Dan. Only the rare ones like your ma see past their own prejudices."

Danny nodded, recalling his mother's words: *If the world had known the truth I would have been deemed a fallen woman. I would have ended in the street ... or at best working for Lil.*

"I'm curious. What's your story, Nell?"

"Why would you want to know?"

"I know my mother used to help you and the others, and I come across working women in my legal practice."

Nell smiled. "And what would a high and mighty gentleman like yourself have to do with working girls?"

Danny caught her inference. "I represent them in court if you must know. I never... patronize..." A sudden heat rose in his face. "Every woman I meet has a different story, but one thing they have in common is their work was not of their choosing. It was forced upon them by circumstance."

She shrugged. "Since you're an old friend and just between us, I was left as a bairn with the local workhouse in Bradfield. Don't know who my parents were. Someone came to the workhouse offering passage to Australia for girls who were happy to be servants. Anything was better than where I was so I hopped on a boat."

Her face betrayed nothing, but Danny caught the catch in her throat as she said, "Turns out the man I was indentured to was more interested in what was under my skirts and if I fought back I copped a hiding."

"How old were you?"

"Sixteen. As soon as I could I legged it to the city, but like you said, what choice did a young, uneducated girl like me have? Only one way to earn any coppers, and that was on my back. So now you know." She took a swig of her beer. "Not many I've told that to, even your ma."

"Thank you," Danny said. "I appreciate your confidence."

She nodded. "Blame it on your friendly face." She looked into her empty mug. "Have to lay off the grog or I'll start crying into your expensive jacket, me lad." She glanced past him and smiled. "Here's your friend."

Bertie emerged from the stairwell, his jacket over his shoulder and a smug smile on his face. Danny suppressed a shudder. He didn't share his contemporary's casual attitude to women. He was no monk but he looked for more than just a carnal encounter.

Nell rose to her feet and cast Danny a quick glance. "Double, you say?"

Danny grinned and watched as Bertie settled the bill without a quibble.

Danny paid for his own drink and they watched one of the girls dancing to the tuneless piano before stepping out into the cold night air. Beside him, Bertie hummed tunelessly.

"Bit pricey," he said at last.

Danny ignored him. The last thing he wanted to invite was a conversation about Bertie's hour of entertainment.

They reached the Britannia and went straight up to their room. Danny declined Bertie's offer of a whisky and, genuinely tired from the long day of travel, collapsed gratefully into his bed.

As he lay in the state between waking and sleeping, he could have sworn he heard the door to their suite open and close. He wondered if Bertie had gone out for some fresh air. With that thought, he turned over, conscious that the long-forgotten *doof doof* of the many batteries of stampers scattered through the valley had ceased. It must be past midnight on a Sunday morning and the silence was overwhelming.

FIFTEEN

As the bells of the competing churches rang out across the valley on Sunday morning, the two young men presented at Sones Livery Stables. Bertie was immaculately dressed in tweed riding clothes, and Danny, more practically, wore moleskins and an oilskin over the blue, woollen pea jacket that he normally reserved for visits to the family property near Mansfield.

Before leaving, he reached under his mattress and pulled out the Colt. He unwrapped it and stood looking at it for a long time before sliding it into his belt. It dragged on his belt, a cold, dead weight. He dropped a handful of ammunition into a pocket and shrugged on the oilskin.

Yorkie Oldroyd provided them with a rough lunch and an exhortation to watch the weather and make sure they were back in town before dusk.

As promised, Amos produced a pair of sturdy geldings, bred in the hills that surrounded Maiden's Creek and a far cry from the thoroughbreds that inhabited the stables of both Danny and Bertie's family properties. Danny selected a black with a white star and two white fetlocks, while Bertie, who had been born for the saddle, took the more lively chestnut.

Relying on his memory and instructions from Amos, Danny led them south along the rough track that wound through the narrow valley cut by Maiden's Creek. The track, hewn by hand by the early gold seekers, clung to the side of the hill, with a sheer drop to the creek. On the far side of the valley, in a feat of monumental engineering, the train line had been cut into an almost vertical cliff face.

Free of the smoke and stench of the town, Danny breathed in the cold, fresh eucalyptus-tinged air. How could he have forgotten how much this part of Victoria was a part of him, part of who he was?

Three miles from Maiden's Creek, the mighty Thompson River cut through the granite chasms as it had for millennia. In its winter spate, it was fast-flowing and deep, as it leaped and danced across the ancient rocks. A wooden bridge now spanned the river supporting the train line. It seemed a fragile construction as the swollen river tugged at its foundations and supports.

The men found a clearing in the winter sun, with a good view of the wild river. They dismounted, tethered their horses, and sat on the bank to eat the sandwiches packed by the hotel. Danny pulled his sketchbook from his coat pocket and tried to catch the raw power of the river and the dark, almost threatening valley, while Bertie snoozed with his hat over his face.

In this deep valley, the sun did not linger long and it soon moved away from their clearing. A chill breeze blowing off the river reminded Danny that a warm fire and tea and cake waited for them back in Maiden's Creek. He nudged the dozing Bertie with his boot.

"Time to go," he said.

Bertie shivered. "When did it get so cold?"

"You'll warm up on the ride."

"I'm freezing."

"Take this." Danny handed him the oilskin and Bertie pulled it on with muttered thanks.

Danny gathered up the remnants of their lunch while Bertie unhitched the horses. "Let's make it interesting," Bertie said. "I'll race you back to town. Last one back buys dinner. To make it fair, I'll take your horse. He's a bit slower."

"Don't be ridiculous. These tracks are treacherous—"

But Bertie had already swung himself into the saddle of the black gelding and had gone with a yahoo and a wave of his hat. Danny was not going to play stupid games that diced with death. He was stuck with the skittish chestnut and a wet and slippery track pocked with potholes. He had too much respect for his neck and the health of his horse to risk either for the sake of a few shillings.

As Amos had taught him all those years ago, he had a few respectful words with the horse before swinging into the saddle. Bertie was well out of sight and Danny blew out a breath and shook his head. Grateful to be alone, he took the ride slowly, enjoying the unfamiliar scent of the damp humus, the distant cries of bellbirds and whipbirds, and the screech of parrots.

The sharp crack of a rifle echoed off the hills. The flighty chestnut started at the sound, nearly dislodging him from the saddle, and Danny's own heart skipped a beat. It took him a few moments to calm both himself and his horse and he paused, hardly daring to breathe, listening. But he heard only the sounds of the bush.

He put his heels to the horse and put it into a gentle canter, picking a safe course along the track. As he rounded a sharp bend, his worst fears were realized. Bertie lay face down on the muddy track, his left leg bent at an unnatural angle, and there was no sign of his horse.

Danny flung himself off his animal, hurriedly tying the reins to a nearby tree. He hunkered down beside his friend. Bertie had lost his hat, and his hair was matted with blood. Hardly daring to breathe, Danny touched his fingers to his neck, letting out a breath as he felt Bertie's pulse, strong and clear.

Gently he turned the man over, wiping the mud and blood from his face with a clean handkerchief. Bertie's eyes flickered open.

"Where am I?"

"You've had an accident. Where are you hurt?"

Bertie began to shiver, and beneath the smears of blood and mud, he had gone an alarming shade of white.

"My leg," he said between gritted teeth. He swore volubly as Danny conducted a quick examination and concluded that Bertie's lower right leg, encased in an expensive English riding boot, was broken.

"Someone shot at me!" Bertie's outrage seemed to overcome his pain. "I felt the bloody bullet go past my ear."

He turned Bertie's head to one side and confirmed the blood on his friend's face came from a nick in his right ear. The bullet had just missed him. A cold shiver ran down his spine.

"You're bleeding like a pig," he said, "but it's just a cut. Where's your horse?"

"Don't know. It dumped me and took off."

Hopefully, the animal would find its way back to the stable and Danny wouldn't have to explain a missing horse to his friend.

He handed Bertie his clean handkerchief and guided his hand to the injury on his ear. "Here, hold this to it."

"Ouch! Who the hell is shooting out here?" Bertie sounded affronted.

"Probably a 'roo shooter with a few whiskies under his belt," Danny said. "We're not in Collins Street."

Bertie's response would have made Nell blush.

Danny stood up and considered his options. They were an hour's ride out of Maiden's Creek. He'd just passed the turnoff to the Italian wood-chopping settlement at Wildman's Point. With a mumbled apology, he hauled Bertie off the track onto a piece of dry ground and propped him up against a fallen tree.

Bertie grasped his wrist. "What are you going to do?"

"Get some help from the settlement up the river. I won't be long."

Bertie's eyes widened. "Don't leave me. Someone is trying to kill me."

"Don't be ridiculous," Danny scoffed. "Who wants to kill you? No one knows who you are."

But even as he said it, a cold shiver ran down his spine. Bertie had been wearing his coat and riding the horse Danny had left town on that morning. Was it possible that he had been followed to Maiden's Creek? He scanned the thick bush on the slope above them but nothing stirred. Whoever it was had ample opportunity to make good his escape.

He pulled the Colt from his belt and loaded it.

"What the hell's that for?" Bertie asked, his eyes wide.

"For you," Danny said, handing him the weapon. "We need to get you out of here before dark," he said as he swung into his saddle.

"Hurry," Bertie said.

"I will."

Putting his heels to the horse, he turned back to the track leading to the Italian woodcutters' settlement. He had distant memories of a shantytown of tents and bark huts but the intervening years had seen basic split-plank cottages spring up where the bark huts had stood.

A heavily pregnant young woman came out from one of the cottages. She looked up at him with a questioning look in her eyes.

Danny spoke rough Italian, the legacy of his travels. It might have been a little rusty but the woman understood.

"Nico!" she called, and a young man of about his own age came out of the cottage.

"What is it? Who are you?" The man addressed him in English.

Danny introduced himself and explained the situation again, this time in English.

The man nodded and pointed to himself. "Nico Alberti. Wait here, I'll get help."

Nico wasted no time summoning the assistance of two other sturdy young men. A rough stretcher was produced, and a pony hurriedly hitched to a cart. Nico's wife threw blankets into the back of the cart.

Up close, Danny could see the scars of old burns marring one side of her face. Catching his curious glance, she touched her face and Danny apologized for his rudeness.

She shook her head. "I am lucky to be alive. Did you say your name was Hunt? That was the name of the doctor who saved my life."

Danny smiled. "My father."

"He will not remember me, but my mother and I thank God for his skill."

"I'll tell him. What is your name?"

"Maria. I was Maria Capelli and I was two when the accident happened. Mercifully I do not remember it."

"Enough talking!" Nico said. "It will be dark before we can get the man to the hospital."

Nico took the reins of the cart and two others saddled up their sturdy ponies and followed. Danny drew his horse abreast of the cart.

"Do you get kangaroo hunters around here?" he asked Nico.

Nico shook his head. "Not much game around here."

"Someone was shooting this morning. That's what spooked my friend's horse and a bullet grazed his ear."

The other man looked at him. "Does your friend have enemies?"

Danny shook his head. "No."

But I do, he thought, and a cold chill ran down his spine. Surely Micah Allen could not have followed him?

As the party neared the place he had left Bertie, he rode on ahead and shouted his friend's name. He didn't want Bertie shooting at him or his rescue party.

Bertie hadn't moved. He held the Colt gripped in his right hand but barely looked up as the rescue party neared. Danny swung off his horse and hunkered down beside his friend.

"What took you so long?" Bertie said, his voice low and tight with pain.

"Lucky for you it's a Sunday and the men were all at home," Danny said.

He retrieved the Colt, removing the ammunition and returning it to his belt as Nico and the rescue party arrived.

Danny stood up and gestured to the men. "Bring the cart over here."

It took the efforts of all four men to get Bertie into the back of the cart. Nico threw a rough blanket over him.

"I am sorry, my friend," he said. "It is going to be a rough ride." Nico gestured to his friends. "You go back. Tell Maria I will spend the night in town and return in the morning."

Nico clicked the sure-footed pony on with Danny following. It was clear both driver and pony knew the track well but they still made slow progress into town, punctuated by groans and complaints from the patient.

It was dusk before they turned up towards the hospital on the hill above the church.

Danny remembered Caleb and Adelaide had come to Maiden's Creek for the opening of the new district hospital five years previously.

He'd seen the newspaper reports and photographic images of his parents standing on a verandah at the front of the building with nurses in starched white aprons and men in stiff collars on either side of them.

The building looked smaller than he had imagined, but appeared to be well cared for. Neatly tended rose bushes hugged the front of the two wings and an old eucalyptus shaded the windows of one of the wings, dropping leaves and bark on a rough lawn.

Danny swung off his horse and jogged up the path to the front door, pulling hard on the bell pull. It was answered by a woman in a dark blue gown, starched white apron and neat white cap perched on shining dark brown hair. It struck Danny that she seemed young to be wearing the uniform of a matron.

Her eyes widened and her lips parted for an instant, as if she recognized him, but within a heartbeat she was once more the consummate professional.

"What can we do for you?" she asked.

Danny gestured back at the road. "My friend fell from his horse. He has a broken leg—"

She glanced at the cart and the man waiting patiently at the pony's head at the gate to the hospital, and she nodded. "Bring the cart around the back. We'll get him inside and see to his injury."

"Thank you, Sister—"

She straightened. "Matron O'Reilly to you, Mr Hunt."

The door shut behind her and as he turned back to the cart he realized he had not given her his name—yet she had known it.

Sixteen

Charlie shut the front door and leaned against it for a long moment to regain her composure.

He didn't recognize me.

She didn't know why that thought disappointed her. After all, she had only really met Daniel Hunt on one occasion, and that was ten years ago. Now, that young man who had been so kind to her had come to the door of her hospital, older and with no recognition in his light gray eyes.

She shook herself into action. She could see no reason why he would recognize her and besides, now was not the time for reunions.

Outside in the courtyard, Alf came out with a hospital stretcher. Charlie sent Eddie to fetch a doctor, and Daniel Hunt and the young man who had been at the reins of the pony cart carried the stretcher into the hospital, depositing the patient on the treatment table and into the care of Sister Keegan. The patient swore volubly, and Charlie winced in sympathy. She did not need a doctor to tell her his leg was broken, and the blood on his face caused her some concern. A head injury she should be concerned about?

"What's your name?" she asked.

"Robert Campbell." He grimaced. "Where's my goddamned sister when I need her?"

"No swearing," Charlie said, automatically.

She turned to Daniel Hunt, who hovered in the doorway, his hat in his hand. "What does he mean about his sister?"

"Margaret Campbell. She's a nurse here I believe."

Charlie nodded. "Of course. She mentioned her brother had arrived in town. She'd asked for tonight off to have dinner with him."

"Stop chattering, woman, and fetch Margaret," Robert Campbell said.

Charlie bit her tongue. If it had been anyone other than Margaret Campbell's brother, she'd have been tempted to give him back as good as he gave.

"Mr. Campbell, my name is Matron O'Reilly and I am in charge of this hospital. Injured or not I trust you to mind your manners and speak to me civilly. I can see your leg is injured. Are there any other injuries?"

Bertie managed a strangled grunt and touched his right ear. She frowned as she examined the wound. It was more than a cut and accounted for the blood on his face. It looked like a chunk had been taken off the upper part of his ear. That would be a story for his friends, she thought.

A heavily aspirated sigh came from behind her and she turned to look at the man leaning against a wall. Daniel Hunt had a ghastly white tinge to his face.

"Are you all right?"

"Mmm..."

"If you're going to faint, do you mind stepping outside?"

The door slammed behind him.

She administered a dose of morphine to Robert Campbell and while she waited for it to take effect, she stepped out into the hall. Daniel Hunt sat on the bench outside her office, his head back, eyes closed and his hands hanging loosely between his knees. She fetched a glass of water and stood in front of him.

"Feeling better?"

His eyes flickered open and she handed him the water, grateful to see the color come back to his face.

"Sorry about that," he said, handing her the empty glass. "There's a good reason I didn't follow my father into medicine."

"What happened?" she asked.

He straightened and cleared his throat. "I heard the shot and found Bertie on the ground. Looks to me like the bullet nicked his ear."

Charlie stared at him. "He's lucky to be alive." She frowned. "A shot?"

Daniel shrugged. "Probably nothing more than a stray shot from a 'roo shooter."

"Did you see anyone?"

"No."

There was something in the hard set of his mouth that intrigued her. There was more to this story than he was telling.

"Do you know his sister?" she asked him.

He nodded.

"She lives with the Butlers at Banksia Cottage just down the lane from here." She glanced at her watch. "Perhaps you could make yourself useful and go and fetch her?"

Danny stood up and took a deep breath. "

That is something I can do."

She let him out by the front door, watching for a long moment as he walked out into the cold night before she turned back to the patient who needed her help.

The morphine had taken effect and Bertie Campbell drowsed as Sister Keegan cut the expensive riding boot from his injured leg. She ran a hand over the fine, well-polished leather.

"This would feed a family of four for a year," she said.

Charlie glared at the nurse. "Sister! Concentrate please."

Keegan flushed and set the ruined boot down. It had done a fair job of keeping the bone splinted but it looked like both the tibia and fibula had snapped. While they waited for the doctor, they made Robert Campbell as comfortable as they could and washed the worst of the mud and blood from his face and hands.

Margaret Campbell appeared at the door, admitting a blast of cold air.

"Bertie Campbell! What have you done?"

Campbell turned bleary eyes to his sister and something like a smile twitched the corners of his mouth.

"Mags. Glad to see you. Do you know everybody here?"

"Of course, I do. I work here. Trust you to fall off a horse. I suppose you were riding recklessly?"

Bertie frowned and touched his now bandaged ear.

"Someone shot at me," Bertie said. "Horse threw me."

Margaret looked at Charlie. "Danny didn't mention a shooting."

"He said something about a 'roo shooter," Charlie replied.

"That's ridiculous. How do you mistake a man on a horse for a wallaby?"

Charlie had no answer for that. She gave Margaret a quick summation of her brother's injuries and Margaret crossed to her brother and laid a hand on his shoulder.

"I think you are going to be our guest for a little while."

Bertie shook his head. "No. Going back to Melbourne tomorrow. Don't want to stay here. People bloody shoot at you..."

The youngest of the three town doctors, Doctor Dixon bustled in, his arrival interrupting any further discussion. He confirmed Charlie's diagnosis and set the leg. With the limb encased in plaster of Paris, the nurses saw their patient installed in one of the beds in the men's ward, where he drowsed off the effects of the morphine they gave him.

"If it's all right with you, Matron, I'll sit with him a while," Margaret said.

Charlie nodded. "I'll stay on for a bit," she said. "Let me know when he's settled."

She paused at the door to survey the ward. She currently had three male patients, including Bertie Campbell. The other men had come in over the last few days with injuries from the mines. In the women's ward she had a woman with dropsy and another heavily pregnant girl who had arrived on the doorstep that morning. It had been a busy day and she needed to write up the records so she turned towards her office.

"Matron?"

Daniel Hunt rose from the bench in the front hall.

"Visiting hours are from two until four tomorrow, Mr. Hunt," she said.

He ignored her.

"How's Campbell?"

"He'll be fine but he won't be going anywhere for a few weeks."

"A few weeks?"

Charlie shrugged. "A broken leg is just that—broken."

She pulled the envelope with Bertie's coin purse, wallet and hotel room keys from her pocket.

"I think you should look after these," she said. "Not that I don't trust anyone here, but I don't like to risk temptation."

Danny took the envelope, peering at the contents, before stuffing it into the pocket of his jacket.

"Thank you for fetching Sister Campbell," Charlie said.

"We're old friends." A smile caught at the corners of his mouth. "If he gets difficult, Matron, Margaret will deal with him."

"That's good to know. Does Mr. Campbell's injury affect your plans?" she asked.

Danny shrugged. "He was intending to return to Melbourne tomorrow, but I was planning to stay on a little longer."

She shivered. "It's cold out here. Do you want to come to the kitchen for a cup of tea?"

Danny hunched his shoulders and nodded. "That would be good."

Charlie installed him at the table in the hospital kitchen and set the kettle to boil.

While she busied herself putting together tea and sandwiches, she sensed him watching her.

As she turned to him with a cup in one hand and a plate in the other, he said, "Do I know you? You seem very familiar."

Her heart skipped a beat and with deliberate care she set the items on the table in front of him while she wondered how best to answer his question.

As she straightened, she said, "We did meet once, but it was a long time ago."

He frowned and his mouth curled in a smile. "The girl behind the potted palm!"

She stared at him. "I didn't expect you to remember."

Danny laughed. "You were the most memorable part of the evening."

Charlie sat down and poured tea for them both. "Not all that memorable. You had promised me a dance but when the time came you took another girl for a partner."

No one else had asked her for a dance that night—it seemed her status as Mrs. McLeod's grace and favor case had been firmly fixed. She had stood beside Eliza McLeod, her heart hammering with anticipation as the time had come for the promised dance. Her stomach lurched and shaming tears sprung to her eyes as Danny led another girl out onto the dance floor.

He picked up a teaspoon and stirred the tea, even though he had not put any sugar in it.

"I'm sorry. That was shameful of me. In my defense, my mother seemed to have lined up every eligible young girl in Melbourne for me to dance with that night."

She shrugged away the old humiliation.

He looked up. "I would rather have danced with you than anyone else in the room."

But you didn't.

"Eliza McLeod meant well, but I never belonged to your world, Mr. Hunt."

And that night confirmed it.

"Danny," he said. "My friends call me Danny."

"Kind of you, but I'm not your friend, Mr. Hunt."

He smiled. "I think anyone who shared a glass of warm champagne with me on the floor behind a potted palm can call themselves my friend. Don't you agree?"

Charlie momentarily shut her eyes. Two lonely people who had shared such a brief encounter hardly qualified for first-name terms. He could call her Charlie, but she couldn't bring herself to call him Danny. The social distance yawned between them.

"Besides," Danny continued, "I believe we share two people in common for whom I have the highest regard. Are you the Charlie O'Reilly that Netty Burrell talks about?"

"That's me. Charlie O'Reilly. Amos and Netty were very good to me when I was a child," Charlie said, adding with a rueful smile, "Not that I was a very easy child."

Danny frowned. "I'm sorry, but I don't recall you from the school."

"No, I think we must have arrived not long after you left," Charlie said in a flat tone. "Everyone still talked about the amazing Doctor Hunt and how he saved the town from smallpox." She paused. "They still talk about him."

Danny chuckled. "So I believe. Caleb does tend to make an impression. Was your father a miner?"

That was a difficult question to answer, and Charlie had to think how best to answer that question. Her mother had run a grog shop on the Aberfeldy road and her paternal uncle Black Jack Tehan had been a charming rogue who had disappeared from their lives on the night her sister, his daughter, had been born. Daniel Hunt did not need to know her family history.

She shook her head. "I just had my mother. She's remarried now and very happy being a farmer's wife down Korumburra way."

"Oh good, tea!" Margaret Campbell walked into the kitchen and Charlie had never been so pleased to see her.

"How's the patient?" she asked.

"Asleep. I'll leave him in the care of Sister Keegan. She won't take any of his nonsense. He's not going to be an easy patient, particularly when it dawns on him that he is stuck here."

She poured herself a cup and sat down, fixing Danny Hunt with a hard look.

"He keeps going on about how someone shot at him. That doesn't sound likely. Why would anyone shoot at Bertie?"

"I heard a shot," Danny said, "but I didn't see anyone."

Margaret's eyes widened. "He was lucky. I think it should be reported to the police."

Danny shrugged. "That's up to Bertie. As far as I am concerned, it was just an unfortunate accident. Some idiot with a few too many under the belt out shooting 'roos."

Charlie studied his face and noted the flicker of uncertainty behind his eyes.

"I think you should report it," she said. "If only for the police to issue a warning about random shootings."

A knock on the door prevented his response. Margaret answered it to the Italian who had brought Robert Campbell into the hospital. He leaned against the door jamb and smiled at Margaret Campbell as he raised the nurse's hand and kissed it.

"Ah, just the beautiful lady I was hoping to see."

To Charlie's surprise, far from being outraged, Margaret colored.

"Enough of that," Margaret said with no rancor in her voice. "You've had a few drinks, Nico."

The Italian grinned and nodded his head in Danny's direction. "My friend over there gave me a few shillings for my trouble so I have had some drinks and now it is too late to go home so I will take a room at the hotel but first I had to see the beautiful Sister Campbell."

Charlie rose to her feet. "Are you going to introduce us?"

Margaret turned to Charlie. "This is Nico Alberti," she said. "He was a patient a few months ago."

Nico grinned and pushed his sleeves up, revealing a long, freshly healed scar on his muscular forearm. "My cousin's saw slipped," he said with a shrug.

"Looks nasty," Charlie said.

"It was," Margaret said.

"But it is all good now," Nico replied. "Thanks to the care of the good Sister here."

Charlie stood up. "Sister Campbell, I think that is enough socializing. You are letting the cold air in."

"Goodbye, Sister Campbell. Goodbye..." Nico gave a cheerful wave and turned away.

Margaret lingered at the door as Nico Alberti turned and was swallowed up by the night. She sat down at the table, but her tea sat untouched and her gaze did not move from the kitchen window.

"Your tea is going cold," Charlie said.

"Sorry... I was woolgathering," she said. "I'll have to telegram my parents with the news about Robert, but it can wait till morning." She drained the cup and pulled a face. "My mother will create the most fearful fuss."

The bell in the women's ward rang on the board above the door. Charlie grimaced and rose to her feet.

"You can go home, Margaret. Sister Roberts will be here presently and you're not needed till morning."

"I'll walk you back, Margaret." Danny Hunt was on his feet. "Margaret?"

Margaret's attention had wandered back to the window. She gave a start and turned to Danny with a smile on her face.

"Thank you. If you're quite sure you don't need me, Matron?"

"I gave you the night off, Sister," Charlie said but she hadn't missed Margaret's distraction.

Danny waved at the door with a slight bow. "After you, Miss Campbell."

"Why, thank you Mr. Hunt."

Charlie glanced from one to the other, seeing the familiarity in Margaret's smile as she passed him.

She supposed if Daniel and Margaret's brother had been friends since schooldays then Margaret would have been very much part of their circle. Old and familiar friends.

As the door closed behind Danny and Margaret, Charlie saw to the patient and made herself a fresh cup of tea. As she sat at the table, she thought about the kindness shown by a young man to a girl too terrified to move from behind a potted palm. Had he really wanted to dance with her, or had he just been saying that to ease her disappointment, a disappointment that still rankled ten years later?

She shook her head. She hadn't belonged to his world then and she certainly didn't now.

SEVENTEEN

D anny retrieved his horse, looping the reins over his arm as Margaret slipped her arm into the crook of his elbow. Arm in arm, they strolled down the lane towards Margaret's lodgings.

"Do you know our new matron?" Margaret asked.

"I don't... not really. We've met on at least one occasion, that I can remember, but we know people in common. That's what we were discussing when you joined us."

"She's hardly your sort," Margaret said.

"What do you mean by that?"

"Her mother ran a sly grog shop up on the Aberfeldy road? And from what I hear, grog wasn't all she sold."

There was something unpleasant in Margaret's tone that caused Danny to stiffen. "Who her mother was and what she did is none of our business and certainly of no relevance to who Miss O'Reilly is today."

"She was in Louisa's year at school," Margaret said. "She was only there because she had some sort of scholarship. She was terribly clever, but she never really fitted in, if you know what I mean. Did you know her when you lived here?"

Danny shook his head. "I think she must have come after I left." The talk of Charlie O'Reilly made Danny oddly uncomfortable. It was time to change the subject. "What about you? Are you content working here in the back of beyond?"

Margaret shrugged. "I have found some interesting challenges but I had hoped they would offer me the job of matron in Matron Birch's absence. I'm just as qualified as O'Reilly and I know the hospital and the town better."

"We can't always have what we want, Margaret," Danny said.

They walked on in silence.

"Why did you really come to Maiden's Creek?" Margaret asked at last.

"I had some business in Maiden's Creek. Caleb sent me to check the old mine."

That was not a lie, he told himself, even if it was just one of several reasons.

"Did you suggest Bertie accompany you or was it the other way around?"

"It was his suggestion," Danny said with complete candor. "It's been some years since I was last here and I had no other plans, so I thought, why not?"

Margaret gave him a sidelong look with narrowed eyes. "No other reason?"

"None." Now he lied, uncomfortable with her line of questioning. "Why? Should there be?"

Margaret shrugged. "I thought maybe... you might want to... Ignore me. Just being silly."

He took a moment to appreciate her discomfort. Perhaps she was remembering her short, sharp dismissal of his suit, but that thought was unworthy.

Margaret looked up at him. "Do you ever wonder if you had made a different decision, how your life may have turned out?"

Danny stiffened. "What do you mean?"

Margaret stopped and faced him. "What if I had agreed to marry you?"

"But you didn't."

"But if I had... would I now be a beautifully dressed society hostess in a nice house, organizing servants and charity drives? That is my mother's and sisters' lives. I would have hated it... or at least I thought I would have hated it."

Danny had no answer to that.

Margaret stopped and dropped her grip on his arm. "Would renewing our friendship be so terrible, Danny?" she asked.

It was too dark to read her face and Danny chose his words with care. "We will always be friends, Mags."

When she had refused his offer of marriage, he hadn't understood her reasons. He'd wanted to rail at her. What was wrong with him? He had everything a girl could want—wealth, good looks (or so he'd been told), a genial personality. He even had a respectable profession on top of his considerable private income. Yet she had still said no. What did she want of him now? Or he of her?

They had reached the gate of the little cottage where Margaret lodged and she turned to face him.

"This is me. Goodnight, Danny."

He took a breath. "Margaret, tell me honestly, why did you turn me down?"

She looked at him. "Really, Danny... it was nothing against you."

When he didn't respond, she looked away for a long moment before turning back to face him, her face shadowed in the dark.

"Very well. I really did want to experience something of life. Make my own way in the world... not eke out my existence as someone else's chattel."

"I never thought of you that way," Danny blurted out.

"I know, but that was the expectation of my parents and I just thought there was something more for me in the world."

She hefted an audible sigh and Danny wondered if she had found what she had been looking for. He doubted it existed in these hills.

Margaret's gaze slid to the gate behind him. "It's cold and I would prefer to be inside. Will you be returning to Melbourne tomorrow?"

"I never intended to. I have that task from Caleb, and besides, I can hardly desert poor old Bertie in his hour of need."

"Good. Then we shall be seeing each other regularly." She caught his hand. "Perhaps we can find each other again, Danny?"

He gently disengaged her fingers. "I shall be busy, Mags."

She stiffened. "Visiting hours at the hospital are between two and four. As for Bertie's hour of need, I shall be putting him on a train back to Melbourne as soon as can be arranged. He's going to be the worst patient."

Danny laughed. "I fear you might be right."

She kissed him lightly on the cheek. "Goodnight, Danny. I'm glad you're here."

Surprised by the gesture, he hadn't formed a response before the front door to the cottage shut behind Margaret and he was alone.

He stood looking up at the stars in the frosty night, his breath blowing white in the cold air, his hands thrust deep into his pockets. He had forgotten how clear and bright the sky could be, each star like a brilliant cut diamond, glinting in the broad sweep of the Milky Way.

He glanced back at the cottage and thought about Margaret's words. Over the years since her rejection, he had harbored a memory of Margaret Campbell that he realized now was no more than hurt pride. Seeing her again stirred nothing more than the pleasure of seeing a familiar face in a strange place and there had been another familiar face that had stirred more in his heart than Margaret Campbell had.

He had seen the hurt in Charlie O'Reilly's eyes when she had reminded him of that lost dance all those years ago. If nothing else he had to make amends to her for his caddish behavior. He allowed himself a small smile. There was no hurry to return to Melbourne. He had all the time in the world.

EIGHTEEN

After leaving Margaret, Danny returned his horse to Sones Livery Stables. Amos was at home but his stable lad, Johnny, assured him the other horse had returned uninjured a couple of hours earlier. Word had already reached town of an accident on the Thompson River track so he hadn't felt the need to raise an alarm or bother Amos.

Thrusting his hands in his pockets and pulling up his collar against the cold night, Danny walked up the quiet main street to the Britannia, his immediate thoughts fixed on a warm meal and a blazing fire. The nagging suspicion that the shooting of Bertie Campbell had been deliberate tugged at his conscience and he hurried on, half wondering if every darkened doorway harbored Micah Allen. Unconsciously his hand went to the butt of the unloaded Colt.

He stopped as he reached the police station. A light burned in the window but he didn't have the energy to deal with the police. It could wait till the next morning. He turned towards the Britannia where lights burned brightly from the front bar.

As he walked through the bar he heard his name... but not his name. A name no one had called him for twenty years.

"Danny bloody Greaves."

He froze and turned slowly to see who had hailed him. A bearded miner seated at a table with three mates raised a half-empty glass of beer. When Danny didn't respond, the man rose to his feet.

"Don't you recognize me, Greaves?"

Danny straightened his shoulders. He would have recognized Bert Marsh anywhere and in that moment he could have been ten years old again. The man's ginger hair may have begun to thin and the lines on his face were highlighted with the ingrained dirt of the mine, but the hard eyes that raked him were those of his childhood nemesis.

"How are you, Bert?" he said.

"Heard you was in town," Bert said. "Come back to slum with us, have you Greaves?"

"Hunt," Danny said. "I go by my stepfather's name."

Bert nodded. "Good bloke, Caleb Hunt, but you'll always be Danny Greaves to me. Come and have a drink with us, Greaves, or are you too high and mighty to rough it with a bunch of miners."

Danny's instinct was to turn and run. He glanced at the bar where Joe gave him a nod of reassurance.

"Set up a round for the table, Joe," Danny said.

Bert pulled a stool to the table and Joe carried the beers over with practiced ease, compensating for his limp and not spilling a drop as he set them down.

"So, Bert," Danny said, hoping the men didn't hear the tension in his voice. "I hear you're doing well up at the mine."

"Foreman of the D shift. This here's some of my crew." He introduced the three other miners. "Married a pretty little thing from down Moe way and we've three nippers. How about you, Greaves?"

Danny shook his head. "No wife or family yet."

"Look at you with your fancy city clothes and your parents donating money to build the hospital. You fell on your feet, Greaves. No earning an honest living like the rest of us."

"I'm a lawyer," Danny said, oddly grateful that he could name a profession.

"I said, honest living," Bert said and his comrades laughed.

"You a good lawyer?" Bert said when the joke was done.

"I think so."

"So why are you here? Haven't seen you for twenty years and here you are."

"I came to check on the Shenandoah and visit friends," Danny said. "The Burrells," he added for good measure.

Bert nodded his approval. "Fair enough," he said.

Danny drained his beer and pushed his stool back.

"It's been good to see you, Bert." He held out his hand.

Bert didn't move. He looked up at Danny with narrowed eyes and a look that made Danny's blood run cold.

"Tell me, are the stories true?"

Danny's breath caught in his throat and he dropped his hand.

"What do you mean? What stories?"

"It was all over town. For all your ma's fine ways, you was a bastard and your father was that English cove who got caught in the fires?"

Danny felt the blood drain from his face. "That is none of your business."

Bert stood up to face him. Danny stood nearly half a head taller than the miner, but he would be no match for Bert if it came to fisticuffs, and he doubted Bert would abide by the Marquess of Queensberry rules.

To his surprise, Bert held out his hand. "I liked you a hell of a lot better for being a bastard," he said.

Danny took the proffered hand and Bert clapped him on the shoulder.

"My da was a hard man," he said. "Too much drink and he'd lay into Ma and us kids when he got home." He picked up his hat from the table. "Always envied you for not having to face that every night."

Bert had envied him? He thought back to Bert's stories about going fishing with his father and how he had wished he had a father to take him fishing. But he also remembered the bruises, dismissed by Bert as rough and tumble with his brothers or an accidental fall while out in the bush.

"I'm sorry," Danny said.

"Yeah, well, he's dead now and I made a vow on his grave that I wouldn't be like him." He looked around at his friends. "Better get home or the little lady will raise hell. Night gents."

Bert tipped his hat and strode out of the bar.

Danny bid the other miners good night and with a quizzical glance at Joe, he retired to his sitting room.

Joe followed him upstairs with a tray of supper and as he bent to light the fire, he said, "Bert's not a bad sort, Dan. His dad—

"I remember the bruises."

Joe sat back on his heels. "They're hard men, the miners. Even my Dad could be a bit free with his belt if he had a few too many. You were lucky."

Except my father tried to kidnap me and left me for dead in the middle of a bushfire, Danny thought.

He thanked Joe for lighting the fire and waited until he heard Joe's uneven tread descend the stairs before closing the curtains against the dark night and tucking into the thick, hot soup and fresh bread on the table. After he had eaten he settled down in front of the fire with his copy of *Mystery of the Hansom Cab* by Fergus Hume, which he intended to loan to Bertie when he visited the next day.

Danny had known Fergus Hume, a law clerk in adjoining chambers to his. Hume had left Melbourne a few years earlier but not before he and Danny had shared several alcohol-fueled dinners when they had talked of nothing but books and writing.

The book had been a prodigious success since it was first published some six years earlier. Although he'd read it before, several times, Danny started at the preface, lingering on Hume's description of how he had come to write the book; asking a bookseller what his most popular seller was. On being told it was a particular detective story, Hume wrote *"... I determined to write a book of the same class; containing a mystery, a murder and a description of low life in Melbourne..."*

He tapped the book thoughtfully. Maybe that's what he was doing wrong. Much as he loved writing his stories of derring-do, all of which resembled the last Rider Haggard he had read, perhaps like Hume he needed to take a more scientific approach. If detective stories were selling, perhaps that was what he should consider writing.

Exhausted by the day's events, he felt his eyelids begin to droop and drifted into a half sleep where he dreamed of faceless men and blazing rifles and a girl in a green dress.

NINETEEN

R obert Campbell's continual high-handed demands for a private room and better food and drink interrupted the Monday morning routine at the hospital. Even Sister Keegan failed to calm him. When Danny Hunt turned up during visiting hours, Charlie took him to one side and told him in no uncertain terms that if Mr. Campbell did not behave himself, he would get his wish and be evicted from the hospital and into his friend's care.

Danny marched into the ward and Charlie followed at a discreet distance under the pretense of seeing to one of the other patients. She was curious to see how Danny Hunt dealt with his difficult friend.

Danny slammed the book he had brought on the table beside the bed and glared at Campbell.

"What's this I hear of you causing trouble for the hospital staff?"

"For God's sake get me out of here, Hunt." Campbell pushed himself up on his elbows. "The food is vile. The women are all harpies, including my sister and—"

"You should count yourself fortunate that you are here, Campbell,"

Danny said. "In my day there was no hospital. If you were lucky you would have been carted over the mountains on the back of a cart. If you were unlucky you would end up at the Australis Hotel being fed gruel. Your leg would have turned gangrenous and..."

Charlie coughed and Danny looked up. Charlie indicated the poor man whose foot had been recently amputated.

"And you would probably be dead," Danny finished sotto voce.

Bertie subsided onto the pillows with a grunt.

"How long am I going to be here?" he mumbled.

Danny turned to Charlie and she joined him at Campbell's bedside.

"You will have to stay here until the break has healed enough for you to be transported safely. At least a couple of weeks," Charlie said. "Until then I ask that you respect my nurses and your fellow patients." The bell by the front door jangled and Charlie drew herself up. "Now excuse me, gentlemen, I have others to see to."

Lizzie Ryan beat her to the door, turning as Charlie approached. "Constable Smith asking for you, Matron," she said.

The policeman standing on the front doorstep whipped his cap from his head.

"Afternoon sister."

"What can I do for you, Constable?"

"We've a problem down in the cells," he said. "Picked up Martha Drew, drunk and soliciting. She's coughing fit to burst a lung so the sergeant asks if maybe someone could come and take a look at her. Doc Linacre available?"

Charlie shook her head. "He's running a clinic up at Aberfeldy. I don't expect him back until tomorrow but I'll come and have a look at the woman."

"Suit yourself, Sister—"

"Matron."

Constable Smith ducked his head with an apologetic "Matron."

As Charlie packed a bag with medical supplies, Mary Keegan stood watching, her arms crossed. "Martha Drew is the town nuisance, Matron. Good luck with her."

"I'm sure I've met worse in the slums of the cities," Charlie said, reaching for her coat.

"If you're not careful, she's more likely to scratch your eyes out," Keegan said.

Charlie followed the young constable down the path to the police station. The sergeant at the front desk looked up from his paperwork. Sergeant Maidment, who had been the law when she was a child, must have long since retired or moved on, and at first, Charlie did not recognize the solid man as he, in turn, looked her up and down.

"Who are you?"

Charlie held out her hand. "Matron O'Reilly. Pleased to make your acquaintance, Sergeant...?"

"Prewitt."

She started at the familiarity of the name. During her childhood, the law had been represented in Maiden's Creek by the cadaverously thin Sergeant Maidment, a sensible and much-respected police officer.

Prewitt had been one of Maidment's constables and had been, in all respects, the opposite of his superior. It seemed he had remained in Maiden's Creek and the years had not lightened his girth. His brass buttons strained over a massive belly and his self-important face held an unhealthy high color.

"Were you a constable here twenty years ago?" she asked.

He narrowed his eyes that were almost lost in rolls of saggy flesh, closely resembling two poached eggs.

"I was. Do I know you?"

Charlie was saved from answering by the broken strains of "Annie Laurie" coming from the back of the police station.

> Maxwelton's braes are bonnie,
>> Where early fa's the dew,
>> Twas there that Annie Laurie
>> Gave me her promise true.
>> Gave me her promise true

The woman's voice was surprisingly sweet and all three turned to look at the door leading through to the cells.

> Which ne'er forgot will be,

And for bonnie Annie Laurie
I'd lay me down and—

The song cut off to be replaced by crashing and foul language, interspersed with violent coughs.

Prewitt grunted.

"Smith here found Martha down by the Miner's Arms Hotel, begging for coin for her next drink. Fortunately, most of the town knows her and her bad habits, but it doesn't stop her trying. If it were me, I'd have let her be, but Smith's got a soft heart and thought she needed the doc."

"Where does she live?"

The young constable answered, "She's got a hut out near the Chinese gardens. Vile, stinking place it is too. Her husband built it on the site of a place that was burned down owing to smallpox. Got the land for a song 'cos folk reckon it's haunted."

Charlie shivered. She had passed the site of the smallpox house, as it was called, on her way to and from school. When she reached it she would always break into a run for fear of the ghost of the woman who had died of smallpox, who was said to haunt it.

"Where's her husband?" Charlie asked.

"Fell down a mine shaft five years ago. He was no great loss. Drunken brute of a man. He was pretty free with his fists, broke her arm once. Left her with a bairn that died of typhus the following summer. Been all downhill for Martha since then."

"Poor woman," Charlie said.

"You haven't met her," Prewitt said with a snort. "Take the sister through to her, Smith."

The cells at the back of the property were little more than caves, cut into the rock and secured by heavy grills. The stench of vomit, and worse, hit Charlie as soon as the constable opened the door. The area was lit by a single kerosene lantern hanging from a hook by the door so at first it was hard to make out which cell the woman was held in until she lunged at the grill door like an unbroken animal, spitting obscenities at the policeman.

The constable instinctively took a step back. "Blimey, what a mess.

You better settle down, Martha or you'll get another bucket of water. I've brought the nurse from the hospital to see to you."

"I don't need a nurse," the woman said. "I just need a drink."

The effort of speaking provoked a paroxysm of racking wet coughs.

"I'm going to let the sister in to take a look at you. Behave," Smith said.

The constable lit a second lantern and handed it to Charlie. He unlocked the grille and Charlie stepped into the cell.

The woman, crouched on the floor, looked little better than a bundle of filthy stinking rags. Long strands of unkempt hair fell around her face and her arms were wrapped around herself as she tried to stem the coughing.

"Give me a hand here," Charlie said to the constable.

With a grimace, he stepped into the cell. "I'll have to clean this mess up," he grumbled as he helped Charlie lift the woman to her feet and guide her to the rock-cut platform covered in a lumpy hessian mattress that served as a bed.

"She's soaking wet," Charlie said.

The constable shuffled his feet.

"Only way to calm her down," he said.

Charlie set the lantern on a stool and raised the woman's head.

"A dousing in this weather is more likely to kill her. Let's look at you."

The hair fell away from a ravaged face that looked ten years older than the woman's true age. A face that even through the grime and marks of dissipation, Charlie recognized.

"Good God," she blasphemed. "Martha Mackie."

The woman stiffened, her chin coming up, and for a fleeting moment Charlie caught a glimpse of her nemesis from school, the prissy little girl in her immaculate pinafores who had called Charlie's mother a whore... and worse.

"No one's called me that for a long time. Who the hell are you?"

"Don't you recognize me, Martha?"

"Nuh."

"Charlie O'Reilly."

The woman's mouth fell open. "Mad Annie's daughter?" She

snorted and looked away. "Who'd've thought Mad Annie's daughter would come back here? Now I'm the whore and they call me mad and you're the one in the nice clothes who smells of soap."

She doubled over, coughing again.

"I'm going to take you up to the hospital, Martha. You need a bath and a square meal," Charlie said.

"I need a bloody drink," Martha spat back. "Leave me be."

"I'm not leaving you here. It's cold and damp and you need a doctor to see to that cough and some decent wholesome food."

Martha leaned back against the wall, studying Charlie through half-closed eyes.

"So Mad Annie's little girl did all right for herself. All that sucking up to the McLeods paid off."

An old, ugly, familiar knot gathered in Charlie's stomach.

You are not ten years old. This woman has no hold over you, she reminded herself.

She turned to the doorway. "Constable, will you help me get Mrs..." She turned back to Martha. "What is your name?"

"Drew. My name's Martha Drew."

"Help me get Mrs. Drew up to the hospital."

"I don't wanna go..." Martha dug her fingers into the mattress. "People die there. I've seen 'em. He comes for 'em at night."

The constable cast Charlie a knowing look and made a drinking motion with his hand.

"In and out of the hospital she is. They get her fixed up and within a couple of months she's back there again. Come on Mrs. Drew, let's get you out of here," he said, prying Martha's hands away from the mattress.

It took both Charlie and the constable to drag Martha to the front desk and secure her release. Outside, the young constable took her by one arm and Charlie took the other. Martha resisted them all the way up the hill, screeching her protests to the world.

Margaret Campbell came out to meet them.

"What a racket," she said. "Mrs. Drew, if you don't calm down you will disturb the patients and they need their sleep."

"I don't want to be here. You can't make me. He'll be coming for me next."

"What's she talking about?" Margaret asked.

"People die here!" Martha screeched.

"It's a hospital, Martha, people die," Charlie said.

The constable beat a retreat to the police station, leaving Charlie and Margaret to wrestle Martha out of her damp, filthy rags and into a warm bath. The woman was pitifully thin, the bones of her shoulders, hips, and ribs clearly visible, and Charlie wondered when Martha had last eaten a decent meal.

Once in the warm water, all the fight went out of her, and she allowed the two women to minister to her. Her hair was tangled beyond redemption and she moaned but made no attempt to stop Charlie as she attacked the tangled mess with scissors, cutting it to shoulder length.

The coughing subsided in the steam from the bath and by the time they got the woman into a clean nightgown and put her to bed in the women's ward, with hot milk and a bowl of soup, Martha was as docile as a lamb.

"It won't last," Mary Keegan said. "As soon as she's got her strength back, she'll be back to her old ways."

Privately Charlie agreed. She'd met too many Marthas on the streets of Melbourne and London, but while she was in her care she would see that she got respect and kindness.

"Nought to be done for women like that," Sister Keegan continued over tea in the hospital kitchen. "It would be a kindness just to let the lung fever take her."

"Where's your Christian compassion?" Charlie countered.

Mary Keegan regarded her with her cold, hard eyes. "I was born at a time when memories of the potato famine were still fresh. Me ma lost six brothers and sisters and her da. There was precious little compassion for our suffering."

Charlie nodded. "All the more reason to show compassion now when we can. Martha gets the very best care we can give her."

Sister Keegan snorted and stood up. "I, for one, won't take any nonsense from her."

"And a little bit of that is probably what she needs," Charlie conceded.

After her shift ended, she left the hospital and made her way up the hill to her little cottage. As she crouched beside the fire, encouraging the first flames, she thought she should feel vindication or even glee that Martha, who made her childhood so miserable, had fallen on hard times.

She didn't feel either of these emotions, just a tremendous sadness.

TWENTY

After he left Bertie, Danny returned to the hotel with the intention of making the most of the daylight to turn one of the sketches he had made on the ill-fated Thompson River excursion into a painting. But as he sat flicking through his sketchbook, he reached for his pencil and began to make a rough sketch of Micah Allen.

Since the shooting incident, he found himself scanning the faces of the people he passed in the street, but if Allen was in Maiden's Creek he remained out of sight. The frustrating thing about the man, Danny thought as he drew, was his very ordinariness. It took a couple of tries but after an hour he thought he had a good enough likeness to ask around. He'd start with Joe Trevelyan, who might well have seen the man in the bar of the Britannia.

As if he'd been summoned, Joe knocked at his door to ask if he wanted supper in his room. Danny glanced at his watch.

"No, thank you. I'm expected at the Burrells' for supper. I completely lost track of time."

Joe glanced at the piece of paper in Danny's hand. "You an artist?"

"Not at all. I just dabble." Danny held the drawing out to Joe. "Have you seen this man at all?"

Joe took it and studied it, a frown creasing his brow. "Hard to say. What color's his hair?"

"Brown."

"Does he have a name?"

"Micah Allen. He may have been asking about me?"

Joe's eyes widened. "Aye, there was a man. Came in Saturday night. Wanted to know if you were staying here."

"What did you tell him?"

"Told him what I tell everyone. Who's staying in my hotel is private."

Danny thanked him with a heavy heart. Micah Allen could be anywhere, waiting on another opportunity to exact his revenge, and if the man was following him, he'd know by now that Danny was staying at the Britannia.

"If he comes in again, what do you want me to do?" Joe asked.

Danny shook his head. "Don't give away the fact that I've alerted you to him. I would be interested in knowing where he is staying."

Joe shrugged. "Easy enough." He handed the drawing back. "I don't need that, not now I've remembered the bloke." He stepped back into the hall. "Goodnight, Mr Hunt."

"I was Danny at school," he said. "Drop the 'Mr Hunt', Joe."

Joe nodded. "Aye, you'll always be Danny to those of us who knew you then."

And this was why one should never return to your childhood, Danny thought as he shut the door behind Joe. When he had reached adulthood, Danny had tried to become Dan or Daniel Hunt to new acquaintances, but only Caleb ever called him Dan, and over the years, he accepted he would always be Danny to those who knew him well.

His gaze lingered on the door to Bertie's room and he glanced at his watch. He wasn't expected at Netty and Amos's for a little while yet and he had the excuse of rustling up something of Bertie's to take to the hospital tomorrow. Bertie wouldn't be returning any time soon. What would a quick look through his trunk cost?

He retrieved the envelope Charlie had given him and found the key to the trunk. One of the housemaids had been into the room and made the bed and done her best to tidy up the mess of clothes, socks and shoes that Bertie had left strewn around the room. He was a man too used to having servants to pick up after him.

He tossed the key in his hand as he stood looking down at Bertie's trunk, remembering its weight as they had carried it between them up the main street of Maiden's Creek. Had it contained the mace of the Parliament of Victoria?

He told himself that the mace wouldn't fit in Bertie's trunk—unless it had been reduced in size. He blew out a breath and, pushing all feelings of guilt to the back of his mind, turned the key in the lock.

He rifled through the already jumbled clothes to the bottom of the trunk. If a five-foot long, solid, silver mace had been concealed in Bertie's possession it was no longer there. Danny sat back on his heels, unsure whether he felt relief or disappointment. He did a quick scan of the cupboard and drawers, but they were empty. If Bertie had brought the mace with him, he had disposed of it sometime in the twenty-four hours between arrival and his accident.

He gathered up a selection of clothing suitable for a prolonged hospital stay, along with Bertie's shaving kit, and closed the door to Bertie's bedroom. He set the bundle of clothing to one side and returned to his own room to tidy himself up for dinner.

As he stepped outside, he paused, looking at the brightly lit police station across the road. Was there any point in reporting his suspicions that Micah Allen had followed him to Maiden's Creek and may have been responsible for the shooting that had resulted in Bertie's injury?

Even as he rehearsed the conversation he would have with the constabulary, it sounded far-fetched and implausible. He needed something more tangible and until he had that, he had to look out for himself. Maybe carrying Caleb's revolver with him was not such a bad idea?

For the moment, one of Netty's home-cooked meals beckoned, and to hell with Micah Allen.

TWENTY-ONE

The heavenly scent of roasting meat and a bright, welcoming light in the window greeted Charlie as she walked down the path to Netty's front door.

Amos opened the door to her knock and she stepped gratefully into the warm, cozy parlor. Netty was bent over the stove while a man stood beside her, a cloth in hand ready to receive the roasting pan.

Danny Hunt looked around and smiled. "Good evening, Miss O'Reilly," he said.

"Mr. Hunt." She returned the greeting. "I didn't know you were expecting anyone else for dinner, Netty."

"Time you two met and I may as well cook for four as two," Netty said. "And here in this kitchen you are Danny and Charlie. I won't be having any Miss or Mister nonsense."

Charlie gave Danny a rueful glance. There was no arguing with Netty, who had clearly arranged for both of them to be present for dinner for her own reasons. Still, an evening getting to know Daniel Hunt a little better gave her an unfamiliar warm glow.

"Sit down everyone. The food will go cold."

Charlie picked up the rotund Flossie from her chair and scratched her ears.

"She hasn't got long now," she said.

"Is that your professional opinion?" Netty asked, setting down a heaped bowl of steaming vegetables.

Charlie sat across from Danny. A smile caught at the corners of his mouth and she found herself smiling in response as they bent their heads for the grace.

"I'm sorry Bertie Campbell is being so difficult," Danny said as he passed her a bowl brimful of new potatoes, doused in melting butter.

Charlie shrugged. "We've dealt with worse."

"I heard you've got Martha Drew up there," Netty said.

"We only admitted her this afternoon. Word travels fast."

Netty shrugged a shoulder. "This is Maiden's Creek. Martha's a sad case. Did you know her, Danny? Martha Mackie as was."

Danny nodded. "There were several Mackie sisters. I don't remember Martha specifically."

Netty glanced at Charlie. "But you would."

"Oh yes, as you well know, Netty, Martha and I crossed paths... and swords on many occasions. But I was sad to see what had become of her when she had so much promise."

"What happened to her?" Danny asked.

Netty clucked her tongue. "Tom Drew was a bad 'un but silly Martha fell for him. No one could tell her otherwise. Family disowned her when he got her in the family way. He did at least make an honest woman of her, but he made her life hell before he fell down a mine shaft and broke his neck. Too late for Martha. The bairn had been born sickly and didn't see out a year and she'd fallen into the demon drink. The town turned on her, and her family had long since moved away, leaving her with nowhere to go and no friendly faces."

Charlie thought of the prissy little girl with her golden curls and lace-edged pinafores.

"Another woman who fell for the charms of a rogue," she said, her thoughts straying from Martha to her mother... and herself. She was just as susceptible to the charms of an unsuitable man as Martha. She could count herself lucky that he hadn't been violent—just married to some-body else. "I don't believe any of us have a right to throw stones. I've seen too many broken women."

Netty nodded. "Martha's in the best place for the moment so let's talk about other matters. Danny, what are you planning to do with your friend in the hospital for a little while? Go back to Melbourne?"

He shook his head. "No. I want to spend some time in the bush. Do some painting perhaps. I promised my parents I would check out the Shenandoah, see that it has been made safe—"

Charlie straightened. "The Shenandoah?"

Danny looked at her. "You know it?"

Charlie almost laughed aloud. "I knew it well. My uncle was the mine manager up there for a while."

"Her uncle was Black Jack Tehan," Netty said. "Talk about rogues."

Charlie rounded on her friend. "Jack wasn't bad." She paused, and added, "Not in the sense we were discussing."

"You have me intrigued," Danny said. "What did this Black Jack do?"

Charlie shrugged. "Let's just say when he saw an opportunity he grabbed it." She glared at Netty. "He was good to my mother and me."

"Aye and when did your mother last hear hide nor hair of him? Abandoned her and the bairn he did."

He had, but Charlie felt bound to defend her uncle's honor.

"He had his own reasons for having to leave the area."

"And we all know what those were. Avoiding the law, and his responsibilities," Netty said.

"Your uncle...?" Danny asked.

Charlie stabbed a piece of potato as she mumbled. "He's my sister's father. His brother was my father."

Danny lifted an eyebrow. "That makes for a complicated family."

Charlie shrugged. "Doesn't matter. Jack took off after my sister was born, no one's heard from him in ages."

"And your ma is a respectable married lady with a new bairn of her own," Netty said.

"Not so new. Amy is five now," Charlie said. She looked up at Danny. "If you're going to the Shenandoah, I would love to go with you."

"Why would you want to see an old mine?" Netty asked.

Charlie shrugged. "Silly I suppose, but it holds memories." She held up a hand. "I quite understand if you don't wish for company, I can go up there at any time."

"No. That would be fine," Danny said. "I would be glad of the company. When would you be able to spare an afternoon?"

"I can take some time on Friday afternoon," she said. "Can I borrow a horse, Amos?"

"Of course," the old man said. He shook a finger at Danny. "I warn you, lad, this one can ride. Taught by her uncle and he was born in a saddle I reckon. Not your namby-pamby English riding-school ways, like your friend."

"In fairness to Bertie, he was brought up on a Western District property. He's a better rider than me," Danny said.

Amos snorted. "Too hard on the reins." He leaned forward. "Now, are you going to tell me what happened up there? Gave my lad the fright of his life, a riderless horse turning up at the stables. He says the horse had blood on its neck."

Danny shrugged. "The horse threw Bertie after it was startled by a shot."

"A shot that took off the top of his ear, which would account for the blood," Charlie added.

Amos looked from one to the other. "Someone hate your friend?"

"Why would you say that? It could just as easily have been a stray shot from a hunter," Danny said, and Charlie thought she detected an element of defensiveness in his tone.

Amos grunted. "Aye, well there's still some wild types living out there on the Thompson. Could've been a stray shot."

Charlie gave Danny a narrow look. There was far more to this story than Danny was telling, and he had piqued her curiosity, but he had turned his attention to the plate.

She turned to Netty and changed the subject. "I paid a call on a certain Nell Taylor."

Netty laughed. "Did you indeed?

"She's done all right for herself," Charlie said.

Danny glanced at Charlie. "Do you know Nell?"

"Everyone knew Nell," Charlie said. "Even you, apparently?"

He smiled. "I renewed my acquaintance with her too."

The conversation turned to Nell and the scandalous goings-on at the Maiden's Creek Tavern, and when the time came to leave Danny offered to walk Charlie back to her cottage. She hesitated before shrugging her acceptance.

They stepped out into a cold, clear night.

Danny shivered. "I forgot how cold it gets up here."

"Keeping the hospital warm is a challenge," Charlie said. She looked up at him. "Tell me, is something bothering you about Mr. Campbell's accident?"

The momentary hesitation gave lie to his next words. "Nothing. It was an accident, nothing more. What makes you think something bothers me?"

Charlie persisted. "It is my job to understand people," she said, "and you have a face I can read like a book."

Danny responded with a noncommittal grunt and for a fleeting moment she thought he might be about to confide in her, but he shrugged his shoulders and said with a laugh, "It's nothing. I'm jumping at shadows."

"There are always shadows," she said.

"True," he agreed and looked up at the hills around them, "and ghosts."

Charlie straightened and looked at him. "Is that why you have returned to Maiden's Creek?"

He shrugged. "I would be lying if I said I didn't have some unanswered questions about my past that lie buried here."

Charlie nodded. "It seems that everyone comes to Maiden's Creek to escape or to forget. Not many return."

He regarded her for a long moment. "So, why have you returned, Miss O'Reilly?"

To escape... and to forget... she thought.

"The hospital needed a matron," she said. "This is my cottage. Goodnight, Mr. Hunt... Danny."

He took her hand and half bowed over it. "Goodnight, Miss O'Reilly."

Charlie closed the front door behind her and leaned against it.

Friendship was a luxury she had shared with few people. Her upbringing had made her wary of people, but occasionally she encountered someone who had something special, a way to get around the walls she built around her heart, and she wondered if perhaps Danny Hunt might be one such person. In which case she needed to redouble her defenses and keep Mr. Hunt at a distance.

Twenty-Two

After the busy, bustling wards of the Women's Hospital, a hospital with only two wards and at most eight patients was hardly taxing, and Matron Birch had left everything running smoothly. It hadn't taken long for Charlie to feel she knew the workings of the hospital and the staff who kept it running.

The four nurses were competent and while they had their strengths and weaknesses, Charlie quickly worked out how to play to their better qualities. Sister Keegan handled difficult and recalcitrant patients with frightening ease, and Sister Becker and Sister Roberts were best with children and frightened women.

Sister Margaret Campbell remained a bit of an enigma. In a way she reminded Charlie of herself, except she had come to this work from a background of privilege. She was well educated, well-spoken and bright, and would have excelled in a busier environment, but she resisted all Charlie's attempts to elicit the reason for her choice of such a small, isolated community.

With the exception of Doctor Linacre, she hardly saw the other town doctors, except when they had patients being treated at the hospital. She never saw the other hospital committee members and they left the running of the hospital to Charlie. She appreciated the autonomy and the trust they put in her.

She had discovered that the role of matron required far more administrative work than she was used to. She ordered audits of all the stores and had taken it upon herself to go through the financial books of the hospital. April Birch had been impeccable in her bookkeeping and she found nothing untoward. She'd always preferred figures to words and she was deep in preparing the budget for the coming month.

"Matron?"

Charlie looked up from her ledger. Sister Janet Becker hovered in the doorway, a letter in her hand. She held it out as she entered the room.

"This came for you."

Charlie took the letter and glanced at the address written in an immaculate copperplate. Recognizing the hand, she dropped the letter to her blotter as if it had scalded her. She looked up to see Sister Becker regarding her curiously.

"Is there something else, Sister?"

Janet took a step into the room and closed the door behind her.

"I was wondering if I could change my day shift on Friday?"

Charlie grimaced. With only four nurses and herself, there was little room for maneuver when it came to the roster.

"May I ask why?"

Janet's mouth twisted into a shy little smile. "My beau has a free afternoon and we thought... that is... we hoped we could go for a picnic, maybe up at the Maiden's Falls if the weather is fine."

Spare me from young love, Charlie thought.

She reached for the roster. "You can have the afternoon off if I swap you with Sister Keegan but you'll have to do her night shift on Friday and Saturday night."

Janet smiled. "That would be grand."

Charlie gestured at a chair. "Sit down for a minute, Sister."

Janet Becker's eyes widened in alarm. "Am I in trouble?"

"Not at all, I just thought if you had a moment and I had a moment, we could talk for a minute or two."

Janet perched on the edge of the chair, her back rigid. So much for a cozy conversation, Charlie thought.

"Where are you from?" she asked.

"My parents are on a farm outside Wangaratta."

"Why did you choose nursing?"

Janet shrugged. "I've eight sisters and two brothers and I didn't want to go into service, or marry one of the local lads and end up on a farm. I thought nursing would give me a bit of independence." She grimaced. "I might have been wrong about that."

"What do you mean?"

"I love my work," Janet said, rather too quickly, "but the hours are long and, well, it's hard to make a life away from the hospital."

"For some of us, it's a vocation."

"Not for me. I want to get married, have a family, but to do that I have to leave nursing, don't I? I don't see why women must give up a job they love just because they have a ring on their finger. Especially as the money would be useful."

"You found yourself a beau," Charlie said. "That's something. Joe Trevelyan is a good man."

A flush of pink rose to Janet's cheeks as she nodded. "He is."

"Do you think you'll marry him?"

"We've talked about what we would do if we were married but he hasn't asked me properly yet." Janet smiled and gave a self-conscious giggle. "Maybe he will this Friday?"

"And then?"

"We'll be off to the city. Both of us have had enough of small towns."

"I never thought Joe would leave the valley," Charlie said.

Janet shrugged. "He's got nothing to keep him here except a loyalty to Yorkie Oldroyd but Yorkie's got his own children to see him right so Joe is free to do as he chooses."

"I'll be sorry to lose you," Charlie said, rising to her feet as a signal the interview was over. "It is nearly time to do my rounds. I shall see you presently, Sister Becker."

Janet nodded. "Better tidy up." At the door she stopped and looked back at Charlie. "That Martha Drew... she's a handful. How long have we got to put up with her?"

"As long as she needs our care."

"She was creating something terrible this morning. Wanted a drink, she said. She upsets the other patients."

"I know. I heard her. She deserves our compassion, not our condemnation, Sister."

Janet sniffed. "If you say so, Matron."

"I do. Off you go."

Janet closed the door behind her leaving Charlie alone... alone with a letter on her blotter.

Charlie picked it up and huffed out a long breath.

The missive had been addressed to *MISS C. O'REILLY, Maiden's Creek District Hospital*. He couldn't even bring himself to use her proper title.

Holding the letter between her thumb and forefinger, she turned to the fire in the grate behind her. For a fraction of a moment she hesitated, half curious as to what Dr William Fitzgerald thought he could say or do that would change anything.

She closed her eyes, took a deep breath, and cast the letter onto the coals, watching as it caught, the corners curling, the black of the ink leaping from the burning paper as it dissolved into ashes.

Stupidly, she felt the pricking of tears behind her eyes and dashed them away with her hand. What right did the man have to keep pursuing her to the ends of the world?

None.

None at all.

She needed fresh air, needed to clear her head of the taint of William Fitzgerald. Without further thought, she grabbed her coat and hat and stepped out into the chill of the afternoon.

"Matron.... Your round..."

She turned to see Lily Roberts standing at the kitchen door. "I'll be back in half an hour," she said. "Urgent matter..."

Through the shaming tears she walked away from the hospital, seeking the one place in Maiden's Creek where she knew she could be alone with her thoughts, even if it was just for half an hour.

The cemetery.

TWENTY-THREE

Danny spent a restless night, his mind churning with his childhood memories.

The events of those last months in Maiden's Creek had been a maelstrom from which he had been whisked away to begin a new life as Daniel Hunt. He needed to make sense of those events and in doing so, maybe then he could find that part of himself that he had lost. He'd already gleaned a sense of Richard Barnwell from Nell and Netty but he had one last place to visit before he felt he could walk away from the man who had called himself his father.

The overnight rain had turned the path to the cemetery into a treacherous muddy hazard of gullies and potholes full of water. Danny's expensive leather soled, city-made boots slipped several times, nearly sending him to his knees, and he reflected ruefully as he grabbed at the nearest bush to steady himself that he should invest in a pair of sturdy nailed boots if he was going to be staying any length of time.

Built into the side of a steep hill, the cemetery had been terraced with just enough width on each terrace to allow for a grave plot and a narrow path. The number of headstones and crooked crosses on untended graves stood as a testament to the uncertain life expectancy in the harsh conditions of the mountains.

The gate to the cemetery stood open and he passed under newly planted pine trees of a sturdy variety that would probably one day frame the entrance. Now they jostled with bright yellow wattle bushes for space and attention.

He stood looking up and down the slope, wondering where he would find the grave he sought.

A woman in a heavy overcoat and red woolen tam-o'-shanter sat on one of the tombs a little way up the slope, her back to him, her head bowed and a sprig of wattle, no doubt plucked from one of the bushes near the gate, clutched between her fingers.

He scrabbled up the path to her level.

"Excuse me, madam," he called out. "I'm sorry to disturb you, but would you be able to help me?"

The woman started, coming to her feet and turning to face him.

Charlie O'Reilly.

There was no trace of the confident, self-assured nurse he had dined with on the previous night. If he was not mistaken she had been crying, her face pale and her eyes red-rimmed. In that fleeting moment before she composed herself, he sensed a curious vulnerability and realized that for all the responsibility she carried, she was still young.

"I didn't mean to intrude."

She looked down at the wattle in her hand. "You're not intruding. I came to put these on Will Penrose's grave." She straightened, once more the brisk, no-nonsense nurse. "What do you need help with?"

"I'm looking for a particular grave and I would be grateful for another pair of eyes," he said and told her which grave he sought.

Together they scrambled up the muddy paths and along the lines of headstones until they found the grave Danny sought, tucked into a lonely corner of the cemetery. A plain headstone made of good-quality marble stood resolutely in place, unlike many of the fallen memorials.

Danny stooped and wiped the moss from the name with his handkerchief.

"*Richard Aloysius Barnwell*," Charlie read aloud. "*Born 13 October 1840, died 19 February 1872.*"

Charlie stood back with her head to one side, considering the gravestone. "Why the interest in Mr Barnwell?"

Danny thrust his hands deep into his pockets and hunched his shoulders. Why was it so difficult to say *He was my father?*

Something about this woman invited a confidence.

"Richard Barnwell was my father," he said.

She looked at him expectantly but he couldn't bring himself to confide the whole story and the moment passed.

Charlie straightened, glancing down the slope.

"I'll leave you to have a few quiet words with the late Mr Barnwell. There's someone else I need to visit."

Danny stood looking down at his father's grave, his hat in his hand. He thought he should say a prayer or something... but nothing would come, only the memory of the wild-eyed man who had all but killed him in his desperate bid to escape from Maiden's Creek. Barnwell's escape route had taken them into the teeth of a bushfire. Barnwell's death, as a result of the burns he sustained in the bushfire, had come as a relief.

And in that moment any further curiosity about Richard Barnwell evaporated as he recalled his own terror and the way Barnwell had abandoned him. No father with a claim to that title would ever have left their child. All for money, not love.

No, he had only one father and that man was Caleb Hunt. He had been the one to brave the smoke and flames to rescue the frightened boy and it was Caleb who had saved his life following a snake bite.

He laid a hand on the cold marble.

"I forgive you," he said aloud and turned away from Richard Barnwell's last resting place.

Charlie crouched beside a grave a couple of rows below him, pulling weeds, and he slithered down the slope to join her. She looked around as he joined her, a question in her eyes. He smiled and nodded, wanting to reassure her that everything was all right with him.

He turned his attention to the gravesite she had been tidying.

The simple granite gravestone was inscribed: *Cecily Brown, Born Melbourne 3 June 1849 Died 19 September 1873 Maiden's Creek. He that is without sin among you, let him first cast a stone.*

"Interesting quote. Whose grave is this?" he asked.

Charlie stood up, dusting her hands.

"You probably didn't know her. She was one of Lil's girls... she called herself Sissy."

Sissy. Of course he had known her. She had been dead nearly twenty years yet her death hit him like a blow to the stomach.

"I knew Sissy." He glanced up the hill and pointed out a large rock at the summit. "My mother used to hold reading lessons for Lil's girls... Sissy, Nell and the younger one... I don't recall her name."

"Probably Jess. I don't know what became of her. I must ask Nell," Charlie replied.

"Lil's girls were always kind to me," Danny said.

"And my mother and I," Charlie said. Her eyes screwed shut as if she was in pain. "There were those in town who labeled my mother a whore. She wasn't." He detected a catch of old pain in her voice. "She just wanted to make her own way in the world. It didn't stop men from presuming... If it hadn't been for Jack—" She broke off, her shoulders straightening. "You don't need to know that. It's history."

Danny glanced back up the hill at Richard Barnwell's lonely grave. "But it is our history that makes us who we are, Charlie. We can't pretend it never happened."

She looked at him. "Believe me, I have never forgotten those who were kind... and those who were not. But for every unkindness there were multiple kindnesses and that's why I'm here. My friend, Eliza McLeod, asked me to see to her brother's grave."

She turned to the handsome grave beside Sissy's, marked with an ornately carved headstone and iron railing. The last resting place of William Josiah Penrose.

"I knew him well. Will Penrose and Caleb were great friends. His death was a tragedy," Danny said.

Charlie looked up at him. "Any death so young is a tragedy in its own way."

She stooped and set one sprig of the yellow wattle at the foot of Sissy's headstone and the other on Will Penrose's grave.

"They could never be together in life but Eliza ensured they were together in death. She didn't have to do that."

Danny laid a hand on Will's handsome headstone, a wave of genuine grief threatening to overwhelm him. "Without Will Penrose there would have been no Shenandoah mine," he said. "We owe him a great debt of gratitude."

Charlie thrust her hands deep into her coat pockets and hunched her shoulders as a cold gust of wind came sweeping down from the high country. "After Will Penrose died, my uncle, Jack, took over the management of the Shenandoah."

"Strange how our paths have crossed and diverged over the years," Danny said.

Charlie huffed out a breath that clouded in the cold, damp air. "But isn't that life?" She looked up at the graying sky. "I had better get back to the hospital." She paused and gave him a small smile. "I'm glad I ran into you, Danny."

"Is there something troubling you, Charlie? I thought you might be upset—"

She shook her head. "No. Nothing important. Sometimes I just need a little time away from the hospital." She smiled. "I am looking forward to our visit to the Shenandoah."

Danny looked up at the gray sky. "It will be an adventure if it rains."

She looked him up and down. "In which case I suggest a visit to the general store for a more practical wardrobe might be called for."

He nodded and she turned away with a hurried goodbye.

Clutching the tam-o'-shanter with one hand and her skirts with the other, she picked her way down through the treacherous paths to the gate. At the gate she paused and turned to look up at him. He raised his hand and she ducked her head in acknowledgment before disappearing from view through a line of cottages. A short cut, no doubt, to the hospital.

The wind had picked up and had a bite to it that Danny had forgotten, as it blew across the snowy plains high above them. He turned up the collar on his coat and searched in his pockets for his gloves. A cup of tea would not go amiss and he knew just where to find one.

Netty's parlor was warm and comfortable, with a fire blazing in the hearth and a small, round tabby cat asleep on the rug in front of it. Danny crouched down and scratched behind the cat's ears. It didn't move, but the attention provoked a rumbly purr.

"She's a great-granddaughter of Charlie's cat," Netty said, setting the teapot on the table. "I thought I'd kept her out of the way of the local toms but her kittens are due any day." She shrugged. "Fortunately she comes from a good line of mousers so I won't have any trouble finding homes for them."

"I've been up to the cemetery," Danny said.

"You keep cheerful company. What took you up there?"

"Richard Barnwell."

Netty stopped in the middle of pouring tea, only composing herself as hot liquid spilled into the saucer.

"He's dead and gone and good riddance," Netty said with a sniff. She studied him with narrowed eyes. "Are you done now? Did you find the answers you came for?"

He nodded. "I'm done."

The cat stood up and stretched, eyeing Danny's lap. He patted his knee invitingly but it took an effort for her to jump up. He tickled her under the chin, a distraction as he said in as casual a tone as he could manage, "I met Charlie O'Reilly at the cemetery. It seems strange that Charlie and I both know so much about this town but nothing about each other."

Netty pushed a cup across to him. "What do you want to know? I knew Charlie when she was a bairn like yourself. Amos and I took her in when her ma couldn't manage for a time." She smiled fondly. "A strange, wild child she was too." She shrugged. "After her sister was born, her mother settled and did piecework for me till she married and Charlie went off to that grand school in Melbourne where your sister goes now." She raised a warning finger. "But if you want to know more, it's for her to tell, not me, and I'd say the same thing to her if she asked me about you." Netty picked up her cup and took a sip. "And I suggest you're going to have to be honest with her."

"I'm always honest," Danny said and then, catching Netty's meaning, he added, "You mean a respectable woman would be horrified if they knew my mother was unmarried and my real father was a... a..." Danny paused. "What exactly was he, Netty?"

"Richard Barnwell was an opportunist," Netty said, "with the devious cunning of a weak man. He was a seducer, a kidnapper, a—"

Danny held up his hand. "Enough. You didn't like him."

"Oh, he could be charming when it suited him," Netty said. "He certainly turned it on you."

Danny closed his eyes, remembering the man sprawled on the floor of the post office residence, explaining the Battle of Waterloo with the set of lead soldiers he had given Danny. Yes, he had been charming but, as his subsequent actions had demonstrated, it had all been for show.

Danny set his cup down and checked his watch. "Visiting hours. I better go and check on Bertie. Thank you for the tea."

As he stood to go, Netty reached up and touched his cheek. "You're so like your mother," she said. "One day you're going to have to let someone in."

"What on earth do you mean, Netty?"

Her eyes twinkled. "How old are you? Thirty, and not settled down yet? Haven't you found any nice girls in your travels?"

He smiled. "Plenty of nice girls and some not so nice."

But only one he had asked to marry, and she was here in Maiden's Creek.

TWENTY-FOUR

Despite a lowering sky, Friday afternoon promised to stay fine. Charlie dressed for the excursion to the Shenandoah in a full, plain skirt of brown wool and a loose mannish jacket and soft felt hat over hair secured in a long plait and wound into a knot in the nape of her neck.

Danny arrived on her doorstep with two of Amos's saddle horses. He was dressed in the moleskins and pea jacket that he had been wearing on the day he brought his friend into the hospital.

She smiled and held up a bundle wrapped in a cloth.

"Shall we go? I have food."

Danny dismounted and handed over the reins of a neat, surefooted mare to her. He stooped, cupping his hands to give her a lift into the saddle, but she swung up without his assistance.

"Amos doesn't run to side saddles," Danny said.

Charlie laughed as she gathered up the reins. "I have never ridden side saddle in my life. I couldn't imagine anything more dangerous in these hills."

"My mother sometimes used to take the mail to the outlying settlements. Netty and I would worry all day until she got back." He smiled. "She wore men's clothing for those excursions."

"I can't imagine your mother in trousers," Charlie said, remembering the tall, elegant woman at the long-ago party.

Danny smiled. "She is quite a surprising woman, my mother."

He secured the provisions in his saddlebag and swung into the saddle. As he did so, his jacket fell away and she glimpsed the butt of a large revolver protruding from his belt.

"What's that for? If you're planning on shooting wallabies, a rifle would be easier."

The color drained from his face and he touched the butt of the weapon. "You mean this?" He shrugged, jerking his jacket back over the weapon. "Just a precaution."

"As long as you know how to use it," she said, wondering what he felt he needed to take precautions against. From the haste with which he took to conceal the weapon, he clearly was not going to elaborate.

They set off at a gentle pace down Main Street, turning north, following the Aberfeldy Road past Lil's Place and the Chinese gardens.

"I used to walk this road every day to get to school," Charlie said when they were clear of the town.

"From where?" Danny asked. "I don't recall anything much on this road between here and Aberfeldy."

"I'll show you when we get there." Charlie looked up at the cold, wintry sky above them. "It was a good three miles and I was invariably late."

"Emerton wouldn't have liked that."

Charlie chuckled. "He didn't and neither did his successor, Miss Donald." She shuddered. "She was a tartar."

"Miss Donald?" Danny frowned. "Didn't she teach the younger children? Her brother was the Presbyterian minister."

Charlie nodded. "Emerton had a heart attack and she took over the school. She made my life hell. She was rather too fond of her cane and a ghastly strap called a tawse." She cast a glance at Danny. "I imagine you were one of those good, obedient children."

"Painfully so," Danny agreed. "But there was one boy, Bert Marsh, who made my life pretty miserable. I encountered him in the bar of the

Britannia the other day. He's a foreman up at the Maiden's Creek Mine now."

"Bert was all right," Charlie said. "I haven't crossed paths with him since I've been back but people can change, you know. I met Flora Donald and her son in the street. All these years she has haunted my nightmares and really she's just an ordinary woman. She no longer frightens me."

As they rode, she noticed Danny seemed uneasy, glancing around him—up the slopes into the vegetation and now and then behind him.

"Is someone following us?"

He hunched his shoulders. "Ignore me. City habits, Charlie. That's all."

They crested a rise and below them, a fast-flowing river cut the road.

"Goodness," Charlie said. "I've never seen the Aberfeldy River look like that. There must be a lot of rain in the high country."

She stared at the angry torrent, grateful they didn't have to cross it. She glanced at Danny. He was staring at the water, his face expressionless.

"Danny?"

He recollected himself and managed a half smile. "Sorry. Memories, Charlie. The last time I saw this river, I was escaping a bushfire."

"That's Australia," Charlie said. As they descended the steep track towards the river and the well-marked turn-off to Pretty Sally, she glimpsed the remains of a slab hut. It had fallen in on itself, the only discernible feature being the solid chimney constructed from river stones.

Charlie stopped. Rising in her stirrups, she pointed to the remains of the hut.

"My childhood home. Strange isn't it? I expected it to be unchanged."

Danny looked from the broken remains of the building to Charlie and back again. "You lived by yourselves all the way out here?"

She lowered herself back into the saddle, leaning forward and resting her forearms on the pommel as the memories, good and bad, came flooding back.

"Ma didn't want to live in a town. She provided food and drink for travelers on the road to Aberfeldy or Pretty Sally." She glanced at her companion. "It may sound strange to you, but I was happy here. There were plenty of miners going up and down the road and I ran wild. I had a dog..." Her gaze flicked to the place where her uncle had buried her beloved friend.

"It's been twenty years, Charlie."

"I know." She straightened, turning her horse towards the Pretty Sally track. "No time to linger on the past, we need to get a move on if we're going to get to the Shenandoah and back before dark."

The road up to the ridge where the settlement of Pretty Sally had grown up was rutted, potholed, and slippery, and they had to dismount to lead their horses around the worst of it.

"Doesn't look like much traffic goes up and down here anymore," Charlie said.

"I used to see the reports," Danny said. "Most of the goldmines supported by Pretty Sally have been worked out and abandoned in the last few years."

The settlement showed the same signs of neglect as the road. Gaps between abandoned buildings or tumbled chimneys showed that many of the structures had been removed or fallen into disrepair. Only the general store still stood intact, the weatherboards rotting and moss-covered.

A woman in a filthy apron over a gingham dress leaned against the doorway, straightening as the two riders approached.

"Anything I can do for you, guv?" She addressed Danny, pointedly ignoring Charlie.

"Can you point out the track to the Shenandoah?" Danny asked.

"The Shenandoah? It's been closed these two years past," the woman said. "What's your business down there?"

"Just that—MY business," Danny replied.

She shrugged and pointed along the road. "A couple of hundred yards past the burned stump," she said. "Can't miss it."·

"You didn't have to ask her. I know where the Shenandoah is," Charlie said. "These gullies were my back garden. I had a shortcut from our hut to the Shenandoah. Took me half the time it took to come by the road."

Danny stared at her. "Netty told me you were rather a wild child," he said.

She smiled. "I was."

They rode on in silence, taking the overgrown track that led down to a gateway, the gates hanging half off their hinges. A neatly painted but faded sign attached to one gate announced:

Shenandoah Mine
Enquiries to Mine Manager's Office.

They rode through the main gate and stopped, both of them looking around.

The site bore little resemblance to Charlie's memories of the once-thriving goldmine. Most of the structures were gone, the iron walls and roofs removed to be used elsewhere. Only a rusting waterwheel, a couple of boilers and a ten-head stamper bore testimony to the once productive mine it had been.

Danny let out a low whistle. "When I first came here, it had known only prospectors," he said. "It was rather beautiful. Caleb taught me how to pan for gold. I was so excited when I found my first few specks. Now look at it. All this destruction wrought by my family."

"At least they had some success," Charlie said. "There's many that don't. My uncle, Jack, had gold fever. He swore it would be the answer to our prayers. His fortune was always going to be in the next pan."

Charlie slid off her horse and led it across to a hitching post, tying the reins securely. The years sloughed away and for the first time since her return to Maiden's Creek she was once more the scruffy chid who belonged to this wild, neglected place where young trees and ferns grew among rusty buckets and the detritus of twenty years of industry.

She left Danny inspecting the workings and taking notes and headed towards a man-made cave cut into the side of the slope. The dark opening had been the original adit, excavated by the first miners who had tried their luck at this place. In later years it had become a storeroom for the explosives and other mine equipment.

She barely broke step as she entered the dark maw, her fingers working along the rugged wall, seeking the old hiding place in a niche in the wall. With the strange quirk of memory, her fingers closed without hesitation on the hard, straight planes of the old tobacco tin.

"What are you doing in here?"

She turned at the sound of Danny's voice. He stood just outside the entrance, his back to the light, his face in shadow.

"It's still here," she said aloud, hardly able to contain her excitement as she held up the tin. "I can't believe it."

"What have you found?" he asked.

She looked at the rusty tin in her hand. "Nothing important, just a memory from my childhood."

"Are you hungry? I've unpacked our lunch. Come and join me and you can show me what you have."

She watched him walk away from her, his hands in the pockets of his old jacket. He seemed to move more easily in the rough clothes—almost as if he had shed an uncomfortable skin and found one more to his liking.

She joined him, the old tin rattling as she walked, and they sat on a large boulder looking out over the silent mine.

"That's what you came out here for?" He pointed his sandwich at the tin in her hands.

She turned it over in her hands, her fingers running over the rust and the pitting.

"You will think this is foolish," she said, "but Uncle Jack and I used to leave messages for each other in this tin."

She tried to open the rusty tin, cursing in a most unladylike way as she broke a fingernail in the effort. Danny took the tin and, using a folding pocket knife, pried the lid loose, handing it back to her.

The tin contained a folded square of paper and a string of wooden beads with a carved bone cross hanging from them. She unfolded the note, written in a barely legible scrawl, she had left for her uncle when she knew she would be leaving Maiden's Creek.

Dear Uncle Jack, I has to leave to go to scool in Melburn. Miss P has been teachin me spelling and such but I is not very good yet. Write to me. I miss you. Love C xxxxxxx.

"I really was bad at spelling," she said with a laugh.

She handed Danny the note and he read it, a smile catching at the corners of his mouth.

"So if the note is still in your tin, does that mean he never came back?"

"Yes, he did," she said.

She carefully extracted the rosary from the tin, her fingers working the beads, worn smooth by many fingers over long years. Yes, Jack had returned and found her note and left her a present.

She let the beads fall through her fingers.

"My grandmother's rosary. He used to have it hanging up in his cottage over there." She twisted, indicating the former mine manager's cottage that still stood firm and intact.

Danny turned the note over. "Here... He did leave you a message."

The few short sentences were written in a faint pencil on the back of Charlie's note, so faint she had missed them.

These were my grandmother's. I've nothing else to give you. Tell your Ma that you lot are always in me thoughts and me heart. J.

Danny held out his hand. "Can I see the beads?"

She handed the rosary to him.

"You're Catholic?" he asked, letting the beads click through his fingers.

She laughed. "With a name like O'Reilly, did you think I'd be Methodist?"

He shrugged and handed the beads back to her.

"I suppose it hadn't crossed my mind," he said.

"No reason it should. I'm not the best Catholic in the world and you won't very often see me at church... in fact mostly there weren't any churches nearby when I was a child but once Ma moved into town after Sarah was born, she found her God and started going every week to St Mary's. I refused to go but in the last few years I've drifted back and I try to get to mass when I can—Christmas and Easter mostly. You, I suppose, are Church of England?"

He nodded. "I am, although my father is not much of a churchgoer. I think the war did that to him."

She replaced the rosary in the tin along with the little note, stowing the tin in her pocket.

"I'm glad I came up here, Danny."

"Was that the only reason?"

She pondered that question and nodded. "It was nothing more than curiosity to see if Jack had found my message. It's reassuring to know he did."

She reached for a sandwich and they sat munching in companionable silence.

"Where does your mother live now?" Danny asked.

"She married a dairy farmer down Korumburra way. He needed a mother for his three children and Ma needed a father for Sarah. He's a good, kind man and treats her well. No one calls her Mad Annie anymore."

Danny's eyebrows shot up. "Is that what they used to call her?"

"And worse, but she nearly died giving birth to Sarah and that tamed her... and Netty Burrell."

"At dinner the other night you mentioned a much younger sister?"

Charlie's heart lurched but she schooled her face. "Ma and Joshua had a late child. Amy. She's five now. Ma calls her, her little miracle. What about you?"

"I've two younger brothers and a sister. Like your little sister, it's a big age difference."

Danny brushed the crumbs from his knees and pulled a pocket sketchpad out of his jacket pocket. Charlie sat watching as he roughed in a sketch of the abandoned site.

"You're very good," she observed as the drawing came to life under his pencil.

"Thank you. There's a certain beauty in the derelict industry, don't you think?"

Charlie looked around at the rusting machinery and failed to find it remotely beautiful. She bit into an apple as Danny flicked over the page in his sketchbook.

"Don't move," he said.

"Are you drawing me?"

"Maybe," he replied.

"No one's ever drawn me before," she said.

"It won't be very good. I am better at landscapes than people."

They sat in silence for a couple of minutes while Danny's pencil scratched at the sketchpad.

"It sounds like you had a rough childhood," he said at last.

Charlie shrugged. "You don't know any better," she said. "I look back now and wonder how—and why—my mother did what she did but I guess I was luckier than some. My mother loved me, and I knew it."

"Did you know your father?"

Charlie shook her head. "No, Matt Tehan died when I was too young to remember him. Ma took up with another man. He beat her and worse. When he turned on me, Ma had enough. With the help of Matt's brother, Jack, we escaped from Tasmania to Victoria. Spent some time on the Bendigo goldfields, before coming to Maiden's Creek with Jack."

"Sounds like your uncle played a big part in your life."

She laughed. "He was a rogue but I adored him. To his credit, he did ask Ma to marry him but she turned him down. Said he wasn't reliable." She gave a dismissive shrug. "But you're right, he was as good to me as any father and I missed him... still do."

"Do you really not know where he is?"

"Queensland, I think. Took up with a woman in northern Victoria. Married her, so Ma tells me. She must have been an amazing woman to tame Jack." She looked up at the sky and rose to her feet, brushing down her skirts. "I think we'd better leave, Danny. It's going to rain before we get back to town." She craned her neck to have a look at the sketchbook but Danny turned it away. "Can I see?"

Two spots of color appeared on Danny's cheekbones as he handed over the sketchbook.

"I told you I'm not good at people."

Charlie stared at the image, rendered in a soft pencil that obliterated the hard lines that she had built around herself. He had caught a shadow of the girl he had first met behind the potted palm. She looked up at him.

"Can I keep it?"

The spots of color deepened and he gave a dismissive shrug. "If you want."

"I think my mother might like it," she said.

"Let me tidy it up a bit and I'll give it to you before I leave," he said.

He pocketed the notebook and helped her to her feet.

"Do you have what you came for?" she asked.

He nodded. "I think I can report that the mine is well and truly shut down. The only possible danger is from that old mine adit but it looks pretty solid to me."

They returned to the horses and Danny held out his hand to help Charlie mount. This time she accepted his help. Their fingers clasped for only a moment, but the touch of his long, strong fingers stirred something in Charlie she had put away, consigned to a dark corner of her life. The magnetic attraction of a man and a woman.

It had drawn them together nine years earlier in a fleeting moment of connection and here it was again—and it had to be resisted at all cost. Like her mother, she had been flawed in her choice of men in the past and she was not going to allow herself to be hurt again, however strong the attraction to this particular man might be.

They rode away, passing through the crumbling remnants of the Pretty Sally settlement. The slatternly woman from the general store had gone back inside and there was no one to be seen. Smoke curled from barely a half dozen buildings. In a few years it would be nothing but a few crumbling chimneys and broken bits of iron.

Charlie glanced at the man riding beside her. He seemed lost in his own thoughts and she wondered what he was looking for, what had brought him back to Maiden's Creek. The grave of his father or something else? Something he had left here, as she had left a note in a tobacco tin, that had to be found before he would have peace?

She took a deep breath and her fingers closed on the tobacco tin in her pocket—her last tie to this place.

TWENTY-FIVE

Dusk and rain had descended by the time they got back to town. They parted at the hospital with a quick farewell and Charlie, damp and cold from the ride, decided a cup of tea in the warmth of the hospital kitchen would revive her before returning to her cold, dark cottage.

She opened the door to the kitchen, completely unprepared for the sight that met her.

"Sister Becker!"

The man and the woman entwined on the day bed started as if they'd had a bucket of cold water poured over them. Janet Becker jumped to her feet, straightening her starched collar and trying to restore her hair beneath her starched cap. She stared at the ground.

Her partner moved a little more slowly and they stood before Charlie like two recalcitrant children.

Charlie looked from Janet Becker to Joe Trevelyan.

"Matron, I..." Janet began, her face scarlet.

"Later, Sister. Get back to your duties. Now!"

Casting Joe a lovelorn look, Janet hurried out of the room, leaving Charlie alone with Joe.

"Joe! Really?"

Joe looked down at his feet. "Janet and I have been keeping company for months now, Charlie. Sometimes the only chance I get to see her is if I come up here and have a cup of tea with her."

"The hospital is not the proper place for romantic assignations," Charlie responded. "And that was a little more than a cup of tea."

Joe looked up. His eyes shone and a smile curled his lips.

"She's agreed to be my wife, Charlie."

Charlie huffed out a breath. "Congratulations, Joe, but there are rules in a hospital, and I have to maintain standards. What if there had been a patient needing help?"

"Lily Roberts said she'd look after things."

"Did she indeed?"

"Lily's a good friend."

Charlie pointed a finger at him.

"And you are playing on my friendship, Joe."

His face dropped into grave lines and he looked down at the toe of his worn but well polished boot.

"I suppose I am. I'm sorry, Charlie... Matron."

Charlie could never stay angry with Joe and she smiled.

"I'm glad she's accepted you and, for the sake of our friendship, she'll get a scolding but that's all. Don't let me catch you up here again, Joe."

Joe gave her a grateful smile before gathering his coat and hat and disappearing into the dark night.

Charlie summoned the two nurses. They stood before her, eyes downcast, prepared for the sort of telling-off that had put the fear of God into them as students.

"I am very disappointed in both of you," Charlie said. "This is a place of work, a place of healing with sick people who need your full attention. It is not a rendezvous for young lovers. I am not going to take this any further, Sister Becker, but if I hear of you and Mr. Trevelyan meeting again on these premises there will not be a second chance. And as for you, Sister Roberts, you are older and more sensible. However well-intentioned you may be, you are doing yourself and your patients no help."

"Yes, Matron. Sorry, Matron," both girls chorused.

"Back to work. I'm going home and I will see you in the morning before the shifts change," Charlie said.

Both nurses scuttled out of her presence with as much speed and decorum as they could.

Charlie made herself the promised tea and sat drinking it in the empty kitchen. As she set the cup to wash in the sink, she thought she should tell the girls she was leaving for the night and made her way out into the main part of the hospital. She heard voices coming from the linen cupboard. The door stood ajar and a light spilled out into the hallway. She stopped when she heard her name mentioned.

"Don't take on," Lily Roberts was saying. "Matron's bark is worse than her bite."

An audible sniff from Janet Becker. "She thinks we should be like her, devoted to nursing and have no life outside."

"Aye, well, she and Keegan are cut from the same cloth," Lily replied. "She'll end up a dried-up old spinster, mark my words. You've got a chance to make a life for yourself, Janet—you and Joe..."

Charlie didn't wait to hear more. She turned and hurried back to the kitchen.

A dried-up old spinster? She wasn't even thirty and that's what they thought of her?

Shaming tears prickled at the back of her eyes and she left the hospital.

Lizzie Ryan had laid a fire in the hearth of the cottage, and a pie stood on the table covered in a cloth. Charlie busied herself with her evening routines and only after she had eaten, and sat in the battered armchair by the fire, did she allow herself to reflect on the day.

She let her fingers play through the well-worn beads of her grandmother's rosary and thought of her mother and her life before and after Maiden's Creek. Then there was Joe and his Janet. They had all found happiness. Wasn't that what everyone sought?

Nobody had ever really looked at her the way Joe had looked at Janet, and she longed for that intimacy with a man. She had fancied herself in love once and had been deceived. She had sworn that she would not be so easily taken in again. No, she told herself firmly. She had her work... her career... her vocation. She had to find her own happiness in her decisions and would not give up what she had worked so hard to attain for a man.

But Lily Roberts' words came back to her.

Dried-up old spinster...

At the back of her heart, she felt the tug of loneliness.

TWENTY-SIX

After returning the horses and helping the stablehand to groom and settle them, at Amos' insistence Danny took supper with Netty and Amos and it was past nine before he returned to the Britannia. A crowd of rowdy miners filled the main bar of the Britannia and Danny paused only long enough to scan the faces for Micah Allen.

From his position behind the bar, Joe raised his hand and made an eating gesture to inquire if Danny required food. Danny shook his head and took the stairs. After the noise, light and warmth of the bar, the rest of the hotel had an almost sepulchral gloom. The corridor upstairs was dark and quiet, the doors to the residential rooms shut firmly. The only light came from a single gas lamp at the top of the stairs.

For no reason he could explain, the hairs on the back of Danny's neck prickled and his boot heels echoed in the silence as he walked towards the suite at the end of the corridor. As he reached for the key in his pocket, his hand brushed the butt of the Colt and he had to stop himself from pulling it from his belt, telling himself he was being ridiculous.

But the door he had locked before leaving hours before now stood ajar.

He stopped, straining to hear any movement from within the room, hardly daring to breathe. With shaking fingers, he pulled the Colt from his belt and the ammunition from his pocket, cracking the weapon open to load it.

He took a deep steadying breath and kicked the door wide open, jumping to one side in case someone within took aim as the door burst open. When nothing happened, he stepped into the room, holding the revolver high and firm as Caleb had taught him. Curtains flapped at an open window, but otherwise, from what he could make out in the gloom, the room seemed still and empty. Danny took a breath and checked the two bedrooms, including the undersides of the beds and the wardrobes. Satisfied that no one lurked in the shadows, he set the Colt on the mantelpiece and lit the paraffin lamp that stood beside a box of safety matches.

Holding the lamp, he scanned the room again. Except for the open window nothing in the room seemed to have been touched. The only discordant object lay on the round table in the center of the room.

An envelope.

Danny set the lamp down and picked it up but he knew what it contained even before he opened it.

A single rifle bullet fell to the table with a metallic *thkk* before rolling onto the floor. Danny peered into the envelope but it contained nothing else. He stooped and picked up the bullet, holding it to the light. It appeared to be identical to the one he had received back in East Melbourne.

If he'd lacked the proof before, he now held it in his hand. Micah Allen had followed him to Maiden's Creek and had already made one attempt on his life, catching out Bertie Campbell by mistake.

He replaced the bullet in the envelope, stuffed it in his pocket, and walked over to the window. His foot crunched on glass. The open window had been broken to allow a hand to slip the catch. Danny unlocked the door and stepped out onto the verandah. The end of the verandah faced out onto a narrow lane and here a large barrel had been pushed across to the wall of the Britannia. It would not have taken an agile young man much effort to swing himself onto the verandah with no one seeing. The sound of breaking glass would have been muffled by the noise coming from the bar below. All the scoundrel had to do was unlock the door to the room, using Bertie's keys that Danny had left on the mantelpiece, and leave.

Danny returned to the room, pulling down the window. A cold, damp breeze blew in through the broken pane and he shivered. He would tell Yorkie or Joe in the morning. Now there was nothing he could do except go to bed. Allen had made his point. He would be waiting and watching for the right moment and Danny would not see him coming.

Even though he doubted Allen would return, Danny lay down on his bed, fully dressed, pulling a blanket over himself, the loaded Colt in his hand.

TWENTY-SEVEN

A sharp rapping woke Charlie from a deep sleep. For a moment she thought it was the wind and the rain and lay staring at the ceiling while her heart raced. When she had convinced herself she had misheard, it came again, more insistent.

"Matron! Matron!"

She all but fell out of bed, groping for her slippers and dressing gown before opening the door. Her breath clouded in the damp air.

Janet Becker stood in the shelter of the verandah overhang, almost unrecognizable in a large oil slicker and hat.

"What's the problem, Becker?"

"A woman's turned up at the hospital with a sick child. Roberts and I thought you should have a look before we send for the doctor. You know how they don't like being called out at night."

Charlie, awake now, nodded. "Go back. I'll be there as soon as I'm dressed."

In the cold her fingers were so numb they barely managed the fastenings on her uniform dress. She coiled her hair into a bun at the nape of her neck and pulled on her oilskin and rain hat. The heavy rain made the path and steps down to the hospital courtyard treacherous. Even with the lantern she had to pick her way carefully.

A light burned in the kitchen and she found both nurses waiting for her. Roberts took her oilskin, hanging it on one of the hooks by the door.

"Where's the patient?"

"We put her in the doctor's office," Roberts said.

"I lit a fire," Becker added.

A woman sat in the doctor's chair beside the fire, her head bent over a child in her arms. Even in the poor light of the fire and the kerosene lamp Charlie could see the child was gravely ill. He hung in his mother's arms, his face covered in a mottled rash.

"Matron's here," Roberts said. "She'll have a look at the bairn."

The woman looked up and Charlie's stomach lurched. Flora Donald. What was her name now? Fraser?

"I want a proper doctor, not her," Flora said.

Charlie steeled herself. "Let me be the judge of that, Mrs. Fraser. Now what's wrong with Archie?"

Flora's lips tightened but she said no more as Charlie knelt beside her and checked the boy's pulse and scanned the little body. The rash extended from his face, down his body. She'd seen it before many times and had no doubt that this was a bad case of scarlet fever.

"When did it start?" she asked.

"I noticed it yesterday," Flora said. "But I didn't think much of it. What do you think it is?"

Charlie shook her head. "There have been a few cases of scarlet fever in the town."

Flora's brows drew together in an all too familiar scowl of disapproval. "That would be the Marsh boy. I've forbidden Archie from playing with Thomas Marsh but I caught them up on the old tram line a few days ago."

Charlie bit back a sharp retort about children finding friends where they could.

"Is the Marsh child unwell?"

Flora shrugged. "Three children in a tiny cottage in the most unsanitary conditions."

Charlie made a note to herself to pay a visit on Bert Marsh's family.

Bert was one of the few from her schooldays she had not crossed paths with yet.

"I know nothing about the Marsh children but there was a child presented at the hospital with it two days ago," Charlie said. "Doctor Linacre informed the school."

Flora's eyes widened. "Aye, the school's been closed these few days past. It's bad, isn't it?"

"I think," she said carefully, "it presents differently with different children. Archie's fever is very high. I wish you'd called the doctor earlier. It is easier to quarantine the child at home," she said. "But now he's here, we will need to keep him away from the other patients and do what we can to get that fever under control." She looked at Sister Roberts, who hovered in the doorway. "Is the bed in the private room available?"

"I need to make it up."

"Get on with it," Charlie said. "And make sure that there is plenty of carbolic soap and a wash stand in the room."

The skin around Flora's nose pinched tight. "He's all I have, Charlie. I cannot lose him."

Charlie... Flora Donald had called her Charlie.

"Your husband...?"

"Died two years ago. He had a weak heart."

"I'm sorry," Charlie said.

Sister Roberts appeared at the door.

"I've made up the bed. Do you want the fire lit? It's perishing cold in that room."

Charlie shook her head. "We want to get the child's fever down so we'll keep the room cold." She turned to the mother. "Go home, Mrs. Fraser. There's nothing you can do here. I'll sit with Archie till morning when we can get the doctor in to see him."

Flora's mouth worked. "I canna leave him."

Charlie laid a hand over the other woman's... her left hand, the hand Flora had beaten so unmercifully with the tawse. She forced Flora to look into her eyes.

"Trust me in this. I will do everything in my power to keep Archie safe, but you will be more use to him in the morning if you are rested. Go home."

The tears that brimmed in Flora's eyes spilled and she nodded. "You were a strange wee bairn, Charlie O'Reilly, but you had a good heart and I couldn't see that." She dropped her gaze, her fingers tightening on Charlie's. "I'm sorry."

Charlie gave the bony fingers a squeeze and extracted her hand, taking the child from his mother's arms.

"Sister Roberts will see you to the door and make sure you wash and clean everything Archie might have touched with carbolic soap."

A flurry of cold air and icy rain blew into the front hall as Flora left. Charlie waited a long minute before carrying Archie through to the private room. It was so cold that her breath clouded in the air. Sister Becker brought in four kerosene lamps and the two nurses stood by while Charlie laid the child on the bed and gave him a thorough examination. Archie was hardly conscious and made no attempt to resist the prodding and poking.

When she was done, they restored the child's nightshirt and tucked him into the bed.

"Is it scarlet fever?" Sister Becker asked.

"The symptoms of diphtheria are frighteningly similar but given the other cases of scarlet fever in town, I think we are right to assume that is what it is. Let's hope there are no more."

"Do you want me to fetch Doctor Linacre?" Lily Roberts asked.

Charlie shook her head. "No. I need you both to take turns to sit with him until morning. He needs to be bathed with cold water to try and bring the fever down. If he gets worse fetch me at once and we'll send for the doctor. Otherwise he can wait until the morning. Sister Roberts can you fetch a bowl and cloths."

Lily Roberts left the room and when a distant bell in the kitchen rang, Janet Becker rolled her eyes.

"That'll be Martha Drew," she said. "The weather's unsettled her. She wants to go home."

"I'm sure you can deal with her," Charlie said.

Sister Becker huffed out a breath and straightened as if preparing for battle and left Charlie alone with the child.

Lily Roberts left the room, returning with a bowl and cloth.

"Still here, Matron?"

Charlie looked up at the nurse. Lily Roberts was probably a year or so older than Janet Becker. She lacked Janet's inherent prettiness and if one was to pass her in the street, she would be unremarkable.

"Just waiting for you to return," Charlie said. "I didn't want to leave the lad alone."

"Becker's dealing with Martha Drew," Lily said as she gently applied the dampened cloth to the boy's forehead. "I had a little brother about Archie's age."

"Had?"

Lily looked up. "He died of diphtheria at the orphanage." She stroked Archie's hair. "Had red hair too."

"I'm sorry. How did you end up in an orphanage?"

Lily shrugged. She continued to stroke Archie's hair, not taking her gaze from the boy's face. "Our parents died on the voyage out from England and we landed in Sydney having no kith or kin to take us in, so Richie and I were taken to an orphanage. Richie died after six months but I lived there till I was fifteen and old enough to go into service. A doctor's family took me in and he was good enough to encourage me to take up nursing."

Charlie studied the girl. "You've done well. You're a hard worker, Sister Roberts."

Lily looked up and smiled. Her smile brightened her plain face. "Thank you, Matron. That means a lot."

"What brought you from Sydney to Maiden's Creek?"

Lily sponged the boy's wrists. "Time for a change, Matron. Isn't that what brings us all here?" She looked up. "I like working in a small hospital. I get to be more responsible. I hope that I might be in charge one day."

Charlie smiled. "Be careful what you wish for, Lily!"

Lily's eyes were dark in the gloom of the room. "I like working for you Matron. Miss Birch didn't have the patience to teach us but I'm learning ever so much from you."

"That is kind of you to say. Now Archie seems to have settled, I might leave you. I'll be no use to anyone in the morning if I haven't had any sleep."

Lily smiled. "You do that, Matron. Archie'll be just fine with me." She paused. "Me and Janet, we'll look after him."

TWENTY-EIGHT

The rain that had begun the previous evening had set in by morning, steady, heavy and relentless. Rivulets of water ran down the slope from the cottage to the hospital, cutting gullies in the hard earth of the lane and, as Charlie discovered when she reached the hospital, overflowing the gutters and finding every possible weakness in the iron roof.

The nurses had set buckets and bedpans under the worst of the leaks, and Alf Kimble and the boy, Eddie, had the ladder out, trying to clear the gutters. She dispatched Eddie to bring Doctor Linacre up to the hospital.

Lily and Janet had been replaced by Margaret Campbell and Mary Keegan, who brooked no nonsense from the patients, made restless by the rain and the flurry of activity around the hospital.

Bertie Campbell had fresh complaints about everything from the food to the snoring of the miner with the amputated foot in the bed next to him. Charlie had been tolerant of his behavior for Margaret's sake, but now she told him in no uncertain terms to keep his complaints to himself or he would find himself sleeping in the woodshed. He demanded to be moved to a private room, but even if it had been available, Charlie had had her fill of Bertie's claims of privilege and entitlement and left him where he was.

She left Bertie and turned her attention to Archie Fraser. Flora Fraser had arrived at first light and Charlie had waived the visitor's rules to allow her to be with her son. She sat hunched on a chair beside the bed with a blanket wrapped around her and her first words to Charlie were a complaint about the temperature of the room.

Charlie ignored her, giving her whole attention to the boy. Despite their best efforts during the night, Archie's fever had not abated. The scarlet rash that covered his little body almost seemed to glow red, hot, and angry in the morning light.

"Your nurses refuse to light the fire. The fever's to be sweated out," Flora said.

Charlie straightened her shoulders and looked the woman firmly in the eye.

"That is old-fashioned nonsense. The boy's fever needs to be brought down and the best way to do that is by cold. If you wish to be useful, Mrs. Fraser, could I request you keep applying the cold water to Archie's forehead and wrists? Doctor Linacre will be here presently."

Before leaving the room she scrubbed her hands with the carbolic soap. She had read the articles on the control of infection and it was all they had.

After the chill of Archie's room, the warmth of the kitchen came as a relief. Young Eddie sat at the table being fed tea and a bun by Geraldine Ryan. Geraldine's new baby slept in a basket on the daybed.

Charlie picked up a bun from the plate on the table and bit into it.

"Doc Linacre wasn't answering his door," Eddie said, mumbling through a mouthful of bun. "I left a message for him but his housekeeper didn't say where he'd gone or how long he'd be. Doctor Elliott is up at one of the mines, and Doctor Dixon is in Melbourne."

Charlie bit back an oath that would have made the most hardened miner blush. Three doctors in this town and none of them where they were needed. She glanced at the window. Cold, hard fingers of rain lashed the panes without any sign of letting up. She had a bad feeling that every able-bodied person would be needed before the day was out.

The front doorbell rang and she frowned. She had quickly discovered that none of the locals used the front door. Everyone came to the back door. Eddie half-heartedly rose to his feet but she waved him back into his chair.

"I'll see to it."

She brushed crumbs from her skirts and strode to the door with the speech about visiting hours on her lips but her blood froze as she opened the door to the well-dressed but damp man who stood in the shelter of the verandah.

"What are you doing here?" she said through stiff lips.

Beneath his mustache and immaculately groomed beard, the man's mouth curled in a smile, not echoed by his eyes. "Now, now, nurse, is that any way to greet your superior?"

"It's Matron, and you are not my superior."

The smile vanished and he shrugged. "I am cold and wet and you are not going to keep me standing on the doorstep, are you Charlotte."

It was an order, not a question, and she had no choice but to stand aside and admit him.

"Why are you here, William?"

Doctor William Fitzgerald looked around the front hall and turned back to her with a look that managed to combine both surprise and hurt.

"Doctor Fitzgerald in public, Charlotte. Didn't you get my letter?"

Charlie thought of the letter she had consigned to the flames. "No," she lied. "And it's Matron in public... and private, doctor."

Fitzgerald straightened. "If you had received my note, you would know I am here to conduct an inspection on behalf of the Registration Board."

A myriad of angry questions flooded Charlie's mind.

She settled for. "Surely the correct person to have advised of your visit is the chairman of the hospital committee, and Mr. Sloan has said nothing to me."

"That is because these inspections are supposed to be a surprise." He held up his hand before she could say anything. "I only wrote to you out of courtesy, knowing you had just taken the position," he paused and his eyes narrowed, "and out of respect for our previous acquaintance."

Charlie closed the door behind him. "Come through to the kitchen," she said. "You are, as you say, soaked, and the least I can do is offer you a cup of tea."

"Very gracious," Fitzgerald said with no warmth.

She found Margaret Campbell in the kitchen, pouring tea from the battered teapot. The nurse looked up, her gaze going from Fitzgerald to Charlie.

Charlie recollected herself. "Sister Campbell, this is Doctor William Fitzgerald."

Fitzgerald divested himself of his coat, hat, and umbrella, holding them out for Charlie to take as he turned his charm on Margaret. Charlie resisted the temptation to throw his dripping garments back at him, instead hanging them from the hooks by the kitchen door.

"Campbell? Are you Angus Campbell's daughter? He mentioned he had a daughter in the nursing field."

"That's right. Do you know my father?" Margaret replied.

"Melbourne Club... and we sit on a couple of committees, and I know your brother, of course. How is Robert?"

"My brother is a patient here," Margaret said. "He came on a short visit and managed to break his leg. The silly sod."

Fitzgerald cast a glance at Charlie. "I trust he is getting the very best of care."

"He is getting the same excellent standard of care we give all our patients," Charlie said.

"How do you take your tea, doctor?" Margaret hefted the teapot and poured tea for them all.

Fitzgerald sat at the table and took the teacup, crossing his legs with studied elegance, as if he were in the salon of a gracious Melbourne hostess, not the functional kitchen of a rural, cottage hospital.

"Where will you be staying?" Margaret asked.

"I have taken a room at the Empress," he said. "I was told it was the best hostelry in town. It is hardly the Menzies, but it will do. I was just telling your matron that I am here to conduct an inspection," he said. "I came in on the morning train and I must say I am less than impressed with the welcome. There was no one at the station to escort me."

"We didn't know you were coming," Charlie said. "Besides, we are extremely busy. We have a very sick little boy and this heavy rain makes life here extremely difficult. We have been unable to contact any of the town's doctors. Two of the town's doctors are unavailable and the chief medical officer, Doctor Linacre is... out on a call," Charlie lied.

Fitzgerald set down the cup.

"Then perhaps I may be able to assist with your patient?"

Margaret cast Charlie a curious glance, which Charlie ignored. Whatever else he might be, William Fitzgerald was an excellent doctor, and she owed Archie Fraser the best possible diagnosis.

"I believe it is scarlet fever. I am aware of a few milder cases in the town. The school has been temporarily closed as a precaution."

Fitzgerald nodded. "Sensible. Now let me have a look at the boy."

Flora sprang to her feet as Charlie stood aside to admit Fitzgerald into the room.

"Who's this?" she demanded.

"This is Doctor Fitzgerald. He is visiting from Melbourne and is one of Melbourne's leading physicians, Mrs. Fraser."

Flora sank back on her chair and watched intently as Fitzgerald examined Archie with professional thoroughness.

He straightened and looked at Flora Fraser. "Matron O'Reilly is quite correct in her diagnosis. It is scarlet fever, and your lad has a very bad dose. Best keep him here and isolated for a few days."

"I told Matron that the fever needed to be sweated out," Flora interposed.

Fitzgerald considered her for a long moment. "The current treatment is exactly what I would prescribe, Mrs. Fraser. The modern thinking is that the temperature has to be brought down. Sweating a fever went out with bloodletting."

Chastened by the voice of authority, Flora looked down at her hands folded on her lap.

"Mrs. Fraser, if you wish to stay with Archie, the best thing you can do is to keep bathing him with the cool water," Charlie said. "That will free my nurses to see to the other patients. I will check in on the hour to see how he is faring."

Fitzgerald gave Flora the benefit of his most charming smile and just for a fraction of a moment, Charlie was reminded that he was an excellent doctor whose patients adored him.

"Thank you, Doctor," Charlie said. "Now, perhaps we could talk in my office?"

She ushered him into her office and shut the door, leaning her back against it. He turned to face her and smiled. Her heart skipped a beat. That smile could win over the most recalcitrant patient... or the most naïve young nurse.

She had been such a nurse. She had convinced herself that she hated him but now he stood in front of the fire in her office, the same man who had convinced her that he loved her and intended to marry her. She had believed him, imagining her life as a doctor's wife, helping with his practice, raising their children. A dream that had been shattered when a colleague had pointed out the engagement announcement in the newspaper. She had fled to London to escape the duplicity of this man. She had hoped that on her return to Melbourne she could avoid him but he had seen her in the corridor of the Women's Hospital and the intervening years had slid away beneath her feet, leaving her once again the naïve, trusting girl who had fallen for his charms. She had known then and there that Melbourne was too small and the medical profession even smaller. She would always encounter him and always be reminded of what he had taken from her.

April Birch's letter had come as a blessing. Maiden's Creek would be a stepping stone. With her experience in a matron's position she could go anywhere... Sydney, Brisbane, Adelaide... anywhere except back to Melbourne.

And now here he was, smiling at her, expecting in his arrogance that she would be pleased to see him, would throw herself into his arms and forgive him.

"Charlotte, I've missed you."

She ignored the velvet tone. "Why are you really here, William?"

"To conduct an inspection, as I said in my letter."

"I told you, I never received it."

His eyes narrowed. "I know when you are lying."

"And I know the Registration Board would never send someone of your seniority to a small cottage hospital like this one."

He shrugged. "An opportunity presented and I took it. I thought we should talk. I have to explain—"

"There is nothing to explain, William."

"Ever since your return from London, you've been avoiding me and now you've hidden yourself away here in this godforsaken town."

She glared at him. "I want nothing to do with you, William. You are a married man with children."

"You know the circumstances. It was a marriage convenient to me and my wife's family. It doesn't mean anything."

She stared at him, aghast. "Doesn't mean anything? What sort of monster are you, William Fitzgerald? How many more nurses have you seduced since you stood in a church and vowed fidelity to your wife?"

"Charlotte, that is unfair. What we had was different."

Charlie uttered a word that would have made her Uncle Jack blush.

A muscle twitched in Fitzgerald's temple and the smile faded. "That was uncalled for, Matron." He drew himself up, his eyes now hard and professional. "Remember, I am here to conduct a formal inspection and we are not off to a good start."

Charlie took a steadying breath. "Doctor, your timing is unfortunate. May I suggest you return to your hostelry and rest from your travels? Perhaps tomorrow you can do what you came to do and be gone."

His lips tightened. "I can see you are in a mood, Charlotte, so perhaps I will take your advice and return in the morning when you have had time to organize yourself professionally and personally. I would hate to give the hospital a poor report based on the welcome I have received."

It was the words he left unspoken, the inference that a good report would be forthcoming if Charlie were a little more accommodating, that enraged her. She all but slammed the door behind him, subsiding into the chair behind her desk with her head in her hands.

She hardly heard the gentle knock as Margaret Campbell looked around the door.

"Are you all right?"

Charlie hastily wiped at the shameful tears. "I'm fine, Sister."

"No, you're not. Is it Doctor Fitzgerald—has he upset you?"

"We have history, Sister. Nothing more. I want this hospital to receive a glowing report. Can you and Sister Keegan ensure that everything is in order before he returns tomorrow?"

Margaret glanced out of the window. "Matron, I think we might have a bigger problem than the inspector. Alf reckons if the rain doesn't let up, the creek will have burst its banks by tonight."

"Then we are going to be busy. Get to work, Sister."

TWENTY-NINE

After lunch, Charlie stood at the window of her office, watching the rain lashing the windows. It looked like Alf's gloomy prediction might come to pass. Eddie had returned from running an errand with the news that the creek had broken its banks in the upper part of the valley, flooding the Chinese gardens to the north. Residents with properties close to the riverbank would be under immediate threat. Netty and Amos had only a small garden between the house and the creek. Charlie bit her lip, wondering what could be done to protect them.

Apart from Archie Fraser, the hospital had three patients in the men's ward and four in the women's ward. Of the women, Martha Drew, while still far from well, was the most disruptive and difficult. The hospital staff had spent the morning preparing spare beds and gathering their store of blankets, spare mattresses and clothing that might be needed in the next few days if the predictions came to pass and the town flooded.

Satisfied that everything in the hospital was as organized as it could be, Charlie pulled on her oilskin and braved the torrential rain. The drains, rudimentary at best, were overflowing, the water-filled potholes merging with a continual flow of water pouring off the slopes. She hopped and skipped across as best she could with her skirts held high to avoid the water but managed to end up ankle deep in water and her boots and the bottom part of her skirt were mired and soaked before she reached Main Street.

Netty's shop had a *Closed* sign in the window and she made her way around to the side, pausing to glance at the small yard with its chicken pen and neat rows of vegetables. The creek had already begun to lap the lower reach of the garden.

Netty answered the door, standing back to admit Charlie to the warm, comfortable kitchen.

"Sit down, Charlie. When did you last eat?"

Charlie shook her head. "I had lunch at the hospital. I can't stop, Netty. I just came to see how you are and to warn you that the creek's already flooding and it won't take much to reach you here."

"Pish," Netty said. "We've had floods before and it's never reached us."

"It looks bad, Netty."

Netty frowned. "But this is my home. Where would I go?"

"I've thought about it and I have a plan. You and Amos have to come up to my cottage," she said, and when Netty started to protest, Charlie held up her hand. "No argument. You can't stay here. The best you can do is lift everything off the floor. Hopefully if the water gets in nothing too precious will be lost."

"What about Flossie?" Netty lifted the pregnant cat from her place by the hearth and cradled her in her arms.

"Bring her, of course."

"And Amos and the stables? He won't leave the horses," Netty said.

Charlie shook her head. "The stables are as much at risk as the cottage. There's an unused block beside the hospital. He can bring the horses up there. It will serve," Charlie said.

Netty frowned and she looked around her cozy parlor.

"I can't leave—"

Charlie swallowed her exasperation. "Netty, you have no choice. I hope I'm wrong but everyone I speak to says the creek is nowhere near peaking yet."

Netty reached for Charlie's hand.

"I know you're right, and it's a kind offer. You're a good girl, Charlie O'Reilly, but let's hope it doesn't come to that."

Charlie squeezed the older woman's hand. "And you are one of the very best of people, Netty. I'll make sure nothing happens to you. "Now I must go."

She bent over Netty and dropped a kiss on her forehead.

They had been easy words to say but as Charlie stepped back into the murk and damp she realized she had other competing priorities she couldn't drop just to see Netty and Amos safe. Maybe this was one responsibility she could delegate to another.

At the Britannia, she found Yorkie Oldroyd polishing glasses in the deserted bar.

"You can't come in here," he protested as she walked up to the bar. "Ladies not allowed."

Charlie looked around the empty space. "I don't think there is anyone here to be offended."

"That's not the point." The tips of Yorkie's ears were turning a pretty shade of puce.

"Is Daniel Hunt in?"

Yorkie jerked his head towards the stairs. "Up in his room. Number 3 at the end of the corridor."

As Charlie turned away, she heard the publican mutter something about "No shame," and she smiled to herself. It still gave her a perverse pleasure to shock people.

She knocked sharply on the door of number 3.

"Who is it?"

"Charlie," she replied.

"Wait a moment."

She frowned at the unmistakable sound of furniture scraping the floor as if something heavy was being dragged away from the door.

The key turned in the lock and Danny opened the door. A side table stood to one side of the door at an angle that suggested it had been pulled out of place. Danny followed her gaze and gave her an awkward shrug of his shoulders but no explanation.

"May I come in?"

He stepped back, pulling down his shirt sleeves with fingers stained with ink, and ran a hand through hair that probably hadn't seen a comb all day. The table in the middle of the room looked to be the center of a hive of industry with balls of screwed-up paper, a pen and inkwell and a pile of closely written pages, held down by the Colt revolver.

"What are you writing?" she asked.

"A story," he mumbled.

"You write stories?"

He hunched his shoulders and gave her a sheepish grin. "Yes. Do you read *The Bulletin*?"

"Sometimes."

"I'm Thomas Pike."

Charlie stared at him. "I love his stories... Is that really you?"

A faint flush of color rose to his cheekbones. "Yes."

"I thought you were a lawyer?"

"I am but I harbor foolish aspirations of writing novels."

She considered him for a long moment. "Why is having a dream foolish?"

He gave a self-deprecatory chuckle. "Because no one wants to print my work. The last publisher described it as 'derivative drivel.'"

Charlie flinched in sympathy. "But your Australian bush stories are so good. What's this one about?"

Charlie slid the top sheet out from beneath the revolver, peering at the closely written and largely illegible handwriting.

"A nosy nurse who should know better than to go prying into other people's business." Danny snatched the page back and restored it to its place under the revolver.

She smiled. "Couldn't you find a better paperweight?"

"No."

"You are out of sorts," Charlie said, her gaze drifting meaningfully to a half-empty bottle of whisky sitting amid the papers.

"Why are you here, Charlie?"

"Netty and Amos," she said. "The creek is rising, and I am afraid their cottage will be inundated. I've spoken to Netty and we have a plan, but could I ask you to look after them? Make sure they make it safely to my cottage before it is too late?"

Danny's gaze moved to the window where a piece of cardboard had been stuck over a broken pane. He unlocked the door to the verandah and stepped out. Charlie joined him.

In the preternaturally gloomy light, they had a good view of the sweep of Main Street and the steadily widening and roiling water of the normally sedentary Maiden's Creek washing over the nearest footbridge that spanned the creek.

He swore and apologized, running his hand through his hair.

"I've been so preoccupied with... with my own matters, I had no idea it was getting so bad. Of course I'll see them to safety."

"Thank you. I have my hands full with the hospital." She looked at him. "Is something wrong, Danny?"

He smiled, but the expression was not echoed in his eyes.

"Nothing. I just slept rather badly last night and thought I'd have a quiet day today." He laid a hand on her shoulder. "I'll look after the Burrells, I promise."

"Thank you. I have to check on Bert Marsh's children."

"Why?"

"I believe one of Bert's children has scarlet fever and we have a serious case up at the hospital. The school is closed and I'm hoping it is only a few cases and not an epidemic."

At the door she turned, her gaze moving from the displaced side table to the revolver on the table. "Danny, is something bothering you?"

He shrugged. "Go, Charlie. I'm fine."

Thirty

As the door closed behind Charlie, Danny let out his breath in an audible sigh. No, he wasn't fine. What was he doing—blocking the door, sitting with a loaded revolver?

He had got as far as the main desk of the police station that morning, but the young constable on duty had been dealing with another matter so Danny left, intending to return later. Now he just felt ridiculous. He couldn't barricade himself in his room indefinitely.

He returned to the table and picked up the closely written pages, a story of a lonely child, living in an isolated hut in the Australian bush with her mother, roaming the creeks and gullies... The words had poured from him but the problem was he didn't know how to end it. Did the child become tamed or did she continue her life of freedom, unrestrained by convention? Or was the conclusion somewhere in between?

The more he got to know Charlie O'Reilly the more he felt drawn to her, to discover her story, learn the secrets she held so close to her heart. He read through what he had written in the knowledge that the ending was something he had to find for himself.

He glanced at his watch. Nearly four. He had been given a mission and he had to see to Netty before it got dark.

As he stepped outside the Britannia he almost collided with a man clad in an ankle-length oilskin, holding an expensive umbrella.

"Ah, Hunt. Just the man I was coming to see."

The last person Danny expected to encounter in Maiden's Creek was William Fitzgerald. He knew the surgeon in passing from the Melbourne Club and the occasional social gathering of his father's medical acquaintances.

"Good to see a familiar face." Fitzgerald seized him by the hand, wringing it as if he was a long-lost friend. "I ran into your father in Collins Street, and when I said I was traveling up to Maiden's Creek, he mentioned you were here. What on earth are you doing in this godforsaken town?"

The same could be said for you, Danny thought, but he kept his peace as he shook the man's hand.

"I came up with Bertie Campbell," he said. "His sister's working up at the hospital."

"Oh yes, I saw her briefly this morning. Did I gather her brother is a patient?"

"He had a fall from a horse and broke his leg. I am sure you will find him full of complaints."

Fitzgerald's eyes narrowed. "That's interesting. Is he not happy with the care he is receiving?"

Danny had the feeling he had been caught out saying something wrong. "Bertie is always full of complaints," he said hurriedly. "The care he is receiving at the hospital is excellent."

Fitzgerald gestured at the Britannia. "Time for a drink?"

Danny shook his head. "No, thank you. I have to see to a friend, but I am curious. Why are you here?"

Fitzgerald smiled. "Hospital inspection," he said.

"My father didn't mention that there was any formal inspection to be undertaken," Danny said.

Fitzgerald hunched his shoulders under the heavy oilskin. "Nothing to do with your father. The health board prefers these inspections to be unheralded. That way issues come to light quickly."

Danny cast him a curious glance. "You seem a little senior to be undertaking that task?"

Fitzgerald's mustache twitched. "Good to keep my hand in."

"And are there any issues with the hospital?"

"I haven't had a chance to make any assessments yet. Met a rather hostile reception from the matron and I'm damned if I can find the doctor in charge."

"The matron? Char... Matron O'Reilly?"

"That's right. Do you know her?"

"You know how it is with Caleb. Friends of friends."

"Of course, I knew her when she was working at the Alfred Hospital a few years ago. Personally, I wouldn't have said she was suitable for such a senior position at her age, but out here I suppose needs must." He made a dismissive gesture as if Charlie O'Reilly was a piece of lint on his coat sleeve. "How are your parents?"

"Both well. Father is in town at present as you know. Parliament is sitting."

"Oh yes, the whole place is still in an uproar about the missing mace, I gather."

Danny had forgotten about the mace.

"Any theories?" he asked.

"Probably at the bottom of the Yarra River," Fitzgerald said. "Do you think the stories about it last being seen at a place of ill repute may be true?"

"I have no thoughts on the subject whatsoever," Danny replied.

Fitzgerald leaned in and lowered his voice. "On the subject of places of ill repute. You're a man of the world, Hunt. How much further is the Maiden's Creek Tavern?"

Danny's fingers clenched. He knew Fitzgerald had a wife and children in a fine house in Toorak and yet here he was sniffing out the local brothel.

He gestured up the road. "A couple of hundred yards in that direction."

Fitzgerald put his fingers to the brim of his hat and Danny watched him make his way, his attempts to avoid the puddles giving the comical impression the man was skipping.

Putting thoughts of William Fitzgerald to one side, he headed across the road to Netty's cottage. Before knocking on the door, he did a quick assessment. The little cottage had been built up high on stumps, prob-ably with overflow from the creek in mind, and while the water had certainly risen to the level of the backyard, it seemed for the moment Netty and Amos were high and dry.

As he could have predicted, she refused his offer of help to vacate.

"I told Charlie we've had high water before and it's never reached us," Netty said. "I don't see how this is any different."

"I think the peak of the flood is still a way off, Netty. If it's pouring like this in the mountains, it will be making its way down the valleys and you're right in its path. The water will rise faster than you know."

Netty raised her chin in a gesture Danny remembered all too well.

"Well, you just keep your eyes peeled, young man, and if I need your help—and that of Charlie O'Reilly—I'll ask. You know I don't take charity from no one."

"This isn't charity, Netty. Its common sense and friendship."

She sniffed. "That's as maybe." She ran a hand down her skirt and straightened her shoulders. "Seeing as you're here, I've a bit of roast lamb in the oven. Might as well take a meal with us."

There was no arguing either with Netty or the mouth-watering smell of roasting lamb. Danny stayed for the meal and repeated Charlie's plan to Amos. With a full stomach, he stepped into the cold, wet night.

As he stood on the edge of the sodden boardwalk, contemplating the best way to cross over to the Britannia, a shadow passed behind him and a voice whispered in his ear.

"Did you get my message?"

Danny froze for a long moment, groping in his coat pocket for the revolver but he'd left it in his room. He turned on his heel but if it had been Micah Allen he had melted into the gathering gloom of the damp evening.

THIRTY-ONE

Before returning to the hospital, Charlie visited the Marsh children. She was disappointed to learn that Bert was on shift but his wife assured her that they only had one child ill with the fever and Charlie satisfied herself he was on the mend. Bert's wife directed her to a couple of other children who like the Marsh boy were showing symptoms of scarlet fever. It was hard to recommend isolation when the families were crammed together in tiny cottages and all Charlie could suggest was everyone in the household had to regularly wash their hands with carbolic soap. In all cases, the mothers had the situation in hand and the children seemed to be faring well. Only poor Archie Fraser seemed to have succumbed more seriously.

Back at the hospital, the unrelenting rain continued into the evening, and along with it came a steady trail of people to the front door of the hospital seeking shelter as the floodwaters rose, washing away bridges and cutting people off from their homes or inundating homes on the banks of the creek.

Superficial injuries were seen to, but no one seemed to be obviously unwell or injured and Charlie directed the displaced to the church of St

Thomas on the Hill, which had opened its doors to take people in. Lily Roberts and Janet Becker came on duty at six to relieve Mary Keegan and Margaret Campbell, who both returned to their respective homes.

While the nurses lodged on the same side of the valley as the hospital, the Ryans lived on the far side of the valley, and with the bridges under water neither Lizzie nor her mother had been able to get to the hospital that evening, leaving it to the nurses to prepare supper for the patients and themselves. Their offering of a rather watery soup and yesterday's bread had not been received with enthusiasm by the patients.

Charlie stayed on until the patients were settled and there were no more people at the door. Archie had improved a little during the day and was now asleep. When Charlie suggested Flora return home, Flora shook her head.

"My home's on the far side of the valley. I can't get back until the flood subsides."

The nurses set up a mattress and blanket beside the bed for Flora to rest.

Satisfied everything was under control, Charlie braved the rain to return to her cottage. In her absence, several leaks had developed, and she found containers to place under the drips. She changed the sheets on the bed in case the Burrells arrived and made up a pallet in the living room. As she could do nothing else, she lay down on the pallet fully clothed, pulling her mother's old quilt over her. Long years of practice enabled her to fall asleep without effort and, lulled by the rain, she was asleep within minutes.

For the second night in a row, she was woken from a deep sleep by a frantic knocking on the door. Wrapping a blanket around her shoulder, she opened it to the shadowy figure of Lily Roberts engulfed in an enormous oilskin.

"Lily?"

"Matron, it's Archie Fraser. He's taken a turn for the worse."

Charlie straightened her uniform and grabbed up a lantern and her own oilskin. A quick check of her watch told her it was two in the morning. She and the nurse picked their way carefully down the now treacherous path to the hospital.

Flora stood by her son's bed and the face she turned to Charlie had such a look of desperation, Charlie's heart fell. What if Archie could not be saved? Scarlet fever was a killer.

"It's his breathing," Lily said.

"I was asleep on the bed the nurses made for me," Flora said. "But I was woken by Archie crying. Sister Roberts was already trying to get him to breathe."

Charlie glanced at Lily.

"It was lucky I checked on him when I did. His throat's swollen," Lily said.

Charlie examined the child. His symptoms were puzzling. The boy's breathing was labored but his fever was down. His throat looked nasty but wasn't so swollen as to prevent breathing. Her main concern was his heartbeat, which was weak and irregular.

She looked up at Flora Fraser. "He is critical. I'll sit with him. Sister Roberts, can you move Mrs. Fraser's bed to the doctor's office." Before Flora could protest, she held up her hand. "Mrs. Fraser, there's nothing you can do and you are just in the way."

Flora opened her mouth but the fight had gone from her. She let Lily Roberts put an arm around her shoulders and escort her out of the room to the peace of the doctor's office.

Charlie did what she could to make the boy comfortable and sat to watch.

Sister Roberts looked around the door. "She's exhausted but I've given her a sleeping powder. That will see her through till daybreak. Do you need anything, Matron?"

"A cup of tea would be good," Charlie said, "and where's Sister Becker? She's supposed to be on duty with you."

Lily froze, her hand on the doorknob. "She... she stepped out."

Charlie stared at her. "Stepped out? It's two in the morning in the middle of winter—in the middle of a rainstorm. Where has she stepped out to?"

Lily's eyes flicked to a corner of the room. "I'm sure I have no idea. She went out about midnight and said she'd be back before the hour. I lost track of time and I was starting to get worried when the crisis with Archie happened."

Charlie frowned. "Why would she go out?"

Lily swallowed and looked down at the polished toe of her boot. "She had been complaining about a headache. She said she was going home to lie down for a bit. I told her it would be all right. Nothing doing here that I couldn't manage."

"Do not make excuses for her, Sister Roberts. Headache or not, she should not have abandoned you. Now you will have to see to her work as well as your own. When Sister Becker deigns to return to her place, I want to see her straight away. That girl will be looking for a new job next time I see her..."

The pent-up emotions began to spill and it took a deep breath to bring herself back under control. There was no more time to waste on thinking about Sister Becker. Charlie had a very sick child on her hands and caring for Archie took every moment of her attention. His sudden relapse had her puzzled, but she'd have to wait until morning before she could discuss the strange symptoms with Doctor Linacre. She pulled a blanket over her shoulders and set herself to watch and wait.

THIRTY-TWO

The rain continued to lash the building unabated all through the night and a grey, wet dawn broke over Maiden's Creek. The stampers had been silenced for the Sabbath and an eerie silence settled on the valley, broken only by the thunder of water from the swollen creek.

Charlie had hardly moved from the hard, unforgiving chair beside Archie's bed, except to tend to the boy and now she lacked the energy to wash her own face. It was Margaret Campbell who knocked on the door and entered carrying a cup of tea. She looked fresh and bright eyed, everything Charlie was not.

"Lily said you'd been sitting with him all night," Margaret observed. "You should go home and get some rest."

Charlie stood up, stretching her stiff, complaining back. "Is Mrs. Fraser still sleeping?"

Margaret nodded. "I peeped in and she's dead to the world."

Charlie thanked the nurse and as she drank the very welcome cup of tea she briefed Margaret on Archie's condition.

"Can I leave him with you for a little while? I need to organize one of the doctors to attend him."

"And get some breakfast," Margaret said. "I left Mary Keegan making porridge."

"Has Janet Becker returned?"

Margaret's eyes widened. "What do you mean?"

"She went out in the middle of the night. Was she here when you and Sister Keegan arrived?"

Margaret shook her head. "No. When did she go out?"

"Lily said about midnight."

"That's not like Becker."

"On the contrary, I believe she and Joe Trevelyan used to meet regularly. Did you know about their assignations?"

"On Saturday nights? It was usually only for ten minutes at the most."

A spark of anger kindled in Charlie's breast. "Did everyone in this hospital turn a blind eye to it?"

Margaret bit her lip but said nothing.

Charlie sighed, too tired to let the anger settle.

"I'll send Eddie to her lodgings," she said. "Lily said she had been complaining about a headache. I don't need her to be ill."

Charlie left Margaret with the boy and went to the kitchen for a fresh cup of tea to try to instill some warmth into her cold, stiff limbs, her thoughts only on Archie Fraser and what needed to be done to get him through the day.

Mary Keegan stood at the stove, stirring the porridge. Charlie glanced into the pot at the grey, unedifying mess and grimaced.

"Beggars can't be choosers," Mary said. "When I was a babe in Ireland, we counted ourselves lucky to have a stale crust of bread to break our fast."

"You are not alone in having an impoverished childhood," Charlie replied. "Many's the time I went to bed with an empty stomach."

Mary Keegan stopped stirring. "I thought with your fancy education and the like you came from the well-offs, like Campbell?"

"Not at all."

Charlie didn't feel inclined to explain her life story to the nurse. She refreshed the tea in the teapot and poured a cup, sinking into the comfortable armchair by the fire, her eyelids already beginning to droop.

A piercing scream ran through the building, causing Charlie to start, slopping hot tea over the cup and saucer and her hand. Cursing, she set the tea down and hurried out of the kitchen, colliding with Sister Roberts.

She grasped the nurse by the forearms as Lily stared at her with wide eyes, her mouth opening and closing.

"Pull yourself together, Sister. What on earth is the matter?"

Lily pointed wordlessly at the ward from which a chorus of high-pitched screams now emanated.

Charlie had been told that nurses never ran but she threw that ancient advice to one side and ran to the women's ward. The three ambulatory women, including Martha, were gathered at the window, wearing only their nightdresses. Two of the women clung to each other, alternately screaming and sobbing.

Charlie clapped her hands.

"Back to bed, this instance, before you all catch your death," she said.

As one the women turned, parting as Charlie walked towards the window, trying to make sense of what she saw in the grey morning light.

Beyond the window, the large gum tree stood unmoved by the wind and rain, ordinary and familiar. Except for the object that hung from its large lower branch, sodden by the rain to the point of anonymity and swaying in the cold, unforgiving rain.

A body—a woman in a blue dress and white apron, darkened to grey by the rain—hung by a rope, her head lowered, her feet only inches from the ground.

"Jesus, Mary and Joseph!"

Beside her, Mary Keegan crossed herself. Charlie resisted the instinctive need to do the same.

"Get the women back into bed, Sister," Charlie said, trying to keep her voice steady and authoritative.

Charlie pulled the curtains across the windows, hiding the horrible sight from the view of the patients.

She turned and glared at the women. "Back to bed and I don't want to hear another sound."

"It's that young nurse, isn't it?" Martha said, her eyes hard with an old defiance that Charlie recognized only too well.

"Bed," she said and pointed. "You already have a bad chest infection and it isn't getting better standing in the cold."

To her surprise, Martha obeyed. She hunched down in the bed.

"It's him," she said, pulling the blanket up to her chin. "He'll be coming for me next. I told you, O'Reilly..."

"Be quiet, Martha. You'll frighten the other patients," Charlie snapped. "I've no time for your fairy stories today."

Leaving Mary Keegan to settle the patients, Charlie found Lily Roberts standing where she had left her in the hallway, her arms wrapped around herself, her teeth chattering.

"I just went to open the curtains," Lily sobbed. "It's Janet, isn't it?"

"Pull yourself together," Charlie ordered, wondering if she was going to have to deliver a good hard slap to get any sense out of the girl. "We have to put our patients first, and you need to go home and get some rest. You've been on duty all night."

"What's happening?" Margaret appeared at the door to the private room.

"There's been an unfortunate death—"

"It's Janet." Lily flung herself at Margaret Campbell, sobbing into the woman's shoulder.

Charlie softened her tone. "We don't know for certain that it's Janet. Margaret, can you take Lily into the kitchen?" She sniffed—the smell of something unpleasant burning was issuing from the kitchen. "The porridge needs dealing with too."

"What are you going to do?" Margaret put an arm around Lily's shoulders.

"I... I..." She stumbled on the next words. How did you say, 'deal with the body'? She settled on, "I'm going to wake Alf and we'll get her down."

She pulled on her coat and grabbed the umbrella they kept by the back door. Nevertheless, her boots and the hem of her skirt were soaked in the short distance to Alf's quarters across the courtyard. She hammered at the man's door and he opened it, bleary eyed and wearing nothing more than a rather grubby set of combinations.

"Get dressed, bring a ladder and a sharp knife."

"Wassup?" Alf scratched his head, causing his spiky grey hair to stand on end.

"We have a dead body hanging from the gum tree."

Alf's eyes widened. "A dead 'un. Sure he's dead?"

"She—and I'm certain. Hurry, Alf."

"Shouldn't we fetch the police?"

"I can't leave her hanging there, Alf. We'll cut her down and secure her somewhere safe and dry first, and then you can go for the police."

Charlie waited in the shelter of the front verandah, hardly able to take her eyes from the slowly swaying body. She'd seen death in many forms but this—stark and horrible—was almost too much to bear.

It seemed an age before Alf stomped around the corner of the building, clad head to boot in an oil slicker and carrying a ladder and long, wicked-looking knife. They crossed the sodden lawn to the tree.

Up close Charlie was in no doubt that it was Janet Becker and she had evidently been there for hours. Her uniform dress was soaked through and her hair had come down from its bun and hung in dripping rats tails around her lowered head.

Alf swore under his breath, whipping off his hat, despite the rain, in respect for the dead.

"Oh no," he said, "not poor Sister Becker. She were a sweet lass."

"Get on with it, Alf."

He set the ladder to the tree. "You'll need to catch her, Matron. Can't have her just fallin' to the ground."

Charlie wrapped her arms around the woman's legs, taking her weight as Alf sawed through the rope. As the rope gave way, Janet's full weight descended on Charlie and she went to her knees, steadying the body as she laid her down on the ground. Her stomach lurched as she looked into the woman's face. Janet's eyes were open and staring, already filming with death.

Charlie had seen hanging victims and it struck her that Janet looked like none she had seen before. Hanging was not pretty, leaving the victim swollen faced, often with protruding tongue and red-streaked eyes. But Janet's face was pale and untouched by the normal signs of strangulation.

"Poor lassie," Alf said. "We can't leave her out here."

"You take her shoulders, I'll take her legs. We'll put her in the operating theatre for now."

Rigor mortis had set in and even with two of them carrying her over a short distance, it took them a while to negotiate their way across the verandah and in through the front door. Mary Keegan must have been following their progress as she hurried to open the door into the operating theatre.

They laid Janet on the table and Mary Keegan went to undo the rope that still circled Janet's neck.

"No," Charlie said, "leave it. The police will want to see it."

"Why? It's plain she took her own life," Mary Keegan said. "'Tis a mortal sin and there'll be no rest for her soul."

"I don't think she was Roman Catholic, Sister," Charlie said, again resisting a sudden urge to cross herself.

Her heart broke for the pretty little nurse with her future in front of her. A future beside a good man who would have to be told that his betrothed had taken her life.

She sent Alf to fetch the police and Doctor Linacre, shut the door to the theater, and turned the key. She needed privacy to see to the body.

Automatically, she picked up a towel and gently dried the girl's face. As she ministered to Janet, she thought back to the moment when she had waited for Alf, looking at the gently swaying body. Something about the tableau had seemed wrong and it dawned on her exactly what it was. Surely, for Janet to have done the deed herself, she would have had to stand on something, even a block of wood, but there had been nothing beneath her feet or in the vicinity that she could have kicked away.

Her blood ran cold as the implications of that simple observation ran through her mind. Had someone else hung her from the tree?

She pulled a sheet over the corpse, left the room, and locked the door behind her. Composing herself, she found the three nurses gathered around the kitchen table.

"Matron?" Lily Roberts turned an ashen face up to Charlie. "What do we do now?"

All three nurses were looking at her, needing guidance and reassurance. Charlie was not sure she had any to give. She felt helpless... and afraid.

To cover her own inadequacy, she made to look at her watch, which she normally wore pinned to her shoulder but it was missing. In her hurry to dress in the middle of the night she had left it in her cottage. She suddenly felt desperately weary. She'd had barely three or four hours sleep before Lily Roberts had woken her.

"Sister Roberts, you are off duty. Go home, we will need you rested for tonight."

Lily's lower lip trembled. "I don't think I can. We shared a room, Janet and I."

"You can and you will. As for the rest of us, Sister Keegan, please retrieve what you can of the porridge and serve the patients their breakfast. Sister Campbell, how is Archie Fraser?

"The noise woke his mother. She's sitting with him now and he seems a little easier."

Charlie nodded and straightened.

"Ladies, there is nothing we can do for Sister Becker and we have living patients who need our strength and calm. I will deal with the police and whatever needs to be done for poor Janet," she said. "Sister Keegan, Sister Campbell, we will do what we do every morning. Give our patients tea and breakfast and see to dressings and medication. You are to say nothing to them and if they ask, just tell them there has been an unfortunate accident and it is being dealt with."

When no one moved, she clapped her hands.

"Pull yourselves together. You are nurses and you have responsibilities. See to them."

THIRTY-THREE

Fortified by a hasty and unpleasant breakfast of burned porridge, Charlie took a moment to compose herself, ensuring her uniform and every hair was in place, before sallying forth to face the patients.

The women's ward was full of questions and Charlie fended them off with the agreed explanation that an unfortunate death had occurred during the night and was being investigated.

"It was that pretty nurse," the oldest patient, Mrs. Grimes said. "Why'd she go and do a stupid thing like that?"

"I don't know," Charlie said. "But that is none of your concern."

Martha glanced at the window where the curtains were still shut.

Her mouth quirked. "I've thought about offing myself but it takes courage and I don't have that kind of courage."

Charlie laid a hand on Martha's bony shoulder. "try to rest, Martha. It's a sad day, but you need to concentrate on getting yourself well."

Martha looked up at her.

"Why? I've no reason to get well, no reason to get up in the morning and no one to mourn me if I went."

"I'd mourn you, Martha," Charlie said and turned away before Martha could see the tears that had started in her eyes.

She composed herself before entering the men's ward. Bertie Campbell was sitting up in bed, his face puce with anger.

"What's going on? What's all that bloody noise about? I've been ringing for bloody hours and no one's come. Where's that pretty Sister Becker?"

"Please do not use bad language, Mr. Campbell." Charlie was not above a bit of bad language herself when she was alone and privately would have liked nothing more than a quiet corner and a good round of swearing at that moment but appearances had to be maintained. "We have had a death in the hospital that has to be dealt with and is taking priority this morning."

She delegated Sister Keegan to deal with him and assured the men that breakfast was coming but it would be late.

Flora Fraser looked up as Charlie entered Archie's room and in the woman's ashen face and grey, hollow eyes, Charlie read utter despair.

"What was all the fuss this morning? Sister Campbell couldn't tell me."

Honesty being the best policy, Charlie replied, "There's been an unfortunate death that alarmed one of the patients. Everything is under control, but we are desperately short-staffed, so if you can stay with Archie that would be appreciated."

Flora's back stiffened. "I'm not going anywhere," she said. "Have you seen the creek? No way I can get home even if I wanted to."

Charlie ran a hand over the boy's forehead and forced a smile. "I think the worst has passed. He seems much better this morning."

A door slammed and a man bellowed, "This is deplorable. Where is the matron?"

Charlie's breath caught. She had forgotten that Fitzgerald had threatened to return today of all days.

She gave Flora a reassuring smile and left the room, closing the door behind her.

"Doctor Fitzgerald," she said. "Please modify your tone. We have enough to deal with this morning without your presence here. Could I request you delay your inspection?"

Fitzgerald's eyes glittered. "Then what would be the point of an inspection, Matron?"

Charlie glared at him. "One of my nurses was found dead this morning. Our cook and domestic servant are stranded on the far side of the valley and breakfast is delayed and the patients are understandably upset."

She looked past Fitzgerald's shoulder to the kitchen door where Margaret Campbell was signaling to her.

"I'm sorry to interrupt but Sergeant Prewitt is here," Margaret Campbell said. "He's in the kitchen."

Charlie looked at Fitzgerald. "Whatever your business here, this takes priority. You can wait in my office. Sister Campbell can bring you a cup of tea presently."

Fitzgerald's eyes blazed. "I'm not going to be dictated to by a nurse."

Behind his back, Margaret pulled a face that would almost have made Charlie smile, had the circumstances not been so dire.

"Suit yourself," she said and pushed past him to greet the policeman who stood warming himself in front of the fire, his sodden oilskin dripping from the hook by the door.

"Sergeant. Thank you for coming so promptly."

"What's all this about?" Prewitt demanded. "Your man wouldn't tell me. Creek's rising and I've important work to see to."

"One of my nurses was found dead this morning," Charlie said.

Prewitt's eyes widened. "Dead? How?"

"In what I can only describe as highly suspicious circumstances," Charlie said. "She was found hanging from the tree at the front of the hospital—"

"I didn't see a body."

"I removed her and she has been laid out in the operating theatre. Would you care to accompany me?"

Prewitt rubbed his bulbous nose. "This is highly irregular."

Charlie put her hands on her hips. "Everything about it is highly irregular."

"What's this about a dead nurse?"

Fitzgerald had followed her into the kitchen and stood at the door, a scowl creasing his forehead. Charlie ignored him and pushed past him with the policeman following.

Unlocking the door to the operating theater, she stood back and let

Prewitt enter the room. Fitzgerald had followed and short of slamming the door in his face she had no choice but to let him in as well. She closed the door behind them.

It was almost as if they took appointed places on either side of the table, allowing Charlie to fold back the sheet covering Janet Becker. The intervening hour had dried her clothes and hair but the rope around her neck told its own story. A wave of sadness washed over her, and she gently pushed a stray lock of hair from the girl's forehead.

Prewitt whipped off his cap and shook his head.

"Poor lass. Where did you say you found her?"

"Hanging from the tree at the front of the building. I left the rope so you can see where it occurred. Nothing else has been touched. I just couldn't leave her hanging there... in the rain and in full view of the hospital and the patients."

"Seems simple enough to me. She took her own life," Prewitt concluded.

"I can't see how—there was nothing beneath her feet," Charlie said. "She could hardly have hoisted herself off the ground and I've seen hanging victims before. They generally look..." She struggled for the words.

"Swollen, mottled..." Fitzgerald put in.

Prewitt shrugged. "It's my experience that folk can be mighty canny when they want to do themselves in."

Fitzgerald leaned over the body, gently easing the rope away from Janet's neck. He looked up at the portly sergeant. "I think it would be prudent for me to have a closer look at Miss Becker," he said.

"Who are you?" Prewitt demanded, as if he had only just noticed the stranger in the room.

"Doctor William Fitzgerald. I am often called in by the police in Melbourne to assist in such matters."

Prewitt's gaze shifted to Charlie. "Is he what he says he is?"

Charlie nodded, but added, "I think we should wait for one of the local doctors to attend."

Fitzgerald shot her a quick glance. "And when is that likely to be? I suggest I be authorized to conduct the post-mortem. Don't concern yourself, Sergeant, my fee will be reasonable."

Prewitt scratched his head, replaced his cap and huffed out a breath. "Very well, Doctor Fitzgerald. Makes no difference to me. You can do the post-mortem, but for now, I'm putting it down to death at her own hand."

Charlie stared at him. "Don't you want to interview witnesses? See where it happened—"

"I'll give it a look on my way out," Prewitt said. "But it's not my priority right now. If this rain don't let up, the creek will be in full flood by this afternoon and the buildings on Main Street will go under."

Charlie left Fitzgerald with the corpse, retrieved Prewitt's oilskin, and saw the man to the front door, pointing out the tree with the cut rope hanging from it. Prewitt stamped around the tree, stopped to look up at the branch, bid Charlie a cursory farewell, and left without even taking notes.

Charlie returned to the operating theater. Fitzgerald had removed his coat, rolled up his sleeves and donned the surgeon's smock that hung from a peg on the back of the door.

"You don't waste time," Charlie said.

He looked up at her with no rancor in his eyes. "Can you assist me, Matron?"

"I'll get one of the other nurses."

"They're busy and I know how you work... please, Charlotte, for her sake, if not mine."

Charlie took a deep breath. He was the only person in the world who habitually called her Charlotte and it grated.

She donned a smock and joined him at the table. The deft movement of his hands and the small crease of concentration between his brows, the faint scent of expensive tobacco caused the years to slip away, and once again she was a young nurse, working with a doctor she admired professionally—and loved privately.

He looked up from an examination of the girl's face. "I agree with your conclusion, Charlotte. This girl did not die from hanging," he said. "Help me turn her."

With the greatest respect, they turned the girl and Fitzgerald parted the matted hair.

He grunted. "There you go. That's what killed her."

The rain had washed away the blood, and Janet's thick hair concealed a hideous wound on the back of her head.

"She was most likely dead before she was strung up," Fitzgerald said. "Something struck her," his fingers explored the wound, "more than once I wager."

He stood back and straightened his shoulders before he gave Charlie a nod and they turned Janet on her back again.

With care, Fitzgerald cut the rope away and set it to one side.

"Do you mind removing her clothing and then we can conduct a proper examination," he said.

Charlie drew a deep breath as she looked down at the body of the young nurse.

Fitzgerald shot her a sharp glance. "It's hard when it's someone you know."

She nodded but couldn't bring herself to make eye contact with the doctor. She didn't need this unexpected kindness and understanding from this man.

He turned his back, his attention on laying out the instruments as Charlie carefully removed Janet's clothes, folding them neatly on a chair by the door. She pulled the sheet up and stroked Janet's cold cheek.

"Are you able to continue?" Fitzgerald asked.

She nodded and took a breath, steeling herself for the procedure that followed. Leaving aside her antipathy to the man, she had to respect the medical professional. Fitzgerald knew exactly what he was doing and what he was looking for.

The autopsy confirmed what had been obvious to the observers. The nurse had died from a massive blow or blows to the back of her head. Whether she was alive or dead when the rope tightened on her throat was impossible to say but the conclusion was inescapable.

Janet Becker had been murdered.

When he had done, Fitzgerald removed his smock and turned to the washbasin, scrubbing so hard Charlie feared he would remove his skin.

"Did you know her well?" he said without looking up from the hand washing.

"Not really. I've only been here a few weeks. She was a lovely girl...

she was engaged..." Her voice cracked. "Someone has to tell Joe. I will need to organize the undertaker and advise her family—"

Before she got any further, the door flung open and Linacre stood in the doorway, quivering with anger, his hot furious gaze fixed on Fitzgerald.

"Who the hell are you and what is the meaning of this? You have no jurisdiction in my hospital."

Fitzgerald didn't flinch in the face of his colleague's fury. He calmly wiped his hands, handing the cloth to Charlie.

"William Fitzgerald, chief physician at the Royal Melbourne Hospital. I would have presented my credentials when I arrived yesterday, but you could not be found." He gestured to the shrouded body. "This young woman has died in particularly bad circumstances. I happened to be here when the police attended and Sergeant..."

He looked at Charlie. "Prewitt," Charlie supplied.

"The sergeant requested I undertake the autopsy, the matter being somewhat urgent, in view of the crisis the town is currently facing."

Linacre opened and shut his mouth in impotent fury.

"Doctor Fitzgerald is here on a Registration Board inspection," Charlie said.

Linacre's eyes widened. "An inspection. No one told me about any inspection."

"The element of surprise is the point. I assume you are Linus Linacre?"

"I am. I am the medical director of this hospital." Linacre's gaze went to the body on the table and back to Fitzgerald. "Right now I don't care if you are God Almighty. You have no right to interfere in this hospital's business. A dead body could have waited. It was not for you to just walk in here and perform an autopsy. Who the hell is it and what were they doing hanging themselves from a tree outside the hospital?"

Linacre crossed to the table and flicked back the sheet from the girl's face. He took a step back. "Good God, it's Becker."

"Didn't Alf tell you?" Charlie asked.

"Alf? No. I sent him away with a flea in his ear while I finished my breakfast," Linacre said. He looked up, all anger gone, his eyes moving from Fitzgerald to Charlie.

"What happened?"

"The girl was hit over the head with a heavy object and I suggest the crime was staged to look like suicide by hanging," Fitzgerald replied. "As you are now here, I will leave you to your patients and return to my lodgings and write the report for the good sergeant who, I might add, authorized me to conduct the post-mortem." As he pulled on his coat and straightened his tie, he inclined his head to Charlie. "Matron, thank you for your assistance. Perhaps you could take tea with me later today?"

"I don't think so, Doctor. I am rather short-staffed at present. If you could give me some idea when you will return for your inspection, I will ensure everything is ready for you."

Fitzgerald's gaze flicked over her and he smiled. "Nothing less than what I expect, Matron."

"Do you know that man?" Linacre demanded when they were alone.

Charlie straightened. "I worked with him in Melbourne a few years ago. I am no happier to see him than you are. Apart from poor Janet's death... murder." She shivered. "The Ryans couldn't get here. Mary Keegan burned the porridge... and the whole place is in uproar."

Linacre sniffed. "And the last thing we need is a visit from the Registration Board." His lips twitched with a wry smile. "Timing is everything, Matron."

He glanced at Janet Becker again and gently replaced the sheet over the girl's face.

"Murder. Here... I can't believe it." He straightened. "Where's her family?"

"Wangaratta."

He nodded. "She needs to be buried sooner rather than later. With the weather, it's unlikely they'll be able to get here. If you've a moment, Matron, show me where she was hit?"

Charlie went over the findings of Fitzgerald's post-mortem. When she was done Linacre stood back and nodded. "Definitely murder," he said. "Poor girl. But it's in the hands of the police and we do have something of a crisis on our hands."

"I'm now one nurse down and the patients are understandably unsettled by... by the death," Charlie said.

"I think we should do a round together, Matron. How is young Mr. Fraser?"

"He had a turn of some sort during the night, but he seems a little better this morning."

Linacre shut the door and Charlie locked it. She took a moment to tidy herself in her office before she and the doctor did the rounds of the two wards. For the first time she saw a different side to Linus Linacre. He was professional and his presence had a calming influence on the patients as he explained that the death of Sister Becker was being investigated and it was likely that the police may have questions for the patients.

He went so far as to suggest that each one write or dictate to the nurses exactly what they remembered of the events of the night and if they had heard or seen anything out of the ordinary. Complaints about the food were quickly quelled as Linacre went on with the news that the rain was causing extensive flooding. One of the railway bridges had been washed out and the likelihood of fresh supplies getting through to the town in the next few days was doubtful.

Even Bertie Campbell seemed subdued and Charlie started to feel some warmth towards him until he blurted out, "Then how the hell am I ever going to get out of this bloody town?"

Linacre quelled him with a look that would have frozen water.

"Mr. Campbell. I understand your predicament, but you are only one of several patients and potential patients. Your needs do not come before those of your fellow human beings in suffering. Now, I will thank you to keep a civil tongue in your head and treat the other patients and the nurses with decency and compassion."

Bertie subsided in his bed, his brow furrowed mutinously, his arms crossed.

When the rounds were done, Charlie sat with Linacre and Margaret Campbell and they put together plans to get them through the next few days. When she was done, Charlie left Margaret in charge, looked up details of Janet Becker's next of kin and composed the most difficult telegram of her life.

THIRTY-FOUR

Regret to inform you that your daughter Janet died this morning in tragic circumstances. Funeral details to be advised. C. O'Reilly Matron Maiden's Creek District Hospital.

I t seemed so cold and impersonal. Charlie imagined Janet's parents reading the words. The grief, the questions, and no one to answer them. She would write a letter to provide more details but for now, it was all she could do.

Thrusting her hands deep into her coat pocket she braved the rain and, being careful of her footing on the wet and slippery slope, made her way down to Main Street on what turned out to be a fool's errand. Although the rain had begun to ease, the water spilled down from the high country, turning Maiden's Creek into a brown, churning weapon of destruction. The foot and wagon bridges that spanned the creek had all been swept away or were well under the water that now sent out fingers of stinking brown water, seeking new pathways of escape and taking with it the more insubstantial outbuildings and settling on the lower ground of Main Street. Barrels, boxes, trees, shrubs and even dead animals were carried along in the foment. If it kept rising, even the buildings on the far side of the street would go under.

Despite it being Sunday, the bells of the churches were silent and the postmaster, roused from his Sunday lunch, looked at Charlie's telegram and shook his head.

"Telegraph's down," he said. "No idea when it will be fixed. Not with the railway bridge out as well."

Charlie stared at him. "How am I going to get this message through?"

The postmaster took the paper and read it with a deepening frown. He shook his head.

"All I can do is promise to send it the moment the line is repaired. Leave it with me."

Charlie thanked him and sloshed down the street to the undertaker across the road from the livery stables who promised he would collect the body by evening.

"Can't leave her sitting in your morgue," he said.

Charlie thought of the cold, gloomy and no doubt damp outhouse behind the hospital and agreed that the sooner Janet could be properly dealt with the better.

The undertaker glanced at the window.

"I'm a bit concerned about the flooding. Don't know when we'll get her in the ground."

Dispirited and borne down by the death and her inability to see Janet properly buried, as well as by the appearance of William Fitzgerald, Charlie felt a terrible need to speak to a friend and she made her way to the Britannia.

Danny opened the door to his room, the smile on his face changing to a look of deep concern.

"Charlie, what's happened?"

Charlie, who rarely cried, had to choke back a sudden irrepressible urge to lay her head on Danny's expensive waistcoat and bawl. Instead, she straightened and spoke in a low voice.

"We've had a... a tragic death at the hospital."

"When you say tragic, I would have thought death fairly commonplace at the hospital," Danny said.

"One of my nurses." Her voice cracked. "We think she was murdered."

Danny stopped and looked down at her. "How? Who? Come in and sit by the fire. You look half frozen."

He stepped away from the door and ushered her into a chair by the fire. He hunched down in front of her and took her hands in his.

"What's happened, Charlie?"

His touch sent something warm and reassuring shooting down her spine. She, who relied on no one, who had fostered a fierce independence, wanted nothing more than to let him take her in his arms and tell her it would all be fine.

But it wasn't fine. Janet was dead and William Fitzgerald was haunting the corridors of her hospital.

"Janet Becker. Someone struck her over the head but..." A tear trickled down Charlie's cheek. She pulled away from Danny and dashed it away. "If that wasn't enough, the bastard then hung her from the big tree in the front of the hospital to make it look like she'd hanged herself."

Danny's lip curled. "That's appalling. Did you find her?"

Charlie nodded. "Only after my nurses and the women's ward had witnessed it. Alf and I had to cut her down."

The tears were coming too easily and no amount of sniffing and wiping stemmed them. Danny handed her a large, well-laundered handkerchief.

"This is ridiculous. I never cry," she said.

"You've had a terrible shock," Danny said.

"She was a sweet girl. It's a terrible, terrible thing," she said.

"Is there anything I can do?"

Charlie blew her nose and managed a crooked smile. "What do you think you could possibly do?"

"For my sins, I am a lawyer. I may be a little useful."

"You're probably more use than that idiot policeman." Charlie said. "Sergeant Prewitt wants to put it down to suicide and forget about it."

"Prewitt?" Danny stood up. "Wasn't he a constable here when we were children?"

"The same."

"He couldn't find his own nose, let alone a murderer," Danny said with feeling.

"My thought too but in fairness he has got a lot to deal with. The creek is flooding and the town in chaos." Charlie looked up at Danny. "I want to do the right thing by her ... and her family. I have to know who killed her."

"There will have to be an inquest," Danny replied. "That might flush out the murderer."

Charlie gave a humorless laugh. "You assume Prewitt will have done a decent investigation. Time is slipping away already."

"Charlie, there is a process..." Danny began. "But you may be right about Prewitt. Very well, let's put together what we know starting with ... who knew her best?"

"Joe Trevelyan."

"Joe? That's right, he was her beau." Danny frowned. "Poor Joe."

"He asked her to marry him on Friday." The tears threatened again. "With everything going on in town, I doubt anyone's taken the time to tell him."

Danny held out his hand and helped her stand. "He's downstairs. We're his friends, it will be best coming from us. How about we go and talk to him?"

THIRTY-FIVE

Heedless of the prohibition against women entering the main bar, Danny pushed open the door and ushered Charlie in, causing a small group of men sitting at a table by the window to raise their voices in protest.

Joe Trevelyan stood behind the bar pouring a beer.

He looked up and shook his head. "Charlie, you can't be in here—"

"We need to talk to you, Joe," Danny said, adding, "somewhere private."

Joe finished his task and pushed the tankard across the bar to the waiting miner. He directed them to a door on the right, which led into a room that Danny recognized as once having served as Caleb's rudimentary surgery. It seemed to have reverted to being a general office and going by the layers of dust it was not in much use.

Joe looked from one to the other and tried to smile.

"What's happened?" His face sobered. "It's bad. I can see from your faces."

Charlie reached out and took Joe's hand.

"It's Janet," she said. "She's dead."

"No!" Joe snatched back his hand and shook his head as if denying it would make the statement untrue. "She can't be dead. We're getting married. She..." He slumped back against the desk and lowered his head into his hands. "She can't be..."

Danny laid a hand on the other man's shoulder. "I'm sorry, Joe."

Joe swallowed and looked up, his eyes brimming with unshed tears. "How...?"

Danny glanced at Charlie and she straightened her shoulders. He wondered how many times she had to tell someone their loved one had died.

"We found her this morning, hanging from the big, old tree at the front of the hospital. We thought maybe she'd taken her own life but when we looked at her, we realized..." Her chest rose and fell as she took a breath. "Joe, someone took her life."

Joe frowned. "Are you saying she was done in? My Janet? She wouldn't hurt a soul. Why would someone do that?"

Danny shook his head. "We don't know."

"Did you see her last night?" Charlie asked, and when his mouth tightened she went on. "Apart from the incident on Friday, I know you've been seeing her on the sly when she's on night duty. Sneaking out of her duties to meet you is a serious breach of the regulations, but none of that matters now. Lily Roberts said she left the hospital about midnight claiming she had a headache. Did you come up to see her again last night?"

Joe's mouth worked. Danny recognized the look of a man wrestling with his conscience.

"No. Yorkie needed me to move some barrels in the cellar and it was well after midnight before I finished. Besides, you made it clear that I had to stay away." His face crumpled. "Janet—"

Joe's self-control gave way and Charlie took the man in her arms and held him as he wept.

"I'm so sorry, Joe," she said, and when she looked up at Danny he saw the tears in her eyes and wondered if they were for the dead nurse whom she hardly knew or this man.

"What's going on? Joe, lad, I need you back at the bar."

The door burst open and Yorkie Oldroyd stood in the doorway. Joe stiffened and pulled away from Charlie.

Yorkie's gaze went to Danny.

"Mr Hunt?"

"We've just had to break some bad news to Joe," Danny said.

"Is it about that lass up at the hospital? I just heard." Yorkie frowned. "But I don't see why you need take on so lad, you didn't know her."

Joe dashed his tears away with his sleeve. "Know her? I was going to marry her."

And with that, he pushed past the men out into the street. Yorkie made to go after him, but Danny caught his sleeve.

"Let him be, Yorkie."

"I don't understand. What did he mean about marrying her?"

"I think that's a question you need to ask him, Mr Oldroyd," Charlie said, "but from what Janet told me, they had been stepping out for some time."

"But why didn't he say summit?" Yorkie scratched his nose in genuine disbelief. "Did he think I'd disapprove?"

Danny cleared his throat. "He may have thought you might disapprove of their plans to move to Melbourne."

"Oh, the stupid lad. Why'd he think that? It's his life, I've no right to interfere in it." Yorkie sagged against the doorframe. "That he'd think so badly of me..."

Charlie and Danny exchanged glances.

Yorkie straightened. "Aye, well... I'm glad he heard it from you first then."

"Look after him, Yorkie."

The old publican nodded. "He's a grand lad. I'll see he's all right."

Danny and Charlie left the hotel and stood on the verandah, looking out at the unrelenting rain.

"That was something I hope I never have to do again," Danny said. He looked down at the nurse beside him. "I suppose you have to do it all the time?"

Charlie nodded. "Telling a relative their loved one has died is the worst aspect of the job," she said. "If you have time, I would be grateful for your company. Next to Joe, Lily Roberts was her closest friend. I think I should check on her and talk to their landlady."

Danny returned to his room, retrieved his coat and umbrella and laced on his stout boots. Outside he opened his umbrella and Charlie huddled beneath it.

"This would cover a cricket team," she said.

"Not quite, and I don't think even a fine product of Manchester such as this will keep this rain out for much longer."

Janet and Lily's landlady, Mrs Cole, opened the door to them,

Her eyes red rimmed from tears, her fingers twisting a sodden handkerchief, she said, "I gave young Lily a sleeping draught. She was in a terrible state when she got in this morning. Couldn't believe what she told me... poor young Janet. Came back as happy as a sandpiper on Friday. I've got a secret, Mrs. C, she told me. You'll hear soon enough but you may have to find yourself a new lodger."

"Joe Trevelyan had asked her to marry him," Charlie said.

Mrs Cole dissolved into tears again. "That's what Lily said. Poor girl... terrible thing..."

When she recovered her composure she asked between sniffs if Janet's parents had been informed.

Charlie assured her a telegram had been organized and a suitable funeral would be arranged.

There was nothing more to be done. Danny would have liked to suggest Charlie search Janet's belongings for a diary or letters but with Lily asleep in the same room, there was no point even asking.

As they made their apologies, Charlie laid a hand on the woman's arm.

"Mrs Cole, please can you ensure that Sister Roberts is in a fit state for duty tonight. I really need her."

The woman sniffed. "Aye, you'll be busy. What with this..." She waved a hand at the rain.

Charlie nodded. "And I have no one else to do night duty."

The woman straightened. "She'll be there."

They thanked Mrs Cole and stepped back outside into the unrelenting rain.

Danny raised his umbrella. "If you don't mind me saying so, Charlie, you look done in. I'm going to walk you home and suggest you get some rest."

Charlie nodded. "I didn't get much sleep last night. But I'm going to need to reorganize the roster to put Keegan on duty with Lily Roberts so I'll have to stay on duty for now and let Mary get some rest."

"Sounds complicated," Danny said.

Charlie smiled up at him. "It is."

At the hospital, Danny felt obliged to call in on Bertie and found him in a foul mood.

"It's disgraceful," Bertie said. "No one tells me a damn thing. What's this about a nurse killing herself?"

Danny lowered his voice. "She didn't kill herself."

Bertie leaned forward. "You mean, she was..." His eyes widened. "There's a murderer on the loose?"

Danny put a finger to his lips. "Keep it down, Campbell."

"Is Margaret safe?"

"Without knowing why the nurse was killed, I can't say."

Bertie's fingers closed on Danny's arm. "You've got to get us both out of here, Hunt. First, someone tries to shoot me and now this..."

"We're going nowhere. Even if we could move you, the train's not running and the telegraph is down. We're just going to have to sit tight for a few more days."

Or weeks...

Bertie swallowed. "I don't mind telling you, Hunt. This whole thing is unnerving. I'm just a sitting duck here."

Danny stood up and patted his friend on the shoulder. "No one is trying to kill you, Campbell." He leaned forward and spoke in a low voice. "But it could be useful if you could keep your eyes and ears open for anything suspicious."

Bertie nodded. "Righto. I can do that. Are you coming back tomorrow?"

Danny smiled. "Who knows? The whole town is descending into chaos. For now, I need to winkle a stubborn old lady out of her home or she will be floating away in a few hours."

He left the hospital by the front door. As he crossed the verandah a female voice hailed him.

"Danny Greaves."

He turned on his heel to see who had spoken. One of the windows to the women's ward stood ajar and a woman with a thin, pale face and lank fair hair, cropped to her shoulders, leaned against the casement.

"Were you talking to me, madam?" he inquired.

"Don't recognize me, do you? Martha Mackie."

"I—"

She waved a hand. "Don't pretend. I'm a ruin. Not everyone falls on their feet, Danny Greaves."

Martha crooked her finger, beckoning him over. When he was within arm's length, she pointed to the large gum tree and lowered her voice, her eyes wide and fearful.

"Did you hear about the dead nurse?"

"I did."

"I saw her first, you know. When the nurse pulled back the curtains it was me that said, there's someone hanging from the tree."

"That must have been dreadful for you," Danny said.

"He did it... I saw him."

"What are you talking about?"

She looked over her shoulder into the ward and lowered her voice. "Death. He comes at night and takes them."

Danny frowned. "Martha, what are you talking about?"

"Martha Drew, close that window and get back into bed this instant," a strident voice with an Irish accent commanded.

"He'll be coming for me next," Martha said in a low voice.

She gave Danny one last fearful glance and closed the window.

Danny stared at the window and shook his head.

Martha Mackie. He had only vague memories of Martha and he thought of her as rather a prissy little girl with her hair in ringlets and a spotless pinafore. He couldn't reconcile that memory with the scarecrow he had just seen. She was right, some people did fall on their feet—and others had the ground swept away from underneath them, he thought as he walked away.

He crossed the soggy grass to the old gum tree and looked up at the sturdy limb from which Janet Becker had been found hanging. The cut rope still hung from the branch and he grimaced, imagining the sight that had greeted Charlie.

Even from where he stood he could clearly see that the rope had been fastened off on the branch. There was no way that anyone could even begin to think anything other than a crime had been committed, and he felt a mounting anger with the useless Sergeant Prewitt.

Criminal law was his area of expertise and he knew enough about the investigative process to do a scan of the entire area around the tree, but it had been well trampled by Charlie and Alf and more recently by a man in heavy boots—Prewitt he guessed. There were the marks of a ladder but he guessed that had been the ladder used to cut the woman down. If a ladder had been used to fasten the rope and hoist the nurse's body to an appearance of a hanging, any trace had been washed away, along with the culprit's footprints or any useful evidence.

Rain trickled down the back of his neck, reminding him he had an important task to perform. Investigating Janet Becker's death would have to wait.

THIRTY-SIX

On her return to the hospital, Charlie found two women sitting on the bench outside her office. The younger woman was heavily pregnant, and from her red eyes and woebegone expression, she had been weeping.

She ushered both women into her office and shut the door. The pregnant girl lowered herself onto a chair while her mother remained standing.

"I'm Mrs Smith and this here's my daughter, Sally." Mrs Smith cast the girl a hateful look. "Stupid little bitch got herself in the family way with some miner who's skipped out on her. I've hid her shame from the neighbors, but the little bastard is nearly due and I don't want her in my house."

"Ma!" The girl protested. "I got nowhere to go."

"You should've thought of that before you spread your legs for that no-good man."

The tears started and Charlie found herself momentarily unable to move or to think and for some reason the inscription on Sissy's gravestone came back to her.

He that is without sin among you, let him first cast a stone.

"Nurse?" Mrs Smith was looking at her curiously.

Charlie let out her breath, unaware that she had even been holding it. She ignored the mother and turned to the distressed girl, helping her up from the chair and putting her arm around her shoulders.

"It's all right, Sally. We'll look after you here."

Without even looking at the mother, she opened her office door and started to guide Sally towards the women's ward.

"Tell the little bitch she can come home but not if she's trailing her little bastard," the mother shouted after her, provoking a fresh round of tears from the pregnant girl.

Charlie pulled screens around the bed and examined the girl. The baby's head had dropped. She looked up at Sally and smiled.

"Baby will be here any time soon."

The good news did not have the desired effect, and the girl began to cry again.

"How old are you?"

"Seventeen," the girl said between sniffs. "He said he'd marry me but as soon as I told him I was in the family way, he up and left. Don't know where he's gone."

"Bastard." Martha Mackie's voice came from the other side of the screen.

"They're all bastards," Mrs Grimes put in.

"Ladies, mind your own peace, please," Charlie said, addressing the patients beyond the screen.

She turned back to Sally Smith and summoned a reassuring smile. "The important thing is that you and the baby are safe and well."

She left Sally in the capable hands of Margaret Campbell, who soon had her tucked up in bed with a cup of tea.

"Why do women do this to themselves?" Margaret said half an hour later as she joined Charlie in the kitchen for their own well earned cup of tea.

"Do what?"

"Give themselves to men with such free abandon. Surely they know the consequences?"

"They fancy themselves in love," Charlie said.

The tea slopped from Margaret's cup onto the saucer as she snorted, "Love!"

Charlie gave the woman a curious glance. "Have you never been in love, Margaret?"

She detected a momentary hesitation before Margaret shrugged. "I thought, maybe..." She glanced out of the window and said with a laugh, "The worst thing a nurse can do is fall for a patient."

But her laugh sounded forced and Charlie remembered how she had looked at the young Italian who had brought her brother to the hospital.

Margaret appeared to recollect herself, reaching for the tin of biscuits.

"No biscuits," she said. "We need Geraldine back."

"What about your life before nursing?" Charlie prodded.

"That was years ago. My mother thought I would make a good match for Danny Hunt. He even asked me to marry him."

Charlie took a breath. "But...?"

There was a degree of coyness in the little half smile.

"I said no."

Charlie turned away under the pretense of placing her cup and saucer in the wash basin. She didn't want Margaret to see her face and the conflicting emotions churning in her heart. Unlike Margaret Campbell she barely knew Danny Hunt but he had stirred something in her that she had thought long forgotten. Margaret might scoff at the mention of love, but unless she had ever really been in love, she could not know how painful and terrifying and yet wonderful it could be... if it was reciprocated.

"And is that a decision you regret?"

"I wonder, sometimes..." Margaret mused. "Seeing him here the other day gave me quite a jolt. I had forgotten how much I had once cared for him." She paused. "Perhaps I could find those sentiments again."

"No one else since then?" Charlie asked.

Margaret put her hand to her throat, fiddling with the button on her collar. "No... no one else, or at least not anyone my family would approve of."

The frantic ringing of the women's wardbell put an end to the conversation.

Charlie rose to her feet. "Enough chat, Sister. We have work to do."

THIRTY-SEVEN

By late afternoon the floodwater had turned Main Street into an extension of the creek. Churning brown water rushed down at an alarming rate, forming eddies and whirlpools as it hit obstructions. Danny stood on the verandah of the Britannia and considered the inundation. It would not be long before the boardwalks and the buildings fronting the street went under.

It was time to fetch Netty.

Pulling the hood of the oilskin over his head, Danny slipped, slithered and sloshed along the boardwalk. To reach Netty's cottage, he found himself wading knee-deep in fast rushing water. The water had crept up her yard and now lapped at the top step.

She answered his frantic knocking. The normally imperturbable Netty clutched at his coat, her eyes wide with fear. "I don't know what to do. I've been trying to keep the water out but it's coming up between the floorboards."

He put a reassuring arm around her. "There's nothing you can do, Netty. The water's going to come in whatever you do. Have you packed dry clothes and some food?"

"I have but I don't want to leave." Netty's voice was high and filled with panic.

Danny put his arms around her and held her close. This woman had brought him up and was as precious to him as his mother and he was painfully aware of how much he had neglected her friendship in the intervening years.

"Charlie says I am to take you to her cottage."

"I know she said that, but I couldn't impose—"

"Don't argue," Danny cut across her.

Netty straightened and wiped a hand across her eyes. "Give me a moment."

She reappeared from the bedroom carrying a large carpetbag. On top of the clothes she stuffed the contents of her larder... a pie, bread, jam and cake.

"What about Flossie?" she said.

Danny looked at the pregnant cat, watching them closely from her perch on the table.

"She comes too, of course," Danny said.

Netty found a basket and they settled the cat in, putting a blanket over her so she wouldn't be spooked by the drama outside.

Please stay put, Danny silently begged the animal.

Netty clutched the cat basket as Danny took the other luggage from her and propelled her by the arm out onto the street. Netty squeaked in alarm when she saw how high the water was.

"You're going to get wet," Danny said. "It's unavoidable, but I've got your hand. We'll get there together."

As Netty hesitated, Danny told her to wait and carried the luggage across to the far side of the street. He set it down out of the rain and water, and went back for Netty, who stood holding the basket with the cat.

"Remember how you used to give me piggybacks when I was a boy?" he said, taking her hand. "Now it's your turn."

"I couldn't..."

"Stop arguing. I won't drop you."

Bunching her skirts, he settled Netty in his grasp. Clutching the cat basket precariously in his hands, he carried her across the street. The water was rising by the minute, and the current tugged at his feet and legs, threatening to overthrow him and dump them all in the filthy stream.

They reached the safety of the other side of the street and Danny let Netty down. She gathered up her basket, cooing reassuring words to the cat, as he took the rest of her luggage in one hand and her arm in the other. In the dark and rain the treacherous lane up to Charlie's cottage had become little more than a fast-running creek as it rushed down to join the main watercourse The little woman nearly lost her footing on the steep hill and it took Danny all his strength to keep a grip on her. They made slow progress, arriving at the door of the cottage muddy and bedraggled.

Charlie had left the door unlocked. Danny lit the kerosene lamp on the table he found a note underneath it telling Netty the bed was hers and to make herself at home. A single mattress had been laid on the floor in the living room, which he presumed Charlie had made up for herself.

Netty sat down heavily on a chair, the cat basket still clutched in her hand as Danny lit the fire, breathing it into life.

"That girl is so thoughtful," Netty said and burst into tears. "Don't mind me."

He patted her inadequately on the shoulder as she snuffled into her handkerchief with a "Take no mind of me."

She gave a final sniff and pulled the cat out of the basket, setting it on her knee. Flossie crouched, glaring balefully at the humans who had upset her routine while Netty stroked her and made comforting noises.

"There, there, Floss. You'll be safe here."

Danny was unsure whether Netty was actually talking to the cat or trying to reassure herself.

"Where's Amos?" he asked.

Netty looked up. "He and the boy were going to move the horses up to the block beside the hospital."

Danny gave her what he hoped was a reassuring smile.

"I'll see he is safe."

Netty set Flossie down on the rag rug in front of the fire and stood up, running her hand down her damp skirts.

"Tell him, and the girl, that I'll have supper on the table."

"I will." Danny paused at the door. "You're safe here, Netty."

She smiled. "I knew you'd not let anything happen to us, but I'm not such a fool as to think that our little home by the creek will be there for us when the water goes down."

Danny arrived at the back door to the hospital, muddy and thoroughly chilled. His knock was answered by Sister Mary Keegan.

She scowled at him. "Boots!"

"I'm not coming in. I just want to know if Amos Burrell is here."

Charlie stood at the stove stirring a pot. She turned to look at him.

"No. He called by an hour or so ago to say he and his lad were moving the horses up, but I've not seen him since. Netty?"

"Netty's at your cottage. I'm going to fetch Amos before..."

Charlie's eyes widened. "How bad is it?"

"It's bad," Danny said. "The whole of Main Street is going under."

Charlie handed the spoon to Sister Keegan.

"Keep stirring," she ordered the nurse. She addressed Danny. "Have you eaten tonight?"

"Not yet."

"I'll save something for you," she said.

"Netty said she had food for you."

Charlie shook her head. "I won't get up there. I think it's going to be a long night. Now go, you are letting the cold air in."

Danny nodded. "I'll let you know when I have Amos safely up in the cottage."

"Thank you." She looked up at him, her eyes heavy with exhaustion. "Be careful, Danny."

He smiled. "I will be."

THIRTY-EIGHT

On his way down to the livery stable, Danny passed Amos's stable hand with four of the horses on leads and directed him to the vacant block beside the hospital.

"Amos is trying to move the last two horses," the boy said, "but the water's really coming in now. I hope you get to him in time. He's a stubborn old coot and he won't leave without 'em."

With a growing sense of dread, Danny reached Main Street. The raging torrent slackened off at the bend in the road, which allowed him some leeway to cross to the livery stables, but he lost his footing halfway across and found himself dunked in the cold, dark water and swept along, until he was able to get a purchase on a hitching post and haul himself upright. He kept imagining the hidden objects being borne along by the water, remembering stories of snakes washed from their hiding places.

Snakes were his worst fear.

He dragged himself back towards the livery stables where he found Amos knee-deep in water, wrestling with a temperamental mare.

"Leave her," Danny said above the roar of the water.

That was about the worst thing Danny could have said.

"I'll not leave any of my horses," Amos said, his bushy eyebrows shooting up in outrage. "There's just Missy here and old Sam. I'll bring the mare if you can manage Sam. He's a good chap. He won't give you no trouble."

Old Sam was one of the coach horses Amos still used to take day trippers out on excursions up to the Aberfeldy River or down to the Thompson River. Large and solid, he stood obediently, dipping his head to allow Danny to buckle on the halter and leading rein. It only took a gentle tug on the leading rein to encourage the old horse to following him out into the now completely submerged yard, the water sloshing around his knees as he plodded forward.

Amos had finally got a halter onto the mare, but she was refusing to move. Seeing Old Sam, however, her resistance seemed to diminish, and she allowed Amos to lead her on. Out in the street, the water tugged at Danny's legs and he lost his foothold, finding himself pushed back against the coach horse, who remained rock solid against the surging water. Only Danny's tight grip on Sam's rope prevented him from being swept away.

Above the roar of the water, he heard a sharp whinny from behind him and turned in time to see the mare plunging in the water, kicking and screaming and breaking Amos's grip on the lead rein. The old man fell face forward into the water and the mare took off into the dark and rain.

"Amos!" Danny screamed but there was no answer.

With difficulty, he scrambled onto the big horse's wet, slippery back and with only the lead rein to guide the horse, managed to turn him back the way they had come. If Amos had lost his footing, he would be swept downstream and Danny's chances of finding him in the dark and the surging water were slim.

He kept calling Amos's name and had nearly reached the Maiden's Creek station when he heard a faint reply.

"Over here, lad."

He found Amos clinging to a tree with one arm wrapped around a sturdy branch as the water dragged at his feet and legs. Danny exhaled with relief and Sam, recognizing his master, dutifully came alongside.

Danny reached out a hand but Amos shook his head.

"That bitch of a mare, snapped me wrist," he said.

Danny grasped a handful of Amos's sodden clothing. "I've got you," he said with more confidence than he felt. "Let go of the tree."

Amos obeyed and his weight almost pulled Danny from the horse. He dug his knees into Sam and somehow managed to drag Amos across the horse's withers. Amos lay there breathing heavily, like a sack of sodden wheat, and Danny once more turned Sam into the deluge. If the water rose any higher, Amos would have his face in the water. Even a horse the size of Sam struggled against the flood. The water had risen to Sam's quarters and Danny could feel the big horse straining against the current as he took one cautious step after another, making instinctively for the high ground.

As they passed the Empress, its lower floor already well under water, Danny heard a cry for help.

He looked up and saw William Fitzgerald hanging over the iron lace balcony.

"You there. I'm stranded. Take me to safety."

In the dark and wet, Fitzgerald would have been hard put to recognize his own mother let alone Danny, and Danny was in no mood for civilities.

"Sorry, mate," Danny said, affecting a hardened accent. "Got an injured man here. Got to get him to the hospital."

"I'm a doctor, I can take him."

"You're right enough where you are, mate."

"You can't just leave me here."

"Didn't say I would. I'll come back for you."

"I'll pay..."

But Danny had already moved on. Sam had seen the road rising up past the church to the hospital, the first high ground, and his instinct took him sure-footed and eager on to the relatively firm ground.

Danny slid off the horse and took the lead rein while keeping one hand on Amos, who managed to get a leg across the broad back and pull himself upright, gripping Sam's mane with his good hand. They made slow progress up the ruined lane, where the water had cut the surface into deep runnels as it poured off the hillside.

They reached the hospital, and Danny let out a heavy breath. What had once been the garden was at least still holding firm and beyond it was the gate to the paddock, where Amos's other horses clustered in a sodden, depressed bunch, their heads hanging down.

Lights burned in the windows of the kitchen and Danny led the horse into the courtyard. He banged on the back door.

"Help here!"

Charlie threw open the door, carrying a lamp. "Danny, thank heavens! Are you all right?"

"I'm fine, but Amos isn't."

Without stopping to pull on a coat, Charlie pushed past him. Together they eased the old man off the horse and with Amos's good arm around Danny's shoulder, they helped him inside.

"Danny, you're soaked. Come into the kitchen—" Charlie began

"I can wait. Got to get back. Your pal Fitzgerald is stranded at the Empress."

"You can leave him there," Charlie responded.

Danny gave her a curious glance but whatever enmity lay between the doctor and the nurse could wait. He couldn't in all conscience leave the man to his fate in the flood.

Sam waited patiently in the hospital courtyard, his head drooping as Amos's stable lad, Johnny, stroked the animal's long face in a way Danny had seen Amos do a hundred times. That affinity between man and horse was something Danny had never quite mastered.

"I was just about to take the old chap round to the paddock," Johnny said.

"It'll have to wait. I've got to take him back into town. There's a bloke stuck in the Empress and I think Sam's the only chance we have of getting him out."

"I can do it."

"No. You see to the other horses and yourself. You've done enough tonight."

The lad looked up at him. "Will Mr Burrell be all right?"

"I think it's just a broken wrist and he's in good hands, but you're in charge. Can you go up to the matron's cottage and tell his wife that he's at the hospital and if she tries to come back with you, lock the door on her. The nurses have enough on their hands already."

"I'll have a good feed for you," Johnny told Sam, reminding Danny that he could use a good feed too.

Danny pulled at the leading rein but Sam laid his ears back and for a couple of long moments refused to move, despite urging from Johnny. Like a human, he gave a resigned snort and turned back to the running creek that now formed the lane. They took it carefully. Both man and horse had to feel for every foothold as the water tugged at their legs.

Using a half-submerged stone wall, Danny climbed back onto Sam's back and they plunged into the water.

Only a faint light from the upstairs verandah of the balcony gave them any indication of how far into the inky blackness they had to go. As they drew closer Danny could make out the shadow of a man on the verandah, holding a kerosene lamp.

Seeing the man and horse, Fitzgerald waved. In an indignant voice tinged with fear, he shouted across the noise of the torrent, "Thank God. You came back. I was asleep this afternoon when the hotel was evacuated. No one thought to wake me. The whole building is creaking and I thought I heard cracking."

Danny considered the options for Fitzgerald to escape the Empress and concluded he had no choice but to climb over the balcony.

"I have a small trunk with me," Fitzgerald said.

"Don't be ridiculous," Danny replied, almost dropping his accent in his indignation. "Just you. I can't hold the horse steady for much longer."

Sam snorted in agreement, shifting his weight as the water dragged at his sturdy legs.

The building gave an ominous creak and a shudder and Fitzgerald had no more argument. He climbed over the balcony. Danny edged Sam closer.

"You'll have to drop lower."

"I can't—"

"You can. You've no choice."

Fitzgerald began to lower himself, agonizing inch by inch, his fingers clawing into the ironwork of the balcony until he was low enough for Danny to catch his legs. Fitzgerald scrabbled for a foothold on the horse's back, twisting himself and dropping down behind Danny. He almost slipped off, taking Danny with him, but Danny ground his hands into Sam's mane, pulling himself back up.

Fitzgerald hauled himself up again, his arms around Danny's waist so tightly that Danny could hardly move.

"Thank you, my good man," Fitzgerald said, his voice tight with fear. "I'll not forget this."

Evidently, Fitzgerald had not recognized Danny beneath the sodden oil slicker and shapeless felt hat, and for that Danny was grateful.

Danny's plunge into the floodwaters had not gone unnoticed and there were plenty of willing hands to see them to safety. As they reached higher ground Fitzgerald was assisted off the horse, a blanket placed around his shoulder and two men dispatched to take him up to the hospital.

"Isn't that Amos Burrell's horse?" A lantern was held up and Danny was relieved to see Bert Marsh grinning at him. "Well, well, Daniel bloody Greaves. I don't know whether to congratulate you or not. Bloody stupid idea, thinking you could get that man out of there."

Now the crisis had passed, the cold and wet was taking over and Danny shivered.

"I don't think the Empress will see out the night," he said, and as if in answer to his words, over the roar of water came a crack and they turned, holding up their lanterns as the best hotel in Maiden's Creek appeared to go down on its knees, one whole side collapsing under the weight of water.

Bert shook his head. "First of many," he said. "Rain's letting up but the water's got to come off the high country yet. Tomorrow will be the worst." He held up the lantern to Danny's face. "You look like death. Get up to the hospital before you fall off that horse—it's a bloody long way to fall."

Johnny was waiting for him, more anxious about Sam than Danny. However, he had the grace to catch Danny as he slid from the horse.

"You're done in," he said. "Nurses just took in the cove you rescued. Looks like you need to get yourself into the warm and dry too."

"What about you?"

Johnny shrugged. "Me ma's cottage is above the water. I've a home to go to. I'll see to this old chap and then head off there myself."

Danny dragged his leaden feet to the kitchen door. He leaned against it and knocked. Every muscle ached and he was cold, so cold...

To his relief it was Charlie who opened the door to him.

"Danny! Thank God. You're soaked through. Come in."

She guided him to the fire and he stood, impotently holding out his icy hands to the flames, his teeth chattering uncontrollably.

"Here." She tossed a towel to him. He caught it and stood looking at it. "Get out of those wet things before I have you in here with pneumonia. I've got some old clothes we keep for an emergency. They're clean and dry."

Danny had no strength to argue. His numb fingers fumbled with buttons and catches, and the exercise took longer than he would have wished. The clothes Charlie found for him were intended for a larger and shorter individual, but they were warm and dry, and he supplemented any inadequacy with a woolen blanket.

Charlie gestured at the table. "Sit down. I've got some soup left and I'll make you a cup of tea."

Only when she had set the food down in front of him did she pour herself a cup of tea and collapse into the chair with a heartfelt sigh.

"Where's Fitzgerald?" Danny asked.

"I've made up a rough bed for him in the doctor's office. I left him in there with dry clothes, some soup and a fire. I don't think he'll move." She smiled and quirked an eyebrow at him. "Had some story about being rescued by a ruffian on a horse."

"I wasn't in the mood for niceties," Danny said.

She reached out and put her hands over his.

"You could have died, Danny. It was a foolhardy thing to have done."

"The Empress collapsed. If I'd left him there, Fitzgerald would have been dead by morning. Not sure I had much choice."

He looked down at her hands... the long, strong fingers and fine bones. They were work-roughened hands, not the hands of a lady. Impulsively he tightened his own fingers around hers and brought his gaze up to her face, remembering her as he had seen her the first time with her dark hair in fashionable curls and those extraordinary green eyes looking up at him. They were both older and her hair had been pushed up into some sort of ugly linen cap. Dark circles smudged her eyes and lines of strain deepened around her mouth but right at that moment she had never looked more lovely.

She pulled her hands free, tucking a lock of hair back into the cap. "How bad is it?"

Danny shrugged. "Morning will tell but I'm betting Main Street will be almost completely under. Buildings are beginning to collapse. No telegraph... no trains..."

Charlie let out an unladylike whistle. "We're already short of food."

"What about clean water?"

"We've got a substantial water tank out the back. As long as that holds up to the deluge, we should be right."

They sat in silence for a long moment as the enormity of the disaster came home to them both.

"How's Amos?" Danny asked to change the subject.

"We've made him comfortable but I am waiting on Linacre to come and set his wrist properly."

"Can't Fitzgerald see to it?"

"I'm not going to risk another war in my corridor over jurisdiction," Charlie said.

She pushed back the chair and stood up.

"I have other things to worry me right now. Danny, you look done in. When you have finished your tea, there is a rough bed in my office. The fire is lit. You should be quite snug."

Danny nodded and stood, his legs hardly able to hold him up. He stumbled to the room she indicated and fell fully clothed onto the mattress that had been made up on the floor. Dimly he was aware of Charlie pulling the blanket over him and he was asleep within minutes.

THIRTY-NINE

T he clock in the front hall had struck one in the morning as Charlie paused on her rounds to check on Archie Fraser.

With Fitzgerald now installed in the doctor's office, they had provided a mattress for Flora in Archie's room but Charlie found the woman awake and seated in the chair by her son's bed. She looked up as Charlie entered the room. In the poor light of the lantern, Flora's face was sharp planes and shadows.

Charlie checked the boy's temperature and pulse. "I won't lie, Flora. He's not out of the woods yet."

"I've been praying."

Prayer was as good as anything at this point in time.

Linacre had checked in on the boy when he had got to the hospital around ten. He had been tending to a woman further up the valley and had arrived home to find water lapping at his front door. Faced with the inevitability of inundation, he had brought a change of clothes, with plans to stay at the hospital. He had been less than pleased to find William Fitzgerald snoring in his office and had ungraciously taken a spare bed in the men's ward.

There had been little rest for Charlie. Apart from a few catnaps taken when she could, she'd been on her feet since Janet Becker had knocked on her door on Friday night. Easing her aching back, she made her way to the kitchen to make a cup of tea. Lily Roberts joined her and the two women sat in silence listening to the rain beating on the roof. Charlie's eyelids droop and her weary body cravedoblivion. She hated this time of night when the dark engulfed her mind and body, with a seemingly endless time yawning until daybreak. She folded her arms on the table and laid her head down, giving in to the need for rest.

A loud rapping on the door brought her awake with an unladylike curse. Lily opened the door to reveal a group of four women, clutching carpetbags and dripping water. A tall woman stepped into the kitchen and threw back the hood of her oilskin.

"Nell!" Charlie looked around at the dancers from the Maiden's Creek Tavern. "What are you doing here at this hour of the night?"

Nell sniffed. "The tavern's under six feet of water and we've nowhere else to go. Those do-gooders at the church turned us out but I said to the girls, that Charlie O'Reilly will see us right."

Charlie didn't know what to say to that.

"Mary Keegan will have kittens," Lily Roberts said.

Nell shot the nurse a sharp glance. "We're not after charity," she said. "Word is you need help here and we'll make ourselves useful. Eileen here is a dab hand with making ends meet with food, and Peg and Elsie don't mind a bit of hard work—sweeping, changing beds and things like that."

"I'm not going to deny we need help," Charlie said, "but where am I going to put you?"

"Oh, don't mind us. We'll fit into a corner somewhere."

"There are a couple of spare beds in the women's ward and we've got blankets," Charlie suggested, conscious of a sharp intake of breath from Lily.

Nell turned to her girls. "See, I told you Charlie'd look after us. Come on girls, let's have a quick kip and then we can give the nurses a hand. They look dead on their feet."

Nell and one of the girls rolled, fully clothed, onto the beds in the women's ward. The other girls dragged the spare mattresses into the ward onto which they subsided, too tired to even loosen their corsets.

Charlie retired to the kitchen with Lily.

"You don't approve," Charlie said.

Lily took a breath. "I'm a good Christian," she said, "and the good Lord had time for the less fortunate among us, but I'm not sure having four ... four ... ladies of the night lodging in the hospital is going to meet with the approval of the hospital board."

"You are quite correct. It is our Christian duty to take in these girls, particularly after they have been turned away from the church. You should know, Sister, it is not our role, or that of the hospital board, to pass judgments."

Lily pursed her lips.

"And we need the help... desperately," Charlie continued. "If they want to cook, clean bedpans, and make beds, I'm not going to say no."

"Needs must," Lily said with a shrug, "but Mrs Taylor's right, you're dead on your feet, Matron and now we have some assistants on hand. Why don't you go up to the cottage and grab some sleep. If I need help I'll send someone to fetch you."

Charlie reached for the oilskin that hung from a hook by the door, her thoughts on falling onto the pallet in her cottage. Her hand stopped as a rumble followed by the cracking of wood and a crash came from the courtyard.

"What was that?" Lily grabbed at her arm and Charlie threw open the back door, peering out into the cold, wet night.

At first she could see nothing in the dark but as her eyes adjusted she could make out an amorphous mound that should have been the outbuildings. She lit a lantern and ventured out under the shelter of the back verandah, holding up the lantern. She gasped.

The bank behind the outbuildings had slipped, bringing down a mudslide and rubble on to the buildings.

"Alf!" Lily screamed.

Charlie handed the nurse the lantern and pulled on her oilskin.

"Wake Mr Hunt and the doctors. We're going to need every able-bodied man," she shouted as she ran into the courtyard, heedless of the water that now poured like a waterfall from the bank behind the hospital.

She came to a halt, staring helplessly at the part of the building that had been Alf's crib. It had been completely crushed and submerged in mud and rocks. She called the man's name and, getting no answer, cast around for something to use in the digging. Mercifully, Alf had left a spade and mattock propped against the wall beside the kitchen door from his earlier work, digging a ditch to divert the water away from the building.

She began digging in the spot where she thought the man's bed might have been, all the time calling his name. As fast as she dug, more mud and water slid down to fill the hole she created.

"Charlie, stop! We need to bolster the bank to stop the mud slipping further."

At Danny's voice, she looked up. "We don't have time. Alf is under here. We've got to get him out."

The courtyard filled with people. Doctor Linacre and one of the sick miners from the men's ward were joined by Nell and her girls, who huddled under the shelter of the back verandah.

"We can use this timber," the miner said, pointing to the crumpled remains of the outbuildings. "The doc and I can work on sheering up the wall while you keep digging."

Charlie straightened and pointed at the miner. "Back to bed. Thanks for the advice but we don't need you risking your pneumonia."

The miner hesitated with a glance at Doctor Linacre, who nodded. That left them with two men and the tavern girls.

The remains of the woodshed leaned lopsided against the surviving outbuildings and Danny found shovels and mattocks as Linacre and two of Nell's girls began pulling the strongest timbers away from the pile. Nell took one of the shovels and joined Danny and Charlie as they worked on the muddy heap.

Danny straightened and held up his hand. "Quiet everyone."

Everyone froze, their collective breath held.

"Get me outta here!" Alf's strident tones, faint but unmistakable, came from beneath them.

Charlie almost laughed with relief, and going down on her knees, she scrabbled in the mud until her fingers touched cloth and the warmth of a still live body. She looked up at Danny and Linacre. "He's still alive. Can you get him out?"

The two men joined her, digging away the mud with their hands to reveal a pair of legs. The rest of Alf appeared to be under his still-intact bed.

"Are you hurt?" Linacre asked.

"Don't think so," Alf replied.

Linacre felt both legs but didn't elicit a pain response. He gave Danny a nod and they hauled on Alf's legs, pulling him out from under the bed.

Carrying Alf between them, they made their way across the court-yard to the kitchen where Lily Roberts waited. They sat Alf on a chair at the table with a blanket over his shoulders as Lily busied herself pouring pannikins of hot, strong tea laced with sugar.

Alf looked like a man made of mud from the top of his head to his feet as he sat at the table, the undrunk tea in his mud-coated hand.

Lily looked around the circle of helpers. "You should see yourselves."

Charlie stepped forward. "Alf's the priority. Get him cleaned up, Roberts, and into a bed in the men's ward with a hot-water bottle," She gave her odd-job man a smile. "You had the luck of the devil with you tonight, Alf Kimble."

The man had begun to shake with cold and shock. "I heard the noise and managed to get underneath me bed when it all came crashing down," he said. "Had just enough air to breathe." His gaze swept his saviors. "Thank you. I thought I was a goner for sure."

"Let's get you to bed," Charlie said. "Ladies, there is a bathroom off the women's ward. The water will be cold but at least there is a bathtub and you can wash the worst of the mud off. Gentlemen likewise. Sister Roberts, can you help me with Alf?"

She looked at Danny and Linacre. "Where's Fitzgerald?"

Lily snorted. "Told me in no uncertain terms that he wouldn't be coming to help," she said. "He'll still be tucked up nice and warm and dry."

Danny shook his head. "I think we need to secure that bank a bit more. We don't want it sliding into the hospital itself. I'm going back out."

Linacre nodded. "I'll come with you."

Charlie lit some more lanterns and held the door for the two men.

At least the rain had eased but any thought she might have had of getting some sleep had evaporated. Oddly, she didn't feel quite so weary anymore.

She caught a glimpse of her reflection in the mirror by the door and grimaced. She may as well have been rolling in mud. It was caked in her hair and smeared across her face. She sank into the chair by the fire and buried her face in her hands. Her day had started with a dead nurse and now it had nearly ended in the death of another staff member.

FORTY

Charlie did the best she could to clean the mud from her face and hands and stripped off her filthy uniform dress. She found a faded brown gingham dress to fit from the hospital's stock of charity clothes. She had no alternative but to wear her own sodden boots and stockings and just hoped they would dry.

From the kitchen window, she could see Danny and Linacre had moved their efforts on to digging a trench using the fallen mud and rocks from the slide to raise an embankment to divert the water, which still poured from the slope above, away from the building.

But the water defeated the attempts of the two men, destroying the embankment and running towards the door. Charlie threw it open and beckoned them in. "Come in. We'll try and stop it at the door."

Danny gestured for Linacre to go in. "I'll try and buttress the door," he shouted. "I'll knock on the window and climb in when I'm done."

Linacre disappeared to the men's ward to wash and try to get some sleep, and Charlie shut the kitchen door as long fingers of water began to thread their way across the red tiles. She hastily rolled towels and set them against the bottom of the door. From the other side she could hear the thud of dirt against the door and gradually the water flow slowed and stopped.

A sharp rap on the window announced Danny was done and Charlie flung the sash up to allow him to climb in. He looked worse than Alf, with mud from his head to the toes of his boots.

"I've done both doors," he said. "The rain's easing right off so hopefully the water will slow and we will avoid it getting into the hospital."

Charlie refilled the tin basin she had used to wash herself with warm water and set it in front of the fire. "Strip off those filthy things. I'm not sure that I have anything more to offer you in the way of clean clothes."

"Bertie Campbell's clothes will fit me," Danny said. "That would be an improvement on nothing!"

The men's ward was still but far from quiet as a chorus of snores ranging from a stentorian rumble to a high-pitched squeak came from the occupied beds. Charlie scrabbled in Bertie's locker and retrieved a set of clean clothes.

She found Danny standing by the window, a towel wrapped around his shoulders and another around his waist, peering out into the darkness.

"Seems to be holding," he said. "And unless I'm mistaken the water flow does seem to be dropping away. Hopefully we're over the worst."

"Come and stand by the fire," Charlie said. "I've some clean, dry clothes for you."

He stood staring into the embers of the fire as she set the clothes on the chair. The firelight reflected off the bare skin of his torso and a frisson of something Charlie had not felt for a very long time ran down her spine. She'd been a nurse too long to be awed by the male anatomy but attraction exceeded the merely physical and she'd known from the first moment they'd met that Daniel Hunt stirred something forgotten within her—desire.

She coughed and Danny started, wrapping the towel closely around his shoulders and apologizing with a fetching flush to his cheeks that made her smile.

"You don't have anything I haven't seen before," she said.

Danny's eyes widened.

"Charlie, I..."

She grinned. "I just like embarrassing you," she said. "Now once again I shall discreetly turn my back and you can make yourself decent."

While he dressed, she sat at the table and unlaced her own sodden, muddy boots, stuffing them with newspaper to help with the drying.

"I've told Sister Roberts to try and get some rest," she said, setting the boots by the fire. "I'm afraid she's asleep on the bed I allocated to you."

Danny shrugged. "I'm not sure I feel like sleep just yet. You don't happen to have any medicinal brandy lying around?"

"It's in the doctor's office and I don't want to disturb Fitzgerald. Looks like it's tea."

Danny shrugged. "Is that all there is to drink in this town?"

Charlie made a pretense of thinking. "Just tea, copious amounts of tea. The panacea for all ills."

Danny smiled. "Charlie, you are exhausted. Sit down and I'll deal with the tea."

She took the seat he offered, wriggling her cold bare toes as the warmth caused pins and needles to shoot through her frozen feet. As he deftly dispensed tea, she cast a glance at him as if seeing him for the first time. He hadn't quite got all the mud out of his hair and it stuck up in spikes in place, and the gray shadows beneath his eyes spoke of his own physical exhaustion.

The girls at school had considered him one of the better-looking catches of the season but she saw more than just the veneer of good looks. Danny Hunt had kind eyes and for Charlie that meant more than a handsome face.

How had he avoided the marriage market? Was it true that he had proposed to Margaret Campbell? She wondered what had happened between them. Had Margaret been the reason he had accompanied Bertie to Maiden's Creek? Had something rekindled between them? Something about the conversation she'd had with Margaret about love came back to her... *Seeing him here the other day gave me quite a jolt. I had forgotten how much I had once cared for him or could again.*

She shrugged off all thoughts of Margaret and dismissed the small knot that gathered in her heart and which she recognized vaguely as jealousy. What transpired between Danny and Margaret was no business of hers. She had no call on Daniel Hunt's affections and it was foolish to think she did.

"Mr Campbell's clothes suit you," she observed as he carried the pannikin of tea across to her.

"We go to the same tailor." He sat down in the other chair and huffed out a breath. "This may sound strange, Charlie, but in a way I feel more at home in the clothes I wear around the farm than all the fine suits in my wardrobe."

Charlie studied him for a long moment. He certainly seemed to move more easily in the rough workman's clothes, as if he had shed an uncomfortable skin and found one more to his liking.

"Little wonder Fitzgerald mistook you for a town ruffian," Charlie said with a laugh.

Danny plucked at the fine wool of Bertie Campbell's trousers. "Unlike Bertie, I wasn't born to money. My mother worked hard for every penny."

"Mine too," Charlie said, "and for her efforts, the men called her Mad Annie and the women of the town called her a whore."

Danny looked at her. "That must have been rough."

"She used to dress me in boy's clothes," Charlie said. "Said it was easier. It was only in more recent years that I came to understand just how it was easier. It made me safer."

"From what...?" Danny began and she saw the realization leap into his eyes.

"From unwanted attentions," she said. "But it didn't make me safe from the bullies at school," Charlie said. "Martha Mackie and the others... they made my life hell."

"Mine too." Danny slumped a bit further in the chair. "It was hard not having a father."

"Tell me about the man in the cemetery. You said he was your father."

Danny shook his head. "There was no marriage. Mother believed he had died at sea—at least that was the story she told me. I used to imagine all sorts of adventures for him, but when he actually came into my life, the reality was rather different. It's a dreadful thing to say, but his death was a relief. He would have made Mother and me very unhappy."

Charlie studied his profile in the flickering firelight, seeing the pain that exhaustion could no longer hide, etched into the lines around his mouth and eyes.

"You know my story," she said. "I've never had any curiosity about my father. Too busy just surviving to worry about a dead man. I doubt my parents were married. I must ask Ma next time I see her."

Danny cast a glance at her, a wry humorless smile twisting his mouth. "So does that make us a pair of fatherless bastards?"

She held his gaze. "It does, but I think unlike you, I have always known who I am and where I come from."

He turned to look at the fire again. "You might be right and part of the reason I am here was to lay that last link with my past to rest. But what about you, Charlie? Why are you here?"

She hadn't the energy for lies and prevarication. She shrugged. "Running away from a certain doctor who does not accept rejection."

Danny glanced at the door. "Fitzgerald?"

"Yes. You don't like him, do you?"

"No, I don't like him. I know his type and I'm not surprised he's tracked you down. He likes to win at everything he does and that includes the women in his life."

Charlie set the cup down. "He is a brilliant doctor," she said and her mouth twisted, "but a vile human being. You're right, he thinks he is a god for all women to worship and when they don't, he tries to destroy them."

Danny stared at her. "Is that what he did to you?"

Charlie chewed her lip. "He would have done, but I took the coward's way out and ran away. I went to England five years ago to escape him."

"What did he do?"

She shook her head with a self-deprecatory laugh. "I made something of a fool of myself in the mistaken belief that he intended marriage." She straightened her shoulders. "He married someone else. I wasn't the first and I won't be the last. I thought enough time had passed and I could return to Melbourne."

Danny frowned. "He's come to Maiden's Creek and I would bet it is not just to inspect the hospital. He wants something from you, Charlie."

Charlie straightened. "He wants me to go back to him. He thinks I should just fall at his feet. Well, he shall go away disappointed." Her bravado leached from her and she leaned forward, burying her face in her hands. "I can't keep running away from him, Danny, but he holds all the cards. He can destroy me personally, and my career, and I've worked too hard to see that happen."

She regretted the words the moment they were out of her mouth. If only she hadn't been so tired and if the problem of Fitzgerald hadn't been weighing on her so heavily.

"Forget what I just said," she said. "He's my problem, not yours."

Danny said nothing, but he reached out across the space between their chairs and took her hand. A simple gesture but the touch of his fingers sent a warm glow to her heart. She closed her own fingers around his, conscious of her work-roughened hands. His were little better; the hard work with the shovel had raised several blisters and the dirt was ingrained around his nails. He had come a long way from the Melbourne toff who had first arrived in Maiden's Creek.

They sat together in a comfortable silence. Charlie became aware of the tick of the clock on the mantelpiece, and she released Danny's hand, turning to look at the window, beyond which the night still lowered. She turned her gaze to the ceiling and the bucket in the corner where the steady drip from a leak seemed to have slowed to the occasional plop.

"The rain," she said. "It's easing."

Danny huffed out a breath. "Thank God."

"Matron!"

Charlie all but jumped from her chair, whirling around to face Flora Fraser, who stood in the doorway, her hair a disordered bird's nest and her face grey with exhaustion and grief.

"Mrs Fraser?"

"It's Archie. I think he's... come quickly."

Leaving Danny by the fire, Charlie hurried to Archie's room. She leaned over the still, little figure on the bed and looked up at Flora and smiled. "It's all right, Flora. He's not dead. He's sleeping peacefully. The fever has broken."

Flora sank down on the uncomfortable chair by the bed. She folded her arms on the side of the bed and lowered her head, weeping uncontrollably.

Charlie hesitated for a long moment before crossing to the side of the bed. She laid a hand on Flora's shoulder.

"He's going to be fine, Mrs Fraser," she said. "You've done a wonderful job. Now lie down and get some rest yourself."

She eased the woman to her feet but Flora fell against her, her tears soaking Charlie's shoulder.

"You're exhausted," Charlie said, easing the woman off her. "The doctor can take a proper look at him in the daylight."

Flora nodded and stepped back, wiping her eyes with one of the cloths she had been using to bathe her son. "And you, Charlie. You must be done in."

"I'm used to it."

She helped Flora onto the lumpy mattress on the floor and covered her with a blanket, before taking the lantern and going to wake Lily Roberts.

"We'll do the rounds and then I'm going to rest for a little while," she said.

They found the wards quiet. Both Amos and the miner were snoring fit to outdo each other and the other patients in the men's ward, including Bertie Campbell, were also asleep.

In the women's ward, a cold breeze circled Charlie's ankles. Beside her Lily shivered. They passed Nell and her girls who were dead to the world. Of the three remaining beds, two contained the patients of the hospital, Mrs Grimes snoring louder than Amos Burrell. The third bed, Martha Mackie's, was empty, the bed coverings thrown back and the sheets cold. The window next to the bed stood wide open; the curtains pulled back.

Charlie pulled it shut and stood peering out into the cold and damp, wondering when Martha had escaped.

"She was here when I checked on them at two," Lily said, answering her unspoken question.

So she had probably been gone a good couple of hours. A woman with a chest infection had absconded into the cold and rain wearing, as far as Charlie could tell, nothing except a hospital nightdress. She swore in a manner that would have made her Uncle Jack blush. It certainly made Lily Roberts take an indrawn breath but Charlie was too tired to care.

"Nothing we can do until daylight," she said.

She closed the window and pulled the curtains back across the window. If Martha was intending to return, she could come in by the front door.

In the kitchen Danny had fallen asleep in the chair by the fire, his head thrown back. Hardly the most comfortable position to sleep but needs must, she thought. Charlie found a blanket and draped it over him. He stirred but didn't wake.

"Go and lie down," Lily Roberts said. "It will be dawn in a couple of hours."

However used Charlie was to the rigors of night duty, the past twenty-four hours had been trying and she found her head buzzing with exhaustion. She took Lily's place on the rudimentary bed in her own office and was asleep before she could count to ten.

FORTY-ONE

For a long moment Danny thought he was back in East
Melbourne.

"Just tea and toast," he murmured.

"Tea and toast? You'll be lucky to get porridge like everyone else,
your nibs!" came the response from a woman who was definitely not
Mrs Brown.

He opened his eyes and met the fierce gaze of a nurse in a stiffly
starched apron and cap, her hands on her hips, glaring down at him.

"Margaret! What time is it?"

"Gone six. What happened here last night?"

Danny sat up straight. Sleeping in a chair was not to be recommended, he thought as he stood up and stretched his stiff and aching
limbs. The physical exertions of the night were taking their toll.

Margaret handed him a cup of tea and he drank it while filling her in
on the events of the night.

Lily Roberts came into the kitchen, falling into one of the chairs at
the dining table.

"Am I ever pleased to see you," she said to Margaret. "What a night."

"Where's Matron?"

"Oh no, I was supposed to wake her an hour ago."

Lily dashed out of the room, returning with Charlie.

Charlie's borrowed gingham gown was crumpled and her dark brown hair was coming down from her customary coil. She was hollow-eyed with exhaustion but when she turned to smile at him, for a fleeting moment, Danny thought she had never looked more beautiful.

"What's the state of the town?" Charlie asked Margaret.

Margaret shook her head. "Hard to tell. It was still dark when I left to come here but from what I can see Main Street is well under water and it's flowing fast."

Charlie nodded. "I don't know much about floods but let's hope it goes down as fast as it rose." She clapped her hands. "Ladies, we have patients to see to. Sister Roberts, go home. Sister Keegan will be doing night duty with you tonight."

"What about today?" Margaret Campbell said. "I can't manage alone."

"I will be here," Charlie replied.

"Matron, with respect—" Margaret began but was quelled by a glance from Charlie.

"There is no one else. Besides, we have some additional hands to help with the menial work today."

The youngest of Nell's girls, Eileen appeared in the doorway, looking remarkably fresh in her borrowed, faded blue cotton gown with a clean white apron tied over it and her hair scraped back from her face.

"Nell says I'm to make breakfast."

Margaret's eyes widened. "Nell? Nell Taylor's here?"

"She is, and the girls are happy to help," Charlie said.

Margaret turned to the table to pour herself a cup of tea and Danny doubted anyone but himself caught her scowl.

He glanced out of the window where the grey early-morning light revealed the full extent of the night's damage. The woodshed and Alf's crib had been flattened, and only a broken wooden wall still stood to indicate there had been any building at all. The courtyard was covered in mounds of mud, rocks and gravel. A broken chair lay in the middle of the detritus.

"I'll change back into my work clothes and make a start on cleaning the mess outside," he said.

"At least clearing a path to the back door would be a start," Charlie agreed.

Danny flexed his fingers, the blisters tightening in protest. Charlie grabbed his hands, turning them over to inspect his palms. Her touch was cool and firm and he had a vague recollection of that same touch last night when they had sat in front of the fire.

"Those blisters are nasty," she said. "Before you do anything, I'll dress them. We don't want to make them worse."

"You can't ask him to clear the yard," Margaret said. "It's not appropriate."

"She's not asking, I'm volunteering," Danny said, "and if the rest of the town looks like this, every able-bodied man and woman is going to be needed."

"What the hell is going on?" The angry male voice caused every person in the kitchen to freeze.

William Fitzgerald stood in the doorway. He looked no better than anyone, in a crumpled, patched and faded shirt and corduroy trousers that were too short for him.

He looked around at the startled faces, his eyes widening when his gaze landed on the girl at the stove. His mouth opened and closed. She returned his horrified gaze with a cheeky smile, leaving Danny in no doubt that the two were acquainted. Danny glanced across at Charlie and she met his eyes with a quick nod. She'd seen it too.

Fitzgerald turned back to Charlie, covering his lapse with a snarled, "Matron, where are my own clothes?"

"Still drying," Charlie replied.

"Fetch them."

No please, no thank you.

Danny stiffened but Charlie, still holding his hands, gave them a warning squeeze before releasing them and drawing herself to her full height.

"Good morning, Doctor Fitzgerald. You will find your clothes in that room." She pointed to a door beside the fireplace.

"And you are a disgrace, Matron. Where is your uniform?"

"Like your clothes, my uniform is in the drying room." She turned to face him. "We had a serious incident last night. A mudslide which nearly resulted in the death of one of our staff members. We could have done with your assistance."

Fitzgerald held up his hands. "I don't do manual labor of any sort. If I were to damage my hands, I would be no use to anyone. Now I would like eggs and bacon and toast, just lightly browned—"

"You will get the same as everyone." Charlie's voice rose. "Porridge. The town bakery is under water so there will be no bread and I very much doubt our hens, if they survived the night, have laid eggs."

"I would like a decent breakfast," Fitzgerald insisted. "I had no supper last night, apart from some sort of watery soup."

"Porridge'll be a few minutes," the girl at the stove said.

Danny laid a hand on the man's arm. "Do you have a moment, Fitzgerald?"

Fitzgerald hesitated but turned and followed Danny to the doctor's office.

Danny shut the door behind them both and turned to confront the older man.

"I don't care for the tone you took with the nursing staff," he said.

"And I don't care for your interference, Hunt."

"It is not interference. Do I need to remind you my family has an interest in this hospital? Besides which, we saved the hospital from being inundated with floodwater last night, saved a man from dying in a mudslide, and if things are not to your satisfaction this morning it is because you chose not to help when your help was needed."

Fitzgerald's eyes narrowed. "I've had my fill of this filthy little town. I am going to conduct my inspection and I will be gone on the first train."

"Good luck with that. With all the water we've had down the creek, I wouldn't be surprised if the train can't run for weeks." He paused. "What do you mean you will conduct your inspection?"

"I said I would do an inspection today and I damn well will and my report will reflect what I can already see. Slovenly standards, lack of personal discipline... and who knows what else."

"Not today, Fitzgerald. The matron has had next to no sleep in two days and the whole town is in chaos. It is hardly a normal situation."

"That should make no difference."

"If you are trying to punish Matron O'Reilly for something that passed between you—"

"How dare you," Fitzgerald said, his voice low and full of menace. "I don't know what the little bitch has told you but this is about how this hospital is run. It has nothing to do with anything else. Now out of my way, Hunt. I am going to find my clothes."

The man stormed out of the office and as the door slammed behind him, Danny slammed his fist into the desk.

Damn it, he had made a bad situation worse. Fitzgerald was out to wreak revenge on Charlie for whatever was in their past, and between the rain and Danny's interference, he had just given the man the very ammunition he needed.

Before changing back into the damp and mud-encrusted working clothes and tackling the monstrous task in the courtyard, Danny visited the men's ward. Netty was already at Amos's bedside, her hand over his uninjured hand. For a long moment, Danny stood at the door and watched them. He saw that same unspoken devotion in his parents' eyes when they looked at each other and he wondered what it took to find that unconditional love with another person.

"Here he is." Amos saw him and waved him over. "The hero of the night."

"You're here early," Danny said, returning Netty's hug.

"Did you think I'd sit in that cottage a moment longer than I had to knowing Amos was here? As soon as the doctor says so, he's coming back with me."

The other men sat up in their beds. Danny was relieved to see Alf looked none the worse for his adventure. "Just waiting for that tartar of a matron to let me up," Alf said, "and I'll come and help with the cleaning up. You can't do it by yourself."

"You need to rest," Danny told him.

"You saved me life last night and I won't forget that." Alf caught his sleeve. "I remember you from when you was a boy at the post office."

Danny did not recall Alf from the many faces that had passed through his mother's post office, but he smiled and nodded and turned to Bertie, who occupied the bed in the farthest corner of the ward.

"I wondered when you were going to get around to me," Bertie grumbled.

"It was a hell of a night. We were lucky the whole hospital didn't slide down the hill last night. I'm just going out to try and clear the yard."

Bertie glanced out the window at the grey clouds rolling over the hills and Danny braced for another litany of complaints.

"Come closer," Bertie said and Danny obliged, leaning forward as Bertie spoke in a lowered voice. "What do you know about the death of that pretty little nurse? Margaret told me she was strung up in that gum at the front. Made to look like she'd done herself in."

"Apparently."

Bertie shook his head. "You're such a lawyer, Hunt. Won't give anything away."

"When you don't know anything, it's hard to be more specific," Danny said. "When did you last see her?"

Bertie looked back at him. "She came around with cocoa about eight. She wanted to tuck us into bed like good little boys."

"Did you hear anything unusual during the night?"

"Not over his bloody snoring," Bertie said, jerking a thumb at the miner in the bed across from him. "And the rain of course." He frowned. "No wait... I did hear something. I couldn't tell you what time it was. A squeaking coming from outside."

"What sort of squeaking?"

"I don't know, a rusty wheel perhaps? Didn't think anything of it." He jerked his thumb at the door. "Haven't you got mud to shovel?"

Danny grinned. "I do. I'll come by again later."

Bertie rolled his eyes. "At least they don't expect me to shovel mud." He frowned. "I must confess I'm seeing a different side to you, Hunt."

"Really?"

Bertie caught his sleeve. "Before you go, there's something I need you to do—"

"Nurse!" One of the men sat bolt upright in bed, screaming. "Nurse—"

Danny patted his friend on the shoulder. "Tell me later. I better get out of the way."

Mud was one thing but he did not want to be around during any sort of medical emergency.

———

Before he set his shoulder to the task of clearing the mess in the courtyard, Danny stepped out of the front door into the dripping world. The roar of the flooded creek came up the hill and from the edge of the garden he looked down into an almost unrecognizable world where only the roofs of the lower buildings that fronted Main Street could be seen above the angry, rushing brown water of the flooded creek.

The red iron roof of Netty and Amos's little cottage was only just visible. Their world destroyed.

He crossed the grass to the old gum tree and looked at the branch from which Janet Becker's body had been suspended. He stood beneath it, looking up as he considered the mechanics of how the staging had been done. Not so hard for a strong man. All he had to do was to lean the ladder against the branch and wind the rope around several times. On the ground, loop one end around the girl's neck and then haul her up like a flag. Mounting the ladder again, it would have been a simple matter to fasten off the rope. He squinted up at the length of rope that still encircled the branch, tied off with a good sailor's hitch.

He scouted around under the tree but the rain had washed away any lingering evidence of footmarks or ladder imprints.

It seemed obvious to him, if not to Sergeant Prewitt, that Janet Becker's killer could have found everything he needed to arrange Janet's body to hand in the woodshed. But why go to so much trouble? Did he think that the blows to the back of her head would not be noticed or did he want to announce her sad end?

He'd come across murderers in his work, even represented a few, and generally he found them sad individuals, driven to violence by drink and poverty and too stupid to do anything quite so elaborate as Janet Becker's killer had contrived. That thought sent a shiver down his spine.

A path ran around the side of the building. He followed it around to the rear of the building. Like everything else it had been scoured into runnels by the rain and the sheer volume of water coming from the back of the property. Any trace of a wheelbarrow track had gone but the path ran under the window nearest Bertie's bed so it was quite possible that what he'd heard was indeed the squeak of a wheel.

He returned to the men's ward and found Alf sitting up in bed with a cup of tea and a bowl of porridge.

"Mind if I ask you a couple of questions, Alf?" Danny asked.

"Ask away, guv."

"Is there a ladder here at the hospital?"

"Aye."

"Tall enough to reach the tree outside?"

Alf rolled his eyes. "How'd ya think I cut the lassie down?"

"Where do you keep it?"

"In the woodshed next to my crib."

The woodshed that was now buried under a pile of mud and rocks.

"Was the woodshed under lock and key?"

Alf gave him a withering look. "Nah, it's the woodshed."

"So anyone could take it out?"

Alf scratched his beard. "Aye, I suppose so, but if you're asking if it were moved on the night the girl died... now I come to think of it, when I went to get it yesterday morning to do... you know... it was damp. I just assumed the rain had got in. It was getting in everywhere."

"What else do you keep in the woodshed?"

Alf shrugged. "I've a wheelbarrow I use for carting the wood up to the hospital."

A wheelbarrow...? A wheelbarrow that could be used for moving an inconvenient body?

"What about rope?"

"Aye. I had a few lengths of stout rope in there."

"Was it still there on Sunday morning?"

Alf made a dismissive gesture. "I don't know lad. You go and look for yourself."

That simple suggestion required an archaeological expedition. Danny straightened but Alf held up a hand to detain him.

The old man frowned. "There's been something bothering me about the sister's death. I think I need to talk to Prewitt. She was a sweet girl, she was, always brought me out a cup of tea and a biscuit and we'd chat about this and that."

"What about her?" Danny said.

Alf scratched his unshaven chin. "She used to meet her young man on a Saturday night... in the woodshed."

Danny frowned. "Are you talking about Joe Trevelyan?"

"The lad with the gammy leg from the Britannia. He was up here Saturday night as usual."

"You saw him?"

"He passed my window. I recognized him by the way he walks and he has a whistle he uses to let her know when he's here."

"And you are sure he met with Janet Becker that night?"

"I can't say for certain he met with her but he was here right enough."

"What time was this?"

Alf shrugged. "It were late. I'd been working on a little wood-working project of me own and lost track of time." His mouth turned down. "Guess it's gone now."

"How late?"

Alf huffed out a breath. "I can tell the time, young man and the clock on my mantle said it was twenty-five minutes past twelve . I'd just put out me light and was about to hop into bed when I saw him pass the window." When Danny didn't respond, Alf concluded, "It's just I thought the sergeant should know but no one's been to ask me."

A cold, sinking feeling settled on Danny's heart. Joe had lied to him. He'd denied going up to the hospital on Saturday night.

"Mr Hunt?"

Bringing himself back to Alf Kimble, Danny said, "I'll talk to Prewitt but I expect the police are busy."

"But the lassie was done in and it's important."

Danny nodded. "You rest up, Alf. I'll be sure to tell him."

Further consideration of Janet's death would have to wait. He had promised to clear more of the yard and in the daylight, the full extent of the damage to the outbuildings appeared daunting and Alf's survival in the rubble more of a miracle. Eddie turned up to help and, after he had seen to the horses, Amos's lad Johnny lent his back to the task as well.

Danny started clearing the back doors that he had blocked the previous night. Through the window, he could see Margaret Campbell, sitting at the kitchen table talking to William Fitzgerald. They were both laughing and smiling and there was something about the way Fitzgerald leaned in towards Margaret that made his flesh crawl. He wondered if he owed Margaret a duty to warn her about the charms of Doctor Fitzgerald.

As it transpired, the woodshed had not been completely destroyed. Logs of wood neatly stacked against the far wall had probably saved it. The wheelbarrow Alf had mentioned had been thrown upside down but had also escaped the worst of the destruction and he could see the end of the ladder buried beneath the mudslide.

Danny righted the wheelbarrow and experimentally wheeled it from one end of the building to the other. The metal front wheel had been poorly aligned and squeaked as it moved, confirming Bertie's story and his own thoughts as to how the body had been moved. Danny searched every inch of the surface of the barrow but any telltale blood had been washed away.

"How are you this morning, Danny?"

He looked around to see Margaret Campbell watching him from the covered walkway at the kitchen door, a pannikin of something hot in her hand. Steam rose into the cold air and he took it from her. Tea. He could swear that the hospital ran on tea.

"What a mess," she said with a shake of her head. "I can't believe you got Alf out alive. It was nothing short of a miracle."

"A miracle and a stoutly made bed," Danny said.

A bell rang from inside the hospital and Margaret rolled her eyes before turning back inside.

Fitzgerald sauntered out of the kitchen, picking his way between mud and puddles. He wore the clothes he had been wearing when Danny had rescued him but the ensemble looked very much the worse for the dunking.

"You've done a good job," he said and his patronizing tone made Danny's fingers clench.

"At least the doorways are now clear and we should have a path to the gate cleared by lunch," Danny said. "How goes the inspection?"

Fitzgerald shrugged. "At least they have one competent staff member. Are you acquainted with Sister Campbell?" Fitzgerald cast a glance back toward the kitchen.

"Of course," Danny said. "Known her for as long as I've known her brother."

A narrow smile twitched Fitzgerald's once carefully groomed mustache. "You married, Hunt?"

"No." Danny may have sounded rather curt.

"You know that girls only become nurses to snare us doctors," Fitzgerald said.

"Really." Danny could not have been less interested in the direction this conversation was going. "I believe you are married, Fitzgerald."

"Yes. Daughter of an old family friend. Her social standing and a rather generous dowry made her irresistible. She's obliged me with a son and a daughter."

"But you still paid a call on the girls of the Maiden's Creek Tavern?" Danny said.

Fitzgerald's eyes narrowed. "Doesn't stop me having a little fun on the side, if you know what I mean. A bit of harmless flirting, that sort of thing."

"And is that what you are doing with Margaret Campbell?" The words came out before Danny had time to think them through.

Fitzgerald cast him a sideways glance. "Do I detect a hint of jealousy?"

"Not at all. Margaret is an old friend. I would hate to see her hurt."

Fitzgerald fell silent. "Warning heard, old man, and let me return the favor. There is one nurse you don't want to cross," he continued.

"Sister Keegan?" Danny suggested.

"Who? No, the O'Reilly woman."

Danny stiffened. "What about her?"

Fitzgerald's mouth quirked. "Don't let those Irish come-hither eyes fool you. She's a tease, that one. Leads a man on and then lets him down."

Danny's skin crawled. "I'd thank you not to talk about a lady in that tone, Fitzgerald."

"Fancy her yourself, do you? Well, let me tell you, Hunt, she's not for the likes of you. As for being a lady, she was dragged up in a gutter. Her mother was a whore by all accounts."

Danny called on every civilized instinct in his body to resist the urge to punch the smirk off the face of the man.

"Speak of her again in those terms, Fitzgerald and—"

"Doctor Fitzgerald. I've been looking for you."

Charlie stood in the door to the kitchen, her face, pinched with exhaustion and something else. Danny wondered what she may have overheard of their conversation. She had changed into a fresh uniform but even the pristine skirts and starched apron could not hide the strain of the past few days and her own exhaustion.

"Have you indeed, Miss O'Reilly?"

Danny ground his teeth. The man could not even bring himself to address her by her professional title.

"A word please," she said.

"Very well." Fitzgerald turned to her, rubbing his hands together.

Danny gave Charlie what he hoped was a reassuring smile. Charlie's lips twitched and he saw the glimmer of a smile before she turned away.

FORTY-TWO

Charlie showed Fitzgerald into her office and shut the door behind them. The mattress had been propped against the wall, bedding neatly folded on a chair. She had let the fire die. In the current crisis, fuel had to be preserved.

Fitzgerald leaned back against her desk and folded his arms, a smirk twitching the corners of his mustache.

"Well, Charlotte?"

"I would like you to leave the hospital and if you must return, do so when we have had a chance to restore order."

"Believe me, there is nothing I would like to do more than leave this hospital and this town but the fact is, I am stranded here and my luggage is currently inaccessible. The ruffian last night refused to take my trunk."

"I can give you the name of a lodging house, well out of the flood, where you will have a comfortable bed. As soon as the Empress is accessible again, your luggage can be retrieved."

"Thank you for the suggestion. In the meantime I intend to stay right here and see how well you cope in a crisis. I am sure that can be incorporated into my report."

He straightened and moved across to her, a smile on his lips, not echoed by his eyes. He reached over and touched her face, curling a lock of hair around his finger.

"Charlotte, we're friends, we shouldn't argue like this."

His touch sent a cold shiver down her spine. She took a step back, and raised her hand, swatting him away.

"I'm not arguing, William. I'm tired and I have work to do. Work that would be easier without you under my feet. I have, as you have pointed out, a hospital to clean, the back courtyard to clear, and a missing patient to find—"

She saw the spark in his eye and cursed her runaway tongue.

"A missing patient?"

"She climbed out of the window during the night," Charlie said reluctantly. "She has her problems."

Fitzgerald took a step back and waved at the door. "Then don't let me detain you any further, Matron. I will take myself for a walk now the rain has stopped and see if I can get back into the hotel. What is the name of the boarding establishment you mentioned?"

Charlie supplied the name of and directions to the lodging house run by Mrs. Cole and watched him walk away from the hospital with a profound sense of relief.

In the kitchen she found Netty, her sleeves rolled up, kneading bread dough. Nell's girl, Eileen, stood at the stove, stirring a large pot of what smelled like a delicious savory stew. Peg was on her knees, scrubbing the floor.

"Netty, what are you doing?"

"Making myself useful," Netty said. "Amos is asleep and if you think I'm going to sit holding his hand with everything that needs doing around here, you are mistaken."

Charlie set the kettle to boil, sat down at the table, and lowered her head onto her arms. A few minutes of sleep would see her right.

"Where's Doctor Fitzgerald?"

Charlie raised her head to answer Margaret Campbell's question.

"Gone to look for lodgings. It gives us a reprieve to get things in order. Let's start with Martha Drew. Does anyone have any idea where she'd have gone?"

Nell's girls stopped working and looked at each other.

"Her cottage would be well under water," Elsie said.

"We need to look for her."

Nell Taylor entered the kitchen, rolling down her sleeves. "That's the bathrooms clean," she said. "What next, Matron?"

"Matron were just saying Martha Drew's missing," Peg said.

Nell's lips tightened. "Lost cause that one. If you've nothing else for me, Matron. I should go and see what state the tavern is in. While I'm out I'll have a look for Martha."

Charlie thanked her and turned back to Margaret Campbell.

"Sister?"

"I came to tell you, Flora Fraser's taken Archie home. One of the bridges across the creek is passable and Doctor Linacre said that would be all right," Margaret said. "He'll be better off at home now. Frees up a bed."

And a nurse, Charlie thought, with a profound sense of relief.

"Go home and get some sleep," Margaret said. "That's an order, Matron. You're no good to us dead on your feet. Danny Hunt's cleared a path to the back door and there's nothing happening here that I can't manage."

"But..." Her protest sounded feeble even to her own ears.

"Go."

Charlie stepped out into the cold, fresh morning air. The trees and buildings dripped moisture and the stampers were silent. Only the rush of water in the valley and the sound of the bush birds chirruping broke the silence.

Danny was still in the yard, shoveling mud and rocks from the remains of the outbuildings.

"You've done enough for now, Danny," she said.

He stopped and leaned on the shovel. "I saw Fitzgerald leave."

"He'll be back. He's just gone to look for lodgings."

"He's out to cause trouble, Charlie," he said.

"I know," she replied. "All I can do is make sure he has no grounds for complaint."

Danny looked up at the sky. The clouds were parting with glimpses of blue sky, belying the devastation and the roaring watercourse in the valley below them.

"I've been thinking about Janet Becker," he said.

Charlie rubbed her eyes. "Glad someone is... so much has happened."

"I think she may have been killed somewhere out the back here and her body wheeled around the hospital in the old wheelbarrow there," he jerked his head, "and then staged to look like she hanged herself."

"How ridiculous when it would have been immediately obvious she died from a head wound."

Danny shook his head. "The killer may have been attempting a diversion... who knows? I think I need to ask Joe a few more questions. He told us he hadn't come up here on Saturday night but Alf swears he saw him here."

"Alf could be mistaken and I cannot believe Joe is in any way complicit in her death. He loved her." She shook her head. "I'm just going up to the cottage to grab a couple of hours' sleep, if anyone needs me."

He smiled. "You go. I'll talk to you later."

She picked her way across the muddy yard and took the steps cut in the hillside that led up to her cottage. As she stepped into the warmth of her own place, she heard a mewling from beneath the chair by the fireplace.

She bent down and stared into a pair of wide, yellow eyes. Flossie lay on her side, panting as the muscles beneath the smooth fur contracted.

"Oh, puss, is it time for your kittens?" Charlie asked.

The cat mewed again and, tired as she was, Charlie found the old wooden box, lined with a clean, dry towel, that Netty had made up for the cat before encouraging her into it. She lit the fire and set the box in front of it. She sat beside the laboring animal, ready to play midwife as Flossie gave birth to four kittens.

Human or animal, the wonder of birth had never left her and she sat for a long time watching the cat as Flossie cleaned her babies and let them suckle for the first time. The cat closed her eyes to narrow slits and her purr filled the quiet room, her own paws working with contentment. If only human life was so simple.

Charlie stripped down to her chemise and rolled under the quilt on the makeshift bed with a sigh.

FORTY-THREE

After a more than adequate lunch prepared by Netty and Eileen, Danny left the youngsters, Eddie and Johnny, to carry on with the clean-up at the hospital. He was desperate for a change of clothes and a few hours' sleep. A bath would be a bonus.

The ferocity of the water flow still pouring down Main Street caused him to stop and just watch it, awed by the power of nature unleashed. The roof of Netty and Amos's little cottage was barely visible above the roiling brown water and a wave of grief washed over him as he thought about how hard Netty had tried to keep her precious possessions safe. He would have to be the one to break the news to her.

Both the Britannia hotel and the police station looked to have avoided the flood, and Sergeant Prewitt stood on the steps of the police station, his hands on his hips. Like everyone he had mud from his knees to the tip of his boots and his baggy eyes had receded even further.

"How goes it?" Danny asked.

"Hard to know where to start," Prewitt said with a shake of his head. "We've two men from the Maiden's Creek Mine missing. Swept off one of the bridges last night and another two died when their cottage slid into the water during the night. Heard you had trouble at the hospital?"

"The bank behind the hospital slipped onto the outbuildings. It nearly took out Alf Kimble."

Prewitt shook his head. "I dread to think what we'll find when the water goes down."

"Any developments with the death of the nurse?" Danny inquired.

Prewitt rolled his eyes. "I've been busy, Mr. Hunt, but I have read the doctor's notes. Looks like it was murder. Just what I need, but I've got me thoughts," he said. "The girl was stepping out with yon lad. I think I need to ask him a few questions."

Danny followed the man's gaze across the road to the Britannia Hotel where Joe was mopping the front verandah. Danny's blood ran cold. If that was the direction Prewitt's thoughts were going, Alf Kimble's evidence would not help.

Prewitt glanced at him. "Something on your mind? My constable said you came looking for me the other day."

Danny shook himself out of his reverie. In all the chaos of the past few days, he had forgotten about Micah Allen. With any luck he had been washed away with the flood, but even as he had that thought he realized it was foolish. Allen was still here... watching and waiting. And then there was the promise he'd made to Alf Kimble.

He chose his words carefully. "If you can spare the time, I suggest you talk to the staff and patients at the hospital. They may have seen or heard something on Saturday night."

Prewitt pulled a handkerchief from his pocket and blew his nose. "I'll do just that, but priorities, Mr. Hunt, priorities," he said.

Promise satisfied, Danny thought. If Prewitt followed up with all the staff and patients he'd get to Alf. As for Micah Allen... that seemed pointless.

Danny bid the sergeant farewell and crossed the road. Joe leaned on the mop handle and looked Danny up and down.

"You look like you've been rolling in mud," he said. "I heard there'd been a bad incident up at the hospital. You were lucky to get old Alf Kimble out in one piece. Come inside and have a drink. Looks like you need one."

Over a particularly good Scotch whiskey, they exchanged varying accounts of a hard night spent battling the storm and the floodwaters.

"The basement and kitchen went under the water," Joe said, "so if you're hoping for something to eat...?"

Danny shook his head. "I'm fine for now."

"Train and telegraph's out so the council have sent someone on horse over to Rosedale. We're going to need supplies pretty quick or the town'll starve."

"What about water?"

Joe huffed a humorless laugh. "Not short of water, are we?"

"But it's not drinkable."

"Most folks have water butts and the like."

Danny swirled the liquid in his glass. Was it his third or fourth? The world was beginning to swim.

"Joe, did you lie to me?"

Fear flickered in Joe's eyes. "What do you mean?"

"Did you go up to the hospital to see Janet Becker on the night she died?"

Joe shook his head, but his eyes slid away as he mumbled, "No, I didn't."

"You are a terrible liar, Joe. You were seen."

Joe frowned. "Do you mean Alf?"

Danny fixed the other man with a hard gaze and Joe shifted uncomfortably.

"Yes, I was there but I only stayed five or ten minutes and in all that time she didn't come out." His eyes brimmed with tears. "On my honor, I never saw Janet that night. I'd never hurt Janet. I loved her."

Danny laid a hand on Joe's shoulder. "Prewitt hasn't spoken to Alf yet, but when he does, Joe, you better be sure about your own side of the story."

———

Upstairs, Danny lit the fire in his room. Joe brought up some hot water and Danny sank gratefully into a bath that rapidly turned brown. Clean and shaved and feeling relatively human again, he found his sketchbook and a pencil. From the balcony outside his room he had a clear view of the extent of the flood. The water had started to recede, but Main Street was still a brown river, carrying parts of fallen trees and other detritus down towards the Thompson.

He recognized part of a waterwheel tumble past and wondered how long it would take the mines to recover. Surely the lower shafts of the Maiden's Creek Mine alone would be inundated and from what he could see, the boiler house and stamper shed were underwater.

As he sat sketching, the day started to close in and in the gloaming he became aware of a woman in white, standing below the hotel, looking at the water. For a brief heart-stopping moment he thought he was seeing a ghost, but the woman shivered, wrapping her arms around herself.

He jumped to his feet and, grabbing a blanket from his bed, ran downstairs and out into the gathering dusk. The woman hadn't moved; small and slight, barefoot and dressed only in a white nightgown or shift, her short fair hair lifted in the wind.

"Martha! What are you doing out here?"

She didn't answer. He flung the blanket around her and she sagged against him, leaving him no option but to scoop her into his arms and carry her inside, calling for Joe as he went.

It was Yorkie who answered his call, throwing open the door to the residence behind the public rooms. Danny carried the woman into the cozy parlor, where a fire burned in the hearth. Joe rose from the chair he had been sitting in and Danny set her down. It was Joe who knelt in front of the woman, chafing Martha's icy hands.

The woman's eyes fluttered open, her gaze flitting around the three men.

"Got any brandy, Yorkie?" she asked.

"Not for you, I don't," Yorkie retorted.

"I think some brandy or whiskey would be just the ticket," Danny said.

"You don't know her," Yorkie said, "but if you're paying..."

He stomped off and returned with a tumbler of brandy.

"What were you thinking, running away from the hospital?" Danny chided.

Martha pulled herself into a sitting position, pulling the blanket around herself. She coughed—a long, deep cough that rattled and gurgled in her chest—and took the glass in her hand.

She would have drunk the entire contents without drawing breath but Danny pulled it out of her grasp.

"Have you anything to eat, Joe?" Danny asked.

Joe handed him a plate of an unappetizing grey stew and he offered it to Martha but she turned her head away.

"Eat it, Martha," Joe said.

She sniffed and took the plate and spoon from him.

"Only 'cos you're nice to me, not like Yorkie here."

"You haven't answered my question, Martha... why did you run away?" Danny asked.

"'Cos I wanted to go home," she said and lowered her head. Two large tears dropped onto the food in her plate. "It's gone."

"When you've finished eating, I'm taking you back to the hospital," Danny said.

Martha bristled. "So that high and mighty Charlie O'Reilly can look down her long nose at me again? No, thank you, Mr. Hunt." She set the now empty plate down on the floor. "Thank you for the supper, Joe. You're a good man."

She tried to stand, but her legs didn't seem able to support her and she fell forward into Joe's arms.

"That's it," Yorkie said. "She ain't staying here. I don't care how you do it, Mr. Hunt, but get her back to the hospital."

"We can put her in the hand cart," Joe suggested. "It's not very elegant but we can't carry her up that hill."

Martha screamed when she saw the conveyance they intended for her.

"Not that. That's how he does it. I saw him."

"What are you talking about?" Joe said.

"Death."

Martha's limbs flailed, resisting all efforts to get her into the cart, leaving them with no option but to rig up a stretcher and carry her up the hill.

Even though she was skin and bones, it still took the two of them half an hour to haul her up the steep hill, along a road that had rivulets cut into it, down which the water still streamed, their pace aggravated by Joe's uneven gait.

Danny's hands, already blistered and sore, were on fire by the time they reached the gate of the hospital. He had no choice but to lift the woman in his arms and carry her to the back door.

Joe's knock was answered by Margaret Campbell.

"Who've you got there?"

"Martha Drew."

"Thank heavens you found her. Nell's been out looking. Bring her in." Margaret stood back to allow them to enter.

"No," Martha protested feebly. "I don't want to be here. People die here."

"Matron!" Margaret called.

Charlie hurried into the hallway.

"Joe, carry her through to the private room. We've sent Archie and his mother home and cleaned it thoroughly. We can keep a better eye on her there."

Charlie called for Mary Keegan with orders to bring hot water, a clean nightgown and a hot water bottle.

Joe laid Martha on the impeccable bed and she clutched at Danny's sleeve.

"I tell you people die here," she said. "That Sister Becker—she knew and now she's dead too."

Danny looked up at Charlie. "What's she talking about?"

Charlie shook her head. "It's a hospital. No one's died since I've been here." She laid a hand on Martha's forehead. "She's running a high temperature."

Martha's eyes moved to Charlie. "Don't let me die. Don't let 'im come for me like he did the others."

"You will die if you try running away again, Martha," Charlie said. "I can hear from your breathing, that you've made your pneumonia worse."

"Leave her with me," Mary Keegan said, and Joe, Danny, and Charlie returned to the kitchen.

Netty sat in a chair by the fire, peeling carrots. Charlie touched her shoulder.

"Netty, take Amos and go back to the cottage," she said. "Your cat needs you and everyone here is fed. You've worked hard enough for ten people today."

Netty breathed a heavy sigh as she untied her apron.

"Aye, it's been a long day."

Eileen gathered up the bowl of carrots. "I'll finish these, Mrs. Burrell."

Netty smiled at her. "You're a good girl, Eileen."

Eileen sniffed. "Kind of you to say."

Danny helped Netty and Amos back up to the cottage, pausing long enough to admire the kittens, before returning to the hospital. He found Charlie and Joe sitting in companionable silence in the chairs beside the fire. Joe had a cup of tea and Charlie sat with her chin propped on her hand, watching the flames dancing. She straightened as he entered but not before he read the exhaustion and strain in her face.

"Where's Fitzgerald?" Danny asked.

"He's found lodgings at Mrs. Cole's. Her cottage is well out of the water and she was happy to take his coin. Margaret tells me he paid someone to cross over to the Empress and bring his trunk so he has everything he needs." She lowered her voice. "Sergeant Prewitt is here asking questions of the patients. He spent a long time with Alf Kimble. Do you know why?"

Before Danny could answer, Sergeant Prewitt stomped into the kitchen followed by one of his constables. The man's eyes were sunk into pouches of exhaustion.

"Sorry to bother you, Matron," he said.

"What can I do for you, Sergeant?"

Prewitt's gaze went to Joe, who rose slowly from his chair.

"Ah, just the bloke we were looking for," Prewitt said. "Joseph Trevelyan, I am arresting you for the murder of Janet Becker."

He gestured to the constable, who stepped forward, taking Joe by the arm.

"What? I didn't... I couldn't... I loved her." Joe looked from Charlie to Danny. "You believe me?"

"That's enough from you," Prewitt said. "Got a witness said he saw you up here on Saturday night. That's enough for me."

"I was here but I never saw her. I swear—"

"Joe, don't say another word," Danny said. "Sergeant, please—"

"Don't you be telling me my job, sir. Good day to you."

Prewitt tipped his fingers to his hat and nodded to his constable. Charlie and Danny stood at the kitchen door, watching impotently as the policemen took Joe away.

Charlie clutched his sleeve. "Danny, you can't let this happen. Joe wouldn't hurt a soul."

He put his hand over hers. "I know, Charlie. I need to think and I'm so tired."

She didn't move her hand and they stood for a long moment looking at each other, as if trying to find the measure of strength within themselves to face this new challenge.

The kitchen door banged and Lily Roberts entered. "Matron. Sally's baby is coming."

Charlie snatched her hand away and nodded.

"I'll be right there, Sister. See what you can do for Joe and I'll wait for your news tomorrow morning, Mr. Hunt."

Back at the Britannia, Danny found Yorkie sitting in the bar with nothing but a guttering candle for light and a glass of whisky in his hand.

Yorkie waved at the bar. "Help yourself, lad, and sit a while with me."

Danny poured himself a drink and pulled up a seat across from the publican. Yorkie rubbed a hand over his eyes.

"You've heard about Joe?"

"Yes."

"They've put him in the cells." He gestured across the road at the police station. "They won't let me see him." His voice cracked. "You know him, as gentle a lad as ever lived and he loved that lass."

"I know. Joe has a huge heart and he'd never have hurt her. What does Prewitt say?"

The door opened, letting in a blast of cold air. Both men turned to stare at the apparition in the doorway. Bert Marsh, caked in mud from head to toe, his eyes blazing.

"Prewitt? That—" The words that followed would have made a

sailor blush. "Couldn't find his own nose. Is it true? That idiot police-man's arrested Joe? How could you let this happen?"

"Shut the door, Bert. You're letting the cold air in," Yorkie said.

Bert stomped across the floor towards them, leaving muddy foot-prints on the floor Joe had cleaned earlier in the day.

He leaned two meaty fists on the table and looked from one to the other. "Well, Yorkie, what does Prewitt say?"

"Prewitt says he's going to get him before the magistrate as soon as he can and then Joe'll be sent to Melbourne for trial."

Yorkie's craggy face crumpled.

"It's a joke," Bert said. "He was soft on that girl. They were getting married."

"Nowt we can do," Yorkie said.

"That's not quite right," Bert said and fixed Danny with a hard glare. "Greaves—sorry—Hunt here is a top Melbourne lawyer. I've seen his name in the papers."

Yorkie looked at him. "Is that right?"

Danny searched around for some form of self-deprecatory retort. In the end he merely nodded. Hope sparked in Yorkie's eyes.

"So what d'ya think?"

"I think," Danny said slowly, "that Alf Kimble's evidence needs to be looked at more closely. He didn't see them together, only saw Joe walk past his window."

Bert nodded. "Aye, that makes sense." He straightened. "I suppose there's nothing to be done tonight. How are you going, Yorkie? Mine's closed and my crew's been trying to clear the train track. A couple of the smaller bridges are out but mercifully the Thompson crossing is still good. I will be a few days before the train's running again. If you need any help we can spare some time here."

Yorkie looked around the room. "Your crew's needed elsewhere, Bert, but thanks for the offer. We weren't too badly hit. Cellar's flooded but that's the worst of it."

"Just let us know. See ya Yorkie. See ya Hunt." At the door he turned and pointed at Danny. "You got to get him off this charge, Hunt."

The door slammed shut behind the miner and Danny turned to

Yorkie. "If you need any help without Joe, just tell me what you want done."

Yorkie nodded. "Thank you, lad. I'll give you bed and board if you can put your shoulder to clearing the mud tomorrow." He rubbed his shoulder. "Me arthritis don't like this weather and Joe's the only real help I have. Have you eaten? I've a couple of mutton chops out the back I can cook up."

"That'd be grand, thank you."

He ate the simple meal with Yorkie and returned to his room. As he lay in bed, he thought of Joe Trevelyan, languishing in the grim cells cut into the rock behind the police station. Joe's grief had been genuine and overwhelming. What possible reason could he have to kill Janet Becker, the woman who had agreed to marry him only the day before? It made no sense at all.

But he knew that once Joe was sent to Melbourne it would all be over. The best hope he had was to have the case dismissed here in Maiden's Creek and Prewitt seemed to have little interest in exerting himself now he had Alf Kimble's evidence.

Danny closed his eyes and considered the options.

FORTY-FOUR

As a grey dawn broke over Maiden's Creek, Charlie stood beside Martha's bed. The fight had gone from her former nemesis and the infection was deep within her lungs, rattling as she coughed. Martha stood at the crossroads of life and death and Charlie wondered if the woman had the fight to go on living.

Martha's eyes flickered open. "Watcha thinking, Charlie O'Reilly?"

"I won't lie. You're very ill, Martha."

Martha's eyelids flickered. "Death stalks this building, Matron. He's coming to get me."

"Not if I can help it," Charlie said. The woman was clearly delirious but she thought it better to humor her and prevent her becoming agitated.

A small smile flickered across Martha's lips. "I told Danny Greaves. I saw death myself... the night that nurse died."

Charlie stiffened. "What do you mean?"

Martha grasped Charlie's sleeve, her eyes bright and urgent. "I've seen him when I've been here before. He comes at night in a dark coat and in the morning someone is dead."

Charlie held her breath. "What on earth are you talking about? Who has died?"

"He only comes for those that he's waiting for. Old Mrs. Grace, she was one and that baby, Abby Temple's little girl. They were sick... and I'm next."

Charlie sat down and took Martha's hand. "Martha, you said death came for the nurse. What did you mean? She wasn't sick or dying."

Martha coughed and Charlie settled her back again.

"I only know what I saw."

"What did you see?"

"He carried her to the tree in a wheelbarrow and went back for a ladder. He strung her up there like a lantern, a warning that he can come at any time."

"How did you see this?"

"Couldn't sleep. I was watching out the window, wondering when I could make a bolt for it, and I saw him with the wheelbarrow. I thought it was Alf at first but then what would Alf be doing in the middle of the night when it was raining so hard?"

Charlie stilled her breath. "And what did death look like?"

"He wore a dark coat and a hat pulled down round his ears. Didn't see his face."

"A man or a woman?"

Martha frowned. "I couldn't say."

"Was it Joe Trevelyan?"

Martha looked genuinely perplexed. "Joe? No. I'd spot him anywhere with his limp."

Charlie could have kissed the woman. Here was a witness, albeit not a reliable one, who could swear it wasn't Joe who had strung Janet Becker from the tree.

"And you're absolutely sure you saw this person? Saw what he did?"

Martha's eyes narrowed. "I know what you're thinking and you know very well I hadn't had a drink in days, Charlie O'Reilly." Martha swallowed and tears welled in her eyes. "He'll be coming for me."

Charlie laid a hand on Martha's bony shoulder. "He's not coming for you, Martha. Not if I can help it."

Martha gave a shuddering sigh and tossed her head from side to side. "I'm ready for him. Nothing in this life worth hanging on to."

"Martha, don't talk like that. It's been a hard few years but it will get better."

"You don't really think so. You know I'll be back on the grog the moment I'm out of here."

"Not if I can help it."

Martha took a few shuddering breaths.

"Why are you so nice to me? I was a horror to you."

"That was a long time ago. We've both changed."

Martha shook her head. "I haven't, I'm still a horror. Ask anyone in town."

Charlie stood up and straightened the bedclothes. "Death is not coming for you, Martha Mackie, not while I've breath in my body."

Martha coughed, that deep rattling cough that left Charlie in no doubt that if death did come it wouldn't be an anonymous person in a black coat with their hat pulled down. Whoever that had been was no apparition but someone quite corporeal.

Satisfied Martha was settled, she returned to her office and pulled out the ledgers looking for the two names Martha had mentioned... old Mrs. Grace and Abby Temple's baby.

There'd not been many deaths in the hospital, and it didn't take her long to locate the details.

In March Abby Temple's unnamed baby girl had been born four weeks premature, and the notes recorded that for the first few days, mother and baby had been doing well. The baby was feeding strongly and Abby was showing no signs of postpartum infections. The notes recorded an observation at 10 pm that the baby had fed and settled well and Abby would be returning home in the morning.

In the morning the baby was found dead in its crib.

The cold, clinical note sent a shiver down Charlie's spine as she imagined the tragic scene—the still, cold baby and the hysterical young mother. Babies died for any number of reasons and the reason given by Doctor Linacre was respiratory failure. That meant nothing, merely that the little girl had stopped breathing.

A cold shiver ran down her spine. Had 'death' in a dark coat lent a hand in the child's demise?

She flicked through the pages. Two months earlier, Ann Grace, aged eighty-two, had been admitted with a lung infection. Three days later she was dead. Nothing unusual or suspicious about that, Charlie concluded, except for a note that her daughter was concerned that her mother had seemed to be recovering and her death was unexpected.

No one expected their parent to die, but at the age of eighty-two, anything could have carried off old Mrs. Grace.

Just to be sure of Martha's story, she checked the register of all patients at the time of the two deaths and confirmed Martha had been a patient in the women's ward on both occasions.

Pulling out her little notebook, she made a note of the details of both cases and Martha's story of 'death' and the wheelbarrow.

She looked at her watch. She had reassigned Mary Keegan to the night shift with Lily Roberts, leaving herself to cover the day with Margaret Campbell. However, with the aid offered by Nell and her girls, she could leave Margaret for a little while and go in search of Danny.

FORTY-FIVE

Charlie picked her way carefully down the ruined track to the town to the Britannia. She paused on the verandah of the hotel to survey the damage. It seemed incredible that having risen so high, the creek had largely returned to its normal course, leaving a trail of destruction and a stinking mess in its wake. It would take months for the town to recover.

The front door was unlocked and she found Danny and Yorkie in the main bar finishing off a breakfast of what looked like bread and cheese. Both men stood as she entered, a formality at odds with the current situation. There were no other patrons to protest at Charlie's unwanted presence. "Good morning, Charlie. What are you doing here?" Danny said.

"I need to talk to you," she said.

Yorkie picked up the plates and empty cups.

"I'll leave you to it," he said.

Danny waved at the chair vacated by Yorkie.

"Take a seat."

"We need to discuss Joe," Charlie said. "I don't believe for a moment that he had anything to do with Janet's death."

Danny returned to his seat, a frown creasing his brow. "A belief in someone's innocence is hardly grounds for a defense, Charlie."

"I think I've found a witness—"

"Hunt!"

The front door banged and a half dozen men entered the bar. Their dirt-ingrained faces were set and threatening. Charlie glanced at Danny and saw the flicker of unease behind his eyes.

Danny rose to his feet. "Bert?"

The bearded leader stepped forward and Charlie recognized the boy she had once known in the solid miner.

"Good morning, Bert," Charlie said.

The man stared at her and he whipped his hat off his head. "Charlie O'Reilly?"

"The same."

Bert turned to his comrades. "You remember Charlie?"

The other men grunted and murmured greetings and she scanned their faces trying to put half-remembered names to the gang who had followed Bert Marsh twenty years ago.

"How's your son, Bert?" she asked

"He's on the mend, thank you. My wife said the matron of the hospital had been by to check on him. I didn't know it was you."

"What do you want to discuss with me?" Danny said, his shoulders stiff beneath his jacket.

Bert pulled up a chair to the table and sat down, waving Danny back down onto his chair.

"We've been talking, the lads and I." Bert looked around at the men who stood with crossed arms behind him. "I told you yesterday, Joe Trevelyan wouldn't hurt a fly." The miner stabbed a finger into the tabletop. "It's like this, Hunt. You're a lawyer. You've got to get him off." Bert looked around his friends. "We've done a whip-round and we've got a few pounds to pay you."

He flung a handful of dirty, creased notes and an assortment of coins onto the table.

Danny stared at the currency and pushed it back in Bert's direction.

"I can't take your money."

Bert threw back his chair and stood up, his fists curled at his sides. He glared at Danny and turned to address his friends.

"I told you he was too good for us."

"No... that's not what I meant." Danny rose to his feet. "I can't take your money because I won't take your money. I'll do it for free."

Everyone stared at him. "You'd do it for nothing?" Bert said.

"I can be my own judge of a man's character and I don't think for a moment that Joe Trevelyan is a murderer. But I won't lie to you, proving it is the problem. He was seen up at the hospital on the night she died."

"But from what I've heard, they've only got the word of that old soak, Alf Kimble," Bert said. "Prewitt is a lazy sod. Now he thinks he's got Joe, he won't go looking for anyone else."

"I can't make any promises that I will get him off, but I will give it my best effort."

Bert clapped him so hard on the shoulder that Danny had to take a step forward, before turning back to the others. "See, I told you he wasn't a bad sort."

"Thanks," Danny said, straightening his collar. "Now if you'll excuse me, I'd better go and see to my client." He looked at Charlie. "Are you coming?"

Charlie scrambled to her feet.

"I need you," Danny whispered in Charlie's ear and took her arm.

Accompanied by Bert and his crew, the delegation crossed the road to the police station and they would have all gone inside but Danny turned on the step and told them to wait outside. He stood aside to let Charlie enter first.

"What's this then? An illegal gathering?" Prewitt reached for his helmet.

"No. I've come to see my client," Danny said.

"Your client?"

"My name is Daniel Hunt, I am a barrister at law and Mr Trevelyan is my client. Here's my card."

Charlie caught a glimpse of an expensive embossed card, no doubt designed to impress wealthy clients. Danny seemed to have assumed a different personality. Despite his workman's clothes, he seemed taller and more confident. Daniel Hunt, the lawyer.

Prewitt studied the card. "You're a lawyer? I thought you were just one of those city toffs like your mate up in the hospital."

Danny summoned a smile. "Never make assumptions about people, Sergeant. Now, if I am to save my client from a miscarriage of justice, I demand to see him now."

"And her?" Prewitt gestured at Charlie.

"She's taking notes."

"But she's the matron of the hospital."

"And a very good note-taker. Now, my good man."

Muttering to himself, Prewitt admitted them both into the area behind the station where the cells had been dug into the side of the hill. They were cold and damp, and smelled of stale urine and boiled cabbage.

"Trevelyan?" Prewitt said. "You've visitors."

From the back of one of the cells, Joe shuffled into the light. He looked like a man facing death, his usually cheerful face unshaven and haggard, his kindly eyes devoid of hope. They sparked at the sight of Charlie.

"Charlie!"

He gripped the iron bars of the cell and Charlie laid a hand over his.

"We've come to help, Joe."

Joe looked at Danny. "Help? How?"

"I am here to represent you as your legal advisor," Danny said.

"Danny is a famous lawyer in Melbourne, Joe," Charlie said.

"I can't afford a lawyer," Joe said.

"Don't worry about that," Danny said. "I am taking you on, *pro bono publico*."

Joe frowned. "What does that mean?"

"For the public good... for free," Danny said. He turned to the police sergeant. "I require privacy to take my client's instructions. Kindly leave us, Sergeant."

Prewitt shuffled out, leaving them alone with Joe.

Danny and Charlie pulled stools across to the cell and Danny handed Charlie a notebook and a pencil.

"You have some good friends in this town who believe in your innocence, Joe, but you're going to have to be completely honest with me."

"Do you want me to tell you I did it?"

Danny held up both hands. "No! I most definitely don't want to
hear that, although if those are your instructions then I will certainly do
my best to render a good plea in mitigation."

"I didn't do it." Tears started in Joe's eyes.

Danny handed him a handkerchief with a quick "Keep it."

He waited for Joe to compose himself before he began. "Good. Now
let's start with your relationship with Miss Becker."

"We met at the New Year's Eve dance and have been stepping out
since then," Joe said. "I couldn't believe my good fortune that such a
pretty lass as Janet would be seen with me, but we got on real well. On
Friday, I asked her to marry me, and she said yes." Joe glanced at Charlie.
"Charlie'll tell you we were as happy as could be."

Danny cast a glance at Charlie.

"Are you taking notes, Charlie?"

Charlie held up the notebook and pencil.

"Yes."

"We had a plan, Janet and me. We were going to get married and
move to Melbourne and start a business there. A respectable hotel for
travelers and the like with meals. You know the sort of thing."

"That takes money," Danny said.

Joe nodded. "I've a little money saved. I do a bit of prospecting in
my spare time and Yorkie pays me a fair wage for my work at the hotel."

Charlie sensed the disquiet in Joe's eyes.

"But?" she prompted.

"It wasn't going to be enough. Not to buy the place we'd seen advertised so Janet says to me that she has an idea to get some more money."

"Doing what?"

Joe looked down at the floor of the cell and shuffled his feet.

"It doesn't reflect well on Janet."

"How?"

"She wouldn't tell me. Just said she knew someone who would give
us some money, no questions asked."

"Why would anyone do that?"

Joe swallowed. "She said she knew something about someone."

Danny and Charlie exchanged glances.

"Blackmail?" Charlie said.

Joe flinched. "Maybe. I dunno and now she's dead I can't ask her, can I?"

"When was she going to have this conversation?"

Joe licked his lips.

"Saturday night." He sighed. "That's why I went up to the hospital. I wanted to stop her."

Danny refrained from rolling his eyes. "So Alf is telling the truth?"

"If he says he saw me then yes, but I swear to God, I didn't see her."

"What time did you go up to the hospital?"

"We shut the bar at eleven-thirty as normal. Yorkie needed some help moving barrels and after I finished up I went up to the hospital just after midnight."

"And how would she have known you were there?" Charlie looked up from her notebook.

Joe looked down at his hands. "I have a special bird call... an owl. She'd come out and we'd sit and chat in the woodshed about this and that. We never got up to anything."

Charlie coughed and Joe looked shamefaced. "Except for when you caught us on Friday night, but that was just a kiss and a cuddle. Nothing more."

"What happened when you got to the hospital?" Danny asked.

"I gave the signal and waited in the woodshed. It was raining something fierce. She didn't come so I called her again."

"How long did you wait?"

"Ten minutes. No more. The hospital was dead quiet and I thought maybe Lily Roberts would have told me if she was too busy but no one came out. I supposed they couldn't hear me over the rain so I came home."

Danny let out a breath. "It's quite possible she was already dead."

Joe buried his head in his hands. When he looked up Charlie saw the desperation in his face as his gaze swept from Danny to her and back again.

"It's well known that Alf's fond of a tipple on a Saturday night. No one's going to believe him, are they?"

"He puts you at the hospital, Joe, and his account ties in with your version of events. A jury would have no reason not to believe him," Danny said. "Did anyone see you return to the hotel?"

Joe shook his head. "Yorkie was in bed and I have a little room of my own out the back. No one to see me come or go."

"That's a pity. The evidence against you is circumstantial and no one saw you commit the act so a prosecutor still has to overcome that problem. Alf's a poor witness but he could be enough to send you to trial."

Joe raised his hands. "I swear I didn't see her, Mr Hunt."

Danny considered his client. "And I believe you."

"So do I," said Charlie. She wondered if this was the moment to mention Martha's account of seeing the figure staging the hanging. She decided against it. Danny needed to hear it from her first before they dared give Joe any reason to hope.

Joe looked up. "What's going to happen to me?"

Danny huffed out a breath that clouded in the cold atmosphere. "If the magistrate at the inquest finds you contributed to her death, you'll be sent to Melbourne, Joe, and it will take a few months for your trial to come up."

"You mean I'd have to go to prison in Melbourne?"

"Remand, Joe. It won't be pleasant, I'm afraid. Coburg jail is a hard place," Danny said.

Joe looked up at him, tears starting in his eyes again.

"I don't want to go to jail for something I didn't do. Can't you get me out of here, Mr Hunt?"

"I'll see about getting you out until the inquest, and with half the town washed away I've no idea when the inquest will be. That gives us a bit of time."

Danny stood up and Joe held out his hands between the bars of the door. "Thank you, Mr Hunt. Thank you."

Danny took the man's hands. "I promise you I'll do my very best for you, Joe."

Charlie leaned in and kissed Joe on his unshaven cheek and they took their leave.

As they stepped into the street, Joe's supporters were still waiting in the street. Danny assured them he had taken comprehensive instructions and would do his best for Joe. Seemingly satisfied by his response, the little crowd dispersed and Danny and Charlie returned to the Britannia and the warmth of his rooms.

Charlie sat in a chair by the fire in Danny's room while he busied himself, tidying the papers and drawings from the table. He had a fire in his eye she hadn't seen before.

"What now?" she asked.

He sat at the table and pulled a paper towards him. "I'll need to make an application to get Joe released on a recognizance."

"Danny I haven't told you my news. It may help."

He looked up. "What is it?"

"I have another witness," she said. "One who saw the man with Janet's body and who can swear it wasn't Joe."

Danny's eyebrows shot up. "Why didn't you tell me before?"

"In fairness, I haven't had the opportunity but now you are officially Joe's legal representative, you need to know."

"Who is your witness?"

"Martha Drew."

Danny rolled his eyes. "If Alf is unreliable, Martha is ten times worse. Who is going to believe Martha's word?"

Charlie swallowed. "I believe her."

Danny crossed his arms and sat back. "Go ahead. What is Martha's story?"

As she related her strange conversation with Martha, it sounded more bizarre and the frown deepening on Danny's forehead confirmed her growing fear that Martha Mackie was not going to be of much help.

He shook his head. "She said something similar to me and I no more believe death is stalking the corridors of your hospital than I do in ghosts, Charlie. But it's a hospital. People die and your witness is... an ailing alcoholic."

Charlie bit her lip. "I have verified the two deaths she mentioned in her account and she is so specific. A person in a dark coat with a hat pulled down low. Whoever it is, they're no ghost or heavenly being."

"Hardly my vision of the angel of death," Danny agreed. "I hope when my time comes, it is something a little more picturesque."

"Don't joke about it," Charlie said.

"You're right. It's serious. Who has access to the hospital at night?"

"That's it. Nobody. The doors are supposed to be locked."

"But both these deaths occurred in warmer months. Maybe a window had been left open?"

Charlie stared at him.

"You think someone could be breaking into the hospital and killing patients? I don't even know what to think about that!"

Danny shoved his hands in his pockets and wandered across to the window.

"You're jumping to conclusions, Charlie. Martha's evidence could be invaluable to Joe's defense. I suppose she was sober on Saturday night?"

"Completely."

"She was quite sure it wasn't Joe?"

"Absolutely emphatic. No limp."

"Excellent. That's pretty conclusive. I'll need to speak to Martha and get a signed statement from her if it is to have any weight," Danny said.

Charlie grimaced. "She's very sick, Danny. To be honest, I'm not sure she'll see out the week."

He nodded. "I understand. No time to waste but for your peace of mind, more than anything else, we should talk to the women she mentioned who lost loved ones at the hospital."

Charlie glanced at her watch. "It will have to be this evening. I must get back to the hospital. Now Nell and the girls have gone back to the Tavern, Margaret's on her own."

FORTY-SIX

After Charlie left, Danny gathered his thoughts and returned to the police station to do battle with Sergeant Prewitt over releasing Joe on a recognizance.

Prewitt referred Danny to the town magistrate, Elijah Sloan, manager of the Bank of Victoria. He found the bank manager perched on a desk, supervising his staff in clearing a thick layer of stinking mud from the floor of the bank. Sodden ledgers and piles of papers had been lifted onto the counters, but from the look of them, he doubted the important bank records could be redeemed. Danny wondered if the bank had copies.

With half an ear and eye on the cleaning-up operation, Sloan did not take much persuasion as Danny cited the paucity of evidence, the cost of feeding and housing a prisoner at a time when the town was facing dire shortages, and the difficulty in the prisoner absconding, given the ongoing floods. Danny concluded with the offer of a sizeable recognizance, from his own pocket.

Sloan scribbled his signature on the paper Danny had prepared and returned his pen to the desk.

"Prewitt wants the matter dealt with expeditiously," he said. "I'll be convening the inquest in the Mechanics Institute hall on Friday." He pulled a face. "Hopefully it will have been cleaned by then."

"That's very soon."

"I've got four other deaths to deal with, and if this is a murder I want it off my desk and in Melbourne as soon as possible," Sloan said.

"Until Friday," Danny said and left the bank manager yelling at a subordinate who had missed a patch of mud in a corner.

Back at the police station, Prewitt did not seem anxious to let his prisoner go.

"How do you know he's not going to take off? He knows these hills, Mr. Hunt."

"And you know Joe Trevelyan, Prewitt. If he gives you his word of honor he'll keep it, and I'm prepared to stand surety for him."

Joe was produced from the cell and the terms of his release explained to him.

"But I can't take your money, Mr. Hunt," he protested.

"You're not taking it, Joe. I only have to pay it over if you abscond, and I am trusting you not to do that."

Joe nodded. "I won't run off. You have my word on that." He looked at Prewitt. "Both of you."

Prewitt sniffed. "Get out," he said. "I've got work to do."

Danny put his arm around Joe's shoulder and they stepped into the fresh air to a cheering crowd. Word had got around and Bert Marsh and his crew, covered in mud from their efforts at cleaning out the mine's equipment sheds, were waiting for them.

"I knew you'd get him off, Hunt," Bert said.

"Let's be clear. I haven't got him off," Danny said. "He's free till the inquest on Friday and I am going to need some compelling evidence to clear his name. So if anyone knows anything, you know where to find me."

Back at the Britannia, Yorkie took charge, seeing Joe was fed and cleaned up before Danny invited him into the upstairs parlor and sat him down with a whisky to take some proper instructions.

"Let's start at the beginning, Joe, and this time I want the whole story."

Joe nodded and Danny wrote as Joe talked. It was the same story he had told Danny when they had visited him in the prison.

"Mr. Hunt—"

Danny looked up. "Joe?"

"There's something else I haven't told you."

The hair on the back of Danny's neck prickled. "Go on."

"I wasn't meant to meet Janet on Saturday night, not after Charlie O'Reilly gave us what for on Friday. But the more I thought about it, I wasn't happy with her plan to get money. It sounded wrong to me."

"Not to put too fine a point on it, Joe, it sounds like she was proposing blackmail."

Joe flinched.

"I thought I'd found a better way. I told you I had to move some barrels in the cellar that night?"

Danny nodded.

"I found a large parcel in the cellars, wrapped in hessian and hidden behind the barrels." He held up his hands, indicating an object about two feet long. "I'd never seen it before. It was huge and heavy and I thought I should open it. See if it belonged to someone." Joe's eyes widened. "It was silver, Mr. Hunt, and I thought it would bring us some real money if it was melted it down... and I wanted to tell Janet about it."

Danny took a breath. "This silver thing... describe it?"

"It was in three bits about this long." Joe indicated with his hands again. "Two long thin bits and a big bobbly bit with a crown of some sort."

Danny almost groaned aloud.

The mace of the Victorian parliament.

He steadied his breath. "Do you know who put it there?"

Joe shook his head. "I dunno. Never seen it before but it was heavy. Finders keepers, ain't that the law?"

"Not quite," Danny said. "What did you do with it?"

"I put it back where I found it."

"Is it still there?"

"Unless someone moved it." Joe sounded terse. "The cellar's underwater so it isn't going anywhere. Anyway, I thought I should tell Janet and stop her other plan. That's really what I was doing up there that night, but everything else is just what I told you. I never saw her."

Danny sighed. "That thing you found, I'm afraid it's not yours to keep."

"So you know what it is?"

"Yes."

And I know who put it there.

"There may be a reward for its finding," Danny said.

Joe shrugged. "Doesn't matter now. Janet's dead. There will be no pub in Melbourne." Tears filled his eyes. "I should have put my foot down when she said what she was going to do. I should have stopped her. I told her it was a bad idea but she was set. We had a dream..."

Danny laid a hand on the man's shoulder. "I'm so sorry, Joe." He sat back and took a swallow of whisky. A cheap and nasty brew, it burned the back of his throat. "Joe, when it comes to the inquest and you're asked to give evidence, don't say a word about the... the object you found. It's not relevant."

"But it's the truth."

"All the court needs to know is that you went up to see her because you loved her and it was your usual Saturday-night rendezvous."

Joe frowned and Danny sighed. Of all the clients in the world, he had the misfortune to have the most honest man who ever lived. Anyone else would be lying through their teeth, but not Joe Trevelyan.

FORTY-SEVEN

It was already going dark as Charlie and Danny trudged up the hill to Abby Temple's cottage. A light shone in the window and smoke curled from the chimney. A thin woman answered the door. With the light behind her it was hard to make out her face but her greeting was heavy with suspicion.

"Whatcha want?"

Charlie stepped in front of Danny. "Good evening Mrs. Temple, I'm Matron O'Reilly from the hospital and this is Mr. Hunt. If you can spare us a couple of minutes we'd like to ask you about the death of your baby."

"I got nothing to say," Abby said but her attempt to shut the door was obstructed by Charlie's foot.

"I know it's upsetting and I am so sorry that it happened. I'm new to the hospital and I just want to understand how it happened so no other mother has to go through the same ordeal."

"She died. That's it," she said, but there was a catch in the woman's voice. She looked at Danny.

"Who's he?"

"He's been sent by the trustees of the hospital," Charlie said. It wasn't quite a lie. Caleb Hunt was a trustee of the hospital and Danny had been sent by his father to Maiden's Creek.

Abby Temple shrugged. "You can come in for a bit but my husband'll be home soon and he'll be wanting his supper." Her thin shoulders rose and fell. "Not that I've much to offer. Any word on when supplies are coming?"

"No, I'm sorry. We're all in the same position. The patients at the hospital are living on porridge and cabbage soup."

That produced a chuckle from the woman, and she turned back to stirring something that also smelled suspiciously like cabbage soup.

"So what do you want to know?" she said, turning to face them, her hands on her hips.

"What do you remember of that night?"

Abby's gaze went to a point somewhere above Charlie's head.

"Not much to be honest. I fed little June—that's what I called her— and the nurse took her and put her in the crib next to my bed. She gave me a drink, said it would help me sleep. I had this strange dream. You know those dreams when you think you're awake but you're really asleep?"

"Yes. Go on."

"It was like a dark shadow bending over the crib. I tried to shout out and make it go away but I couldn't make myself heard and the next morning June was dead... cold as the grave."

Charlie reached out and touched the woman's arm. "How awful for you."

Tears welled in the woman's eyes. "We'd had the priest in to christen her that morning because she was so little and weak so I like to think she's with God now in a happy place."

"I hope there'll be other babies, Abby," Charlie said.

Abby touched her stomach. "I haven't said anything to Bob yet but I think there's one on the way."

Charlie smiled. "Come and see me at the hospital as soon as you can. I'm a midwife and I can check everything is going well."

Abby shook her head. "Ain't going near that place again, begging your pardon, Matron. Ellen Bushby can see to me."

After the woman's grim experience at the hospital, Charlie could hardly blame her for choosing to stay away.

"Ellen is very good but if you don't mind, I'll come and see you too," Charlie said. "Just to be doubly sure. We'll leave you in peace now."

At the door, Danny turned back to the woman. "You said the nurse gave you a sleeping draught. Can you remember which nurse?"

"Aye, that Irish one."

"Can you remember which other nurse was on duty that night?"

Abby frowned. "I can't remember. One of the young ones. I heard one of the nurses hanged herself. Is that true?"

"It's still being investigated," Danny said.

Abby shivered. "Another reason to stay away from the hospital." Her eyes widened. "If it weren't haunted by the unquiet dead before, it will be now."

"Ghosts and death... not sure I want to go back to the hospital," Charlie said as they walked away. She glanced at Danny. "You're quiet."

"Thinking," Danny said.

"And...?"

"Let's see what Mrs. Grace's daughter has to say."

Unfortunately, the woman was not much help. She hadn't been at the hospital when her mother had died so she couldn't shed any light on what might have happened.

"But you had a suspicion."

The woman frowned. "That's all it was. It wasn't proof. I'd seen my mother that afternoon and she was talking about coming home the next day. She'd not been in the best of health with a weak heart and then the chest infection, but she was a fighter."

"When were you told she had passed away?"

"I got a message to come to the hospital and Doctor Linacre and the matron told me." Her lip wobbled.

"Was there anything unusual about her?" Danny asked.

"What do you mean?"

"About the way she looked," Charlie put in.

The woman frowned. "She looked peaceful but her lips were blue. I thought it was just 'cos she'd been dead a few hours."

"Did you speak to any of the nurses?"

"That Irish nurse spoke to me, told me how sweet Ma was and how sorry she was she had died. She was very kind. Why are you asking? Do you think something might be wrong?"

"We don't think anything," Charlie said. "I'm just tidying up some paperwork that Matron Birch left for me."

"And who are you?" The woman looked at Danny.

"I'm representing the chairman of the board of trustees. We like to make sure everything is running smoothly so we are looking into mortality rates at the hospital."

Charlie didn't think the woman entirely believed him.

She thanked the woman for her information, expressed her condolences again and the two returned to her cottage where Netty had managed to prepare a stew.

"Young Johnny shot a 'roo for the hospital," Netty said. "The patients will be glad of a change from cabbage. What did you find out?"

Charlie swallowed. She was reluctant to voice the thoughts that had been churning in her mind.

"There is a killer in the hospital," Danny said, voicing the conclusion she had reached.

"Danny!" Netty gasped.

"We think there is a killer at the hospital." He modified his statement.

"I don't want to believe it," Charlie said, "but I you may be right. I know of a case when I was working in London. A hospital wardsman. He was guilty of at least three deaths before he took his own life."

"How did they catch him?"

"A doctor walked in and came across him with a pillow over the patient's face. He ran out and jumped from the roof of the hospital. It was all hushed up but word gets around."

"Why did he do it?"

"Before he jumped he told the doctor he was ending their suffering but he didn't live to say anymore."

Danny considered his reply. "Charlie, you need to check who was on duty the night of those deaths. I am betting it was Keegan and Becker."

"I've already checked," Charlie said, hating the thought that a nurse could kill. "One night it was Becker, the other it was Roberts, but both nights it was Keegan. If Janet Becker knew, or suspected, her colleague of involvement with the deaths, could she have tried a little blackmail and ended up dead herself?"

Everyone was silent for a long, long moment.

"You think it's Mary Keegan?" Netty voiced the question nobody wanted to ask.

Charlie glanced at Danny, who shrugged.

"What we think and what we can prove are two entirely different things," Danny said. "It could just as easily be Alf or Doctor Linacre or a complete stranger. We don't know if it was a man or a woman. Whoever it is, we have only a few days to provide a plausible reason why it isn't Joe. Ideally, we might have to do something to draw them out. I just don't know what."

A frantic knocking at the door made them all start. Charlie answered the door to a lad of about fifteen.

"They said at the hospital that the midwife would be here. We need help. Nico's wife is having a baby and it is not going well. They sent for you."

"Nico?" Charlie had to think. "Oh, Nico Alberti from the Italian settlement?"

The boy nodded and Charlie took a breath. In normal times the Italian settlement of Wildman's Point was easily accessible but now...

"How are we to get there? The bridges are out."

"There's one bridge just downstream of the railway station. It's damaged but if we're careful we can get across," the boy said. "That's how I came. The track is out in places but I know the way and I can guide you."

"Take one of my horses," Amos said. "The lad managed to rescue a few saddles and bridles."

"I'll go with you," Danny said.

"Why?" Charlie said. "You're not going to be any use to me."

"He's being a gentleman, Charlie. Be gracious," Netty said.

"I don't need protection," Charlie mumbled. She reached for her coat. "But I've no time to argue. If you're coming, I'm leaving now. I just have to collect my bag from the hospital. You can make yourself useful and organize the horses."

At the hospital, she found Lily Roberts in the kitchen making cocoa for one of the patients who was having trouble sleeping. Mary Keegan sat at the table writing up notes.

"How's Martha tonight?" Charlie asked.

Keegan looked up. "Still with us."

Something prickled at the back of Charlie's neck as she looked into the woman's eyes. Could Mary Keegan be behind the deaths? She glanced at the hooks beside the door but there was no long black coat, just the nurse's rain slickers. Admittedly they were long and black but they made a noise when you moved in them. Martha had said nothing about noise.

"Where are you off to?" Mary asked.

"The Italian settlement," Charlie said. "Nico Alberti's wife is in labour and having trouble."

Keegan smiled, a nasty humorless smile. "That will disappoint Sister Campbell."

Charlie didn't have time to inquire as to why it would disappoint Margaret but she already had a suspicion that Margaret Campbell had something of a tendresse for the handsome young Italian.

With her bag properly stocked, Charlie pulled her heavy oilskin on and ran out into the dark where Danny and the boy from the Italian settlement, who gave his name as Alfredo, waited with a chestnut and the sturdy mare she had ridden up to Pretty Sally. The boy went ahead, holding up a lantern. It was tortuously slow going, as the horses struggled to find firm footing on the slippery, ruined tracks.

The bridge the boy had mentioned was little more than a few wooden planks with no guardrail. They had to dismount and slowly lead the horses across while the angry creek roiled below them. Even the little creeklets that ambled gently down the slopes into Maiden's Creek had turned into raging torrents that had to be traversed.

Danny suggested they use the tramway that had been cut into the slope above them to facilitate the transport of wood into the mines. Alfredo shook his head.

"We thought of that, but it's been washed away in a few places. This is the safest path."

It took nearly two hours to reach Wildman's Point.

Alfredo let out a whoop as they approached the settlement. Nico Alberti ran out of his cottage to help Charlie from her mount. She shooed everyone from the house with instructions to Danny to keep Nico out of the way and slammed the door on the world.

Maria was in considerable distress and exhausted. Her mother had done her best but Maria had still not fully dilated. The woman really needed a doctor's skill but all she had was Charlie and Charlie had to do the best she could.

She shut her mind to all other concerns and applied herself to the problem presenting to her.

FORTY-EIGHT

"She is very bossy, that one," Nico said as he ushered Danny into a neighboring cottage.

"She is also very good at what she does," Danny said. "Your wife is in good hands. Your first?"

Nico nodded. "Is it always like this?"

"I wouldn't know."

Nico found a bottle and poured them both a tin cup of what smelled like some sort of distilled spirit.

"You're not married?" he said, handing Danny the cup.

"No."

Nico grinned. "No nice girls in Melbourne?"

Danny took a mouthful of the drink and nearly choked. It burned the back of his throat.

"My brother's grappa. He sends me a crate every year."

Danny coughed. "Strong stuff."

Nico shrugged. "You get used to it."

"How long have you been married?" Danny asked.

"Maria and I were wed just after Christmas." A sly smile crept over Nico's face. "It was something of an urgent matter. Her father was not best pleased with me but these things happen, do they not?"

Danny wondered if the wedding had involved an actual shotgun.

"And are you happy?"

Nico shrugged. "She is a nice girl and a good housekeeper and she will be a good mother. I have no complaints."

Evidently, love didn't enter the marriage equation.

Nico grinned. "The nurse who came with you. She is the matron of the hospital?"

"That's correct."

"She is too pretty to be a matron. Are you... and she...?"

Danny took a sizeable swig of the grappa to cover his embarrassment. "Ah... no... just a friend."

"Sure, sure," Nico said.

"I recall you saying you were a patient at the hospital recently," Danny said, changing the subject.

"Ah yes, at Easter. An accident with a saw. The doctor there sewed me up." He flexed his fingers. "I have days when the hand doesn't work so well but I manage."

"Were you well looked after?"

Nico grinned. "Very well looked after." The leer in Nico's smile prompted the hackles to rise on Danny's neck.

"What do you mean?"

"It is a lonely life to be away from home," Nico said. "And one of the nurses was particularly kind to me."

He swallowed another couple of mouthfuls of grappa. It improved on acquaintance.

"Any nurse in particular?" Danny asked, against his better judgment.

Nico shook his head. "I would not want to get anyone into trouble with your matron," he said, "but we enjoyed a kiss and a laugh, nothing more."

"You're a married man with a pregnant wife," Danny said.

Nico shrugged. "It was all in good sport," he said. "I meant nothing by it."

Just a kiss and a laugh? Danny wondered if the nurse had felt the same way.

He changed the subject. "Nico, did anyone die while you were at the hospital?"

Nico's eyes widened. "My father used to say that you only went to hospital to die."

"So someone did pass away?"

"It was a young boy. Diphtheria I heard them say." He crossed himself.

"Do you remember the night he died?"

Nico shrugged. "Not really."

"No strange visitors to the ward? In the night."

"In the middle of the night? No. Why do you ask?"

Danny shook his head. "I'm surveying causes of death at the hospital, that is all."

"The boy died. That is it."

He stiffened as a thin wail cut through the silent night. A baby.

Nico jumped to his feet and ran out into the dark. Danny followed.

Charlie stood by the fire, jiggling a wrapped bundle in her arms. She looked up as Nico threw open the door to the cottage and in that brief unguarded moment, Danny saw the wonder in her face, bathed gold by the fire, as she looked down at the baby in her arms.

"You have a son," she said, handing the bundle to the new father. "I must see to your wife." She paused. "Aren't you going to ask how she is?"

Nico looked up from his infant. "My wife? Is she all right?"

"She is a bit sore and sorry for herself. I had to use forceps to persuade your boy into the world. Does he have a name?"

"Luigi, after my father," Nico said without hesitation.

Charlie glanced at Danny. "I'll see Mrs Alberti settled and then we should be on our way."

"It is late and it is not safe for you to go back," Nico said. "We can find beds for you both here and you can leave at daybreak."

Charlie and Danny exchanged glances. The ride from Maiden's Creek earlier in the night had been difficult and it would be worse now that they were both tired. There was some sense to Nico's suggestion.

"As long as we're away at first light," Charlie said. "The hospital is shorthanded enough without me going missing."

"Mary Keegan knew where you were going," Danny said. "She seems quite capable."

"You will stay with my grandmother tonight," Nico said, handing the baby to his wife's mother.

Nico escorted them to a little cottage on the outskirts of the settlement occupied by an elderly lady who greeted them both like long-lost friends with hugs and kisses and effusive outpourings in Italian.

"She says she owes you Maria's life and her home is your home," Nico translated.

"Very kind," Charlie said.

Danny thanked her in his basic Italian, which provoked a stream of colloquial conversation between the woman and Nico.

Signora Alberti plied them with food—the best meal either had eaten in days—and made up rough beds for them, Charlie in the curtained-off area that held the old lady's bed and Danny beside the fire.

The old lady retired to her bed, but Danny and Charlie remained sitting by the fire, fortified by more of the grappa.

"That's strong," Charlie said after her first mouthful.

"It grows on you," Danny said.

Charlie lapsed into silence, scowling into the fire as she sipped the grappa.

"Tell," he said.

"Tell what?" She looked up at him.

"Whatever it is that is bothering you. Are you worried about the baby?"

She shook her head. "No. Mother and baby are both fine."

"Then what?"

"I have little time for wandering husbands," Charlie said.

"Are we talking about Nico or someone else?"

"What do you mean, someone else? Of course, I mean Nico," she snapped. "His wife told me they only married because he got her pregnant and since then it has been a succession of girls, all through her pregnancy."

"Including one of the nurses at the hospital," Danny suggested.

"I suspect as much. In fairness, I don't think she knew he was married and I doubt it went much beyond flirting."

Danny eliminated Janet Becker and Mary Keegan from the flirtation. Lily Roberts or... "Margaret?"

Charlie jerked a shoulder. "It doesn't matter. Nothing would have come of it anyway."

He looked at her. "This is more than just Nico. It's personal, isn't it?"

"What makes you think that?" Charlie studied the grappa in her cup.

"Fitzgerald?"

Charlie looked up and Danny knew he had hit a nerve.

She drained her cup and held it out for more.

"I've never said anything to anyone," Charlie said. "Damn it. It's the grappa."

"Charlie, I'm a friend and I know there was something between you and Fitzgerald. He as good as told me."

Charlie screwed her face as if in pain. "I bet it wasn't complimentary," she said.

"He wasn't married when we first... first..." She trailed off. "I don't want you thinking the worst of me, Danny."

"Why would I do that?"

"There was more to what happened between myself and William Fitzgerald than I have told you... or told anyone. I could say he seduced me, but that would be untrue. Blame my upbringing, my mad mother... whatever, but I fancied myself in love with the bastard. I stupidly thought he would marry me and then one of the other nurses pointed out the engagement announcement in the paper. When I challenged him, he laughed and said it was a marriage of convenience and there was no reason not to continue our relationship. I said I wanted nothing more to do with him and he turned nasty. He could have destroyed my reputation personally and professionally so I thought it might be judicious to leave Melbourne for a while. I didn't expect him to want to just pick up when I returned but he found out I was back and working at the Women's Hospital and I started receiving letters and gifts."

A knot of anger and frustration boiled in Danny's chest. He'd had the measure of Fitzgerald from the first time they had met at the Club. It came as no surprise that the man was a habitué of Madam Brussels... or Nell's tavern. Like Nico Alberti, he thought of marriage vows as merely an inconvenience.

"You are a man," Charlie said. "I don't expect you to understand, but all Fitzgerald has to do is start a rumor that I am in some way a loose woman and I lose everything." Her voice cracked.

Danny recalled the brief conversation he'd had with Fitzgerald and the tone he had taken when speaking of Charlie. Now it all made sense and the urge to smash a fist into the man's smug face redoubled.

"Charlie..." he began but didn't know what to say, how to make it right. "You're right. He is a bastard."

She had confided in him, perhaps now was the time to confide in her.

"I told you about my father... my real father. He was like Fitzgerald... He seduced my mother, left her pregnant, and disappeared."

Charlie stared at him. "But your mother... Adelaide is a lady, not like me. I'm nothing... a nobody."

Danny stared at her. "Don't you dare say that about yourself, and yes, my mother came from wealth but the effect was still the same. She and Netty ran away... as far away as they could go. For all my young life, she told me my father was a gallant sea captain lost at sea. She lied to me. The reality was a wastrel who cared only for our fortune and nothing for either her or me."

He had said it... the words that had been churning in his chest since he had arrived in Maiden's Creek.

"I'm sorry." Charlie reached for his hand, curling her fingers around his.

"But for all of that, it is her lies I remember, not Richard Barnwell's attempt to take me from her."

"That's unfair," Charlie said, and she squeezed his hand so hard the bones grated. "In protecting herself she was protecting you. What life would either of you had if she hadn't woven a story for you both?"

Danny had no response, except an acknowledgment Charlie was right.

"It is always the woman who gets blamed," Charlie said. "Your mother, the young girl at the hospital... Martha Mackie... like..." She released his hand and pulled her knees up to her chin, wrapping her arms around them. "Like me," she said in a very small voice.

She had loosed her hair and secured it in a rough knot in the nape of her neck, but long locks of dark hair escaped in tendrils. The fire added a glow to her face and she looked like the beautiful young woman she was, not the stiff and proper matron in her starched uniform.

"Charlie..." Even to his own ears, his voice sounded husky.

The grappa, he thought, and he coughed.

"Charlie..." he said, trying again.

She looked up at him. Her eyes were dark pools, her lips slightly parted, and he wondered what it would be like to kiss those lips, hold her slight body in his arms. Beneath the starched uniform and the walls she had built around herself, she was still a woman and a desirable woman.

"Danny?"

"You deserve better than the William Fitzgeralds of the world."

She shook her head. "No, I don't. Danny, our roads are set when we are born."

"I don't believe that for a moment! Look at what you have achieved."

"Compared to what I came from? True but I was fortunate, Danny. Fortunate to meet people who saw something in me I couldn't see for myself, but I have to recognize my limitations. I could never hope to study medicine properly and become a doctor so I decided to be the very best nurse I could be."

"And you are," he said. "I've seen you with patients. You have a gift, and why can't you study medicine? They take women now."

She laughed. "Danny, I can't afford tuition fees or not to work and I can't go cap in hand to my benefactors who have already been too good to me. I'm a grown woman of nearly thirty. This is my life." She stood up. "Speaking of which, it is late and I'll be no use tomorrow unless I get some sleep."

Danny jumped up, almost knocking over the stool he had been sitting on.

"Goodnight, Charlie," he said.

She didn't move and they stood looking at each other for a long, long moment.

He took a breath and held it as he reached out, curling a lock of dark hair around his finger. Her lips parted and, emboldened, he stepped forward, letting his hand stray to the back of her head, drawing her in towards him.

Their lips met with the bruising intensity of mutual need and long loneliness. She slid her hands around him, drawing him closer as they explored each other. Only the need to draw breath made them part and they stood in the firelight, arms around each other, hungry eyes scanning faces for the smallest sign that either had overstepped the mark.

It was Charlie who moved first. She stepped back and laid a hand on his chest. "Danny, that was—"

"Wrong? Charlie, I'm so sorry..."

She smiled and pushed him lightly. "No. It was lovely," she said, "but it was a moment that we can't repeat again... ever."

Why not?

He wanted to rail at her. Hadn't she understood what he had been trying to say to her? They were really not so different, and any difference didn't matter.

Instead, he settled for an embarrassed laugh. "Of course, you're right. You go and get some rest. I'll have the horses ready at first light."

"Goodnight," she said, lifting the curtain and giving him a last, lingering smile before slipping out of sight.

Danny lay awake for a long time, his hands behind his head, thinking about Charlie, reliving the exquisite delight of their kiss. He touched his lips, still feeling her touch like a burning brand.

He'd kissed girls before. He'd kissed Margaret Campbell just before he asked her to marry him, but it had never been like that. No woman had ever lit the fire that now coursed through his veins like Charlie O'Reilly had. His whole body ached for her... for more, and the thought that she lay just a few feet away when she could be in his arms only made the agony worse.

He forced his mind to recite Latin legal maxims, guaranteed to cool any man's ardor, but despite his best efforts he found himself going over the confidences she had shared with him.

Ex abundanti cautela. From an excess of caution.

There was a legal maxim for every occasion. Had his whole life been predicated on an excess of caution? Maybe it was time to throw that caution to wind and follow where his heart led.

Whatever else happened, he would never be another William Fitzgerald.

FORTY-NINE

The habits born of many years in nursing meant that Charlie could fall asleep without difficulty even after the most trying day, but she lay awake listening to the gentle burbling snores of the old lady in the bed. Danny lay within a few short paces of her and while she ached to slip beneath the covers of his bed and hold him close, to do so would be madness.

Charlie O'Reilly, daughter of Mad Annie, did not belong to the world of Daniel Hunt. To think otherwise would be to relive the foolish dreams of a younger, more naive Charlie who had believed William Fitzgerald would make good on his promise to marry her.

She cursed herself and blamed exhaustion and the grappa. Now he would think her the sort of woman who gave herself willingly to any man who treated her kindly, and Fitzgerald had done just that. He had singled her out for praise for her nursing skills, lavished the sort of attention on her that she would only have dreamed of as a child, but when she had given herself to him, it had all changed. The letters and presents came less frequently. He had humiliated her in front of her colleagues and patients.

He had, in short, made her life unbearable, and all the while his eye had been fixed on a new and prettier nurse. When she had refused him on that last occasion he had not expected her defiance. No woman defied him. If a relationship ended it was of his choosing and his pride could not take the rejection.

That was why he had pursued her again on her return. He could not accept that she did not want him.

But did her experience with William Fitzgerald mean she should ignore the dictates of her heart? That traitorous heart was leading her down a path that could only end in more tears.

She rolled onto her side and pulled her knees up to her chest, fighting back the waves of nagging loneliness that crept into her thoughts in the darkest hours of the night, until at last, she slept.

She emerged in the morning to a grey dawn. She found herself unable to meet Danny's eyes and any conversation was monosyllabic.

After a quick and substantial breakfast provided by the old woman, Danny organized the horses while Charlie checked on her patient and satisfied herself that mother and baby were doing well. She gratefully received parcels of food that were pressed into her hands and swung into the saddle.

They rode away from the settlement in the damp early morning light, both lost in their own thoughts.

On Charlie's part she had concluded the kiss had been a mistake, an aberration brought on by the stress of the day. She had to put things between them right, even if they could never quite return to the easy friendship that had been developing.

It didn't matter—in a few days he would be gone, returning to his Melbourne life, and if they met again it would be as casual acquaintances, nothing more!

I just have to get back to the hospital, back to work and it will make sense again.

But as they rode, the beauty of the bush folded her in its arms. Wreaths of mist rose from the gullies and the trees, and ferns dripped with moisture. The heady scent of eucalyptus hung in the air and bell-birds tinkled their distinctive cry in the treetops, echoed by the shrill call of the parrots.

"I had forgotten how lovely the bush can be," she said aloud.

Danny did not respond, and she cast him a sidelong look.

"Danny?"

He gave a shake of his head as if bringing himself back from a place far away.

"Sorry... did you say something? I've been wondering how to apologize for my behavior last night." A slow smile curled the corners of his mouth and for the first time all morning he met her eyes. "But the truth is I'm not sorry I kissed you."

"It can't happen again," Charlie said.

His lips tightened. "Why not?"

That had not been the answer she had been expecting.

"This track leads back to our normal lives and... well... we don't belong in each other's worlds."

His eyes narrowed. "Charlie, I don't agree. You are now one of the very few people who know I am a complete sham... a poor fatherless bastard, as people used to say."

"Absolute rubbish," Charlie said. "Richard Barnwell forfeited any right to call himself your father, but you have something many people... me among them... don't have and that is a wonderful man who was probably a better father to you than Barnwell would ever have been. So stop feeling sorry for yourself."

"When did you learn to be so wise?"

"I had it beaten into me as a child," she said, without humor. "But my comment stands. I no more belong in your world than I did at your birthday party all those years ago."

"I disagree," Danny said.

There was no answer to that. He would go back to his Toorak mansion, or wherever he lived, and she would return, if she was lucky, to a boarding house somewhere near whatever hospital employed her next or, if she was unlucky, to the nurses' quarters.

"Charlie—" Danny began, but she held up a hand.

"I don't want to talk about it anymore, not while we have the more pressing problem ahead of us of getting Joe Trevelyan off a murder charge. That requires our full attention. The rest can wait."

They lapsed into silence.

"Nico said a boy died of diphtheria while he was in the hospital," Danny said.

"And?"

"He didn't think anything unusual surrounded the death."

"We can't assume every death is brought on by a third party," Charlie said. "But I will go through the records today and see if there are connections and patterns."

She smiled, thinking of her long-neglected love for mathematics and the puzzle of finding those elusive connections and patterns.

"I think it is looking likely that Janet surprised the person and paid the price," Charlie said.

"If there was some way we could catch this person in the act," Danny mused.

Charlie considered that thought for a long moment.

"There might be. Martha Mackie is still very ill and may be a candidate for the angel's ministrations."

Danny shivered. "That is a terrible thought."

"It wouldn't be hard to lay a trap," Charlie said, and a plan started to form in her mind.

"But we've got no certainty they would fall for it. He or she may have been scared off by the confrontation with Janet Becker," Danny ventured.

"Maybe, but I think we have to try something," Charlie said.

"What are you thinking?" Danny asked and she sensed the reluctance in his tone.

She explained her idea.

"No," he said. "Absolutely not. You will be putting a patient's life at risk."

"No, I won't," she said. "The only life I'm risking is my own."

"Charlie, I'm an officer of the court. I can't do anything illegal."

She cast him a sharp sideways glance. "I don't see how it is illegal. Sometimes we have to push the boundaries, Danny, and if we're going to save Joe and hopefully other lives then we can't just sit back. If Joe is convicted of this crime, the real murderer remains at large, free to go on killing at will."

"I am not going to be a party to such a foolhardy scheme, Charlie."

She glared at him. He had his gaze firmly fixed on the track ahead, a mutinous line to his mouth.

"What would you do? Wait for that idiot Prewitt to miraculously find the murderer? We are all Joe has, Danny."

He turned to her, the anger fading from his face. "Charlie... I don't know what to suggest."

"It could be nothing happens, Danny, and what is the risk in that? But I am almost certain that it has to be someone in the hospital and they have to be stopped. At least three innocent lives, that we know of, have been taken."

"I don't take risks, Charlie. There is a reason I chose law as a profession."

"Then it is time you did," she said. "We don't get anywhere in life without sometimes taking risks and what greater reason can there be than to save a life... Joe's life!"

The horses stopped on the track, looking at each other in puzzlement while the humans glared at each other.

"Learn to take risks, Danny," Charlie said.

"What about you? Running away from Fitzgerald because you won't stand up and expose him for the bully he is?"

"That's different."

"Is it? You talk about taking risks, Charlie O'Reilly, well let me tell you, you are the biggest risk to my health, safety, and sanity I have ever encountered."

Despite the blazing anger in his eyes, Charlie felt a burble of laughter rising in her chest. "But you still kissed me."

"Yes, I did, you mad Irish demon."

"I'm not Irish. I'm Tasmanian."

"Same thing, and yes I kissed you and talk about risks..."

"It was nice," Charlie said.

"It was... Stop it, I'm trying to be angry with you."

Charlie bit her lip to stop the smile. "Come on Danny. Let's give this mad, crazy idea of mine a try. At worst, nothing happens... at best, we catch a killer."

He huffed out a breath. "God help me," he said, looking away from her. When he turned back the last trace of anger had gone from his face. "I want it noted by the court that I strenuously objected to Miss O'Reilly's plan but in the interests of her safety, I felt compelled to agree to cooperate."

FIFTY

It was nearly midday before Charlie returned to the hospital, tired and mud-splattered from the difficult ride. Boards had been laid down in Main Street to allow the horses to pick their way through the gluey, stinking, muddy mess but despite this, both animals stumbled and sunk in potholes, nearly dislodging their riders.

The properties fronting the street had all been inundated. The owners were now faced with trying to clear their floors of layers of mud, and rotting produce and spoiled wares were being tossed out onto the boardwalk, adding to the stench. Charlie put her hand to her nose but it did little to alleviate the smell. Incredibly one structure stood solid against the water that still swirled about its footings... the pretty little bandstand. A symbol of hope and normality in all the chaos.

They stopped to look at Netty and Amos's cottage. It still stood but the impact of the floodwaters had undermined the foundations and the walls sagged and leaned alarmingly.

Charlie dismounted and picked her way down the side to the front door that stood ajar. She pushed it but the doorframe had warped and she could only open it enough just to squeeze through the gap.

"Charlie, be careful. It's in a dangerous condition," Danny shouted after her.

She ignored him. So many happy memories of this kitchen and now it was ankle-deep in mud, the furniture scattered and broken like matchwood.

Danny followed her into the house, squeezing through the narrow entrance.

"This is almost worse than a fire," he said.

"How are we going to break it to them? What are they going to do?" Charlie waved a hand at the irretrievable mess. "Netty's always been here. I can't imagine Maiden's Creek without her."

Danny nodded. "My parents offered them a home years ago but they refused to leave. Perhaps now they can be persuaded to move either to Melbourne or up to Mansfield. I think Amos would like it up there. Plenty of room for horses."

He stooped and pulled something from the mud. Netty's beloved brown teapot. Still intact.

He handed it to Charlie. She wiped it with her gloved hand, remembering happier times.

"It's something," she said. "Now we better get back. I'll need to change before I go to the hospital. You know what you have to do?"

Danny nodded. "Find Bert Marsh," he said.

The decision to involve Bert had brought on another argument but in the end, Danny had been forced to agree with Charlie that they needed an extra pair of hands. Bert could always decline and they would have to make do but Charlie had every confidence in him.

"Don't say a word to Joe."

"Of course not." Danny looked indignant. He huffed out a breath. "Nothing to be done here."

Charlie nodded. "I need to get back to work. Margaret will have been by herself all morning."

They walked the horses up the hill to the hospital, Charlie clutching the muddy teapot to her as if it was made of precious metal.

At the hospital gate they parted, Danny to return the horses to Johnny with the news that the livery stables had been completely washed away. Charlie made her way up the slope to her cottage to wash and change. Smoke curled from the chimney and she glanced through the front window to see Amos and Netty sitting by the fire. Netty, as always, had some sort of needlework in her hand and Amos dozed, his empty pipe between his teeth.

Charlie's heart clenched. She envied them their contentment. They might have lost everything but they still had each other.

She sat down on the bench outside the door and removed her soaking, muddy boots before venturing inside.

Netty was on her feet. "Charlie, lass, we were starting to worry."

Charlie handed her the teapot.

"I'm sorry, Netty. We checked on the cottage. I don't think there's much that can be salvaged and the cottage is irreparable."

Netty hugged the teapot to herself as she nodded. "I feared as much. We'll talk later. You need to get into something clean. The boy from the hospital has been up looking for you several times. Says that man Fitzgerald has been creating merry hell."

Charlie grimaced, her mind racing to all the issues over which Fitzgerald could create 'merry hell'. Her absence being the principal cause of his displeasure.

She washed and changed and, resisting Netty's offer of food, straightened her back and prepared to face whatever new torment Fitzgerald planned to inflict on her.

In the kitchen, she found Margaret Campbell helping Geraldine Ryan serve out the lunches.

The nurse looked up. "Thank heavens you're back. Fitzgerald is here," she said, "and he's not happy."

"Where is he?"

"The office. He's been in there all morning, writing his report."

She took a deep breath and knocked on the door to the doctor's office. Fitzgerald sat at the desk with its usual incumbent, Linacre, seated across from him.

"You wished to see me, Doctor Fitzgerald?" Charlie tried and failed to muster an ingratiating smile.

Linacre half rose as she entered. Fitzgerald remained seated.

"There you are, Sister," he said.

She ignored the intended slight.

"Yes, here I am," she said.

"And where have you been?"

"Attending a difficult birth at the Italian settlement on Wildman's Point."

"All night?" Fitzgerald quirked an eyebrow.

"It was a complicated birth and nearly two in the morning before I was satisfied mother and child were well. Too late to return to Maiden's Creek."

"It's a five-mile ride," Linacre put in, "and the road is treacherous at night at the best of times but particularly at the moment."

"But you got there in the dark?"

"We had an escort with a lantern who knew the road."

Fitzgerald's eyebrows shot up. "We?"

"Mr Hunt accompanied me to ensure my safety."

"Very gallant of him." Fitzgerald's acerbic tone made his thoughts on Danny's gallantry quite clear. "And where did the two of you sleep?"

"Not that I see it is any of your business, but we were accommodated by the community. You can check with Nico Alberti if you doubt me."

Fitzgerald looked down at the papers on the desk in front of him. "I have nearly concluded my report. I was just discussing my findings with my colleague here."

Linacre shifted in his seat and avoided Charlie's questioning gaze.

Fitzgerald cleared his throat. "In summary, Doctor Linacre... since my arrival I have been subjected to blatant insubordination from the matron and staff. The state of the hospital is appalling—filthy floors, leaking roof, lack of decent food. Patients absconding out of windows. There is a lack of discipline from the staff. The nurses' uniforms are a disgrace and the matron was out of uniform... shall I go on?"

"You—" Charlie bit back the profanity that rose to her lips.

"Matron!" Linacre all but shot out of his chair. "That won't help."

"I'll give you insubordination," Charlie continued, ignoring Linacre. She fixed her gaze on Fitzgerald. "You know exactly what pressure this hospital has been under this week. The whole town has been inundated with the worst flood in memory. Food supplies and communication chains are completely cut off and yet instead of writing how magnificently the hospital has managed with these privations, you turn it into a personal vendetta against me—"

"This is nothing to do with you. I just observe what I see."

"Doctor Fitzgerald, I must agree with Matron O'Reilly," Linacre said. "It is unfair to write a report based on this week's events—"

"I write what I see," Fitzgerald said, rising to his feet. "I will tender my report to your hospital board and it will be up to them to act on my recommendations. Now, if you will excuse me, I have arranged some sort of rudimentary transport out of this benighted town this afternoon and I need to pack."

Collecting his hat and coat, Fitzgerald walked out of the room, slamming the front door of the hospital behind him.

"Matron... your language... quite intemperate..." Linacre protested when they were alone.

"You're going to let him put in his report, knowing as well as I do exactly how unfair it is?" Charlie said, rounding on him.

Linacre spread his hands. "It's out of my control. I am one voice on the hospital board but you have my word that I will address the issues with the other members. Let's just see what the final report says before we leap to conclusions." He paused. "What did you mean about a personal vendetta?"

Charlie walked over to the window, trying to compose herself. She couldn't tell Linacre that Fitzgerald would be using his report to wreak his vengeance on her.

"We have encountered each other before," she said.

"That is unfortunate. All we can do is trust to his professionalism in this matter," Linacre said. "Mrs Alberti, is she doing all right?"

Charlie turned to face him. "She'll be fine."

"I'll ride out to the settlement in the next day or two and check on her. In the meantime, I suggest, Matron, that we do a round of the patients. At least he cannot criticize the exemplary care all our patients receive and we will say no more about the Fitzgerald report for the moment."

Charlie opened her mouth to defend herself but one look at Linacre's hard-set mouth and glittering eyes and she thought better of it. Linus Linacre had been banished from Sydney over a suspicious death. That made him as likely a suspect in the hospital deaths as anyone else.

After the rounds, they conferred in his office.

"It is good to see Martha has improved," Linacre said, "but I am concerned there is an underlying consumption. I'd like to have her sent down to the hospital in Sale when the rail opens again."

"I hope she is strong enough to give a statement to Sergeant Prewitt tomorrow."

Linacre paused in pulling on his gloves.

"A statement? What about?"

"She says she saw Janet Becker's killer on the night she died."

"Good Lord? Martha? Is she certain?"

Charlie nodded. "She may have some problems, doctor, but she is quite clear about what she saw."

"Did she say who it was?"

Charlie shrugged. "Matter for the police," she said.

She closed the door on Linacre and leaned against it. Danny was right—she was in enough trouble, and if her plan did not work no one was likely to thank her for what she planned to do that night.

FIFTY-ONE

C harlie stayed late to catch up with the two duty nurses, Roberts and Keegan. As they went through the handover details of each patient, they reached Martha Mackie and Charlie laid the groundwork of her plan to catch a killer.

"She's improved to the point where Doctor Linacre says she can be released tomorrow," Charlie lied.

"Released?" Mary Keegan looked up. "After all our hard work she can go back to drinking and who knows what else? Besides, where would she go? Her cottage is gone, washed away with the flood."

Charlie shook her head. "Not our concern, sister."

"It is if she comes back here again within a few days," Mary grumbled. "What is Linacre thinking?"

Charlie caught her breath. Now was the moment.

"Now she is sober and recovered, she will be able to provide a proper statement to the police about what she saw the night Janet died."

Lily Roberts frowned. "What do you mean?"

"Martha told me that she saw the person who murdered Janet Becker."

The two nurses looked at each other.

"Martha Mackie is not a reliable witness," Mary Keegan said. "Did she tell you who it was?"

"No, but she says she knows," Charlie lied. "I will get Sergeant Prewitt up here in the morning so she can tell him what she knows."

Mary Keegan sat back in her chair and folded her arms. "Just after the attention. You mark my words, she's just making it up."

Charlie shrugged. "Nevertheless, we have to take what she says seriously. Now, if you ladies will excuse me, my bed is calling me."

Charlie rose to her feet, pulled the blind on the kitchen window closed, bid the two nurses goodnight, and checked her arrangements were in order.

At her cottage, she found Netty serving the last of the kangaroo stew to Danny and Bert Marsh. It made for a crowd in such a small space.

"Are we set?" Danny asked.

"Yes," Charlie said, her pulse quickening at the thought of the night ahead.

"Do you know who it is?" Netty said.

Charlie shook her head. "Not really. I strongly suspect Mary Keegan... she seems to have been around the other deaths."

"But she was not on duty the night Janet Becker died," Danny pointed out.

"No, but there are ways to get into the hospital without being the one on duty," Charlie said.

"It could just as easily be a complete stranger," Amos said. "In which case tonight could be a waste of time."

"I don't approve," Netty added. "You could be putting yourself in danger, Charlie."

"Rather me than my patients," Charlie said.

"I don't like this," Netty said.

"Neither do I," Danny agreed.

Charlie sighed. "We've been through this, Danny. It is our only chance. No harm is going to come to Martha."

"I think it's grand," Bert said, spooning up the last of the stew. "Most exciting thing that's ever happened in Maiden's Creek."

Charlie gave him a withering glance, wondering if involving him had been a wise decision, but Amos couldn't help, and they needed an able-bodied man they could trust... that she could trust. Danny still seemed to harbor a certain reticence about the miner. As she knew from her first encounter with Flora Fraser, the childhood trauma of bullying was hard to shake, even in adulthood.

She changed into a dark skirt and blouse. The men were also wearing dark clothing and Bert produced a pair of unsavory woollen caps for them to wear. Danny's lip curled as he held the distasteful object between thumb and forefinger before cramming it on to his head with a grimace.

Without a light the three of them crept with care down to the hospital. In a way it was a mercy that Alf's crib had been destroyed in the mudslide. He'd taken up temporary residence with his sister down in the town, which left no one on site as a casual observer and with the blind on the kitchen window drawn, any comings or goings via the courtyard would be unobserved.

Just to be certain, Charlie crept over to the kitchen window and in the narrow gap between the blind and the frame she could see both nurses sitting by the fire. Lily Roberts was knitting and Keegan was dozing.

She had left the window to Martha Mackie's room off the latch and Danny slid the sash window up. It rolled easily and without much noise. Hoisting her skirts, with Danny's help, she climbed over the windowsill, landing softly.

Martha stirred in her sleep.

"What's happening?" she asked blearily.

"It's me, Charlie," she said.

Martha sat up, clutching the bedclothes to her. "I thought you were the..."

"We're just going to move you up to my cottage for the night," Charlie whispered.

"Why?"

"I need the bed. Now don't make a sound."

Martha seemed to accept Charlie's word and cooperated with Charlie as she bundled her up in a blanket with warm stockings on her feet and helped her across to the window where Bert waited. As they maneuvered Martha over the sill, Bert took the woman in his arms.

They had been over the plan several times and there was no need for any conversation. Bert's role was to carry Martha up to Charlie's cottage where Netty would look after her. He would return to keep watch for anyone coming up from the town and to stay close enough to hear any cries for assistance.

Danny slid across the windowsill into the room and Charlie shut the window, leaving it open far enough to allow Bert access via that route if he was needed. Before she'd left that night, she had moved a chair behind a screen in the corner of the room and Danny took his place out of sight of the door as Charlie pulled an old nightdress over her clothes and donned a nightcap to hide her dark hair.

She slid into the bed, still warm from Martha's body. All they had to do now was watch and wait.

After a long, hard night and day, Charlie dozed but her nurse's instincts had her instantly awake as a floorboard outside the room creaked. She turned to face the door, curled in a sleeping position, watching through half-closed lids as the door opened and a figure only distinguishable as a darker shade of black slipped inside the room, closing the door with the faintest of clicks.

Charlie held her breath as the shape took substance. Someone wearing a long dark coat and a felt hat pulled down low. In the gloom it was impossible to tell gender or height and they made no sound, as if they crept toward her on stockinged feet.

The killer had taken the bait.

Her heart beat a rapid tattoo in her chest, and her stomach churned as she saw a flash of white and realized that the assailant had been carrying a pillow behind their back.

She just had time to scream "Danny!" before the pillow came down on her face and was held there with astonishing strength. She grabbed at her assailant's gloved hands, raking her nails at her assailants hands in a desperate bid to remove the suffocating pillow.

The world started to go black.

Dimly, she heard Danny's voice and another man... Bert? Scuffling and the crack of fist on bone. A woman screamed and quite suddenly the weight on top of her had gone.

She threw the pillow off her face and sat up, gasping for breath.

"You took your time," she railed at Danny and Bert, both of whom were on the floor, holding down a slender figure in a long black coat who writhed and fought their grip.

Danny looked up at her. "Are you all right?"

Charlie took a deep, thankful breath and nodded.

"The honor's yours," Danny said.

Charlie jumped from the bed and pulled the felt hat from her assailant's head. Of all the people she had suspected of the crimes... Keegan or even Linus Linacre... the last person on her list was the woman who stared defiantly at her.

Lily Roberts.

The two men wrestled the struggling, swearing woman to the chair and secured her there with a length of rope Bert had brought with him.

With shaking fingers, Charlie lit the kerosene lamp that stood on the mantlepiece.

Only when they were certain Lily was secure, did they step back and stand together looking at Janet Becker's murderer.

"Lily. Why?" It was all Charlie could think of to say.

Lily responded by attempting to spit at them, but it was a futile gesture. She raised her chin, her hot, angry eyes going from one to the other, but she remained silent.

Danny looked at Bert Marsh. "Fetch Prewitt and tell him he'll need at least one of his constables, the burlier the better."

He wiped blood from a long scratch on his cheek and leaned against the wall beside the door. From the pocket he pulled out the Colt revolver.

"Planning to shoot me, were you?" Lily said.

Charlie stared at the weapon. "I didn't know you had that with you. Is it loaded?"

Danny met her gaze.

"Just in case," he said.

She took a breath and pulled the nightdress off. "I'm going to check on Mary Keegan."

In the kitchen, she found Keegan sound asleep, her head back and a dribble of spittle running from her mouth. She checked the woman's pulse and concluded that she must have been drugged. The nurses' cups had been washed and were neatly stacked by the sink.

Charlie leaned on the table, her soul crushed by the revelation of the night. She had badly misjudged Mary Keegan and failed to see the killer behind Lily Roberts' cherubic smile. Lily, who had been on duty on all but one of the nights Martha had seen her deal out death to her innocent victims.

She had also been on duty the night Archie Fraser had come so close to death. The thought sent a chill down Charlie's spine. Had Roberts been interrupted in her work?

She checked on the patients and found them all sleeping. Bertie Campbell was snoring in tune with the miner in the bed next to him. Probably drugged too, she thought. Satisfied that they were all well, she returned to Lily.

Some of the defiance had gone from the woman. She looked like a trapped animal, her eyes darting around the room, looking for escape but there was none to be found. Charlie crossed her arms and stood looking down at the killer.

"Well?" she said.

Lily took a shuddering breath.

"Is it true what you said about Martha seeing Janet's killer that night?"

"Yes," Charlie said, "and she saw you the night you smothered the baby."

Lily's lip curled. "But can she be sure it was me?"

Charlie shrugged. The answer was no... all Martha saw was a figure in a black coat and hat, but Lily didn't need to know that.

"I would like to know why you took the patients' lives, Lily."

Lily looked away. "It's what we did to animals that were suffering— on the farm at the orphanage. We ended their suffering. That's all I was doing."

"You are not God, Lily," Charlie said, fighting the urge to rail at the woman. She had killed an innocent baby and an old woman, and those were just the ones she knew of. How many others had there been over Lily's career as a nurse?

"What about Janet Becker? She wasn't ill, she wasn't suffering."

Lily's gaze dropped to the floor and Charlie thought she detected a tear. "That was an accident."

"Was it? What happened?"

Lily sniffed. "She guessed. She was on duty the one night I took the risk of helping the old woman on her way. It may have been something I said to her. She was my friend, we used to talk."

"But I am guessing that you drugged the nurse who was on duty with you, like you drugged Sister Keegan tonight, when you planned to..." She struggled for the words and decided to be blunt, "...murder your patients."

Lily flinched. "I don't murder, I help them on their way to God."

Charlie let that pass.

"And Archie Fraser?"

Lily's gaze slid away, but she said nothing.

"What happened to Janet Becker?"

"I wasn't planning on anything that night. Janet and me were talking in the kitchen, just like we always did. Then she turned on me. Said she had worked it out. She knew I had been helping people on their way. She wanted money. I don't have any money, Matron. She accused me of stealing from the people I helped, but I don't. I'm not a thief. I'm doing the Lord's work."

Charlie heard boots on the floorboards outside the room. She had left the door ajar, and the back of her neck prickled, hoping it was the law that had stopped to listen to the conversation.

"Go on."

"Janet was my friend but she was saying awful things, calling me a murderer. I... I just wanted her to be quiet. She turned her back on me so I picked up one of the saucepans and hit her. I didn't mean to kill her but she was dead. I didn't know what to do. She was just lying there on the kitchen floor."

"How many times did you hit her?"

Lily hesitated, looking up at the ceiling. "Three," she said. "She stopped moving after the third time. I heard Joe's owl call so I snuffed the light and he went away. I didn't know what to do, so I sat for a long time just looking at her and crying because she was my friend. Then I thought maybe I could make it look like she done herself in, so I carried her outside and put her in the wheelbarrow and wheeled her round to the front of the building where you found her. A ladder, some rope, and that's where I left her, only I didn't think it through, did I? I should have realized someone smart would realize she hadn't hoisted herself into the tree by herself."

"Or that she had died from a heavy blow to the back of her head," Charlie said.

The door creaked open, and Bert stood there with a disheveled Sergeant Prewitt. The policeman looked like he had been dragged from his bed and the confused expression on his face told her that he was still processing Lily's confession.

Charlie turned to look at them. "Sergeant Prewitt. You heard?"

The policeman nodded. "Miss Roberts, I'm arresting you for the murder of Janet Becker."

"You can add in the attempted murder of myself and at least two patients in the hospital."

Prewitt scratched his unshaven chin. "We'll have to see about that. Right now, I better get this young woman down to the cells."

He summoned his constable, and they removed Lily Roberts.

Charlie woke Mary Keegan but the drugs had left the woman groggy so Charlie suggested she take a bed in the women's ward.

"I'll have to stand duty for the rest of the night," she told Danny as they sat in the kitchen. She would have given her soul for something stronger than tea, but it would have to do.

"You're exhausted, Charlie," Danny said.

She smiled. "Thank you for your concern, Danny, but I'm used to it." She paused. "We did a good thing tonight."

"I'm just surprised it worked," Danny said.

"So am I," Charlie conceded. "And I am so relieved Joe is no longer under suspicion. Speaking of Joe, you can go back to your own bed at the Britannia."

Danny sat back and crossed his arms. "I'm not leaving you here alone."

"That is very gallant of you, but there is no need." Her words belied her impulse to throw her arms around his neck and thank him from the bottom of her heart. She didn't want to be alone in the sleeping hospital.

Charlie ran a hand across her eyes.

"I'm down to two nurses now. I'm don't know what we are going to do."

"That is a problem for the morning, Charlie."

He reached across the table and curled his fingers around hers. She returned the pressure momentarily before standing up in response to the thin wail of a tiny baby.

"I'll just check on Sally's baby. If you want, you can use the day bed and grab some sleep yourself."

"I might just put my feet up for a few minutes," Danny said.

When Charlie returned from seeing to Sally, Danny was sound asleep. She found a blanket and laid it over him, taking a moment to brush the hair from his eyes.

A wave of disappointment and apprehension washed over her.

Now that the problem of Joe was solved, Danny was free to leave Maiden's Creek, and she would be alone again.

Fifty-Two

After the drama of the previous night, Danny found himself unable to settle to anything constructive. He spent the afternoon helping Yorkie and Joe clean the mud from the hotel. They had tried bailing the water from the cellar but had given up for the time being as patrons started drifting back to the bar.

The afternoon being both fine and sunny, he changed into clean clothes and strolled up to the hospital to visit Bertie. He had nothing to take to his friend. Every book in the Mechanics Institute library had been lost in the flood and reduced to a large pile of sodden, stinking paper in the backyard of the Institute. As a writer and lover of books, it broke his heart and he made a quiet resolution to see the library restored.

He found Bertie in a filthy mood.

"What is going on around here?" he demanded. "No one tells me anything. Even my own bloody sister says she's too busy to stop and talk. Is it true that one of the nurses has been killing patients in their beds? What sort of hospital is this?"

Rare anger flashed in Danny's chest. "A very good one. You are lucky to be here."

"Bill Fitzgerald asked me my opinion of the hospital and I was only too happy to share the appalling treatment I have received," Bertie said.

Danny was under no illusion about Bertie's thoughts on the hospital and, with a sinking heart, he knew it would reflect badly on Charlie.

"Did you? I hope you realize that he will be taking every poor opinion you expressed and exaggerating it. This is your sister's livelihood you are talking about."

Bertie glared. "I don't give a damn. The family wants Margaret out of here." He glanced around the ward at his fellow patients. "I say, is there somewhere we can talk? I've got to get out of this damn bed."

Danny, now thoroughly familiar with the hospital, found a wicker wheelchair of some antiquity in a storeroom.

"Where are you going with that?" Margaret intercepted him in the corridor.

"I'm going to take your brother outside for some fresh air."

"Good. You can tip him down the hill if you like. We're all fed up with his moaning."

"Is Char... Matron in this afternoon?" Danny asked.

"She is busy with a birth," Margaret said. "I'm here by myself for the moment. Do you need a hand with Bertie?"

Between the two of them, they got Bertie out of bed and into the wheelchair with his leg propped up on a frame in front of him. Swaddling his friend in blankets, Danny wheeled him out onto the verandah.

Bertie took a deep breath of air. "You've got to get me out of here, Danny. What with murderers stalking the corridors and the like—"

"Tempting as it is, you are quite safe, Campbell. We caught the killer."

Bertie settled back. "Tell me all about it and don't spare the details. I'm dying of boredom."

Danny related the story of the plot to catch the murderer. In daylight it sounded even more harebrained than it had when Charlie first proposed it. But it had worked.

"I'm impressed," Bertie said. "Never thought of you as the heroic type."

"Thanks," Danny said with heavy sarcasm.

"I rather liked that Sister Roberts. Better than that sour-faced Irish woman or my sister," Bertie said at last.

"As soon as they get the train running again, we'll see what we can do about moving you back to Melbourne," Danny said.

"If I could move out of this chair, I would kiss you. You don't happen to have a smoke?"

Danny had come prepared with Bertie's tobacco pouch and he rolled them both cigarettes. Bertie took a deep, thankful draw on the tobacco, watching the smoke curl into the air.

"And this bloke, Joe Whatsit from the pub, he's in the clear?"

"Yes. Dependent of course, on the inquest."

"He struck me as a bit slow."

"That goes to show you are no judge of people, Campbell."

The subject of Joe prompted another thought. Danny took a final drag of the cigarette, coughed, and ground the stub under his heel.

"What were you intending to do with the mace?" Danny asked.

Bertie choked on some smoke. "How do you... how could you possibly...?"

"Joe found where you hid it in the cellar. I haven't been able to get it out because the cellar is still flooded."

Bertie rolled his eyes. "I've been trying to think of a way to tell you about it. It wasn't supposed to be left down there. I was going back to get it the night after we got back from our excursion to the river."

"Why did you hide it down there?"

"I didn't think it was a good idea having it in my luggage," Bertie said. "Can't trust hotel staff."

"So you brought it all the way from Melbourne with you? Why?"

Bertie shrugged. "I thought I could drop it down an old mine or something."

"What an idiotic plan. Are you going to tell me how you came to have it at all?"

Bertie pulled a face. "It was a stupid drunken wager one night at Madame Brussels. Madame had set a scavenger hunt, and top of the list was the mace. We had to meet back in a few days with our haul. I knew the engineer at Parliament House, and I also knew he needed a bit of money, so I paid him to steal the bloody thing."

"I read the reports of him being interviewed, but they didn't find anything at his house."

"Of course they didn't. I had it. I won the scavenger hunt and we had some fun and games with the damn thing but once the hue and cry went up I realized I was going to be in serious trouble. Do you know how hard it is to hide a five-foot mace? I chopped it up and it was still huge. It's been hidden under a spare bed at home but Ma was talking about visitors, so I thought I would bring it out here and quietly lose it in the bush somewhere."

"You could just as easily have dropped it in the Yarra."

"I was being watched. Rumors of the shenanigans at Madame Brussels had begun to get around, and Tommy Bent had the police on us. I had to get it away from Melbourne. Seemed like a good idea at the time." He stubbed out the cigarette and looked at Danny. "What are you going to do? Hand me in to the authorities?"

"Don't tempt me," Danny said. "Tommy Bent is not too happy and you're right, he has you pegged as the chief suspect in the case."

Bertie swore. "If Dad finds out, he'll probably disinherit me." He gave Danny a sharp look. "Were you sent to spy on me?"

Danny ignored the question. "Given everything that's happened over the past week, the fate of the mace seems relatively trivial."

"It doesn't feel trivial. Your mate has already discovered it."

Danny shrugged. "Its disappearance has already taken on a mythic element. It seems to me it makes a better story if its fate remains a mystery. What do you suggest I do with it?"

"Lose it. I don't want to cart it back to Melbourne or get you and your mate into trouble." Bertie's shoulders slumped. "It's one of the reasons I've been so edgy. I had visions of it being discovered and police swarming all over the town."

"The police have enough to do. Leave it with me, Bertie." Danny stood up. "Now let's get inside, it's cold out here."

On his return to the Britannia, he met Charlie toiling up the hill with her leather bag clutched in her hand.

"Everything all right at the hospital?" she asked.

"Seems to be."

"Babies are no respecters of overworked staff. The good news is I have someone to assist Mary Keegan on night duty tonight. Ellen Bushby recommended a woman who used to do some nursing down in Melbourne. I've just been to see her and she jumped at the chance of earning some money." She let out a sigh. "Now that the telegraph is working again, we can get some advertisements in the papers for replacement nursing staff." Her face softened. "I've just seen the postmaster. The telegram's gone to Janet's parents, and the undertaker tells me she'll be buried tomorrow. I just have to speak to the Church of England minister."

"Word at the pub is the train will be running again by early next week," Danny said.

Her mouth quirked. "Does that mean you will be leaving?"

He hesitated. There were so many things he wanted to say, but in reality there was only one answer.

"Yes."

She nodded. "Maiden's Creek will be quiet without you."

"Oh, I don't know, the stampers will be up and running soon enough."

She laughed and the warmth of her smile lit the sparks of the fire he had been fighting for days. He fought back the desire to take her in his arms and kiss her there in the middle of the day in the middle of the town, but he resisted, thrusting his hands into his coat pocket.

"I'll see you at the inquest tomorrow," he said.

And they parted. He turned to watch her until she turned the corner by the church and disappeared from view.

On his return to the Britannia, he went looking for Joe. "Can we get into the cellar?" he asked.

Joe blew out a breath. "Water's still about knee deep. Why?"

"That package you found belongs to my friend. I need to retrieve it."

Joe nodded. "I'll get it for you."

Danny looked around. There were a few hardy souls in the bar, but the last of the beer had gone, and the alternative offerings were beyond the pocket of most working men.

He nodded. "If you don't mind."

"After what you've done for me, Mr Hunt, it is no trouble at all."

Danny lingered by the door of the cellar, waiting for Joe to re-emerge, barefooted and his trousers wet well past the knee. He carried a bulky package wrapped in sodden hessian.

"Sorry, it's a bit damp," he said.

Danny carried it upstairs and set it on the table. One end had been peeled away, revealing the silver head of the mace. No wonder Joe had thought his fortune was made.

He concealed it as far under his bed as he could push it, locked the doors and picked up his pen to draft telegrams to Melbourne, one arranging for the return of Bertie Campbell and the other to his parents advising that he would be bringing Netty and Amos with him when he came home.

But first, he had to decide what to do with the mace of the Victorian parliament.

FIFTY-THREE

Despite the stained and warped panelling and other obvious damage from the flood coupled with an overwhelming smell of mildew and mold, the hall at the Mechanics Institute was packed for the inquest into the death of Miss Janet Mary Becker, nurse at the Maiden's Creek District Hospital.

Lily Roberts had been brought in from the police cells, still dressed in her nurse's uniform, now bedraggled and stained from two nights' incarceration.

Charlie sat with Martha Mackie. Netty had done her best and Martha, pale and thin and still wracked with her cough, was dressed neatly, her shorn hair concealed beneath a hat and a hairnet. Martha clutched Charlie's hand with a strength that belied her frail frame.

Charlie nodded a greeting to Danny, who had dressed for the day in his city clothes. He looked every inch the city lawyer, prepared to go in to fight for Joe Trevelyan.

Proceedings commenced with Mr. Sloan presiding in his role of magistrate and coroner, and Sergeant Prewitt presenting the evidence.

Alf gave his evidence of seeing Joe at the hospital. Joe then took the stand and, guided by Danny, admitted to going up to the hospital where Janet Becker hadn't come out to meet him and he had returned home without seeing her.

When Martha's turn came, she gave her evidence in a thin, raspy voice. Yes, she had seen a figure in a long, black coat and hat hang the body of the nurse from the tree. The small details she remembered gave strength to her testimony and when Sergeant Prewitt held up the coat and hat Lily Roberts had been wearing the night she was arrested, Martha was adamant they were indeed the garments she had seen the killer wearing.

Danny interjected to ask if the person she had seen was Joe Trevelyan. Martha squared her shoulders, looked the magistrate in the eye and said that the person she had seen did not have a limp and could not have been Joe.

When it came to Charlie's turn, her stomach churned and she glanced at Danny. He gave her a reassuring smile and she steeled herself for the questioning.

Prewitt began by asking her what had led to the suspicion that there was something untoward happening within the hospital. Charlie had been through the records and had identified eight cases where the death of the patients had been unexpected. While she couldn't swear that any of them had been caused by Lily Roberts, she noted that Sister Roberts had been on duty the nights the deaths occurred.

This brought the proceedings to the events that had led to Lily Roberts' arrest.

"Why choose that night?" Prewitt asked.

"By that time I was convinced that someone within the hospital was responsible for the death of Janet Becker," Charlie said. "And the only way I could prove it was to catch them in the act."

Prewitt then asked her to recount the events of Lily's arrest. Charlie took a deep breath and told the court about the pillow over her face. "I was only saved by the intervention of Mr. Hunt and Mr. Marsh," she concluded.

Danny and Bert Marsh were called and both corroborated Charlie's evidence about Lily's confession.

At the conclusion of the evidence, the magistrate sat back, his fingers steepled.

He cleared his throat. "It is my finding that Janet Mary Becker died somewhere about midnight between the fifth and sixth of August at the hand of Miss Roberts. However," the magistrate leaned forward, his gaze on Charlie, "I cannot condone the method employed to catch Miss Roberts. Miss O'Reilly's actions were foolhardy and could well have resulted in her own demise or injury, had it not been for the intervention of a third party."

Charlie's stomach lurched. The public rebuke took her back to schooldays and the unfairness of the allegation against her, for which she could mount no defense. She met the magistrate's hard gaze, but she could feel the color rising to her cheeks as the eyes of the audience bored into her back.

But Sloan had moved on. "It is a matter for the prosecution as to whether they pursue an attempted murder charge in respect of the assault on Miss O'Reilly and the further investigation into the other deaths Miss O'Reilly referred to in her evidence. I therefore recommend Miss Roberts be conveyed to Melbourne at the earliest opportunity, Sergeant. Thank you for your attendance and it is a relief to put this unfortunate matter behind us."

After a good morning's entertainment, the crowd filed into the street. Netty took charge of Martha and led her away. Martha had to be returned to the hospital, and her future did not look promising. Doctor Linacre had reached the conclusion that she had succumbed to tuberculosis, and he was making arrangements to have her transferred to a sanatorium. Danny had agreed to pay the cost of her ongoing care, but with that diagnosis and Martha's frailty they all knew it was unlikely she would see another winter.

Charlie joined Danny and they stood watching as Lily Roberts was led from the room to the accompaniment of boos and jeers.

Accompanied by Bert Marsh, Joe Trevelyan joined them.

Bert Marsh clapped Danny on the shoulder.

"I knew you could do it," he said.

"I didn't do much—" Danny began.

"You got Joe off the hook and that would never have happened if it had been up to old Prewitt."

"How do I thank you—" Joe began but Danny raised his hand.

"You have good friends, Joe. Now you can grieve for Janet and decide what you want to do with the rest of your life."

Joe shrugged. "This is all I know, Danny. It was one thing to dream when I had someone to dream with, but I don't think I've the courage, or the money, to go to Melbourne now. Yorkie needs me, and," he shrugged, "life here isn't so bad." He looked at Bert. "And I do have good friends."

Bert Marsh looked from Danny to Charlie and a slow grin creased the corners of his eyes. "You and Charlie O'Reilly here make quite a team."

An unaccustomed flush of heat rose to Charlie's face and she couldn't meet Danny's eyes.

Bert flung an arm around Joe's shoulder. "Let's go and have a drink, Joe. Celebrate your release."

Joe shook his head. "Another time, Bert. They're burying Janet in an hour, and I want to be there."

Mr. Sloan walked out of the doors to the hall, papers tucked under his arm. He looked up and down the street and, seeingCharlie,e he walked over to her. She greeted him with a smile that was not returned.

Ignoring the others, he said, "Matron O'Reilly, a word if you please."

He gestured her back inside the hall and into the now-empty library.

"I have summoned a meeting of the hospital board," Sloan said. "Tomorrow morning at ten in the morning. We expect your attendance."

"May I ask what the meeting will be about?"

He fixed her with a cold, hard gaze. "Your future. Until tomorrow, Matron."

He turned and left her standing in the musty room.

Charlie hunched her shoulders. She'd been in trouble so many times that she recognized the tenor of the meeting would not be pleasant.

"What was that about?" Danny said when she rejoined him.

She shook her head and managed a watery smile. "Just hospital business. Sloan is chairman of the board."

"What would we do without the Sloans of the world," Danny said without amusement. "I heard some good news this morning. The train will resume on Monday. Means we can get Bertie Campbell out of your hair."

And it meant Danny Hunt would be leaving Maiden's Creek, Charlie thought.

Danny glanced at his watch. "It's almost time for the funeral. Are you coming?"

Charlie nodded, and they walked slowly down Main Street toward the cemetery.

"You know, we do make a good team," Danny said.

She looked up at him. She'd seen a different man today. In his city clothes, every inch the lawyer. So polished, so sure of himself. In a few days he would be on a train back to Melbourne and she would be forgotten as the tendrils of his real life closed back around him.

"We do," she said.

"In a foolhardy kind of way," Danny said with a smile.

"That's a bit harsh," Charlie responded. "We caught a killer."

"There is that," he said with a shrug.

They reached the path leading to the cemetery. Charlie looked up at the little crowd already gathering at the gate. "Too late for Janet Becker and too late for the others she helped on their way to God. Will she hang?"

Danny shrugged. "I suspect a good lawyer would mount a defense of insanity. She may not hang but she will certainly spend the rest of her life locked away."

"I don't know what would be worse," Charlie said.

In the meantime she had not only her own future to consider, but that of the hospital. They were now short of two qualified nurses, the hospital was close to unworkable and she had to face the hospital board in the morning.

———

The sheer amount of water that had run off the hill above it had badly damaged the Maiden's Creek cemetery, cutting channels and holes in the pathways, even to the extent of washing the soil from the most recent graves. Mud clung to Danny's city boots and the bottoms of his trousers as he and Charlie picked their way to the row of five freshly dug graves that gaped darkly to the wintry sunshine.

In addition to the nurse, there were four victims of the flood to be buried that afternoon, and a sizeable crowd gathered in groups scattered around the cemetery. The Church of England minister had the grim task of conducting all but one of the burials, and Danny felt that the man rushed through the interment of Janet Becker in his haste to get the grim task done.

Charlie stood with an arm around Joe Trevelyan, who wept openly and without reserve for the girl he had loved and with whom he had planned his future. Yorkie stood on the other side of him, stoically upright but with one hand on Joe's shoulder.

Danny glanced up at his father's headstone in its lonely corner.

Who had attended his funeral? Who had wept for him? No one, he suspected.

He glanced across at Charlie, conscious that she was watching him. He saw understanding in her eyes, and his heart clenched. How could he just walk away from this woman he had shared so much with in the past few days? But he had a very different life to return to, one he saw now, all too clearly, had lacked direction and purpose.

Things would be different from now on. His brothers in the law called him St. Jude for taking on lost causes, but from now on, he would do whatever was in his not inconsiderable power to see some sort of system was established to ensure the Joe Trevelyans of the world did not face the injustices of the legal system alone.

FIFTY-FOUR

SATURDAY 13 AUGUST

Charlie dressed carefully for her interview with the hospital board, ensuring that she had not a hair out of place and her uniform was clean and crisp, but she had seen her future in Councillor Sloan's cold eyes and knew that a decision had already been made. Whatever picture she presented would not change the outcome.

In the hospital kitchen, Margaret Campbell avoided Charlie's eye as she said, "They're waiting for you in the doctor's office."

Before Charlie could ask her any more, the bell to the women's ward rang and Margaret hurried away.

The hospital board members were gathered behind the desk, an echo of the day little over a month ago when she had been interviewed for the post. Sloan sat in the middle with Doctor Linacre to his left and Mrs Crabtree to his right.

Linus Linacre stared fixedly at the desk as Sloan directed her to the single chair facing them. From the grim faces confronting her, the air crackled with tension.

Charlie greeted them with a smile and did as she was told, sitting straight, her hands neatly folded in her lap, presenting, she hoped, a picture of professional competence.

Behind her corset, her heart thumped and her stomach churned.

Don't let them see your fear.

"You know why you're here?"

Charlie met his gaze. "I have some notion but please put your case."

Sloan held up a sheaf of handwritten papers. Even across the desk, Charlie recognized Fitzgerald's writing.

"We have the report from the inspector," he said and slammed the papers down on the desk in a move that made everyone start.

He leaned his elbows on the desk and clasped his hands as he leaned forward.

"We are fully aware of the exigencies under which the hospital operated during the inspector's visit and in other circumstances we would be prepared to treat its recommendation with some reservations. However, Matron, what we find difficult to comprehend are your willful actions of Wednesday night and your willingness to put not only a patient's life at risk but your own."

Charlie swallowed. "There was a killer in the hospital," she said. "What would you have me do?"

"Discuss the matter with Doctor Linacre and ourselves."

Charlie glanced at Linacre, and to her surprise he answered for her. "Matron O'Reilly quite possibly considered me a suspect in the case. All the deceased were, after all, my patients. Am I correct, Matron?"

Charlie forced herself to meet his hard gaze. He had been a suspect. She couldn't deny it.

She cleared her throat. "I just knew whoever it was had to be someone inside the hospital," she said. "The killing had to stop."

Sloan shook his head. "Matron, I don't know what to think. It is fortunate that your foolhardy plan had a favorable outcome, but this willful disregard of our position and authority cannot be tolerated." He looked at his two fellow board members. "I am afraid we have no alternative but to relieve you of your duties."

Even though she had been expecting dismissal, following the tenor of their brief conversation the previous day, his words went to her stomach like a fist. She stared at the clock on the mantlepiece behind him, hardly comprehending the enormity of what he was saying and hoping she wouldn't disgrace herself with tears.

"Matron?"

She brought her attention back to the three people confronting her.

"When do you want me to leave?" she asked, her voice high and tight with the effort of suppressing the tears that welled behind her eyes.

"Your termination is effective immediately," Sloan said. "We expect you will return to Melbourne on the first train."

"And in the circumstances, we are unable to provide a reference," Mrs Crabtree put in.

Charlie blinked. "No reference?"

Linacre half rose to his feet. "Colleagues, I have said this to you privately and I will now say it in her presence. Matron O'Reilly and I have not seen eye to eye in a couple of cases, but she has brought something to this hospital, to this town, that was sorely needed—professionalism and a genuine concern for our patients. How many more people would have died in our care if Roberts had not been caught, beginning with Martha Mackie? She didn't endanger Martha's life, she saved her." He turned to Charlie. "Matron, if the board won't give you a reference, I certainly will."

Charlie looked up at him. "Thank you, Doctor Linacre." Her voice sounded dangerously near cracking.

"Your comments are noted," Sloan's voice dripped ice. "Matron, I am conscious that you are giving shelter to displaced persons in your cottage and we are not completely without heart. You may remain in the cottage until you leave. After that your friends will have to make other plans for themselves."

Charlie swallowed, taking a deep breath as she composed herself. She would not give them the satisfaction of faltering.

"While I appreciate your wish to be rid of me, could I just point out that the hospital is desperately short staffed. We have lost two nurses in the space of a week, which means we only have one qualified nurse for each shift. I have arranged an assistant for the night shift but my plan was for me to provide the coverage on the day shift."

"We have sent to Sale for temporary replacement staff and in the meantime effective immediately, Sister Margaret Campbell will be appointed matron. She will have to make do with the staff she has available."

"An appointment we should have made in the first place," Mrs Crabtree put in, "had it not been for the insistence of Matron Birch."

Charlie felt nothing. Her mind and body had gone numb. Their voices receded into the distance, and she was once again a small child facing an injustice that was not of her making. She half expected one of them to produce a tawse and ask her to hold out her hand.

She rose to her feet with an abruptness that caused the chair to totter uncertainly. "If there is nothing else," she said. "Please excuse me. I am sure you wish to brief Matron Campbell on her responsibilities."

Unsurprisingly, she all but bumped into Margaret Campbell in the hall outside, and the look on her face told Charlie the woman had been listening at the door.

"Charlie, I—" Margaret began

"Don't say a word," Charlie said, fumbling with the keys on her belt. "You'll need these." She thrust the heavy bunch of keys at Margaret and turned and walked away with as much dignity as she could muster. She couldn't bear for the other woman to see the tears that welled in her eyes.

She walked over to the paddock and leaned on the fence, breathing hard to steady her emotions as she watched Amos's horses peacefully grazing. Old Sam ambled over to her and pushed her with his soft nose.

"Sorry, old chap," she said. "I don't have anything for you."

She ran a hand down his long nose and buried her face in his neck. The scent of horse was oddly soothing.

"Miss O'Reilly!"

She inwardly flinched at the sound of her name and straightened, turning to see Linacre striding across the grass towards her.

"Miss O'Reilly, I'm sorry. That was badly done."

Charlie swallowed, hoping the man did not see the tears in her eyes.

"This posting meant a great deal to me, doctor."

Linacre looked down at the toe of his boot. "I do understand, probably better than you think. I am sure you heard stories of what happened in Sydney and I owe you an explanation. I made a mistake... a bad mistake, and a wealthy and influential patient died. It was suggested it would be prudent for me to leave for a while, so I did, leaving my wife and children behind." He swallowed. "It has been a long and lonely year, but I am fortunate to have formed a friendship with a good woman, a widow, and on those occasions I have been somewhat hard to locate, I have been with her."

So that explained his absences and the smell of perfume. The alcohol was probably habitual.

"I am not proud of myself, but my wife has made it clear she does not want me to return to the family home, so I too have been cast adrift. You are without doubt one of the most talented and professional nurses I have ever worked with," Linacre continued. "I know you and I did not agree on a couple of occasions, but I want you to know that Maiden's Creek will be poorer for your departure."

She managed a watery smile. "Thank you, doctor, that means a great deal to me." She held out her hand. "I really do mean it," she said.

He took her hand and gave it a firm, peremptory shake. He was a man not given to extending praise or compliments, and she knew what it had cost him to speak up for her.

He bobbed his head, turned, and walked away.

A chill gust of wind blew down the valley, and Charlie wrapped her arms around herself, shivering in the cold. She had to swallow her pride and face Margaret Campbell with whatever dignity she could muster.

She found Margaret in the matron's office, looking through the paperwork. She looked up as Charlie entered without knocking.

"I am so sorry," Margaret said. "It is monstrously unfair after everything you have done."

Charlie shrugged. "They were right. I acted recklessly, and I should have consulted them." She managed a wry smile. "I've never been good with authority. I suggest that I accompany your brother back to Melbourne when the train is running, and we can make arrangements for him."

Margaret nodded. "That sounds like an excellent suggestion," she said, straightening. "I'll make the arrangements. If he's travelling with you, we won't need to get a nurse up from Melbourne."

"I am staying on at the cottage until I leave."

"I think that's the least they could do," Margaret said.

"I shall expect to hear what arrangements you have made with respect to your brother. Until then—"

The word 'matron' stuck in her throat and she turned on her heel.

FIFTY-FIVE

B reaking the news of her dismissal to Amos and Netty provoked outrage from her friends, and it was all she could do to prevent Netty from marching down to the bank and giving Mr Sloan a piece of her mind.

"It will accomplish nothing and just make a bad situation worse," Charlie said firmly. "And for now, please don't say a word to anyone. As far as I am concerned my priority is to work out what to do with you. Once I've gone, you can't stay here."

Netty's shoulders slumped and she looked at Amos. "We've decided we'll be taking up Adelaide and Caleb Hunt's offer of a cottage on their property out of Mansfield. Adelaide's asked often enough and we've nothing to hold us here now except sentiment."

"There are nicer places in the world to be sentimental about," Charlie said. "I believe Mansfield is quite lovely."

"It's still close to the mountains and Amos will have proper space for his horses," Netty said. "Don't you fret about Amos and me, we'll be fine. We've nowt to keep us here except the horses, and Amos can make any arrangements for those with young Johnny."

"Old Sam's coming with us," Amos said. "The others will find buyers easily enough."

Charlie asked how Amos proposed to move the large, old horse from Maiden's Creek to Mansfield.

"Johnny can bring him over the mountains when the weather fines up," Amos said. "I'd like to see the lad right, and there's always work for a good horse handler."

"It's you, lass, what are you going to do?" Netty said.

Charlie shrugged. "I don't know. I don't want to go back to working in a big city hospital," she said. "Perhaps it's time I looked at the opportunities for a qualified nursing sister, maybe in outback Queensland."

Netty's face could have been framed as a picture of disgust.

"Queensland? It's hot and dusty and uncomfortable. You're a mountain girl. You'd hate it."

Charlie laughed. "Thank you for your faith in me, Netty. I go where I am needed and if it's the outback of Queensland then so be it."

Netty studied her. "You're needed here, lass, but they're too blind to see it."

Any further discussion of Charlie's future was curtailed by a rap on the door.

Netty opened the door to admit Danny. His gaze went straight to Charlie, and she forced a smile.

"Charlie? I thought you would be at the hospital."

"No," Charlie said rather more sharply than she intended. "I'm not needed."

He looked her up and down and frowned. No doubt he was wondering why she was not needed in the middle of the day when they were so obviously short-staffed. She couldn't tell him. The shame of her peremptory dismissal was too raw.

"I'm glad you're here, Danny," Netty said. "We were just saying to Charlie, Amos and me have discussed matters and we would like to take up your mother's offer of a cottage on the Mansfield property. We'll come as soon as the train is running."

Danny nodded. "I hoped that would be the case and I've already telegrammed mother to tell her to expect you both. I'll be leaving when the train runs so it would make sense for the two of you to come with me."

Netty glanced at Charlie with a questioning look. Charlie gave a quick shake of her head. Danny Hunt was the last person she wanted to share her humiliating dismissal with.

Netty's gaze fell on the brown earthenware teapot on the table. "We've nowt much to pack."

Danny laid a hand on her shoulder. "Tomorrow we'll go and have a look through the cottage and see if there is anything else worth salvaging."

Netty nodded but her lip quirked and the eyes she turned away from Danny brimmed with tears only Charlie could see.

"I came to tell you I am borrowing a horse, Amos. I have one last thing I need to do up at the Shenandoah," Danny said.

Amos removed his pipe from his mouth. "I thought you said it was all in order?"

"Just something I might've missed."

"Why don't you go too, lass?" Netty suggested. "A ride in the fresh air will do you a power of good."

"Would you mind?" Charlie turned to Danny.

It would probably be their last chance to be alone together. Her traitorous heart beat a little faster, remembering the kiss they had shared only a few nights ago.

As he appeared to hesitate, a flush of embarrassment overwhelmed her. She had overstepped the invisible line between them that had sprung up again once the urgency of the situation with Joe had passed, and she felt a fresh wave of humiliation.

Then he smiled, and she relaxed.

"Why not? I'll go and organize the horses if you need to change."

As Charlie unfastened her uniform, she realized it would be the last time she wore the uniform of a matron. Any position she would be able to find would be that of a nursing sister again. It had been a brief and inglorious promotion. She had betrayed April Birch's trust in her, and now Margaret Campbell took her place. She had long suspected that Margaret had coveted the promotion. Well, good luck to her. Nothing was ever as easy as it appeared.

Danny returned twenty minutes later with the two familiar horses that had taken them to the mine on the previous occasion and to the Italian settlement. Charlie had changed into a pair of men's trousers, securing her hair in a long plait beneath her favorite soft felt hat. Netty packed freshly made bread along with pickles, cheese and a canteen of fresh water from the rain tank, and Danny secured the food in a saddlebag.

"I just have to fetch something from the hotel," he said as they led the horses down the hill.

Charlie waited in the yard at the back of the hotel as he went inside, emerging with a large, unwieldy and anonymous bundle wrapped in a grey blanket, which he strapped to the back of the horse.

He swung into the saddle, and she glimpsed the Colt tucked into his belt again and wondered again why he felt it necessary to carry the weapon. There had been something he had not told her, and perhaps an afternoon in his company might induce that confidence.

"What's in the bundle?" she asked.

"I'll tell you later, once we are out of town," he said.

"Another mystery to solve?" she suggested as they turned the horses' heads north along the Aberfeldy Road.

"In a manner of speaking," he said.

Mysterious bundles, a revolver at his belt? It seemed Mr Hunt had his secrets.

Fifty-Six

D anny glanced at the woman riding beside him. She'd been silent for an hour, her gaze fixed on the road ahead, her mouth set in a hard line.

"Something troubling you?"

She started and shot him a deprecatory smile. "Sorry. I'm not very good company."

"What happened with the hospital board this morning?"

Her gaze slid sideways and she shrugged.

"Charlie!"

"It's none of your business," she snapped.

Something unpleasant, he surmised, wondering what disciplinary action the board could impose. If she didn't want to tell him right now, it could wait.

They took the turn off to Pretty Sally. The river still flowed fiercely, cutting off the road to Aberfeldy, and all trace of the old wayside hut that had been Charlie's home had gone, even the chimney reduced to a pile of stones. Had Charlie and her mother still been living in the cottage, they would have been washed away.

The ghostly settlement of Pretty Sally looked even more abandoned and bedraggled than it had on their previous visit. The slatternly woman leaned in the doorway of the general store and answered Danny's greeting with a grunt as they rode past.

"Track to Shenandoah's washed out," she called after them.

Danny turned in his saddle and thanked her but she'd gone back inside the store.

The woman had been correct; the track had been washed away, leaving them with no alternative but to leave their horses tethered at the crossroads and slip and scramble down the ruined track. Charlie carried the canteen and the food for their lunch and Danny lugged the heavy and awkward package that Bertie had bequeathed him.

At the first view of the old mine site, Danny's heart sank. The Shenandoah creek had surged through the gully, tearing at the bank and swallowing much of the remaining infrastructure. The waterwheel lay on its side across the creek, forcing the water to find a new course. The side of the hill had also slipped in places and the original adit where Charlie had kept her tobacco tin was now buried behind a pile of rocks and mud. Danny set his burden down and straightened his back. The place looked desolate and in a few years would be totally lost to the bush and the brambles.

"When are you going to tell me what's in your parcel?" Charlie asked as they gained the relatively solid ground of the old encampment.

Danny hesitated. Could he trust her?

He met her eyes and knew he could, without question.

"The mace of the Victorian parliament," he said.

To his surprise she laughed.

"Pull the other leg," she said.

"It's true."

She sobered. "Then what are you doing with it? I read the papers. There's been a hue and cry over it for months now."

"I didn't steal it, if that's what you think," Danny said, sensing the accusation in her tone. "I had nothing to do with it."

Realization flickered in her eyes.

"Your friend, Campbell?"

His silence gave her the answer.

"Then why not just return it to the Parliament? Leave it on a doorstep or something. No one need know it was you."

"I thought about that, but I agree with Campbell. It's too late. It's been badly damaged and its return will only reignite more questions. Better it just quietly disappears."

"Can I see it?"

Danny hesitated, but a part of him wanted to see it for himself.

He undid the string holding the hessian together and turned back the covering, revealing a sad and sorry sight. The ceremonial mace of the Victorian parliament had been sorely used, inexpertly hacked into three pieces, the silver plate dented and coming away in places. He hated to think what services it had been called on to perform at Madame Brussels.

Better for everybody concerned that it just disappeared.

"That's it?" Charlie looked down at the disreputable object and her lip curled. "Can't we rescue the silver? That's got to be worth something."

Danny stared at her. "That would be theft."

Charlie shrugged and for the first time all day she smiled. "I come from a family of thieves and bushrangers," she said.

"Really?"

"Uncle Jack—" Charlie began and stopped.

Ah, yes, Uncle Jack. Danny remembered the stories now. Uncle Jack was not above a little forgery and outright theft—but he didn't need to know any more about her scurrilous relation.

"So what are you going to do with it?" Charlie asked.

Danny glanced at the place where the poppet head had stood over the main mine shaft. Now only the lower supports remained to give any indication of the structure that had once stood there. He gathered up his burden and carried it over to the mine head. The shaft had been roughly covered with heavy logs and he hauled one to the side to reveal the long shaft that went deep into the earth.

Charlie joined him and they stood together looking down into the impenetrable darkness.

"Removing the silver is theft, but dropping it down a mine shaft is acceptable?" Charlie regarded him with her hands on her hips.

"Oddly, yes," he said.

"If you're going to do it..." Charlie said.

He stared into the dark abyss for a long moment before releasing his grip on the mace. He held his breath until he heard a distant, but distinct, splash. Of course, the mine had flooded in the rain. The mace would be lost forever.

He wondered what lie he would tell Tommy Bent.

Charlie leaned against him and he drew her, unresisting, into his arms. She wore many uniforms, this woman—the matron of a hospital, a conspirator, a righter of wrongs. But the woman in his arms was the real Charlie O'Reilly, the wild, lonely child who had roamed these gullies.

She hid her past behind the veneer of respectability that had been furnished by her education, but there were depths to her, vulnerabilities and secrets she still harbored, and he wanted to discover everything about her.

He brushed a lock of dark hair from her forehead, tucking it behind her ear as he bent his head.

"Charlie O'Reilly, I love you," he said.

She said nothing, but her expressive eyes told their own story as she reached up for him.

Their lips brushed before they came together with the hunger that had characterized their brief stolen moments. As they parted, Charlie locked her fingers behind his neck, her forehead resting on his.

"Danny, I—what's that?" She broke contact, her gaze fixed on a point behind his shoulder. "We're being watched. There's someone there. I saw him move—"

Danny turned on his heel in time to get a glimpse of a dark figure ducking down behind a rock on the slope behind them.

"Get down!"

He pushed Charlie to the ground as a sharp crack echoed off the sides of the gully, startling a flock of parrots who rose screeching into the air. A hard glancing blow caught Danny's leg as he fell on top of Charlie. They lay on the cold, wet ground for a long, long moment.

Danny groaned as the pain knifed through him, catching his breath. Micah Allen. He had almost forgotten about the man and his threats in the darkest days of the flood crisis, and yet Allen had got through it all and followed them up here to this lonely spot.

"Danny!" Charlie shook his shoulder. "Danny."

He gathered his scattered thoughts. "Where is he? Can you see him?"

Charlie wriggled out from underneath him. "Oh God, Danny, you're hurt."

He rolled onto his back, a warm rush of blood soaking his trousers. The pain almost blinded him, but he needed to keep his senses.

"The Colt..." he murmured.

She understood, scrabbling at his belt for the weapon. "Is it loaded?"

"Give it to me."

She pressed the weapon into his right hand.

"Help me stand."

With Charlie's help, he managed to get to his feet, groaning as he tried to put weight on his left leg. He pushed Charlie behind him, partly to protect her and partly for support.

A second rifle shot pinged into the ground a few feet to their right. Allen had paused to reload before he slithered down the slope and approached them, his rifle at his shoulder.

"Don't be a fool, Allen," Danny said.

"I've come too far now," Allen replied, and the rifle in his hands shook with the emotion of his words.

He turned the weapon on Charlie.

"I'll start with your girl here. You can watch her die, just as I watched me dad die. Better part of a night it took him to draw his last breath after that bastard shot him. I was with him at the end, and he made me promise to make it right. See the bastard hang. Well, he didn't, did he?"

Danny's right hand, out of view of the man with the rifle, drew back the cocking handle of Caleb's Colt revolver. Using both hands, he raised the weapon.

"Drop the rifle, Allen."

Allen jerked and stopped. He hadn't been expecting retaliation.

The man's eyes widened, but he seemed to gather his composure, continuing his slow walk towards them.

"Fancy toff like you won't know how to use that weapon," he scoffed.

Danny jerked the muzzle of the Colt to his left. "See that piece of tin?"

He took a breath and fired. The tin leaped in the air, and he quietly thanked Caleb for his patient hours spent in the paddocks at the Mansfield property.

The rifle in Allen's hands wavered. Even if he did try to shoot one of them now, the chances of his making a good shot were remote. Danny pressed the advantage.

"I have five more rounds in the barrel," he said. "I will shoot you before you get off one shot."

Allen's breath sounded labored in the quiet stillness of the valley. He raised the rifle higher, sighting it, but he couldn't disguise the shaking in his hands.

"For all your words, you don't want to kill me. You have had ample opportunity to do that over the last few weeks. And as for killing my friend, to kill her, you will have to look into her eyes in the knowledge that she is completely innocent." He paused. "And before you get one shot off, I will have put two into you."

Allen licked his lips.

"Stop talking!" His high-pitched tone made him sound like a petulant child.

"And how do you think you will get away with it? We have friends who know where we are and will come looking for us. They know you have threatened me. Kill us and you will be hunted down and hanged, and there will be no mercy."

The burning pain in Danny's leg threatened to overwhelm him, and the world was beginning to fade around the edges. It took all his concentration to stay conscious and calm. He set his jaw and held the Colt firm.

He continued. "If I shoot you dead, which I will if you so much as shift your position, it will be self-defense. You will have accomplished nothing. Your father is dead. That boy did not kill him. He didn't deserve the noose, but you will, and it will all have been for nothing. Your mother and your brothers and sisters need you, Allen."

"Stop it!" Allen sounded hysterical. "Stop it!"

"I am giving you a chance to drop that weapon and leave. Go home, Allen, and I will say nothing. Go home to the people who need you."

"You're wrong—" Allen began, but he seemed to be struggling for an argument.

The muzzle of the rifle shook beyond use. He gave a strangled cry and flung the weapon to one side.

"Go," Danny said. "Run."

And the man complied, turning on his heel and bolting for the gate.

To emphasize his point, Danny let off a round into the air. Allen started and increased his pace.

Now the criss had passed, the world began to roar in Danny's ears, a black cloud blurring his vision.

He went down on his knees and pitched to his right side.

Charlie caught him, laying him down on the cold, damp ground where he lay looking up at the wintry sky and wondering vaguely if he was dying.

"Who was that man?" she asked from a long way away.

"His name is Micah Allen and he's been trying to kill me..."

He could say no more. Speaking had become a terrible effort and he just wanted to sleep. He closed his eyes as the world turned black and he felt himself falling into a pitiless, dark void.

FIFTY-SEVEN

For a long moment Charlie kneeled beside the unconscious man, unable to move. How, in the course of a few short minutes, had she gone from blissful happiness, hope and the knowledge that for the first time in her life she had the love of a good, honorable man to... this?

She took a deep breath and reminded herself that she was Charlie O'Reilly, a highly commended nursing sister who could handle any emergency. The "might have beens" could wait—she had an injured man who needed her. Now she had to do what she was trained for.

"Danny..." She brushed his face as her fingers sought the pulse in his neck.

She exhaled as she detected the faint but regular beat. At least he wasn't dead.

A growing stain of sticky red soaked the moleskin trousers, and she steadied her breathing, easing the material away from the wound, revealing an entry and an exit wound. She let her breath out. Provided the bullet had not encountered bone or a blood vessel, he would be fine. However, there was a high possibility of infection from the material drawn in by the bullet's trajectory. He needed the hospital and the operating table to ensure the wound was properly cleaned.

She looked around at the harsh, pitiless hills that surrounded her. Not a person within miles; even the birds had fallen silent as clouds, heavy and grey, lowered over the horizon. A heavy silence that could mean only one thing settled on the valley. If it was going to snow, she could abandon any hope of getting Danny back to Pretty Sally, let alone Maiden's Creek.

"Danny!" She slapped him lightly on the cheek. "Danny, come back."

He rewarded her with a groan and his eyes flickered open. "So sorry, Charlie."

"What for? Saving my life?"

"It was me he wanted to kill."

"That much was clear," she said, trying to keep her tone light. "Who is he?"

"Someone with a grievance against me."

"He's gone," she said, looking towards the track and hoping she was correct. "And you will be too if we don't get you to the hospital."

"How bad is it? It feels like hell..."

"Not as bad as it could have been. First, I've got to stop the bleeding."

"Is this where you tear strips off your petticoat?" Danny managed a crooked smile.

"If you haven't noticed, I'm not wearing petticoats," Charlie said, "but you are lucky. I always carry a few medical necessities with me."

She located the saddlebag with their uneaten food and the canvas pouch packed with bandages and gauze pads and carried it across to the injured man.

Danny took a shuddering breath. "It's starting to snow."

Heavy, white, wet flakes caught on his hair and eyelashes.

Charlie swore and brushed them away, pressing the gauze pads against the wounds and winding a bandage around his leg as best she could.

She looked up at the heavy gray clouds above. The snow was falling quite heavily now and she had to find shelter for them both or they would freeze to death.

She brushed a hand across her eyes, straightened, and looked around at what was left of the mine's infrastructure.

"The old mine manager's hut is still standing," she said. "Can you stand if I help you?"

She gathered up the moth-eaten, gray woolen blanket Danny had used to wrap the mace and threw it over her shoulder. She thrust the heavy Colt revolver into her coat pocket, feeling its weight drag on her clothing. It took a nurse's long experience to get him to his feet. With his arm around her shoulder, she steadied him with her arm around his waist. The fifty yards to the old hut, which had briefly been the home of her uncle all those years ago, felt like a mile.

What she remembered of a small but cosy cottage, warmed with memories of Black Jack Tehan's presence, had gone. The door hung drunkenly on one hinge and she pushed it open. The glass in the one small window was broken, and flurries of snow were already drifting in through the broken panes. No furniture remained except an iron stove. Despite the broken window and door, the hut appeared sound. If the fireplace still drew, she could get a fire going, and they should be able to see out the night.

They fell across the lintel and stumbled across to the fireplace. She propped Danny against the wall and lay the blanket down. Danny subsided onto the blanket, his knees buckling like a puppet without strings.

"I'm so sorry, Charlie," he said. "I'm being a frightful nuisance."

Frightful nuisance didn't even begin to describe their predicament.

"Don't be ridiculous," she said. "I'm going to have a better look at that wound. I apologize in advance. It's going to hurt."

Charlie's rudimentary medical supplies did not include a candle or safety matches and the natural light was fading fast. She would have to make do with what little light came in through the doorway and the one grimy window. She took off her coat, whipped off her leather belt and told him to bite down on it while she worked quickly, pulling off the blood-sodden dressing she had placed on the wound only minutes earlier.

Danny removed the belt from between his teeth and looked up at her. "Is it bad?"

She managed a smile. "It's not as bad as it could be but you need a doctor, not me."

He reached for her hand. "I have absolute trust in you, Charlie."

"I will do what I can. The bullet went through, so there's no bullet still inside, and I don't think anything important has been hit. But the exit wound is a mess and who knows what's been dragged inside. A doctor will need to clean it out properly. Until then, I'll clean and bind it up as best I can but I'll need you to stay still."

Using water from the canteen, she did the best she could with her meager supplies. To his credit he bore her ministrations stoically, and when she had finished, he was still conscious but pale and sweating.

He had also begun to shake, probably from a combination of shock and cold. She had nothing to hand to ameliorate either condition.

"Stay awake," she said as his eyes began to close.

"I'll try," he murmured.

She sat back on her heels. "While there's some light, I'm going up to Pretty Sally to send a message for help. I'll be back. Do you have any money?"

"In my jacket."

She reached into the pocket he indicated and pulled out a fine leather wallet. Her eyes widened at the number and value of the notes folded neatly inside. More money than she saw in a year as a nurse. She selected a couple of pound notes to help smooth the way with the residents of Pretty Sally.

Before leaving, she retrieved Micah Allen's rifle. It was still loaded, and relief flooded her—they had been lucky that Danny had talked the man out of killing them. Charlie closed the weapon and left it with Danny. She pocketed the revolver, still loaded with the remaining five rounds. They couldn't be certain Allen had left the area and she didn't want to be surprised by the man on her way up to Pretty Sally.

It lacked barely an hour of daylight and the snow swirled around her as she slipped and slithered back up the hill towards the horses. After a moment's thought, she swung into the saddle of Danny's horse and gathered up the reins of her little mare, leading the animal behind her.

Pretty Sally had closed its doors on the dark, cold evening. A few lights burned in the windows of shacks, but Charlie decided to try the old general store. She found the front door locked and bolted, so she followed a path around the back to the rough lean-to residence and banged on the door.

"Who's there? If you want anything from the store, we're closed." The woman's voice sounded high and tight.

"My name is Matron O'Reilly from the Maiden's Creek hospital," Charlie lied. "My friend has been badly hurt down at the Shenandoah mine. I need someone to go down to Maiden's Creek and fetch the police and some help to get him out of the Shenandoah gully because he's in no fit state to ride a horse."

The door opened a crack and the slatternly woman peered around the crack.

"What do you mean he's been hurt?"

"He's been shot—"

The woman's eyes widened. "Was that the man who rode through just after you? He followed you last time, too. I see everyone who comes through here." She paused. "Rode back just as I was shutting up. Looked like a man with the devil on his tail."

"So he's gone?"

"Aye." Eager for gossip, the woman leaned forward. "So, how did he come to shoot your friend?"

"It was an accident," Charlie said. "Please, I don't have time to waste. Is there anyone who can take a message? I have money—"

A glimpse of the note in Charlie's hand was all the encouragement the woman needed. She summoned a lanky youth of about sixteen, and Charlie gave him the message to take to Maiden's Creek.

The boy scowled. "It'll take me hours to walk down to the Creek," he said. "It's dark and it's snowing. Can't it wait for morning?"

His mother cuffed his ears. "No it can't. There's a dying man needs your help. Besides there's some shillings in it for you."

"I've got a horse you can take."

Charlie gestured at the front of the building and the boy brightened. "No worries," he said. "I'll just get me coat."

"I doubt they'll get anyone up here tonight," his mother said.

"We'll get through the night. First light will be fine."

Charlie saw the boy on his way with the promise of another pound note on his return with help, and returned to the shopkeeper. "I'll go back to my friend and wait out. Can you give me blankets, candles and matches. I've got food and we're dry enough in the manager's hut, but we just need to keep warm."

The woman led her through to the store, and Charlie made some selections. The last of the notes were carefully stowed in the shopkeeper's apron pocket.

Laden with supplies from the store, Charlie made her way back to the Shenandoah track in the dark. She had purchased a lantern and lit it, using it to lead the reluctant horse down the treacherous track. The snow was falling hard by the time she reached the mine. Outside the manager's hut she unloaded the supplies and pushed open the sagging door to the mine manager's hut.

"Charlie, is that you?"

"It is."

She held the lantern up. Danny had pulled himself into a sitting position, his back to the wall, the rifle in his hands.

Seeing her, he cracked the weapon open and set it to one side. He leaned his head back against the wall and let out a heavy breath.

"I was starting to worry," he said. "Starting to hear things."

"Allen won't be back. According to the woman at the general store, he rode through Pretty Sally like a scalded cat. I picked up some supplies. Now we just need to get a fire going."

Not wanting to leave the horse out in the weather, she unsaddled the beast and secured it with a length of rope in one of the few remaining outbuildings with a semblance of a roof, leaving it with a rusty bucket of water. Unfortunately, there was nothing she could offer in the way of feed.

She gathered an armful of dry wood from inside the derelict buildings and carried it back to the hut. Back in the hut, Danny appeared to have lapsed into unconsciousness again. She checked his pulse and decided warmth was what they both needed.

The wood did not catch easily. When it did she held her breath, terrified the chimney would be blocked, but it drew cleanly and she sat back on her heels watching the comforting flames begin to crackle.

She turned to Danny, taking his hands in hers and chafing his icy fingers. His eyes flickered open.

"Help's on the way, but we're here for the night. I've got the fire going and extra blankets." She summoned a smile. "And I'm hungry."

She wrapped the blankets around both of them as they huddled in front of the fire. Danny drank some of the water and a corner of bread but his strength was fading, and Charlie suggested he lie down in front of the fire. She tucked the blankets around him and set herself to watch as his eyes closed.

The firelight lent a warm glow to Danny's face. Holding her breath, she reached out a finger and pushed a stray lock of brown hair away from his eyes. Her touch lingered on his face, and she traced along his jawline, resting for no more than a breath on his lips.

"I love you too, Daniel Hunt," she whispered into the dark, finishing the conversation that had been interrupted by Micah Allen.

FIFTY-EIGHT

Danny woke to impenetrable dark and bone-chilling cold. For a long moment he had no recollection of where he was or how he'd got there. He made the mistake of moving and groaned aloud as the shafts of pain brought memories back in harsh relief.

He caught his breath and turned towards the glow of embers in the fireplace. The fire needed stoking but he couldn't move. It wasn't so much the pain, which was not so bad as long as he lay quite still, but the terrible lethargy, and he was cold—so cold.

As his eyes became accustomed to the dark, he could make out a figure huddled against the wall, a blanket over her shoulders, her knees drawn up and her arms wrapped around herself. Charlie's head slumped forward on her chest. Her hair had come loose from its plait and curled over her shoulders. He nudged her gently with his boot and she started, pushing her hair back from her face as she straightened, arching her back.

"Charlie," he whispered.

She shuffled over to kneel beside him, stroking the hair from his face.

She smiled. "No fever. That is good. How are you?" Her breath clouded in the cold air.

"Sore... stiff... cold... and your hands are frozen."

She nodded. "I'll put some more wood on the fire."

He watched her as she busied herself with that task. The flames leaped up as the wood caught, bathing her hair with gold reflections.

"Where did you find dry wood?" he asked.

"Plenty around in odd spots," she said. "Bit wary of snakes and spiders but didn't see any."

"Too cold for snakes," Danny mumbled, adding, "I hate snakes."

She rubbed her hands together and hunched her shoulders.

He tugged at her sleeve. "I'm going to make a very improper suggestion," he said. "You're cold and I'm cold... Maybe if we...?"

She turned to look at him, a smile curling her mouth. "That is a most improper suggestion."

"I can assure you, your virtue is quite safe."

"You assume I have virtue," she said.

Her smile, reflected in the firelight, belied a sadness in her tone.

She shivered and picked up the blanket she had been using, pulling it over the two of them. She lay beside him, stiff as a broomstick.

"Come here," he said, easing his right arm around her shoulders.

She relaxed, nestling into him, resting her head on his shoulder. A faint scent of rosemary and lavender drifted from her hair and he closed his eyes.

"I warn you, I'm very cold," she said.

She had been correct. He may as well have invited an icicle to join him. He held her closer, and slowly they both began to thaw, drawing comfort as well as warmth from the intimacy.

"Danny," she said. "Who was that man?"

Danny sighed. "Micah Allen," he said. "He was unhappy with a court case I was involved in."

"A dissatisfied client?"

"No. The opposite. I defended the boy accused of killing his father. The jury let him off the murder charge, and Allen thought the jury and the judge were wrong and blamed me. He sent me threats, and to be honest, he is one of the reasons I decided to get out of Melbourne for a while."

"But he followed you?"

"Yes. I'm fairly certain that he mistook Bertie Campbell for me."

Charlie said nothing for a long moment.

"He was going to kill us both."

"I don't think he would have gone through with it. It's one thing to shoot from a distance, but to look someone in the eye and take their life is another matter."

"I don't share your confidence. I saw the look in his eyes—he felt cornered, and that sort of person is dangerous. We would both have been dead and our bodies tossed down the mine if you hadn't talked him out of it."

Danny considered her words. He needed to diffuse her fear... and his own fear.

"Talking is what I do, Charlie."

"Would you really have shot him?"

Danny had been reliving those few fraught minutes. Could he have shot the man? It would have been self-defense, but to take another person's life? He didn't know the answer and hoped he would never be tested again. Caleb could have his revolver back.

"Where did you learn to shoot like that?"

"Caleb... He fought in the Civil War in America and taught me how to handle the Colt." Danny gave an unwise snort of laughter. "My mother did not approve."

"I thought he was a doctor? I didn't know he fought in the American war."

"He served as a doctor, but even doctors needed to know how to defend themselves. Warmer?"

"I think I'm defrosting."

Danny closed his eyes. "I wish I'd known you when we were children."

"You wouldn't have liked me. Nobody did," she said. "Except Joe. He was always kind to me."

Danny drew her closer, his lips brushing the dark hair. He wanted to stay like this forever, holding this woman in his arms. Forever was a long time, but he'd never been so sure of anything in his life. He who carefully considered everything he did knew without doubt that he couldn't let her go.

"Marry me."

The thought had translated into words... words he did not regret.

She stiffened in his embrace and pulled back. "What did you say?"

"Marry me, Charlotte O'Reilly."

She propped herself up on her elbow and looked down at him.

"No," she said.

He frowned, trying to make sense of her answer. No? Had he completely misjudged her?

"No? I want you to be part of my life, Charlie. I don't want to leave Maiden's Creek without you."

She laughed. "When you are not delirious from pain and blood loss, you will regret asking me that question."

"I don't think I am delirious." He flinched. "I am in pain, but it helps focus the mind."

She shook her head, her hair brushing his face. "I can't marry you for two reasons."

"They better be good."

She looked down at him, her face grave in the light of the fire.

"I can't marry you because if I do, I will have to give up nursing, and it is my vocation, Danny."

"Why would you have to give it up?"

"Married women can't work in the nursing profession, Danny."

"That's ridiculous."

"It may well be, but those are the rules."

"You won't need to work, Charlie. I have a comfortable income, a nice house, servants—"

She shook her head. "Danny, you know where I come from. I am the illegitimate granddaughter of a convict. The daughter of a woman who brewed grog for miners. That was my world, and I worked hard to rise above it. Nursing is mine. I've earned it. I would never be happy being the lady of the house, doling out tea to your friends' wives. It would kill me. Besides, can you imagine how well I would be accepted into Melbourne society? It's a small town. It would be common knowledge that you married beneath you within ten minutes of the wedding vows."

Danny frowned. "None of that concerns me. I'm not marrying your grandparents or your mother. It's you, Charlie O'Reilly, I love. And the second reason?"

Her lips quirked. "I'm Catholic and you're Protestant. Neither church will let us marry."

Danny considered that statement for a long time. Would he be willing to convert to Catholicism to marry this woman? Would she convert to Church of England? The roots of those divides went deep.

Before he could formulate an answer, she bent her head and kissed him gently.

"Thank you for asking. I will put your generous offer of marriage down to a fever brought on by the trauma of your wound, and we will never speak of it again. I think you will find that once you leave Maiden's Creek, I will become a distant memory. Now, try and sleep. It's still hours until dawn."

Danny closed his eyes, but sleep did not come easily, even after Charlie's breathing had slowed and she slept.

He held her closer. He hadn't been delirious or joking. There was something wild and untamed about Charlie O'Reilly, and he had been completely serious when he had suggested marriage. It didn't matter where she came from or who her antecedents were or that she would be a terrible grand dame of Melbourne society. As for the religious divide? Surely they could work something out between them?

If she wanted, they would allow her to still follow her dreams and together they would be amazing. Maybe he had to fight a little harder for her.

He'd said it before, and he said it again.

"I love you, Charlie O'Reilly," he whispered into the dark.

FIFTY-NINE

Charlie woke with a start, her heart thumping. A grey light filtered in through the broken window, and she lay for a long moment watching her breath cloud in the air, wondering what had woken her. The horse in the shelter nearby nickered, and an answering whinny came from a distance.

She gently disengaged Danny's arm, which he had flung across her, and slid out from under the blankets, stretching her stiff limbs. A cold night on the floor of the hut, and every bone ached. Danny stirred but didn't wake as she checked his pulse. It was slow but regular, but he did seem unnaturally warm, and she hoped it wasn't the start of a wound fever. She pulled the blanket up around his shoulders and let her hand linger on his forehead.

Definitely feverish.

The distant horse could presage the rescue party, but she didn't want to risk Micah Allen returning so she retrieved Danny's revolver. She'd never handled a revolver before, and the weight dragged on her arm as she stepped out into the cold morning.

Several inches of snow covered the ground, softening the harsh lines of the industrial ruins. A heavy fog hung in the gully, hiding the ruined creek. The world seemed unnaturally still and quiet, every sound muffled.

She placed the revolver in her pocket and rubbed her hands together before thrusting them into the pockets of her jacket, her fingers closing on the butt of the weapon.

A *cooee* reverberated off the cliff faces, swallowed by the fog.

Charlie stiffened and took the revolver out again as half a dozen ghostly figures emerged from the track, picking their way carefully over the broken ground. She dropped her hand as she recognized the portly figure of Sergeant Prewitt, slithering down the last of the track toward her.

"I'm very pleased to see you, Sergeant," she said.

His gaze went to the revolver in her hand, and she shoved it back into her pocket.

He pulled a note from his pocket with his heavily gloved hands. "Didn't quite know what to make of this, Miss O'Reilly."

She realized that she and Danny had not had a chance to discuss the story they would tell the world.

"We think we disturbed a claim jumper," she said, with her fingers crossed in her pocket. "He shot Mr. Hunt but took to his heels. He's long gone now."

"And where's Mr. Hunt?"

"I'm here, Sergeant."

Charlie turned on her heel. Danny stood, or rather sagged, in the doorway of the manager's hut. His unshaven face was an unhealthy gray, with dark circles under his eyes. He propped his right shoulder against the door jamb, his weight on his right leg.

"We need to get him to the hospital," Charlie said.

"Can you walk?" Prewitt asked.

Danny glanced down at the bloodstained bandage around his thigh. "No," he said.

Prewitt nodded and jerked his head at the men behind him. "We've bought a cart, but there's no way we'll get it down here. You'll have to be stretchered up to the road. Lucky we brought one with us."

Prewitt's men set down the stretcher they carried, and Danny made no protest as they loaded him onto it. Charlie covered him with the blankets and saddled her horse, leading it out of the shelter. The animal's laid-back ears and general air of displeasure echoed her own mood. They were both tired and hungry and anxious to be back in their own stables, even if neither she nor the horse had a stable to call their own.

Prewitt pushed his cap to the back of his head and scratched his balding pate. He looked around the desolate site.

"What in God's name were you doing down here?"

That was a difficult question to answer. Disposing of the mace of the Victorian parliament was not the answer Prewitt would have been expecting. Sometimes the simplest explanation was the best.

"Mr. Hunt wanted to be certain that the site had been secured before he returned to Melbourne," Charlie said.

They followed the men with the stretcher as they picked their way back up the track.

"Any word on when the train will be running?" she asked.

"Tomorrow they say. You leaving us, Miss O'Reilly?"

Charlie didn't answer.

Prewitt frowned and stopped in the track, looking at her. "I've been trying to work out how I know you, and now it makes sense. You're Mad Annie's girl."

Charlie flinched at the old soubriquet.

"No one calls her that. My mother is happily married and settled," she said, stiffly.

"Your uncle, Jack. He was a rogue and some," Prewitt laughed. "Reckon we're still looking for him to charge him over the theft of the gold from this mine, and I think there were some forgery charges in there too."

Charlie smiled. "I can't help you, Sergeant. I don't know where he's ended up."

Prewitt shrugged. "Good luck to him. Always rather liked him."

A cart waited at the top of the hill, and the men slid the stretcher into the tray. A couple of them doubled over trying to catch their breath.

Charlie leaned over her patient. "How are you?"

Danny managed a watery smile. "Been better to be honest."

She patted him on the shoulder. "Use the experience in your writing, Mr. Hunt."

He laughed and groaned. "Don't do that, Charlie."

"Do what?"

"Make me laugh... or call me Mr. Hunt."

It was nearly midday by the time they reached the hospital. Margaret Campbell swept in and took charge. Charlie started to follow, but Margaret barred her way, dismissing her with a curt... "Thank you, we can manage from here. You must be exhausted, Miss O'Reilly."

"He's my patient. I need—"

Margaret leaned in toward her. "No you don't. He is not your patient. He's mine. You are no longer employed here." Her eyes glittered. "I don't know what hold you have over him, Charlie, but you don't belong among people like Danny and me, just like you didn't at school. I suggest you move on and leave Danny alone."

Charlie raised her chin and bit back the sharp retort that rose to her lips.

Margaret smirked and shut the door in her face.

With her head held high, Charlie turned on her heel and walked away from the hospital, but exhaustion and a thousand conflicting emotions boiled over, and by the time she reached the cottage, she fell sobbing into Netty's arms. Dimly, she was aware of Amos slipping out of the door. He was a man more comfortable in the company of horses than emotional women.

All the pent-up emotion that had been building over the past week would have explained the storm, but Netty didn't need to know that beneath it all, Charlie's heart was breaking.

The heart she had sworn never to give up again.

Sometime in the dark, cold night, she had given it away, and no matter how she tried to rationalize the words that had passed between them and her firm refusal of his marriage proposal, she had been lying. She would have given up nursing, her religion, whatever it took to be with him.

But as Margaret Campbell had turned her away from the door of the hospital, she knew the decision had been the right one. Mad Annie's daughter did not belong in Danny's world.

Netty took her hands, turning them over.

"Blood," she said. "Danny?"

Charlie looked down at her fingers and her clothes, seeing the dark stains of Danny's blood. She took a shuddering breath and nodded.

Netty grasped her sleeves and shook her. "Charlie. Is Danny...?"

It took a moment for Charlie to understand that Netty had mistaken her tears for grief at Danny's demise.

"He's hurt, but he'll be all right, Netty," she said, wiping her eyes with the back of her sleeve.

Netty's shoulders slumped. "What happened?"

Charlie slumped into the chair beside the fire. The cat abandoned her kittens and jumped into her lap. Charlie let her fingers stray over the cat's fur, to be rewarded with a comforting purr. Netty produced tea and cake, and Charlie related the main events of the preceding day.

"We've been so worried. A strange boy brought back your horse with a message for Prewitt. He had no idea what was in the note, just that some folk were in trouble at the Shenandoah mine."

Charlie set the teacup down and leaned back in the chair. "I'll be leaving tomorrow, Netty. You can come with me, but it is probably more sensible for you and Amos to accompany Danny back to Melbourne. He will need help."

"What do you mean you're leaving? Is it Danny?"

Charlie deposited the cat back in the box with her kittens and stood up.

"I can't stay, Netty. I have no reason to stay. I have lost my job and my home... and as for Danny, I can't see him again. It hurts too much."

Netty shook her head. "I don't understand, lass."

Charlie yearned to tell her the truth, the truth she kept buried deep in her heart. The truth that no one except herself and her mother knew.

The real reason she could not marry Daniel Hunt had little to do with vocations or religion.

Secrets and lies... she couldn't marry him and keep the greatest secret of all from him, so she was left with no choice but to walk away.

Netty took her in her arms, and Charlie let the tears come again, allowing Netty to lead her into the bedroom. She lay down on the bed and, covered with her mother's old patchwork quilt, she slept.

SIXTY

"You're back."

Danny turned his head on the hospital pillow and looked at Bertie Campbell, propped up on his elbow in the neighboring bed, watching him.

"What do you mean?"

"You've been out to the world for the last twenty-four hours," his friend said, "and here I was hoping you would explain the mess you got yourself into."

Danny took a deep breath and stared up at the ceiling. He was conscious of a nagging ache in his leg but no longer experienced the sharp, all-consuming pain.

"Margaret says you got yourself shot. I think you need to change your occupation," Bertie said. "I didn't think lawyering could be quite so dangerous."

"You're right. I think I should stick to property disputes or wills..." He paused. "Although both of those areas of law are fraught with high emotion."

"Prewitt's poked his head in a couple of times. Doesn't look like they've caught the chap who shot you."

Danny was tempted to add 'and you' but held his tongue. Bertie didn't need to know how close he had come to being a victim of Danny's erstwhile stalker.

He gingerly pulled himself up and looked around the ward. He appeared to be wearing a hospital-issue nightshirt of a harsh, scratchy cotton. From the corridor, he heard voices, a man and a woman, and his heart beat a little faster. He needed to see Charlie, assure himself that she was unharmed.

He recalled every word that had passed between them during that dark, cold night, and he was determined to repeat the question he had posed in slightly less confronting circumstances.

The door opened, and he bit back his disappointment at seeing Doctor Linacre. The doctor strode over to the bed.

"How is my patient today?"

"Suitably grateful to be here," Danny replied.

"You were very lucky you had Sister O'Reilly with you. She saved your life," Linacre said.

Danny pulled himself up straighter in the bed. "I owe her my thanks. Is she on duty today?"

Linacre frowned. "Didn't she tell you?"

"Tell me what?"

Linacre pushed his glasses up his nose. "The hospital board in its infinite wisdom dismissed her two days ago."

Danny stared at the man. "Dismissed her? Why?"

Linacre sighed. "The report from the inspector who was here last week and then the incident last Wednesday—"

An unfamiliar white-hot fury rose in Danny's chest. "We caught a murderer!"

"I know." Linacre, to his credit, looked miserable. "I opposed the decision, but the majority were overly concerned with the reputation of the hospital." He ran a hand through his hair and shook his head. "She's a damned good nurse and a superb midwife. One of the best. She is a loss."

"Who did they appoint in her stead?"

"Sister Campbell."

Danny frowned, remembering the conversation he'd had with Margaret when he'd first arrived in Maiden's Creek. She'd expressed her disappointment at losing out on the job to Charlie. It might have only been an acting position, but now she had her wish.

"I'm not here to gossip," Linacre said. "Let's look at that wound. Sister?"

Margaret Campbell walked into the ward, carrying a covered basin.

"Not you," he said to Margaret.

"Danny, I—"

"No. Please can you summon the other nurse?"

Margaret scowled.

"Sister, in view of your personal relationship with the patient, I can manage," Linacre said.

Margaret set down the basin and flounced off. The doctor pulled the screen around the bed, and Danny endured the unpleasant examination.

When he was done, Linacre straightened. "Looks to be healing well. You'll be with us a few days, Mr. Hunt."

Danny sank back against the pillows and lay staring at the ceiling. He had to see Charlie, explain, and make it right between them.

After the doctor had gone, Margaret appeared beside his bed holding a cup of tea. He managed a watery smile. "Sorry, Margaret. I didn't mean to offend you."

She shrugged and plumped the lumpy pillows and settled him back.

"I can heat some soup left from lunch for you," she said.

"I'm not staying. Where are my clothes, Margaret?"

Her eyes widened. "Why? You're not going anywhere. You nearly died."

"But I didn't." He glared at her. "And you can't keep me here against my will."

She crossed her arms. "Go on then, Danny. Walk out of here. I doubt you'll make it to the door."

He had to admit in his present condition, she was probably right.

"Can I get a message to Charlie?"

Margaret snorted. "I believe she left on the first train this morning.

She's gone, Danny, and a good thing too. She would have made your life miserable."

"Why would you say that?"

"I'm no fool, Danny," she said. "I've seen the way she looks at you. People like Charlie O'Reilly and—" She took a quick breath, a slight flush coloring her cheeks. "It's fun to flirt and maybe even go a little further, but they're not for us. You would have just made a complete fool of yourself and been the laughing stock of Melbourne society if you had entertained any thought of marrying the likes of her." Her tone softened. "It's been a difficult few weeks, and you have been thrown together in extraordinary circumstances. I am sure you will find, with a bit of distance, that it is better for you that she made the decision to leave."

She patted his hand, but he pulled it away. She gave him a last, condescending smile and walked away.

He watched her straight back and the flick of her skirt as he fought back the rising anger, not so much at her patronizing words directed at him but at the slur on Charlie. Matron Campbell. She had got what she wanted but he wondered if she wanted more.

The fight drained from Danny, and he slumped back onto the pillow. Charlie had gone without a word. Why? He lay back, trying to make sense of everything that had happened in the last forty-eight hours. Everything that had passed between them... the words, the gestures... the kiss.

"Hunt? Hard not to overhear my sister. She certainly gave you what for."

He brought his attention back to Bertie.

"Was she always like that?" he asked.

"You mean, did Mags get her own way when her mind was set on something? Yes. I know she's my sister, but my God, the tantrums if she was thwarted." Bertie huffed out a breath. "Can I tell you a secret?"

"Another one? I'm not doing any more of your bidding, Campbell."

"It was Mags' idea to invite you along with me. She said it would be nice to see you again, and frankly, I thought it might be worth seeing you two back together again. Mother has never forgiven her for turning you down, and I think Mags may have regretted it."

Danny ground his teeth. That explained the unexpected invitation from a friend he had seen little of in the past few years.

He ignored Bertie's confession. "I have no regrets about coming, Campbell."

Bertie gave a huff of laughter. "Look at us both, flat on our backs. I sure as hell wish I'd stayed in Melbourne. Good news is the train is up and running again, so hopefully the parents can see some way to get me home."

But Danny wasn't listening. "Why did the board sack Charlie? She saved this place..." he said aloud.

"They had a negative report from that hospital inspector," Bertie supplied.

That had certainly contributed to Charlie's departure. Fitzgerald had exacted his revenge. Charlie hadn't stood a chance.

Danny thumped the mattress with an impotent fist and swore under his breath.

Bertie leaned across from his bed and said in a low voice, "Did you manage to... umm... do the thing I asked you to do?"

"Yes," snapped Danny. "Nearly got us both killed."

"It won't be found?"

"Not in our lifetime."

"Thanks. Sorry I dragged you here, Hunt."

I'm not. If I hadn't come to Maiden's Creek, I would never have met Charlie O'Reilly... and now she's gone.

He turned on his side and closed his eyes. "I'm tired, Campbell. Going to grab some sleep."

But sleep didn't come easily as he wrestled with the frustration of being tied to a hospital bed while Charlie O'Reilly slipped further and further away.

SIXTY-ONE

D anny had a stream of visitors that afternoon, starting with Sergeant Prewitt and a wide-eyed constable deputed to take notes. Prewitt wanted a full account of the incident at the Shenandoah, which Danny explained as an encounter with a claim jumper.

Such incidents were not unknown in the rough world of the Maiden's Creek goldfields, but the involvement of such a high-profile visitor as Daniel Hunt provided extra spice to the story, which would, no doubt, do the rounds of every bar and fireside in town for some time.

Prewitt was followed by Netty Burrell.

"When Charlie told me you'd been shot, I feared the worst," Netty said, her gloved hand finding his and holding tight.

"Where's she gone, Netty?"

Netty shook her head. "I don't know. She wouldn't say. Just said she couldn't stay in Maiden's Creek."

"I don't blame her. I will be speaking with Caleb about the shoddy treatment she received here."

"Miss Campbell has oh-so-politely requested Amos and I leave the cottage by tomorrow," Netty said, her mouth twisting. "We've nowhere to go."

Another black mark against Margaret Campbell, Danny thought.

"I have a suite of rooms at the Britannia." He glanced across at Bertie. "Bertie's not using his. You are welcome to take his place."

"Thanks," Bertie said.

"In fact, can you fetch me some clean clothes? I'm not staying here a minute longer than I have to."

Netty frowned. "Are you sure—"

"I'm sure. Please, Netty."

She returned an hour later with a bundle of clothes. She helped him out of bed and he asked her to go in search of a set of crutches while he dressed with difficulty in the bathroom at the end of the ward.

The effort took all his energy and as he sat on the edge of the bath to regain his strength, the door burst open and Margaret Campbell stood in the doorway.

"It would have been polite to knock," Danny said.

"I thought you had collapsed," Margaret said. "What are you doing? Why are you out of bed? And what's all this nonsense about crutches?"

"I'm leaving the hospital. I'll be heading back to Melbourne on the train tomorrow."

"That's ridiculous. You are not strong enough..."

"Apparently, you have evicted the Burrells from the matron's cottage so they will be accompanying me."

"I didn't exactly evict them. Just suggested they may like to look at alternative arrangements. It's my cottage by right—"

It felt as if he was seeing Margaret Campbell for the first time. How had he ever imagined a life with this woman?

"Tell me... are you happy, Margaret? Did you get what you wanted?"

"What do you mean?"

"You wanted to be the matron of this hospital, and now you are. What's next?"

She stared at him, her lips parted. "I don't know what you mean."

"It's only a temporary position in a small cottage hospital. Will it be enough for you?"

She raised her chin. "For the moment." She laid a hand on his arm and smiled. "Danny, I had hoped that you and I could, maybe, go back to where we once were."

"A wise person once told me that you can't live in the past, Margaret. I am happy to part as friends, and I wish you well with your new position."

Ignoring the sharp pain in his leg, he hefted himself onto the crutches and swung away from her. Amos and Netty and Joe Trevelyan were waiting by the door to help him return to the Britannia, and tomorrow he would be on the train to Melbourne.

It was time to go home and try to find Charlie O'Reilly.

Sixty-Two

Joshua Woods' dairy farm was only a couple of miles out of Korumburra but the walk from the station took Charlie over an hour. At the gate she hefted her small valise and walked up the long, rutted and muddy track, past green fields of contented cows, to the neat farmhouse.

Her stepfather, Joshua, sat on the verandah, mending a harness. He rose to his feet as she approached and smiled with genuine warmth. She loved this man. He had been good to her mother, and as far as her sister, Sarah, was concerned, he was the only father she had known. Annie, in her turn, had loved Joshua's three children, all now grown and making their own way in the world.

"Charlie, my girl. Good to see you. Your mother's out the back feeding the chooks. She'll be pleased to see you. I'll go and put the kettle on. Are you staying long?"

"I don't know," Charlie said. "I had to leave my trunk at the station. Can we go and fetch it later?"

"Of course. If we'd known you were coming, we'd have been there to meet you."

He took her valise in his large, capable hand and ushered her through the house.

Annie Woods stood in the center of the large chicken pen, scattering scraps to the brood of hens. A magnificent rooster strutted among the brown and white hens, snatching food from his girls, who responded with indignant squawks.

"G'day, Mum," Charlie said.

Annie started, almost dropping her pan.

"Charlie, what are you doing here?"

"Can't I pay a visit to my mother without a cross-examination?"

Annie gave her a sharp, appraising glance but didn't reply.

She secured the gate to the chook pen and set the basin down before crossing to her daughter. She took Charlie by the forearms and looked up at her before taking her in her arms and giving her a long, hard embrace.

"Charlie!"

Charlie's heart gave a leap as a small girl in a grubby pinafore came hurtling across the cow yard toward her, pigtails bouncing.

"Amy," she responded, sweeping the child into her arms.

Amy's thin arms encircled her neck.

"That's enough, Amy, you'll choke your sister," Annie said.

Sister ... An old, familiar stab of pain threatened to overwhelm Charlie.

"I can never get enough hugs," she said, setting the child down. "I have too many years without those hugs to make up for."

Annie gave her a knowing look.

"Wash those hands and your face and get inside, Amy. You can lay the table for tea."

"She's grown," Charlie said.

"What do you expect? Must be six months at least since you last saw her."

Annie raised a hand and touched her daughter's face.

"You look tired, my girl," she said. "Everything all right?"

Charlie forced a smile. "Fine. I'm fine. What's the news of Sarah?"

Annie snorted. "You think that one would write unless she absolutely had to? Last letter was dances and parties and who knows what else. God help Eliza McLeod's pocket."

"Sarah has an allowance same as I did," Charlie said.

"Let's just hope she marries well because any more education will be wasted on her."

Annie put an arm around her daughter's waist, and the two women walked into the house.

Seated at the well-scrubbed kitchen table, tea and cake spread out before her, Charlie listened attentively as Amy chatted about all the consequential matters of a five-year-old's life—school, friends, which cows had calved... She could have talked until the end of days, and Charlie would have hung on every word.

"Enough, Miss Chatterbox," Annie said at last. "Your sister's tired from her journey. How about you leave her to talk to me for a little while and go and help your pa with the milking?"

Annie waited until the back door shut behind the child.

"She's doing so well," Charlie said.

Annie nodded. "Aye, she's our pride and joy."

She leaned over and laid a hand over Charlie's.

"So why are you really here, Charlie?"

Charlie took a deep breath and, for the first time in her life, said, "I need your advice, Ma."

"You need *my* advice? Well there's one for the books," Annie said.

"Ma... please."

"Don't pay me any heed," Annie said. "What's on your mind. Is it a boy?"

Charlie laughed. "A boy? I'm nearly thirty. I'm long past boys... but you're right, it is a man."

Annie bristled. "It's not that bastard, Fitzgerald? He hasn't taken advantage of you again?"

"No... not directly."

Charlie sat back in the chair and put her arms behind her head as she wrestled with how to put her dilemma into words.

"I've made such a mess of things, Mum."

Annie poured another cup of tea. "Let's start with what happened to this wonderful new job of yours?"

Charlie told her about the events at the hospital and losing her job over the report Fitzgerald had written.

Annie had a suitable epithet, drawn from her days in the grog shop, to indicate her thoughts on Fitzgerald.

"You catch a murderer and that's how they repay you?" Annie said.

"And in doing so broke every rule in the hospital's book. They were right. I endangered patients, and that's the worst thing a nurse could do."

Annie pushed a plate of biscuits across to her daughter. Charlie picked one up and bit into it. She had no childhood memory of her mother making biscuits or anything much beyond kangaroo stew.

"And where does this man fit in? Do I know him?"

"You know of him. Daniel Hunt."

Annie sat back in her chair. The expression on her face could not have been more shocked if Charlie had hit her over the head with a dead fish.

"Daniel Hunt? Oh, Charlie, he's not for the likes of you. The Hunts... well, they're worth a fortune." Annie frowned. "What's he gone and done? If he's hurt you..."

Charlie held up a hand to silence her mother's righteous indignation. "He hasn't hurt me." She took a deep, shuddering breath. "He asked me to marry him."

"And?"

"I turned him down."

Annie blinked. "You turned down a proposal of marriage from one of the wealthiest men in Melbourne?"

Charlie nodded. "I don't care a jot about his money. He's... he's..."

"Do you love the lad?"

Charlie nodded.

"So what's the problem?"

Charlie swallowed. "To begin with, he's Protestant and I'm a Catholic..."

Annie threw her head back and laughed. "When was the last time you set foot in a church, my girl?"

Charlie had to think. "Easter?" she suggested.

Annie reached out and took her daughter's hands between her own.

"Charlie, lass," Annie said. "You were never christened in the Catholic faith. Matt Tehan couldn't find a priest when you was born and then he died and well... what with one thing and another, it just slipped my mind. You, my girl, are a heathen."

Charlie stared at her mother. "You mean...?"

"I mean, you are free to choose whatever religion you wish. They won't marry you in the Church of England unless you're christened with 'em mind you, and that's not such a big sacrifice to make for the man you love, is it? I'm sure they'd be pleased to add another to their flock."

Charlie extracted her hands and diverted herself by pouring a cup of stewed tea from her mother's brown earthenware teapot. Like Netty Burrell's teapot, Annie's was chipped in multiple places but it had been one of the few objects that had survived Annie's tumultuous life.

She sipped slowly without tasting the brew as her mind turned over the possibilities. She thought of her grandmother's rosary, tucked up with the patchwork quilt in her trunk. The habit of a lifetime would be hard to give away, but that was all it was... a habit. It was all the same God. The rest was just ritual.

Annie shrugged. "If it's all that stands between you and the man you love, you do what it takes."

Charlie huffed out a breath. "I'll have to give up nursing."

Annie studied her daughter. "And if you're going to let a commitment to working every hour that God gave you stand in the way of you marrying a good man that you truly love, you're a bigger fool than I thought you. Charlie love, Danny Hunt has enough money to build a hospital. If it's saving the world you want, trust me that's a lot easier when you've money and status, and as Mrs. Daniel Hunt, you'd have both." Annie frowned. "But they're just excuses. You haven't told him about Amy, have you?"

Charlie shook her head. "No, and he doesn't need to know. I told him Amy's your daughter... your little miracle."

Annie sat back and considered her daughter for a long, long moment.

"Secrets and lies, missy. That's no way to make things work. When I married Joshua, I told him everything about me, and as you know, some of it wasn't pretty, but he took me as I was, told me he didn't care what happened in the past, he wanted to make a new life with me." Annie laid a hand over Charlie's and squeezed her fingers. "You have to tell him the truth, Charlie, or it will always stand between you."

"None of this conversation matters. I walked away from him."

"Walked or ran?"

Charlie flinched. "Ran."

Annie shook her head. "You can't keep running, lass. Some day it all catches up with you." She hefted herself to her feet and leaned over her daughter, kissing the top of her head.

"You're welcome to stay here for as long as you need."

Like a small child—like Amy—Charlie wrapped her arms around her mother's waist and buried her head in her apron and cried.

SIXTY-THREE

"I think we should send for Doctor O'Connor." Adelaide's voice came from a long way away.

"Stuff and nonsense. I've forgotten more about bullet wounds than O'Connor's ever learned in his lifetime." Caleb's soft Virginian accent came from the other side of the bed.

"That was thirty years ago," Adelaide protested.

"Trust me, you don't forget battlefield surgery," Caleb replied, the light bantering tone gone, his voice low and grave.

"Stop arguing," Danny said, his eyes still closed. "I trust Caleb implicitly."

"Thank you, Dan," Caleb said. "I'll just go fetch my bag."

The bed sagged as Adelaide sat down. She ran a motherly hand over his forehead.

"You've got a fever," she said. "What were you thinking, risking your life on a journey back to Melbourne? You should have stayed at the hospital."

"Couldn't stay a moment longer."

"You were fortunate to have Amos and Netty with you. I've put them up in the spare bedroom, and we'll take them up to Mansfield when we're sure you'll be all right."

"Honestly, mother, I had very good care, and there's someone I need to find."

Adelaide narrowed her eyes. "What aren't you telling me?"

Danny didn't have the strength to dissemble.

"Do you know Charlie O'Reilly?"

"Eliza McLeod's protégé." Her eyes widened. "Danny, you haven't made a fool of yourself?"

He pulled himself up on his elbows. "What do you mean by that?"

"Miss O'Reilly was a singularly attractive young lady if I remember rightly. Her sister is quite the talk of the town."

"Miss O'Reilly was the matron of the hospital, mother," Danny replied coldly. "And she was with me when I was shot. Without her assistance, I would be dead." He sank back on the pillows.

Adelaide had the grace to lower her eyes. "I'm sorry, I just jumped to conclusions."

Danny grasped his mother's hand. "I would hope that you had more faith in me, Mother. But if, hypothetically, Charlie and I had... umm... formed an attachment...?"

It seemed an interminably long moment before Adelaide replied. "Danny. I have watched a parade of fatuous young girls throw themselves at your feet. Charlie has several virtues none of those girls have... pride, intelligence, education and integrity."

"You have summed her up perfectly." He paused. "I asked her to marry me."

Adelaide's eyes widened. "And?"

"She declined."

His mother's lips quirked. "And what exactly were the circumstances in which you posed this interesting question?"

"It was the middle of the night. I'd just been shot and... it just came out."

Adelaide shook her head. "Have a long think about what you just told me and ask yourself why she would have turned you down."

"Religion and her career, she said."

"Hmm," was the only helpful suggestion that came from his mother.

She made to rise to her feet but he put a hand on her arm.

"I'm sorry for the things I said to you before I left."

"Did you find what you were looking for?"

Danny shook his head. "I found the grave, and I heard the stories. None of them does him any credit. What I did learn was that it doesn't matter. We can't hold on to the past, and I've made my peace with my memories of that time."

Adelaide laid a hand over his. "I'm sorry, Danny. Sorry for holding the truth from you and for never thinking to talk to you about Richard. I... Caleb and I thought it better that we just moved on with life, rather than relive a painful time for us all. I just wanted to protect you." She looked up as the door opened. "Caleb's back and I can see from the expression on his face there's nothing he likes better than a good bullet wound."

His stepfather had come prepared with his shirtsleeves rolled up and a covered tray under which, Danny was certain, were all manner of hideous medical instruments.

"Are you staying, my dear?" Caleb addressed his wife.

"No. I don't need to see you operating on my son. I will fetch Netty. She is much more useful."

"I don't need operating on and I don't need Netty," Danny said to her departing back.

Adelaide took him at his word, and Netty did not appear. Caleb's examination was thorough and unpleasant, but as he finished redressing the wound and stood washing his hands at the washstand he turned to Danny.

"They did a good job, but your mother is right. It was a foolish decision not to stay a few days longer."

"I couldn't."

Caleb sat down on the bed. "Problems at the hospital?"

"Yes and no. The hospital itself is fine, but things went on with the board and the hospital inspector..." He ran a hand over his eyes. "I'll tell you the whole story when I've had some sleep."

"And Tommy Bent's little matter?"

"Resolved," Danny said.

"In what way?"

"No one will ever know what became of the parliamentary mace."

Caleb laughed.

SIXTY-FOUR

Once Danny was on his feet again, Adelaide and Caleb left him to recuperate in the East Melbourne house and returned to the property at Mansfield with Amos and Netty. After the turbulent events of the past few weeks, Danny revelled in the comparative peace of home.

While Mrs Brown insisted on feeding him at every possible interval, he took the time to start writing a story that had been tugging at his sleeve since his return to Melbourne. Forget the bush tales of Thomas Pike—he wanted to write a mystery set in the mountains of his childhood... a wild, untamed child... the ideas spilled out of him, his pen moving so fast he could barely read his own writing.

"What!" He snapped as the door to his room opened and Mrs Brown looked in.

He apologized for his rudeness, and his housekeeper straightened her shoulders.

"You've a visitor," she said, and the tight set of her mouth said a thousand words. "A woman."

Charlie?

Danny got to his feet in such haste that the barely healed scar on his leg caught, and he nearly tipped over his inkstand.

"I see," Mrs Brown said with a raised eyebrow. "She's in the parlor."

Danny pulled on his jacket and limped down the stairs as fast as his still-healing leg would let him.

It took him a moment to recognize the woman standing beside the fire, dressed in a dark red dress set off by a fashionable hat garnished with a red feather, standing at the window, as Margaret Campbell. She raised a hand, clad in a red kid glove, and he nodded in acknowledgement.

"Margaret, this is a surprise. Would you like refreshment?"

"Your housekeeper has already offered, thank you," she said.

He gestured to a chair and they sat while Mrs Brown bustled in with a tray of teacups and freshly baked biscuits. She didn't linger, leaving Danny to pour tea.

"What brings you to Melbourne?" he asked.

"I brought Bertie home at last," she said. "He was driving me to distraction at the hospital, so we made the necessary arrangements and now he's at the house in Toorak driving the servants to distraction instead of me."

"Did you find extra nurses?"

"We had three nurses sent up from Sale, and while I'm in Melbourne, I'll interview a couple of women for permanent replacements."

She took the cup he offered. "How are you?"

"I'm on the mend, thank you," Danny said, ignoring a protesting twinge. "Fortunately, Caleb spent three years of his life dealing with bullet wounds on the battlefields of the Civil War in America. He says I'll live."

Margaret took a delicate sip of the tea.

"Your father is creating a terrible fuss at the hospital. He wrote a letter to the board demanding to see Doctor Fitzgerald's inspection report and the reasons for the dismissal of Matron O'Reilly."

"Good," Danny said with feeling. He didn't wish Margaret ill, but he did want to see justice for Charlie.

"I suppose you've given him your version of the events?" she asked.

Danny said nothing. Beneath her fashionable and composed exterior, he sensed a peevishness in Margaret's tone.

"He asked and I told him. I am sure none of this will affect your position," he said at last.

Margaret nibbled the corner of a biscuit. "I've been considering my position," she said. "It may be time to return to Melbourne. Sister Keegan is long overdue for a promotion and, for some reason, seems to like living in Maiden's Creek. She will make a perfectly adequate matron at the hospital."

"What's brought about this decision?"

Margaret shrugged. "Nursing has lost its allure," she said. "Seeing you and Bertie reminded me of everything I left behind. I am forced to agree with my mother. It is past time I settled down and looked to have a family of my own."

"I am sure your mother will be pleased to hear that."

She smiled, but something in her cold, calculating eyes sent a shiver down his spine.

"I..." She looked down at her lap and then up, giving him a coquettish glance from beneath her lashes. "I feel we parted on bad terms, and I would like to make amends. If I return to Melbourne, I was rather hoping that we could try again."

Danny stared at her as the realization sank in that she was effectively asking him to marry her.

"Margaret..."

"A gentleman would honor his offer," she continued.

Danny set his table napkin down. "You made it perfectly clear that you did not wish to marry me. I'm sorry, Margaret, but too much time has elapsed. I don't entertain the same feelings for you I did four years ago."

"You came to Maiden's Creek—"

"I had my own reasons for going to Maiden's Creek, regardless of your attempt to lure me there. If anything, our reacquaintance has confirmed that you made the correct decision all those years ago."

Her lip trembled.

"But I didn't. I made a decision out of spite towards my parents. I'm older now and I want different things from my life. If... if you think you no longer love me, that doesn't matter. Love can come again."

Danny felt himself being backed into a corner and the only way out of it was to behave like a complete cad.

He stood up. "I'm sorry, Margaret, but the answer is no. There is another woman in my life now."

Margaret's nostrils flared. "That little tart, Charlie O'Reilly? She's no match for a gentleman, Dan. Did you know she threw herself at William Fitzgerald, and I mean in every possible way? She actually expected him to marry her. Can you imagine?"

"I don't give a damn."

Margaret jumped to her feet with such force that her cup fell to the floor, spilling tea across the expensive oriental rug.

"I understand... believe me, I do. There was a man at the hospital. He was handsome and charming, and he made me feel like I was the only person in the world who mattered."

"Did you love this man?"

The pause, the few heartbeats told their own story. She stared at him, her eyes large and unblinking. "I thought I did, but then I found out that he had a wife and realized it didn't matter what I felt. Even if he hadn't had a pregnant wife, it would have been impossible. People like us don't marry people like them."

"Like who?"

"The lower classes. There, I've said it."

The pain was naked on her face, and he understood. He took a step towards her. "Mags—"

She raised a hand. "Don't, Danny. Don't you dare be nice to me. I made a prize idiot of myself and now I've done it again." She took a deep, shuddering breath, and heat flushed her cheeks. "If you marry Charlie O'Reilly—I will see that she is never accepted into Melbourne society."

"That is unworthy of you, Mags."

Margaret stared at him, and the color in her face faded, as if she realized that her words had revealed so much more than she intended. "Danny, I—that was unfair and unkind. You know I didn't mean it." Her lips curved in a shaky smile. "Let's forget this whole conversation.

I'm only in town a few days and we could take in a theater show or supper and perhaps—"

Perhaps we could start again? The unspoken words died on her lips.

He shook his head. "I don't think so. Mags, our moment passed. There is no 'perhaps' for us. I am sure there are plenty of eligible gentlemen who would be delighted to make you their wife. Not me."

"You are no gentleman, Daniel Hunt," were her parting words as she flounced out of the parlor, slamming the front door behind her.

Never said I was, he thought as he stooped to retrieve the teacup and set one of the neat white table napkins down to sop up the spill.

He crossed to the window and looked out at the quiet street. He had to tell Mrs Brown to pack a small traveling bag. He had a train to catch in the morning.

Sixty-Five

Charlie leaned on a fencepost watching Amy playing with the family dog, a mutt called Ben who reminded her of the dog she had owned as a child and who had died trying to protect her mother and herself.

Amy, like Sarah and like Joshua's children, who had been raised by Annie, had something she had never known—stability and happiness. Annie had tried but she had been so damaged by the man who had brutalized her that she hadn't had the time or the energy to spare for her eldest child.

Charlie didn't love her mother any the less for her hard upbringing, but she would never have left Amy with her mother if she thought that the child would spend a single moment living in the fear and neglect she had known as a child.

The fortnight she had spent on the farm had not had the healing effect she had hoped it would. Seeing Amy every day had opened wounds that she had covered up, convincing herself that the decision she had made to surrender her child and go as far away as she could get had been the only sensible solution.

She thought of Danny and his mother. From what she had gleaned from him, Adelaide had chosen her child over social convention, and she had fought like a lioness to protect him when Richard Barnwell had come to claim him. She hadn't abandoned her child.

And yet she, Charlie, had handed over her own daughter, admittedly to her mother and her husband, to bring up as their own. Amy would never know her as anything more than her much older sister, would never call her Ma. The thought made her heart break a little more. It was too late to undo that decision. She had to live with the knowledge that it had been the only decision she could have made. Amy was happy, settled, secure and—most importantly—loved.

"Penny for your thoughts?"

Charlie started, whirling on her heel to look at the man who stood behind her, his hands in his pockets.

"Danny!"

Her heart skipped a beat with the sheer joy of seeing him.

"How... Why?"

"How did I find you? I wrote to your mother to ask if she knew where you were and she replied that you were here with her."

That explained her mother's furtive secreting of a letter in her apron pocket a week earlier.

He continued. "And why? Because you vanished off the face of the earth and I had to see you again." He laid his hands on her shoulders, forcing her to look up at him. "You saved my life, Charlie O'Reilly and you gave me no chance to thank you." He slid his hands down her arms, grasping both of her hands in his. "You also failed to tell me that you had lost your job because of me."

"It had nothing to do with you." She detached his grip and took a step back, wrapping her arms around herself. "I lost my job because I did what I always do, put my pursuit of the truth before everything else. The board was entirely correct in their decision."

"My father disagrees. He has been raising merry hell with the board, and a certain Doctor Fitzgerald has been asked to resign from the inspection board. There is also an investigation into his dealings with the nursing staff at his hospital. A couple of brave girls have come forward with complaints."

"I don't need your father fighting my battles," Charlie said.

"In that case, you don't know Caleb Hunt," Danny said. "He hates injustice and bullying more than you do. I'm not saying you will be offered your job back, but there will be an official apology for your treatment."

"I wouldn't take the job back even if it was offered," Charlie said. "When I left, I knew I would not be back."

He smiled. "What are you going to do?"

"I'm waiting on a letter from a hospital in Mount Isa," she said.

Danny stared at her. "Mount Isa? In Queensland? You don't think you could go any further away?"

Charlie shrugged. "I could have gone back to London. Besides, it's none of your business."

Danny studied her for a long moment and she shifted uneasily under his clear gaze.

"I have had time to think and reconsider a conversation we had on a cold night on the floor of a hut at the Shenandoah mine," he said.

"There is nothing to reconsider," Charlie said.

"I asked you a question, and you didn't give me a proper answer."

She frowned. "What question?"

"I asked you to marry me."

"Danny, you were delirious."

"I wasn't. I meant every word," he said.

"And I told you I couldn't because I was Catholic and I had a vocation..."

He waved a hand. "I have just taken tea with your mother, and she tells me you are, in her words, a heathen, so I have a proposition for you."

She stiffened and glared at him. "I consider myself a Catholic, but go on."

"My mother brought me up with a responsibility to care for those less fortunate than ourselves, but, as you know, I came into a fortune, a condition that causes me considerable difficulty and embarrassment. It is one of the reasons why I take legal cases with clients who can ill afford a lawyer's fees. I have been talking to my father, and Caleb is firmly of the opinion that much more could be done for the women of the poorer classes in Melbourne. He has suggested that a small, privately funded hospital could be established to provide at least rudimentary care for women and children who can't or won't go to the larger hospitals. It needs someone who knows what they are doing, who may be a qualified nurse and a brilliant midwife, to oversee it. I thought I could suggest someone..."

Charlie's lips parted. "Me?" she whispered.

"You. The offer comes without any conditions but," he held up a finger, "I would be honored if you would reconsider your answer regarding marriage to me."

"So it does come with conditions," she said, trying unsuccessfully not to smile. "You sound like a lawyer."

"Because I am. If you were to overcome your scruples and consent to be my wife, I have no objection to you continuing to pursue your career as a married woman. I would even support you attending medical school and becoming a qualified doctor."

"A doctor? But I could never..."

"Yes, you can. As Mrs. Charlotte Hunt doors will open to you and nobody will say no to whatever you want to do," Daniel said.

"But society...?"

Danny uttered an expletive that left Charlie in no doubt as to what he thought of 'society'.

"Charlie...!"

Amy came running over to them.

"Who's this?" Danny asked.

"This is my sister, Amy," Charlie said with practiced ease as the child hid shyly behind her skirts. "Amy, this is my friend, Mr. Hunt."

Danny crouched down and held out his hand. "I am very pleased to meet you, Miss Woods," he said.

Amy giggled as she shook his hand, and a bell rang from the verandah.

"That'll be supper," Charlie said. "Are you staying for a meal?"

Danny shook his head. "There's a train back to Melbourne in an hour. I can't stay."

"I haven't answered your question."

"I don't want an answer now. I want you to think about it. I have left my address with your mother. You will find me at home."

He turned and, with a barely discernible limp, walked away.

Amy leaned against Charlie's leg. "He's nice," she said.

Charlie laid her hand on the child's head, stroking the unruly dark hair, so like her own, as she watched Danny walk away. She stood at the crossroads of her life again. This time did she run or did she stay and face the consequences?

SIXTY-SIX

"Thank you for your assistance here, gentlemen. I will retire to consider my decision."

The Honourable Sir Thomas à Beckett rose from his seat at the judicial bench, prompting the Clerk of the Court to issue a hasty "All stand" followed by the scraping of chairs as everyone present rose to their feet.

Danny inclined his head to the retreating back of the judge and gathered his papers. He paused to exchange words with the plaintiff's legal counsel before turning to leave.

"Danny."

A dark-haired woman in a plain blue suit, relieved only by a row of black buttons and a line of lace at the neck and wrists, rose from the bench at the back of the court. He nearly dropped his files as he hurried across to her.

"Charlie, what a surprise. How did you find me?"

"I called at your address. Your housekeeper told me where you would be," she said.

"How long have you been sitting there?"

She glanced at a watch pinned to her shoulder. "About two hours," she said. "I like watching you in action," she added.

He rolled his eyes. "You couldn't have picked a duller case. A contract dispute..."

She slipped her hand into the crook of his arm.

"You can tell me over dinner," she said, adding, "at the Menzies. I've always wanted to dine at the Menzies."

His eyebrows quirked. "Very well. Dinner at the Menzies. Just let me change first."

His chambers were next door to the court, and she followed him up the stairs to the pleasant office overlooking Lonsdale Street. As he shut the door, she snatched the horsehair wig off his head.

"That's better," she said. "Now you look like Danny."

He took it back from her, arranging it on the wig stand before removing his gown. "That wig cost a fortune. Treat it with respect."

"It makes you look very distinguished."

As he filed his papers, she wandered around his room, pulling the occasional heavy, leather-bound copy of the law reports from the shelf and leafing through the closely printed pages.

"So much to remember," she said.

Danny ran a comb through his unruly hair, replacing the white falling bands and his collar and waistcoat with a tie and jacket.

He proffered his arm. "Shall we?"

They strolled arm in arm along William Street to the Menzies Hotel on the corner of Bourke Street. The call of street vendors and the clang and the rattle of the trams and the press of pedestrians annoyed by their leisurely pace went unheeded as she leaned against his shoulder.

Only when they were seated in the magnificent dining room and their first course of soup was steaming in front of them did he dare ask, "So, Charlie, have you come to tell me you are on your way to Mount Isa?"

She straightened the serviette on her lap and cleared her throat. "I have been offered the post, but I haven't accepted it. I thought there was some unfinished business between us that we needed to discuss before I agreed to take the position."

Danny set the soup spoon down and gave her his full attention.

She took a breath. "Last time I saw you, you asked me a question and asked me to reconsider my answer."

He took a breath. "I asked you to marry me. Do you have an answer for me?"

"It's dependent on what you say next. My mother believes that a marriage has to be founded on honesty, and I've not been completely honest with you."

Danny quirked an eyebrow.

"I went to England five years ago to escape from an unfortunate liaison with a married man."

"I know. You told me that. Fitzgerald."

She bit her lip. "I didn't tell you everything."

Danny's mind raced as he tried to imagine what the 'everything' could possibly be. He did not anticipate what she said next.

"You met Amy..." Charlie took a deep, shuddering breath. Her eyes glistened with unshed tears as she said, "Danny, she's not my sister. She's my daughter. Fitzgerald promised me marriage, otherwise I would never have... but within weeks his engagement was announced and by that time I knew I was," she lowered her voice, "expecting. I confronted him, but he just laughed and told me I was a nurse, I should know how to get rid of it."

A white-hot rage rose in Danny's chest. He wanted to reach across the table and take her in his arms, but something about her stiff back and the wide, frightened eyes held him back. So he let her finish.

"I concealed my condition for as long as I could, but when it got to a point where I could do so no longer, I went to my mother's home. We discussed what to do, and we agreed that the best thing for the child would be for her and her husband to bring it up as their own. She pretended to be expecting so no one would be surprised when she produced a baby." Her lip trembled as she said, "When Amy was born, everyone was so happy for her. I can't tell you how hard it was to pack my bags and walk away, but I couldn't be near her, so I went to England. I didn't intend to ever come back, but I missed Australia more than I could have imagined." She lowered her gaze to her lap and her voice shook as she said, "And I missed my family... my daughter."

Danny, whose life was words, found himself speechless. He tried to imagine the young mother handing over her child and walking away. What if his mother had done that to him? But what choice did Charlie have?

She looked away, her face burning.

"Don't look at me like that."

"Like what?"

"Like you hate me."

Danny found his voice. "I don't hate you." He took her hand in his. "It just makes me love you more."

She managed a wobbly smile. "You're not just saying that."

"I'm not. What will it take to convince you that it changes nothing about my feelings for you?"

Her lips curved in a tremulous smile. "Thank you."

"Does Fitzgerald know about the child?"

She shook her head. "I let him believe I had done exactly what he had told me to do. I didn't think I would see him again, but Melbourne is a small town and the medical profession smaller still, and when I returned from London, there he was, expecting I would fall into his arms. The fact that he had a wife and children made no difference."

"So, you took the job in Maiden's Creek?"

She grimaced. "For all the good it did me." Her fingers tightened on his. "I don't ever want him to know about Amy. I couldn't bear him having any more power over me than he already thinks he does." She swallowed.

"How can you bear it?"

A betraying tear trickled down her cheek, and she wiped it away with her napkin. "I bear it because I know it was the right decision. You and I—we've both known the taint of illegitimacy, Danny, and I don't want that for her. Amy is happy. Annie and Joshua are doing a wonderful job of raising her, and it is better she should think that I am her sister." She took a deep breath. "That's it. That's my terrible secret and the real reason I can't marry you. I just thought you had a right to know."

Danny shook his head. "It changes nothing, Charlie. If anything, it strengthens my resolve. My question still stands. Charlotte O'Reilly, will you marry me?"

She blinked and swallowed. "Yes," she whispered. "I would be honored to be your wife. Are you sure—"

"Of course I'm sure, and if you are agreeable to converting your heathen status to that of the Church of England, I know a perfectly pleasant vicar who would be happy to make you one of his flock."

"And what you said about studying medicine and the hospital?"

"I meant every word, Charlie. I would be beyond proud to have another Doctor Hunt in the family."

Her mouth quirked into a tremulous smile. "Next to being your wife, it is the one thing I want more than anything in the world. And there is something I would like you to do for yourself," Charlie said.

Danny smiled. "What would that be?"

"I want to see you write a book... a proper book. Not just the wonderful stories you pen for the magazines," Charlie said. "Because I think that is what you want to do more than you want to be a lawyer."

He smiled, thinking of the scribbled pages on his desk at home. "How can someone who has known me for such a short time know me so well?"

She held his gaze. "From the moment you sat next to me on the floor behind a potted palm to escape your party, I knew you and I had found each other. It just took ten years to realize that."

"On the subject of potted palms..." Danny straightened and signaled the waiter. "Your best champagne..."

SIXTY-SEVEN

East Melbourne, 14 March 1893

The well-wishers had gone, the reception rooms had been cleared of the wedding breakfast and even the servants had left the house. Danny and Charlie were alone in the East Melbourne villa.

Danny lay sprawled on the bed in the main bedroom, feeling oddly out of place. The house had been a wedding present from Caleb and Adelaide, but some redecoration would be required before it would ever feel like it was truly his home—Charlie's and his home.

He still wore his wedding clothes, although he had ditched the jacket and undone the waistcoat and the neckcloth. He lay with his ankles crossed and his arms behind his head, reliving the day.

He wondered if all wedding days blurred as this one had done. It had been intended to be a small affair, but St James Cathedral had been packed. He had stood at the altar dry-mouthed and beset with more nerves than when he'd appeared before the Chief Justice of the Supreme Court. He had hardly dared turn as Bertie Campbell nudged him, and Charlie entered the church on Joshua Brown's arm, attended by her sister Sarah and little Amy.

Amy... She had performed her duties for the day with gravity, giving in to the company of Danny's young sister Nicia at the wedding breakfast. The older girl had taken her under her wing, whisking her off to play with the magnificent doll's house in the nursery.

And he had known as he watched the two girls running up the stairs hand in hand that this house needed children to really be a home.

"Danny?"

He propped himself up on his elbows and caught his breath.

Charlie stood in the doorway to the dressing room. She had let down the tightly wound curls so that her dark hair hung loose and twisted over one shoulder. The ivory satin wedding dress had been exchanged for a green silk dress of a style long since out of fashion, a particular shade of green that emphasized her extraordinary eyes.

He drank in her beauty, and the memory of the girl in this same green dress crouched behind the potted palm all those years ago, and the circle closed.

"You kept it," he said.

"I couldn't part with it, and amazingly it still fits," she said.

He smiled and patted the bed beside him. "Come here, mystery girl."

Abandoning all pretense of dignity, she laughed and took a run, launching herself onto the bed in a tangle of green silk. He wrapped his arms around her and rolled her over.

"You are more beautiful now, Charlie," he said, silencing any response with a kiss that said everything words could not express.

The kiss was no longer a snatched, cautious moment in time, but a coming together in the sure knowledge that they had all the time in the world to explore each other's bodies and minds.

The soft autumnal night dissolved around them, and Danny woke to the early-morning birds calling to each other in the trees outside the window. The distant rattle of the trams along Wellington Parade and the calls of the vendors took on a new clarity.

He turned his attention to the woman who lay curled up in his arms, dark hair spilling across the fine linen of the pillows. He kissed the pale skin of her shoulder.

She stirred, arching her back against him, and her eyelids flickered drowsily.

"Charlie," he whispered.

"Mmm..."

"There is something serious I want to discuss with you."

She rolled over, their faces now only inches away from each other on the pillows.

"Now? You want to discuss something serious with me right now?"

"Yes."

She ran a finger along his jaw, her mouth curling in a soft smile.

"Go on."

"All my life I lived in the shadow of my mother's secrets and lies, however well-intentioned they were. I don't want that for Amy."

She frowned. "What do you mean?"

"I want her to come and live with us."

She drew away. "Danny. You don't know what you are saying."

"I do."

"She thinks Annie is her mother." Charlie sat up, wrapping her arms around her knees. Lowering her head, she said, "Annie and Joshua are named on her birth certificate. Legally, she is their child and she is happy. I can't just tell her that it was a lie. She's only five years old, and she's only just getting to know me as her sister. She would never understand if I told her I'm her mother. I don't want secrets either, but maybe this is one that we need to keep until she is old enough to understand." She gave him a sideways glance. "You were ten when you found out about your father, and that has haunted you your whole life. If you had been ten years older would that knowledge have had the same effect?"

He shook his head. "Probably not."

"There may be a time when I... we can tell Amy the truth, but for now she needs to know nothing more than that Annie and Joshua deeply loved her and by me, her sister."

Danny ran his hand down her back. "You're right. I know you're right and you are braver than me. Perhaps there is another way. In a few years, if we were to offer the opportunity for her to come to school here in Melbourne and live here, with us, during the term, she can go back to Annie and Joshua during the holidays. Would Annie agree? Is it something you would like?"

She looked up at him, her eyes bright. "More than anything in the world. That is a wonderful idea. Every day I am away from her I think of her and wonder about how I could have made a proper life for her and then I remind myself that it would have been no life." She paused, her lips tight. When she spoke the suppressed emotion shook her voice. "But I am not complete without her."

He reached out to her, curling a lock of hair around one finger and tugging her towards him. "*We* are not complete without her," he said.

Her eyes filled with tears and she smiled at him. "Daniel Hunt, you are an extraordinary man. I am blessed that you walked into my life."

"If I recall rightly, it was you who walked into mine."

She laughed and he bent his head to kiss her.

Author's Note and Acknowledgements

Thank you for reading *The Homecoming*.

THIS BOOK WON THE 2023 AUSTRALIAN ROMANCE READERS AWARD FOR FAVOURITE HISTORICAL ROMANCE!

Those familiar with the previous two Maiden's Creek books, *The Postmistress* and *The Goldminer's Sister*, will recognize the fictional town is based on the little Gippsland town of Walhalla, and while I have moved the timeline forward twenty years, as in the previous books I have incorporated snippets of Walhalla's own history.

Stringer's Creek, the actual creek that flows through Walhalla, flooded in 2020, inspiring this story. Coincidentally, through my research, I discovered floods were common in Walhalla, but most notably a major flood devastated the town in August 1891, destroying buildings and killing four people. Photographic images of this disastrous flood exist, as do numerous newspaper reports and drawings from which I drew my account of the flood. You can find the images on my Pinterest board for this book.

I have based the concept of the hospital on the old Walhalla hospital, which is still extant and sits overlooking the little town. It is now a private home and is reputed to be haunted by the ghost of a nurse who hanged herself from a tree outside the hospital.

Walhalla itself did not get a railway, despite much agitating, until 1909—too late for the declining goldfields. World War I signed the death knell of town and railway. If you visit the town today, a short section of the railway line has been restored and it gives you some feel for the difficulties in bringing the rail to the town (visit the Walhalla Goldfields Railway).

The greatest fun I had with this particular story was incorporating the real-life Mystery of the Missing Mace. This story is absolutely true and I have recounted the evidence of its disappearance based on reports at the time. It disappeared on the night of October 9, 1891, and was never seen again. It was hardly an inconspicuous object, being 1.5 metres in length and weighing 7.5kg. The story of it ending up in a brothel did not appear until nearly a year later, so there is some doubt about its veracity. No one knows what its ultimate fate was, although popular opinion was that it ended up in the Maribyrnong River. Who is to say it didn't end up down a mine shaft?

Which brings me to mention of Thomas Bent. I remember as a child driving past his statue on the side of the Nepean Highway at Brighton and my father telling me the story of the mace. Bent's home, Billilla, in Brighton is still extant and can occasionally be visited. Although he ended up as the Premier of Victoria from 1904 to 1909, his property speculation and other dealings did not make him a popular man. Whether he had anything to do with the missing mace remains pure speculation.

The influence of Florence Nightingale finally began to take effect by the end of the nineteenth century with the establishment of professional training and accreditation for nurses. "Nightingale Nurses" were highly respected. By 1890 formal training hospitals for nurses had been well established in Melbourne and the first women doctors graduated from the medical school in the University of Melbourne in 1891.

The legal system continued to disadvantage the poor right up until the formal establishment of the Legal Aid system in the 1980s. Prisoners and the very poor were able to apply for legal aid on some matters but it was not until 1928 that the Victorian government set up the Public Solicitor's office to provide aid for people worth less than fifty pounds.

Finally, on to matters literary, starting with *The Bulletin*, that popular political magazine/newspaper which gave voice to Henry Lawson and Banjo Patterson and many others. I was delighted to find the "Bulletin Debate" exactly fitted with the timeline of my story. This was a back and forth between Lawson and Patterson about the merits of bush life which Lawson argued Patterson romanticized and Patterson argued Lawson saw only the dark side.

And let us not forget Fergus Hume... the author of *The Mystery of the Hansom Cab*. A qualified lawyer who worked as a law clerk in Melbourne, Hume aspired to be a playwright but after numerous rejections he, as all writers are advised, studied the market and concluded murder mysteries were the way to go. Unable to find a publisher, he self-published the book. *The Hansom Cab* was an instant bestseller, selling over twenty thousand copies in Melbourne. Unfortunately, he sold all his rights for a mere fifty pounds and never saw another cent... nor did he have another bestseller.

Let us hope Danny has better success as a budding mystery writer!
Alison Stuart

———

ACKNOWLEDGEMENTS

No book is produced in isolation and I would like to thank in particular, my wonderful writer's group, The Saturday Ladies Bridge Club, who kept me going when I was struggling to write during the darkest days of the Melbourne lockdowns (2020 and 2021).

My husband, David, had a little less technical input to this story as it did not involve rotating machinery or theories of engineering, but he is, as always, the rock against which I thrash the ideas for the plot.
Alison Stuart

BOOKS BY ALISON STUART

The Women of Maiden's Creek Series

THE POSTMISTRESS

THE GOLDMINER'S SISTER

THE HOMECOMING

The Guardians of the Crown Series

BY THE SWORD

THE KING'S MAN

EXILE'S RETURN

The Feathers in the Wind Collection

AND THEN MINE ENEMY

HER REBEL HEART

SECRETS IN TIME

FEATHERS IN THE WIND (BOX SET)

Regency/World War One

GATHER THE BONES

LORD SOMERTON'S HEIR

A CHRISTMAS LOVE REDEEMED (Novella)

(Writing as A.M. Stuart)

The Harriet Gordon Mysteries

SINGAPORE SAPPHIRE (Book 1)

REVENGE IN RUBIES (Book 2)

EVIL IN EMERALD (Book 3)

TERROR IN TOPAZ (Book 4)

AGONY IN AMETHYST (Book 5)

THE UMBRELLA (A Harriet Gordon Novella)

VISIT ALISON STUART'S WEBSITE